EVIL IS A MATTER OF PERSPECTIVE

EVIL IS A MATTER OF PERSPECTIVE

EDITED BY ADRIAN COLLINS
& MIKE MYERS

GdM

For Tom Smith, for the late night chat from the other side of the world that led to the concept for this anthology.

For Tim Marquitz, Joe Martin, Shawn Speakman and Geoff Brown, for your advice and support.

For Mike Myers, for the countless hours spent editing Grimdark Magazine and the pieces in this anthology.

For the Grimdark Magazine team, whose volunteer efforts over the last three years got us into a position where this anthology could acquire the talent and attention we needed to succeed: Cheresse Burke, Layla Cummins, Kyle Massa, Rob Matheny, Tom Smith, Jeff Suwak, Joe Price, Sean Grigsby, Joey To, Jewel Eliese, Kristy Mika, Matthew Cropley, Shawn Mansouri, and Durand Welsh.

For the authors, who leapt at this project and got so involved in the Kickstarter.

For the grimdark and dark fantasy community who trusted us to create it.

For Kennet Gencks, who we wish was still here to hold this anthology in his hands.

Grimdark Magazine has chosen to maintain the authors'
original languages (eg. Australian English, American English,
Canadian English, UK English) for each story.

CONTENTS

ON THE GOODNESS OF EVIL

A Foreword by

R. SCOTT BAKKER

The world is a circle that possesses as many centres as it does men.
—Ajencis

EVIL IS A MATTER OF PERSPECTIVE.

"There is nothing either good or bad," Hamlet says to Rosencrantz and Guildenstern, "but thinking makes it so." For many scholars, claims like this identify Hamlet as the forebear of the modern individual. We dwell in what might be called the age of 'more or less relativism,' a time when the assertion of universal moral truths can just as easily identify *fantasy* as it can scripture.

This wasn't the case just a few centuries ago. As recently as the Renaissance, assertions of universal good and evil were more apt to sort *friend from foe.* Their universality was given, which meant the imperative to 'destroy evil' included the murder and degradation of fellow human beings.

When people grow up immersed in cultures, the values belonging to those cultures become their unconscious yardstick, their own idiosyncratic angle on the actions of their fellows. Geography turns out to be a good predictor of moral consensus. This is no accident. 'Us good' and 'Them evil' line up so neatly simply because 'Us against Them' is pretty clearly the primary evolutionary function of 'good and evil.' *Infants* display bias for and against at the tender age of three months! The more we study the psychology and neuroscience of good and evil, the more clear their biological bases and evolutionary origins become, to the point where it now takes a genuine leap of faith to say evil is *more* than a matter of mere perspective.

'Evil,' you could say, is the name our ancestors used to label victims.

Which is to say, *to do evil.*

Hamlet's world, the modern world of moral complication, is the one you happen to be sitting in this moment now. 'Evil' is often *evil,* we think, because it licences irrevocable acts on the basis of a hallucinatory universalism. Someone reads some scripture, takes what are, in many cases, absurdly parochial claims, and thinks they apply to the whole of humanity. They think evil is more than a matter of perspective, and people are all too often oppressed, terrorized.

Thus the dark moral to the story of human morality: *we are hardwired to hallucinate universal good and evil.* And we are often most evil when we think ourselves certain of evil. Absent modern civilization, we will generally assume the evil of our enemies to be absolute, not a matter of mere perspective.

Like it or not, the objectivity of evil is part and parcel of our basic moral toolbox, and you find clear evidence of this throughout our culture, on the evening news, in popular political rhetoric, in comedy, but also, believe it or not, on the shelves of your local bookstore—and nowhere more so than the fantasy section.

Consider Tolkien. Part of the difficulty of modern life, the 'malaise,' lies precisely in its moral complication, how it continuously bombards us with unprecedented moral problems, environments unknown to our ancestors and quite beyond the toolkit they have bequeathed us. Middle-earth is possessed of a profound moral certainty, one far outstripping anything our ancestors enjoyed (and they enjoyed a great deal). Heroes question their resolve, their wisdom or even their courage, but they never question the *evil* they are charged with destroying. *Sauron is evil* in an absolute sense.

To dwell in Middle-earth as a reader, then, is to dwell in an *essentially* morally idyllic place. The apocalyptic structure (or 'eschatology') assures that good will prevail, but even if Sauron had regained the One Ring and Middle-earth had fallen into irrevocable shadow, *it would be no less morally simple*. The reader is guaranteed their instinct to universalism will not be betrayed, that those who destroy evil will not themselves be charged with evil. Evil triumphant does not simply amount to an inverted good. Orcs can be killed by the thousands, but no orc can be *murdered*, simply because murder is intrinsically immoral, and to destroy evil is to do good in Middle-earth.

The goodness of 'evil' is what makes *The Lord of the Rings* morally (as opposed to merely magically and spiritually) fantastic, and so genuinely scriptural. It indulges our ancestral predilection for moral certainty, vividly concretizes our instinct to demonize our enemies, blurring, the way our ancestors blurred, the natural and the social dimensions of our environments. It explores a world where our hallucination is as real as real, where fundamental moral structure of the world gratifies our instinct to destroy evil.

The Lord of the Rings exemplifies what might be called *morally fantastic* heroic fantasy fiction. It allows us to escape the moral complexities of modern life, to follow the human drama against a backdrop of absolute moral certainty. And there is comfort in this—at least there is for me! Doing good is difficult enough *knowing the Good*, and quickly seems hopeless when you have scant clue as to what 'good' means. This is the genius in Tolkien's world-building, his instinctive understanding of the way worlds and ideologies rise and fall together in the ancestral mind. The more convincing the world, the more convincing the objectivity of evil.

And this is just to say that *The Lord of the Rings* indulges what has to be, without any doubt, the most dangerous of the many illusions we have inherited from our tribal ancestors. This is why so many critics both within and without fantasy were so quick to condemn the work for its apparent, political *atavism*. *The Lord of the Rings* resembles scripture, and so, they think, promulgates a universalistic mindset, rather than, as was the case in my childhood, revealing such mindsets as fantastic. The interchangeability of Sauron and Satan, for me anyway, made Satan seem more fictional, not less. And the jaw-dropping believability of Middle-earth taught me that reality could be easily faked.

Whatever the political consequence of *The Lord of the Rings*, the larger genre has never wanted for counter-examples, works that are more or less *morally realistic*, while remaining magical and spiritual. Nowadays the inclination is to identify morally realistic heroic fantasy as *grimdark*, but it's important to realize that we are talking about a story-telling *tendency*, here, rather than fixed set of types. 'Grimdark' simply helps us articulate this tendency in the context of other concerns.

In grimdark, then, the storyteller seeks to complicate, even undermine, our instinctively universalistic understanding of good and evil. One of the goals of grimdark, in other words, is to *explore the perspectival structure of evil*, either by jamming the moral intuitions of readers, and/or by depicting morally ambivalent heroes ('rogues') and morally ambiguous worlds. Where morally fantastic heroic fantasy tends to be scriptural, providing a mythologized portrait of the past, morally realistic heroic fantasy tends to be *historical*, providing a demythologized portrait of the past.

The canonical work of morally realistic heroic fantasy has to be George R. R. Martin's *A Song of Fire and Ice*. Where Middle-earth levels moral complexities, Westeros *exposes* them, all the heroisms and the madnesses belonging to our premodern ancestors. In Westeros, moral status is always held in suspense; characters are far more likely to pursue ingroup interests at the violent expense of their 'evil' outgroup competitors. The reader is systematically denied the moral clarity required to do anything more than what they are forced to do in their daily lives: interpret as best they can.

Given the kind of criticism levelled at Tolkien's mythologization of morality, one might think someone, like Martin, who so relentlessly pursues its demythologization would be applauded. The problem is that demythologizing premodern moral contexts entails depicting actions and attitudes that we presently think abhorrent. In circles devoted to the moral and political evaluation of cultural production, description amounts to tacit endorsement, and has the aggregate effect of desensitizing audiences to such occurrences in the real world. So where Tolkien was accused of constructing too sanitary a world, one finds Martin—and grimdark more generally—accused of constructing one that is too unsanitary. Where Tolkien is charged with mythologizing too much, Martin is charged with mythologizing *too little*.

In each case, of course, the critic is making some kind of universal claim regarding the evils of certain forms of representation. The transgression they identify will strike them as *objective*, so they will insist that contrary interpretations are *wrong*, despite the absence of any fact of the matter. The moral nature of their claim suggests they will be incapable of considering their position rationally, that they, like every other moralist on the planet, will endlessly confabulate reasons. But this isn't to say their charges should be dismissed: far from it. Precisely because we are hardwired to be chauvinistic, we need to take all charges of chauvinism seriously.

What it means is that *there will be no decisive way to settle the issue one way or another*. Precisely because the issue is moral, perspectival, we lack the objectivity required to reach any decisive settlement one way or another. What imperative compels a writer to import modern moral perspectives? A *universal* one? What good is served by editing, say, sexual violence out of our reimaginings of our premodern past? Does sexual violence become less prevalent when we ignore it, or does our cultural environment simply become less troubling, less tolerant of difficult topics? King Richard III, forensic historians have discovered, was not simply killed by being stabbed in the head, his body was also subsequently desecrated: someone, perhaps in a bid to humiliate his memory, thrust a sword into his rectum hard enough to notch his pelvis. The suspicion is that he was displayed thus draped over the saddle of a horse. Certainly it would be absurd to suggest that this latter fact does not say something *incredibly important* about Richard's life and times—even humanity itself.

Precisely because brutality characterizes so much of our past, we need to view all demands for mythologization critically. No matter how plain the offending text seems to be, the would-be moral censor has a pretty challenging case to make. First, they need to convince people of their interpretation in the absence of interpretative facts of the matter. Second, they need to convince people that the alleged meaning is indeed *evil*, either intrinsically or in terms of consequences. Given our tendency to hallucinate universality, they will assume their claims and evaluations *obvious*, something that only morally or intellectually defective individuals could fail to see. That self-same programming will lead them to devalue their targets, to think tactics like shaming and threatening and harassment are more than justified. They will believe their good more than rationalizes the systematic devaluation of perceived offenders. They will do *evil*, in other words, to combat what they think 'evil.'

The chances of *rationally* debating and settling the matter are zero. Neither the grimdark critic nor the apologist have any hope of resolving the controversies between them *precisely because their moral debate is a modern one*—complicated. In premodern times, when the objectivity of morality was enforced (if not given), the matter would have been decided by some kind of moral authority. The evil party would have been identified and chastised if not destroyed. Nowadays, *we have no arbiter*, no way, as Nietzsche might have put it, to evaluate competing valuations. The goodness of 'evil,' the ability to *impose* clarity where none can be found, is no longer an option belonging to us. Interminable debate is the inevitable outcome, particularly in those societies possessing guarantees on free speech.

In this sense, *grimdark as much exemplifies as explores moral complication*, daring to represent what many think immoral, worthy only of contempt and scorn. By committing to the perspectival nature of evil, *grimdark writers themselves risk what others call evil.* Grimdark, you could say, contains a commitment to the potential goodness of *evil*, the need to ignore the moralist and to make readers *itch*.

Evil *is* a matter of perspective. To appreciate this fact is to surmount the tribalism that is our inheritance, to join those who refuse, as far as they are able, to play groupish games. To write grimdark, to pursue complicated moralities in fantastic settings, is to risk the universal instincts of one's fellows in a manner no other genre can.

R. Scott Bakker
January, 2017

A LIFETIME OF INSPIRATION

An *Introduction by*
ADRIAN COLLINS

I'M A VILLAIN. AND SO ARE YOU.

From a very early age I found myself drawn to the villains in fiction. As I started to watch and read science fiction and fantasy, I wanted to know why they were the way they were. Why did Darth Vader want to kill the rebels? Why did so many storm troopers follow the Emperor? What made Sauron want to destroy Middle Earth? Why was I so interested in Boromir after he betrayed the Fellowship of the Ring?

In my teens I became immersed in modern history—the Nazis in particular. How could an entire nation turn on the world like that? How could they see their cause as righteous when history tells us it was evil? How could they be the cause of so much death and destruction when the War to End all Wars had already been fought?

As I grew older, I became more cynical and intuitive. I had debates where my mouth went dry as I realised my fervently argued black and white viewpoint was wrong; felt like smashing my face to a pulp on a brick wall when I couldn't even find a middle ground with somebody who refused to budge. I made mistakes I'll likely look back on with shame until the day I go into the furnace. But I learned, and I realised life was all about perspective. There was no black and white viewpoint, just seven billion shades of grey in between.

For every evil act that I read about, hear about, or witness—from a coward punch in the street after a night out to the bombing of a military checkpoint or civilian hospital in the Middle East—irrespective of how reprehensible I see it as, there is somebody out there who sees a history of oppression and hardship and horror and abuse leading to that act and understands it or even views it as heroic. The coward puncher may have suffered a lifetime of physical and mental abuse to make them snap at an innocent that night. The conquering empire— whether I see it as an empire of good or evil—likely has millions of followers firmly believing that I am doing my best to tear it down and they need to defend it with blood and bullets.

This realisation, and my inability to find fiction out there that met this need (not that it wasn't out there) led to a starvation of the stories I hungered for. I stopped reading pretty much all together until one fateful day when I spotted David Gemmell's *Sword in the Storm* in my mate's small luggage he'd left at my parent's house before flying back to the United States. In that book there is a defining series of scenes for the protagonist Connavar that not only goes against my personal moral compass, but drives his character harder in a different direction than I first expected. It's a hell of a twist.

Now, Gemmell is borderline grimdark at best, but that taste of the wrong side of Connavar and the realisation that he was still a person worth barracking for set me off in search of work more like that scene sequence. Give me darker; give me more evil; show me an antagonist who is more than just a dark lord. I found it in the meatgrinder world of *Warhammer 40,000*. I found it in Joe Abercrombie's *The Heroes*. Then in Mark Lawrence's *Prince of Thorns*. Then in Peter Orullian's *A Length of Cherrywood*. The list continues. These authors and many more created the foundation of my love of grimdark fiction, replaced all but a few on my favourites list, and drove me, eventually, to found *Grimdark* Magazine and to create this anthology through Kickstarter.

The more I read characters like Glotka, Zoisa, Jorg, and Cersei the more I understood the villain's perspective, and the more I started to relate that perspective to my life experience. Divorces, broken relationships, ruined friendships, the Western media's obsession with making us hate people, the Australian government's continuous duplicity, social media—it's so easy to jump on a side and scream your anger into the face of somebody on the other side of the fence. It's far, *far* harder to sit down and have a really good think about what led them to stand there, screaming right back at you.

This, more so than many things I've experienced in 31 years of life, enforced upon me that evil, in all its forms, is a matter of perspective, as much as many of us may never accept this cold fact. To somebody—probably plenty of people—I am a villain. To me, you might be one. We are all a shade of grey, which is why I believe grimdark is so relatable. This is why I wanted to share these stories with you, and this is why I know you'll enjoy some of the best authors in fantasy dropping you into the shoes of their antagonists, who make the world of fiction a more complex, interesting, and grim place. Enjoy.

Adrian Collins
January, 2017

THE BROKEN DEAD

MICHAEL R. FLETCHER

— Manifest Delusions —

---

*While this reality is responsive to the madness and delusions of the
Geisteskranken, the sane masses truly define it.
If it's a hell we have only ourselves to blame.*

—Wissenschaftler, Natural Scientist

YOU ARE NOTHING. YOU'LL NEVER BE ANYTHING. I'M
so disappointed.

Anomie fled her home. Her father's words followed, echoing
down the alley.

She ran until she could no longer hear him. She ran until she
could run no more. She ran until exhaustion dragged her down.

When she woke curled in the doorway of a one-story home that looked to have been abandoned for decades, a young man stood over her, hands on hips. Long black hair hid his face in a curtain of shadow. His clothes too were black. A long knife, reaching to the middle of his thigh hung at his side in a well-worn scabbard. The pommel, polished bright, was a grinning death's head.

A thief?

But she clearly had nothing. She'd left home with nothing. She'd never have anything, never be anything.

Anomie sat up, pushing aside the piled garbage littering the entrance to the run-down dwelling. Someone had eaten a lot of those sausages you can buy in the market for a few coppers and the remains of scores of leaf-wrapped meals littered the ground.

Sausages. She couldn't remember the last time she'd eaten. Her stomach burbled complaint. Thousands of rauch butts, smoked to the nub, blanketed the ground.

A slim-fingered hand—*artist's fingers*, she thought—pulled long black hair back, tying it in a cue. Pale blue eyes, jagged shards of chipped ice, examined her.

So cold.

"The world has certainly shit on you." His voice was deep, melodic. He had the bur of an accent she didn't recognize.

Was he from one of those villages tucked in the shadows of the Kälte Mountains? Her father always referred to that area as *the festering arsehole of the world.* There wasn't much in life that managed to earn a kind word from the old man.

Brushing the worst of the dirt from her clothes, Anomie asked, "Do you live here?"

The blue eyes never left her. It was like nothing else mattered, like he thought there was nothing else worth looking at. He drank her with his eyes, devoured her. She prepared herself for the cruel words that would surely follow, held ready for the dismissal she knew would come.

"Are you hungry?" he asked.

That voice is dark chocolate. She nodded.

Blue eyes crushed her. She couldn't breathe under that regard. Anomie found herself desperately wanting to see some hint of acceptance there, anything other than disgust.

He held out a hand, artist's fingers asking her to take them. She hesitated, then reached up to accept the proffered help. It was warm. He pulled her to her feet.

"Come," he said. Releasing her hand, he turned and walked away as if he knew beyond any doubt she would follow.

With the weight of those blue eyes gone she felt guttered. She was nothing; her father was right. Anomie wanted those eyes again, needed to feel their attention on her skin. Crushed was better than empty.

She didn't want to be alone. Had never been alone. Didn't know how to be alone.

If I go with him I'll never be alone again. She knew it to be true.

Anomie followed, jogging to catch up.

"My name is Matthäus," he said when she walked at his side. He glanced at her as if looking for a reaction. "Matthäus Sommer."

She'd never heard of him but thought maybe she should have. Not wanting to seem ignorant or uneducated, she nodded in appreciation, widening her eyes as if impressed.

"I'm Anomie," she said, ignoring her last name. It was her father's and she hated it.

You are nothing. You'll never be anything. I'm so disappointed.

WEARING NOTHING BUT A SWORD ON HER HIP, ANOMIE lay on the floor in an unused sub-basement of the Geborene

Damonen church in Selbsthass. The Schatten Morder—her cadre of Cotardist assassins—lay littered about her. Years of dust covered them, gathered in the hollowed cavity of her gutted corpse.

"Konig demands your presence."

A priest stood over her. She had no recollection of his arrival, no idea how long he'd been standing there, talking.

The Theocrat of Selbsthass and High Priest of the Geborene Damonen, Konig was the centre of her world, her purpose. His will alone kept her from dissolution and she was torn between her need to serve and her desire for an end. She felt like she'd been close this time. Just a few more years and maybe she would finally have faded to nothing.

But this priest, wrapped in soft skin and sweat, wearing his life like an insult, was not Konig. His need didn't matter. His wants didn't matter.

"Why?" she asked, not bothering to rise. The word was a whisper. She hadn't drawn breath in years and her lungs hung slack and empty.

"Someone stole Morgen."

Morgen. The god-child had been kind to her once. He'd touched her like she didn't disgust him and said her loneliness made him sad. Anomie sat up.

"Konig wants you to find the thieves," said the priest.

Konig only ever called on her for one purpose: Death.

Anomie stood and her Schatten Morder, the five corpses scattered about the floor, stood too. All bore swords, but none wore more than shreds of long rotted clothing. None wore armour—such contrivances are for those who fear death. In those rare times when the Theocrat called them into service, they always saw violence. When they became too damaged to continue, Anomie left them where they fell. Someday her own body would suffer enough damage to render her incapable of movement and she too would fall. She didn't fear that moment.

The Schatten Morder gathered around Anomie, feeding off her need. She didn't know their names, didn't care. They knew she wanted to belong, to matter, and they would follow her until she achieved that or they would witness her failure. If they had a preference, they never spoke of it.

"Take me to Konig," she said.

"Dress first," commanded the priest.

She glanced down, saw the rotten ruin of her body. Her lungs hung loose within the bone cage of her ribs. Twisted muscle showed through parchment skin. Dust rained off her with every move. Her breasts hung deflated.

Anomie pinned the priest to the wall with bone arms and choked the life from him. She held him there until the last tremor of life left his body.

I'll find Konig on my own.

She dropped the dead priest to the ground and took the stairs up into the land of the living. Konig needed her.

Her Schatten Morder followed.

MATTHÄUS BOUGHT ANOMIE A MEAL OF SAUSAGE wrapped in perilla leaves, scrounging through his pockets to come up with the few coppers. Judging from the bored expression of the old woman working the stand this was a common occurrence. When he realized he didn't have enough to buy himself one as well he shrugged like it was nothing. Anomie offered him half of hers and he shook his head.

"I write better when I haven't eaten," he said. "Hunger sharpens the mind. Comfort is a distraction, happiness a lie."

She knew his words to be truth. Life had shown her nothing else.

They returned to the abandoned house where he had first found her sleeping. Neither said a word and she felt comfortable in the silence. Matthäus walked through the discarded leaves and countless rotting remains of sausages like he didn't see them. Though he didn't invite her in she knew he expected her to follow and she did.

Why not? What else did she have?

The wood floor creaked and groaned with every step. The walls looked to have once been painted gold. Someone had splashed watery black paint over the top. They'd been sloppy. Threadbare sheets had been crudely nailed over all the windows. Many appeared to be in the process of falling down and hung from bent nails. She could imagine her father's reaction to this place. She knew all too well his look of disgust.

Matthäus removed the scabbarded long knife from his belt, dropped it on a table, and collapsed onto a stained and sagging sofa. Anomie stood, uncertain. He drew two crumpled rauch from an inner pocket, put the tapered ends in his mouth, and lit both, drawing the smoke deep. Blue eyes locked on her. Strands of black hair had worked free of the cue and cut his face in sharp lines. He grinned, exhaling an oily cloud, and offered Anomie one of the rauch. He'd already lit it; she couldn't decline.

She drew fire into her lungs and the world softened, became a little more distant.

Matthäus' gaze flicked toward the sofa beside him and Anomie knew she was supposed to sit. She sat, tucking her legs under her. He watched, drinking her with those sharp shards of ice. Fear and excitement warred within Anomie. She knew that look, knew what it meant. She'd seen it on enough boys to understand.

He'll lean forward now. Put a hand on my thigh—

Matthäus sat back, inhaling smoke and letting it leak out his nostrils in dark curls. He regarded her through that stained lace curtain.

"Is this your house?" she asked. "Do you own it?"

"Own." The word wasn't an answer but rather a gentle mockery of her question. "Tell me how you came to be on my front step," he said.

They talked late into the night. Matthäus listened like no one had ever listened before, blue eyes seldom blinking. He never interrupted, never made those empty noises people make to show they are paying attention while waiting to speak. He smoked, inhaling her words. His expression never changed and he showed no hint of judgement as she spoke of her father and their estrangement. He just listened.

He's soaking it up. Memorizing.

Each time a rauch died he dropped the wet and crumpled wedge of tobacco, still smoking, into an empty wine bottle. It was already two thirds full.

So he can afford rauch but not food? Anomie hated the thought. That was her father: Always judging. Always disappointed.

As dawn lit the mottled sheets draping the windows, he leaned forward as if to offer her another rauch and instead pulled her into a smoky kiss. His tongue, hot and tasting of tobacco, explored hers. His hands roved her body, gentle and firm, devouring her shape.

He undressed her over the course of an hour, touching and tasting everything she was. After more orgasms than she thought possible, they curled together and slept. He hadn't undressed, had made no attempt at pleasing himself. Her pleasure was everything.

She'd never been the centre of such attention.

ANOMIE STOOD IN KONIG'S CHAMBERS, AWAITING the Theocrat's attention. Trepidation and Abandonment, two of the High Priest's three Doppels—hated aspects of his splintered personality that manifested as reality—paced the room, mirroring his poses. Their bald heads gleamed in the light. The third, Acceptance, lurked in the background, beaten and bruised, teeth shattered, face scarred.

Made a play for power, did you? Clearly he'd lost. Doppels always turned on those whose delusions birthed them.

The thick carpeting beneath her feet might as well have been mud. The many luxurious draperies adorning the walls were a thousand shades of grey. The world of the dead was devoid of warmth.

Aufschlag, the Geborene Chief Scientist and pompous twat, stared into the cavity of her torso, squinting at where her lungs hung deflated. He looked like he wanted to ask her a question. When she turned toward him, pinned him with the empty sockets of her eyes, he flinched away from her attention. The fat man was a coward and a fool, clung to his sad life with the desperation of a drowning rat. Aufschlag thought he and Konig were friends and Anomie couldn't understand the scientist's wilful ignorance. Gefahrgeist didn't have friends, they had people they used. Apparently that wasn't enough for Aufschlag.

When Konig finally noticed her she drew breath and said, "We are summoned." Her voice was thin and dry, lungs whistling as air leaked out the many small tears.

"I have—"

"It has been years since you have summoned us." *He doesn't care. You're nothing. You'll never be anything.*

Konig scowled at her, annoyed at being interrupted. "I have not had need—"

"We are worthless." Anomie's lungs deflated as she talked, turning her last words into a dusty wheeze. "Cursed immortal dead. Hated."

"I don't hate you," he said.

She drew breath. "We rot unheeded and unneeded. We fall away to dust. We are nothing and yet denied the nothing we desire."

Konig stood before her, placing his hands on her shoulders, forcing her to meet his flat grey eyes. "You are worthless," he said, "but you serve something greater than yourself. I am your purpose. Your service defines you. Without service you will be denied even a moment of value, the slightest taste of intent with direction. You serve because in those rare moments you find yourself valued."

She knew he was a powerful Gefahrgeist, dedicated entirely to his own needs, but was incapable of caring. Konig's wants defined reality. His words made new truths. She didn't care that he would use her and forget her the moment she'd completed her task. To be needed now, if just for a short time, was enough. It was more than she deserved.

"We will serve," she whispered.

Konig's Captain of the Guard ushered Asena and her coterie of Therianthrope assassins into the room and Anomie spat hatred at the pretty little bitch. Konig clearly preferred the lithe shape-shifter over Anomie's rotting corpse. After briefly bickering with the wolf-girl, Anomie lost interest; she couldn't compete with such vibrant life. *I am worthless.* Only the knowledge that Konig had use for her kept her from crumbling to the ground.

Anomie watched Konig argue with himself, his own Doppels manipulating him, seeking advantage so they might one day bring him down. She watched the Theocrat realize Aufschlag had betrayed him. The scientist had helped three rogues steal Morgen, the Geborene godchild. A thrill of excitement coursed through her when she thought she'd be called upon to kill the scientist, but then Konig murdered Aufschlag, stabbing him in the chest.

Disappointed, she bowed her head and sank into despair.

Life swirled around her, noisy and hurried like bad theatre.

She remembered the few plays Matthäus had taken her to see, how he mocked each one, pointing out the flaws in the writing, the plot holes and poor pacing. His own play, he said, would be better. It was going to be huge, epic in scale. There would be scores of scene changes, a cast of hundreds. *I'll reduce the audience to tears with every death*, he had told her. *I'll be remembered as the greatest playwright of all time.*

At some point Matthäus decided playwrights were pathetic drunkards and focussed on his poetry. His epic play, a stack of hand written papers relegated to the floor when his poetry needed more room, reached to Anomie's knees. She never read it; he wouldn't let her.

One night, several months after he'd found her sleeping in his doorway, while they curled together on the stained and stinking sofa, chewing auslösekugeln mushrooms, watching shadows dance to their shared hallucinations and talking about how much he hated Halber Tod, the famous Cotardist poet, he saw his path. He dedicated himself to the one poem that would make him famous. People would talk about his poem a thousand years after his death. She'd held him tight, happy to be close to such brilliance, glowing in the knowledge that while she might not matter, she could be a small part of something that did.

Matthäus died before he completed his poem, betrayed. Murdered.

"You will slay Morgen," Konig commanded, interrupting Anomie's thoughts and finally giving her purpose. "Bring about his Ascension."

Anomie's past was never far away. There was no forgetting her crime. No forgiving.

"Anomie," continued Konig. "Take your Schatten Morder south, to Unbrauchbar in Gottlos."

Then he deafened both her and Asena with his delusions. He said it was to protect her from the influence of other Gefahrgeist who might bend her to their purpose, but she knew Acceptance manipulated him into doing it to distance Konig from Asena.

Anomie bowed and led her Schatten Morder from the room. There was no need to command her cadre of corpses, they always followed. Who they were—who they had been in life—she had no idea. Sad pathetic souls. Anomie understood all too well.

She would lead her Cotardist assassins south as Konig commanded. They would find those who had stolen Morgen and help the boy Ascend before his kidnappers' filth contaminated the Geborene godling.

He offered to cure me. She remembered Morgen hugging her and asking if she'd like to truly live once again. He'd promised he could make her whole, return her to the bright circus of life. She'd been terrified. *I don't deserve life.* Not after what she'd done. *I'm nothing. I'll never be anything.*

Morgen looked disappointed when she begged him to leave her as she was.

And now I'll repay his kindness with death.

It wouldn't be the first time.

It wouldn't be the last.

YEARS SLID BY, ANOMIE AND MATTHÄUS SLEEPING ON their sagging sofa. Sometimes they'd rut, grunting and clawing like animals, but more often than not he'd take hours to pleasure her with his tongue and fingers never once hinting at having needs of his own. Matthäus always decided, always controlled. When dark moods took him he wouldn't touch her for months, barely seemed to notice her existence. But he always came out of it, always returned to her with his blue diamond eyes. Months of neglect would wash away in a moment of bright need. Matthäus' wants defined their relationship, defined her world. Even though she knew she didn't deserve it, she'd never been so happy. Sometimes she almost forgot her father.

It was the hottest summer in memory and she and Matthäus walked their usual route. The market moved at a much slowed pace. A warm breeze passed through Anomie's thin shirt. Her flowing skirt often caught the wind and showed her legs. Men stared at her as she passed, eyes hungry. Matthäus didn't notice or didn't care; she loved his utter confidence. Still dressed all in black, somehow he wasn't sweating, though his hair wilted and the long cue hung limp down his back. The grinning death's head knife hung at its place on his hip.

"Aren't you hot?" she asked.

"I'm fine." After a week of happiness and sex twice a day his mood was once again turning to black.

She realized she'd never seen him without his shirt in public. He even hesitated to completely undress when they entwined on the sofa.

"You have a great body," she said. "Remember that art gallery where you showed me those nightmare paintings that were never the same twice? There was an exhibit depicting the perfect human form. You're like that. You have nothing to be ashamed—"

He silenced her with a glance. When he spoke his eyes were cold, his words tight and bitten. "I was a fat child. Everyone made fun of me. It scarred me. Forever. No matter what I look like on the outside, I will always be that fat child on the inside."

She pulled him into a hug, feeling the hard muscularity of him against her softness. He didn't react, didn't return the embrace.

I've hurt him.

FIRST THEY VISITED LAGER GLOCKE, MATTHÄUS' FRIEND and dealer, to buy auslösekugeln mushrooms. Matthäus had become convinced that an altered state was required to write truly great poetry. Sanity, he told her one night, was an impediment. 'Look at Halber Tod,' he'd said. 'Look at all the great poets. Not a sane one in the bunch.' He'd grinned at her then, eyes bright. 'I'll be the first great sane poet.'

On Matthäus' insistence she'd tried the auslösekugeln but found the taste awful and the hallucinations worse. She'd puked so hard she thought she'd die and then dreamed she was made of clay and that unseen hands were shaping her to their purpose.

Next they visited the claustrophobic smoke shop, where everyone knew Matthäus's name, and bought a box of rauch. Finally, with what little money they had left, they stopped at the market to purchase a meal.

After finishing their meal, they returned home.

That night he didn't touch her, seemed barely aware of her existence. When she went to bed Matthäus stayed up smoking and writing and eating auslösekugeln. Her dreams danced and flickered, writhing in response to his drug-induced hallucinations.

He woke her in the early hours of the morning when the world felt thin and unreal, like the gods still slept and had yet to fully realize their creation. Matthäus' face was gaunt and pale, his blue eyes bright and ringed dark with exhaustion.

"I know what I have to do," he said, grinning with feverish intensity.

His hair had come undone and she brushed it back from his eyes. She loved these moments when he got excited about a new project. He'd tell her all about it, talking aloud as he thought through the details. She'd listen, her entire being focussed on his words, euphoric he chose to share this part of himself with her. He hadn't yet completed any of his projects. The scrawled sheets of three half-finished novels littered the floor. Countless poems were tucked into every nook and cranny, written and forgotten. He'd sketched pictures with char, painted with oils, and done one piece in his own blood. She stole glances when he was asleep and was amazed at his talent. His work was brilliant, detailed and flawless. In the last year he'd learned to play the lute and three different wind instruments she didn't know the names of. He mastered them all, played and sang and brought tears to her eyes. When whatever drew him to music withered and died, he sold the lute to buy rauch and lost two of the flutes. One he kept and would bring out every now and then, when the auslösekugeln took him away, to play haunting three-note songs.

Anomie was awed by his talent, his ability to master anything he turned his mind to. Someday he would find the right medium to express the incredible depth of his soul. Someday all the world would see his genius and he'd be happy and famous and she'd be there beside him.

Where she was nothing he was everything.

"I'm going to hallucinate a poem," Matthäus said, staring at nothing as he envisioned his masterpiece. "It will be about life and death. It will be about the one struggle we all face, the one struggle shared by all humanity." He dug a crumpled rauch from a pocket and lit it off a nearby candle. After inhaling the smoke deep into his lungs he passed it to her. Tendrils of smoke leaked from his mouth and nose as he talked, oily snakes dancing to his words, hinting at deeper meaning, and fading to nothing. "We live. We die. But we all want to leave our mark. We all want to be remembered after we are gone."

Anomie blinked and said nothing. She'd never given it much thought. *No one will remember me.* Did she even *want* to be remembered? She didn't think so.

You are nothing. You'll never be anything. I'm so disappointed.

"I've been practising," he explained, holding up a nugget of auslösekugeln that looked suspiciously like a dried rat turd.

Anomie remembered the story he'd written about how eating cat faeces turned people into gods but no one was willing to do it so doomed mortals they remained. It had been the funniest thing she'd ever read. She'd been sad when he dropped it, unfinished.

"I can shape the hallucinations," Matthäus said.

He sees things I can't even imagine.

"I need to be better. I need finer control," He added. Blue eyes locked on her, saw her. "I need you," he said, leaning in to kiss her. He tasted of smoke and sausages. "I can't do this without you." He rushed to explain, his words tumbling out. "We are our relationships, the people around us. We are sparks thrown from a dry pine fire, fast and fading and then gone. We are those we leave behind. We are those who leave us behind." He took her hand in his, kissing it and breathing hot on her knuckles. "Together we will hallucinate my poem, for one cannot capture all that is life and death alone. I *need* you."

And that was it. He needed her.

No matter how much she hated the taste of the mushrooms and feared the hallucinations, she could not let him down.

"Of course," she said. "Anything."

Matthäus fed her auslösekugeln. He was her world. Later, after she'd finished vomiting, they made love surrounded by their shared hallucinations. The world twisted to their writhing embrace, exploded into spears of brilliant light with her orgasms.

That night she once again dreamed she was clay.

ANOMIE LED HER SCHATTEN MORDER SOUTH TOWARD Gottlos, a mud and rock shite-stain of a city-state ruled—as were all city-states—by a Gefahrgeist. How sane could the sane really be when they always turned to such self-centred bastards for leadership?

A colossal storm raped the sky, tore the world with madness, and she walked through the downpour without fear or doubt. This, she knew, was the doing of a Geisteskranken riding the ragged edge of sanity, about to topple over the Pinnacle, that moment when their delusions snuffed the last weak flame of sanity.

The world of the dead, already drained of life and colour, had become quiet as the grave since Konig deafened her. The Schatten Morder followed her with no need of commands or orders. She never spoke to them, never had in all the years they'd haunted her each and every step. Ahead she saw a dishevelled camp, hundreds of emaciated bodies cavorting, filthy and uncaring, in the muck and rain. They hadn't bothered to set tents. In the centre of the camp she saw a litter and a grotesquely fat slug of a man sitting on it. She watched as he gestured and the mob bent to his desire. They were helpless, mindless fish in the ocean current of his mad will. She watched them drag down one of their own and beat her to death, breaking her apart with axes and tossing the chunks into a massive cauldron.

Slaver-type Gefahrgeist, she thought. Anomie had heard of people whose desperate need for worship bent those around them to their will, stole freedom from everyone they came in contact with. She hated herself for doubting Konig's reasons for deafening her. Without his wise forethought she would have immediately fallen under the slug's influence. The Theocrat deserved better.

Lightning lit the world bright with fury and though she couldn't hear the answering thunder, she felt it in her bones.

She drew her sword and strode into the camp, mud clinging to the bones of her bare feet. The Schatten Morder followed, weapons drawn. The mob split before them, inviting them in, drawing them toward their master. A scrawny mud-covered savage—a lost soul stolen from the GrasMeer tribes by the look of him—stepped from the crowd. He grinned sparse teeth, brown drool, and utter insanity. His eyes mirrored the storm and she knew this wretch was the cause of the fury savaging the skies above. She killed him, cut him down and stepped over his emaciated corpse.

The world tore.

The hellish madness corrupting the sky unleashed its full power. The man she'd killed may have caused the storm, but he'd also been controlling it. His death set it free.

Anomie didn't care.

In a howling frenzy the mob threw themselves at her and she killed them. These mindless drones, lost to the will of the Slaver, were nothing. They had no weapons to speak of and few wore more than sodden sheets for clothing. The Schatten Morder followed Anomie. Waves of living flesh came at them and they left behind rotting meat. For those who could achieve the Afterdeath, annihilation was a gift. Anomie and her Schatten Morder had many gifts to give. Moving ever closer to the Slaver at the centre of the camp, they climbed mountains of dead and more flocked to receive their alms.

Morgen will be here. She knew it. She'd bring him death as Konig commanded. She'd free the boy to Ascend as the Geborene god he was meant to be.

A familiar figure, fat and tall, rose up to stand beside the Slaver. Bright canine teeth glinted in the flashing strobe of lightning. Anomie knew that bulk, knew those bright teeth.

Gehirn, Konig's pet Hassebrand.

Rippling waves of heat pulsed off the big woman. The hair and clothing of those unfortunate wretches within a half dozen strides burst into flames. Mouth stretched in a scream Anomie couldn't hear, Gehirn lit the world afire.

All those years Anomie lay in the basement of the Geborene church, Konig had been sending Gehirn scampering about the world. *He always calls her before using me.* Seeing the woman out here, knowing she was under the influence of the Slaver, Anomie understood now why Konig had finally made use of her. *He only called on me because Gehirn is beyond his reach.*

Anomie hated Gehirn almost as much as she hated Asena, that fawning bitch of a Therianthrope.

I'll kill her.

With a gesture Gehirn burned a path between herself and the Schatten Morder turning hundreds of enslaved souls to ash.

She wants to die.

Anomie burned. Fire ate the flesh from her bones and still she continued forward.

"You will slay Morgen," Konig had commanded. "Bring about his Ascension."

The Theocrat's will drove Anomie forward. Only in service did she find purpose. She was nothing. Konig was everything. She would not fail him as she had failed Matthäus.

Kill Morgen. Free the boy to be a god. She couldn't see him, but he must be here.

She raised her sword in challenge, and it glowed cherry red and then ran like thick mud to coat her fist in a sheen of molten steel.

Damned Hassebrand. I'll beat Gehirn to death with it.

Fire was nothing to the dead.

Anomie felt nothing.

FOR MONTHS ANOMIE BASKED IN MATTHÄUS' BURNING need. Finally, he knew what he was meant to do. Finally, he'd found his grand purpose. His hallucinated poem would shake the world. Talentless frauds like Halber Tod, those pathetic wretches who relied on insanity for inspiration, would be forgotten, outshone by a new light.

Many nights they went hungry, auslösekugeln, rauch, and cheap wine their only sustenance. In spite of the gnawing hunger she'd never been happier. Matthäus' eyes shone bright with purpose. He was driven, wound tight like a hangman's noose choking all doubt from life. And she would play a part in his poem. She'd stand beside him as he changed the world. It was better than she deserved.

If only father could see me now.

You are nothing. You'll never be anything. I'm so disappointed.

Last night they'd each eaten a fistful of auslösekugeln and twisted the world within their abandoned home with their hallucinations. She'd puked blood. Now, in the shivering light of the morning, the evening was a blur of chaos. Her skull ached and groaned, brain gibbering at what it had unleashed. But she remembered impossible depths of emotion and understanding, the world and all reality making complete sense for the first time. Everything had been perfect and she'd belonged. That feeling was gone, drowned in the agonizing crash that always followed an evening of rampant hallucinations. Today she was nothing.

Matthäus stood over the sofa where Anomie lay, squinting against the light stabbing through the filthy sheets nailed over the windows. His black hair hung loose, falling past his shoulders in tangled knots. Blue eyes, ragged splinters of consuming purpose, swallowed her. He held a half-empty bottle of wine in his fist. That death's head long knife hung at his hip.

He's going out?

He'd stayed up after exhaustion took her and she'd collapsed into dreams of clay. She'd been moulded by the angry hands of a child, shaped into something useful and then dashed against the wall. She'd been crafted specifically to be destroyed.

"I'm ready," he said, taking a long pull from the bottle. "Today is the day." His eyes never left her. "You'll be there with me, right? I can't do this without you. I need you."

Need.

Of course she'd be there.

"What happened last night?" she asked. "I can't remember."

"Everything fell into place. The entire poem. I can do it. But it has to be today while I still have the entire thing in my head." He lit two rauch, passed her one and dragged smoke deep into his lungs. "We have to go now. It has to be now. Now."

"Okay," she said, rising. She wobbled, her legs unsteady, knees like damp clay.

Matthäus pulled her into a smoky kiss and she felt stronger. For him she could do this. For him she would do anything.

He held out his hand, palm open. A half-dozen tough nuggets of auslösekugeln lay there. "Eat these. All of them."

Her stomach threatened rebellion and she hesitated.

"I've already eaten twice this," he said. "I need you to eat them."

Stuffing the lot into her mouth she chewed hard and fast, swallowing while they were still fibrous.

ANOMIE LEANED AGAINST MATTHÄUS AS HE LED HER to the market. It was later than she'd thought. The stalls were already open and doing brisk business. Beggars, mummers, and buskers worked the corners. Matthäus sneered at them. The one time he'd brought his lute to the market he'd made enough to keep them in sausages and rauch for weeks. He never returned a second time, said it cheapened his art.

Matthäus led her to the heart of the market, searching out the busiest intersection. Standing in the centre, forcing people to pass around them, he stood straight, eyes closed. The auslösekugeln rendered the morning sun harsh and white. Translucent images danced in her peripheral vision, gone every time she twitched to look.

Market-goers shot them annoyed looks, the eyes of the men lingering on Anomie. Fear and doubt sank into her, water on cracked earth. She didn't like it, wasn't comfortable being the centre of attention.

You are nothing. You'll never be anything. I'm so disappointed.

"Don't we need…something?" she asked. "Props? A sign explaining what we're doing?"

"No."

Sometimes the mushrooms made the little world inside their abandoned house beautiful. They softened edges, made colours more vibrant, turned the ruined home into a fairyland dream. This wasn't like that. The market was garish and ugly. Too many bright colours and cloying scents. The world hardened like clay left in the sun. *It's going to crack.* The sky grew heavy, pressed on her shoulders, raged its disgust down upon her.

The full effect of the mushrooms had yet to land but Anomie knew this feeling. It was coming. The world would fray apart and she'd lose herself to madness. Her heart stuttered erratically. She breathed in shallow sips, unable to draw air.

"This is a bad idea," she whispered, but Matthäus wasn't listening.

Eyes closed, face to the sky, he lifted a rauch to his lips and inhaled smoke into his soul. Anomie caught flickering hints of hallucinations that weren't hers. A scene played out in the shadows. Young lovers bound together in need. Doomed. The young man was clearly Matthäus, strong and perfect, but the woman was too beautiful to be Anomie. A stab of hurt pricked at her heart at this small betrayal. Shoppers were beginning to notice the hallucinations, jumping at shadows and trying to catch things seen in the corners of their eyes.

Every time a clump of shoppers passed close to Anomie and Matthäus, the hallucinations stuttered and disappeared, and they were just a dirty young couple blocking the thoroughfare. But when the crowd gave them space the hallucinations manifested, stained reality.

"Rutting gods," swore Matthäus, facing her. Exhaustion emptied his eyes. "Too many rutting sane. Their influence is stifling me." Hollow eyes lit with blue fire. He drew another fistful of auslösekugeln, tearing it in half and stuffing his share into his mouth. The rest he held out to her. "Eat."

"No. I'm scared. Let's do this later."

Blue eyes held her. "Scared? Later? This is it. This is the poem that will make me famous. I'll be remembered for all time for this one day." He lifted the dried rat turd nugget of mushrooms, held it under her nose.

She wanted to explain that the last mushrooms she'd eaten had yet to land, but then he'd want to stay here and wait. She needed to get away, flee the devouring eyes. She needed the dark solitude of their home, even if it stank of stale rauch smoke and sour sweat. "It'll be half an hour before these take effect," she said instead. "We'll come back then."

"I *need* you."

"I can't do this. I'm going to puke. I want to go home. Please." *If you love me—*

"Eat."

She ate the auslösekugeln, forcing the mushrooms into her mouth and swallowing the dry nuggets whole.

Matthäus smiled and touched her hair. There was no softness in his eyes. No gratitude. He showed teeth in a grin and for the first time she noticed how stained they were from the wine and smoke. He took her hand in his, squeezed it hard. His eyes closed and the hallucinations haunting the shadows coalesced.

The market stopped. Everyone saw Matthäus' hallucinated poem.

He hallucinated the story of their love for all to see. He showed them how he found this pathetic girl in the entrance to his home. He showed them how he took her in, how he shared his life with her.

The audience saw and they believed.

Anomie watched herself wither as Matthäus grew. She was caught in his shadow. As he shone brighter and brighter she withered and died. He would rise up to take his place among the greats of the world, remembered and worshipped by everyone. She would die, no one and nothing. Her death, however, wasn't without meaning. The loss of her would forever change him. His sadness, the absolute misery at losing her and the loneliness he'd suffer, brought tears to the eyes of all gathered to witness his poem. Somehow he'd have to go on. Somehow he'd find the strength to survive the loss of his love.

But it wasn't real. *Just a dream.* She saw through the lie. For all the heart-rending emotion on display, she knew he felt none of it. Not really.

She hated herself. *You're being cruel, unkind to the man who gave you so much.* Without him—You're nothing. You'll never be anything. I'm so disappointed—she'd never be anything. She owed him so much.

The auslösekugeln coursing through her blood twisted her perceptions and her hallucinations, fed by Matthäus', entwined with his, feeding them and feeding off them. Together they twisted the world to match his vision, to make his poem real.

She saw then the truth: For his poem to truly work, for it to be real, she would have to die. He needed her death.

Anomie glanced at her hands, saw the rot staining her fingertips.

The full force of all the auslösekugeln Anomie had eaten since waking shredded the world like a tornado. She stood at its centre, lost to the madness. Matthäus' shallow imaginings became her reality and her own hallucinations made them real.

He needs me to die.

Decay spread up her arms, peeling flesh from bone.

He needs me.

Turning, she saw Matthäus. Blue eyes wide with fear, he retreated from her. She knew that look, had seen it in her father's eyes so many times: Disgust.

"Please," she begged. "Don't—"

Matthäus' need was gone, stolen. She needed it. Without him she was nothing, would never be anything.

The market, harsh with colour and the sweet stench of sun-warmed fruit, faded to grey. All life and colour bled away. One by one her senses died, distancing her from life.

This isn't real. I'm hallucinating. Her internal organs shuddered and stilled. Terror washed away all but one thought: *I don't want to die.*

Someone screamed and the sounds of the market changed, became tinged with panic and fear. Matthäus' disgust was replaced with growing satisfaction. But he no longer looked at her, didn't seem to see her at all. He had eyes only for the crowd. Grinning in triumph Matthäus bowed with a flourish and a smattering of uncertain applause rippled through the audience. The accolades spread as more folks understood this was theatre.

The rot spread faster, fed by the belief of the scores of shoppers. They applauded the show, but looked upon Anomie with sadness and disgust.

Turning his back to Anomie, Matthäus basked in the crowd's appreciation.

To finish his poem, I must die. He must be left alone to mourn me, Matthäus did this to her. His poem was killing her.

She took his long knife with the death's head pommel and stabbed him. She stabbed him over and over as the market emptied of people, their screams distant and unimportant. Matthäus fell and she pounced on him, slashing and stabbing and screaming.

Quiet, the pattering drip of blood on cobbled stone.

Anomie knelt over her lover, her shirt and skirt soaked through. Knife clenched in a numb and shaking fist, she gazed upon what she had done. Matthäus lay open before her, sundered and torn. *He loved me and I…*

A life-time of self-hatred shaped her thoughts and a massive auslösekugeln overdose made them real.

She killed her reason to live. She betrayed him at the moment when he needed her most.

You are nothing. You'll never be anything. I'm so disappointed.

ANOMIE RUSHED GEHIRN, INTENT ON KILLING THE Hassebrand. The big bitch had fallen under the sway of a Gefahrgeist, betrayed Konig's trust. Anomie would be the Theocrat's vengeance, his avenging fist.

The fat Slaver screamed something at Gehirn and a maelstrom of fire blinded Anomie.

When she could once again see she stood alone in a field of clover, lavender and green.

Colour.

She inhaled the sweet scents, felt the warm breeze on her skin.

Warmth. Skin.

She was whole.

Her skin was flawless, perfect. Her hair hung long, thick and healthy. She breathed deep, felt the steady beat of her heart. She was as she remembered, as she had been on the day of her death.

Anomie laughed, feeling her body shake with the pleasure of being.

Gehirn killed me. She knew it to be true.

This was not the Afterdeath she had expected. She'd killed so many in service of the Theocrat. Shouldn't they be here awaiting her?

"Where are my dead?"

"I'm here."

Even after all these years she knew that voice.

Anomie turned to face Matthäus and stared at him in shocked confusion. *He's just a boy.* He couldn't have been more than eighteen. Now that long knife hanging at his hip looked silly, the affectation of a young man trying to look dangerous.

"I… I've killed hundreds. Where are the rest?"

Dull blue eyes locked on her. "I'm the only one that matters," he said. "And I've been waiting."

She knew that look. Though grey, Konig's eyes shared that flat death.

"You killed me before I completed my poem," said Matthäus. "You and I, we're not finished."

You are nothing. You'll never be anything. I'm so disappointed.

"No," she said. "Leave me alone. Let me—"

"I need you," he said, taking her hand in his and driving his will against her.

"Let me go," she whispered.

"You're here because of me," said Matthäus, kissing her fingers. "You owe me. We're going to finish the poem, you and I. I'll be the greatest poet in the Afterdeath." Blue eyes, cold and dead, never left her. "I can't do this without you. I *need* you."

She'd been on the receiving end of such manipulation all her life. From her father. From Matthäus. From Konig. The needs of others defined her. Every man who'd ever touched her life had used her, bent her to their desires.

You are nothing. You'll never be anything. I'm so disappointed.

With her free hand Anomie took Matthäus' knife.

For Konig she had killed hundreds; she'd lost count years ago. It had long become easy. Death was nothing. Meaningless.

This one however would be different.

This one would mean something.

GLOSSARY OF TERMS

Cotardist: Believe they are dead. Often combined with the belief they are rotting or missing internal organs.

Doppelgangist: Believe a double (called a Doppel) of themselves is carrying out independent actions

Gefahrgeist: Have limited ability to feel for the pain and suffering of others. Sociopaths are driven by their need to achieve and rule in social circles.

Geisteskranken (Delusionist): In a reality that is responsive to the beliefs of humanity, Geisteskranken are capable of believing something so utterly and completely to affect noticeable changes. Under normal circumstances it requires large numbers of people—all believing the same thing—to affect change. The more people who believe something, the more real their belief becomes. Most Geisteskranken are only mildly neurotic and can cause minor or subtle changes. The truly powerful are also that much more deranged.

Hassebrand: Set fires as an outlet for their repressed rage and loneliness.

EVERY HAIR CASTS A SHADOW

TERESA FROHOCK

— Los Nefilim —

Barcelona
May 3, 1937

DRESSED IN A SONG OF SCORPIONS, ALVARO STOOD AT the mouth of an alley and watched Les Rambles, Barcelona's main boulevard. The normally congested area was empty of mortals. Highly unusual given the time of day. Something had happened.

With a flick of his forked tongue, Alvaro tasted blood on the air. He inhaled deeply and smelled the mortals' rage and fear. The street might be deserted, but it did not go unobserved. Eyes watched from every window. The afternoon stillness possessed an ethereal quality, much like the tension just before a brawl.

The scorpions, made restless by the citizens' anxiety, glistened in shades of blue and black as they formed a coat around Alvaro. They clung to his skin and crawled into his hair.

Alvaro soothed them with a whisper and thumbed the heavy signet ring he wore. The wide band sported a black stone shot through with streaks of puce and gray, like an onyx cat's eye. Any Nefilim, whether they were the sons and daughters of angels or daimons, would know Alvaro was the daimon Moloch incarnate. Their souls had merged, forming a new body, uniting the old with the new, and creating a god like the mortal realm had never known.

From another part of the city, the sound of gunshots peppered the stillness. Alvaro glanced to his right and noticed several mortals about two blocks away, busily erecting a barricade of cobblestones.

He contemplated the situation. The Nationalists were still too far south to be a threat to Barcelona, so whatever aggressions the mortals were currently engaged in had nothing to do with them. Judging from the attire of the men down the street, Alvaro assumed the hostilities between the Anarchists and the Communists had finally exploded into open skirmishes. Like the angels and the daimons, the mortals never seemed to tire of war. Of course there was possibly an underlying cause to the mortals' hostilities: the angels' civil war had escalated.

"As above, so below," he muttered. The mortal situation in Barcelona mirrored the angelic conflict in the numinous realms. Alvaro guessed that Los Nefilim, the angels' ground troops, had also been dragged into the conflict.

While he deliberated, a girl and boy ran up Les Rambles, skirting a firefight in the side streets. *Now this is interesting.* Alvaro focused on the youths and adjusted his dark glasses. The mirrored lenses shielded daimonic eyes the color of smoke and nickel from the mortals and the sun.

And that bright, bright angel-girl, he mused. He recognized her. *Ysabel Ramírez.* Thirteen years old and already she had the body of a young woman. Auburn curls flew around her face and threw streaks of gold at the afternoon sun as she darted along the sidewalk, trying first one door and then another, obviously looking for a place to hide.

Don Guillermo must be proud to have begotten such a beauty. Alvaro's rare encounters with the girl had proven that her intelligence matched her charisma. Her allure had certainly brought Alvaro's grandson Rafael under her spell, because the boy followed her, pausing to look back the way they had come.

Merely a year younger than the girl, he was already taller. As dark as Ysabel was light, he was the spitting image of his father Diago at that age.

And look at him move! he thought. *Lithe as a dancer, a thief, an assassin.* Alvaro drank the image of his grandson but also scanned the street for any sign of his son. Wherever Rafael was, Diago couldn't be far behind. He usually kept the boy very close to Los Nefilim's stronghold at Santuari. It was rare to see Rafael in the city.

Diago was absent. Alvaro frowned. This wasn't the time to let two youngsters run loose in the city. At any moment, they could be taken down by a sniper's bullet, or assaulted by angels, or... accosted by daimons.

A smile twisted Alvaro's mouth as he caressed his scorpion coat. Hadn't he once advised a certain Italian by the name of Machiavelli to never waste an opportunity offered by a crisis? And was this not a calamity—two children running through a city at war? What better way to ensure his grandson's allegiance than by saving the boy and his precious angel-girl from certain disaster?

Alvaro's greedy stare slithered back to Rafael and Ysabel.

Deep within the body he shared with Moloch, Alvaro felt the ancient daimon stir. Like a broken conscience, Moloch whispered, *We tried to break Diago's spirit, and we drove him into the enemy's arms. We cannot afford the same mistake with Rafael.*

Moloch was right. Rather than bend Diago to their will, they had merely made him more rebellious. He had wrested Rafael from the daimons and raised him among the angel-born Nefilim to spite Alvaro. Diago had always been defiant. In all probability, Rafael was as recalcitrant as his father. The forceful measures that had failed on Diago would not achieve any greater success on Rafael.

Moloch's voice hissed in staccato beats along the backs of the scorpions, *Diago says his incarnations have changed him.*

"He is not the only one who learns from the past," said Alvaro.

Ysabel paused to speak to Rafael.

Moloch watched her through Alvaro's eyes. *Dangerous little thing. We should kill it.*

Alvaro made no answer and stroked his ring. Almost immediately, he discarded the idea of murdering Ysabel.

"No," he replied. "Rafael grew up with the girl, and they live in one another's shadows. Killing her will turn him against us. We must find a way into his heart that will make him loyal to us."

Moloch fell silent as Ysabel finished her hurried conversation with Rafael. She resumed her search and tried the next door.

That was odd. She had her father's talent for blacksmithing. "Why doesn't she sing her way past the lock?" he muttered. And on the heels of that question came his answer: *because she is hiding her magic from other Nefilim.*

Just as the thought cleared his mind, three Nefilim rounded a corner fifteen metres away. All of them were bright with angel song. The one in the center carried a Spanish Mauser. He was lanky and sandy-haired with a craggy face jagged as a rock. On his left was a skinny boy with an overbite made more severe by his razor-thin lips. The Nefil on the right was heavier and wore the red handkerchief of the Communists.

Alvaro's initial suspicions were correct: a group of angels and their Nefilim *were* behind the disturbance. Apparently they were hunting members of Los Nefilim. Any other day and Alvaro would watch the proceedings with mild interest—Moloch would get his wish, and Guillermo's brat would be taken out of the way. Today was not that day. Not with Rafael beside her.

Rafael had noted the trio. He crouched and aimed a Luger at the other Nefilim. "Stand down! Or I'll shoot!"

He means it. Someone had put a spine on the boy. That had to be his father's gun. Pistols were at a premium, and Alvaro knew members of the militia who would take the weapon if they could. *Where is Diago?*

The Nefil in the center raised his rifle and aimed it at Rafael.

The angel stink grew stronger: stardust and fire and ice.

Alvaro wrinkled his nose. Moloch recoiled from the scent.

Ysabel paled, but that was her only sign of distress. Her back was ramrod straight and a snarl curled her lip. "This is sedition, Antonio! Stand down and I will ask my father to forgive you."

The Nefil in the center, who was apparently Antonio the seditionist, spat on the sidewalk. "Guillermo is finished, little girl. Los Nefilim doesn't need a king anymore. Come on now. We'll make a place for you in a new order of Nefilim."

The skinny boy grinned and made an obscene gesture.

Rafael's eyes went hard and dark. The barrel of his Luger wavered.

"The one with the gun," Alvaro murmured. *Never look away from the gun.*

Antonio took a step forward.

Rafael targeted Antonio and pulled the trigger. The dry click of an empty chamber was loud in the sudden silence.

Antonio laughed. He lifted the rifle to his shoulder and took careful aim.

Without warning, Ysabel produced a note both clear and strong. Her song blazed in coppery hues. Beside her, Rafael added his voice to hers. Deeper vibrations of amber and jade wound into the resonance of her melody. Together, they shaped the pulsations into a sigil. Rafael whirled and kicked his heel against the pavement. A spark ignited their glyph and charged it with cold white fire. Ysabel spun the ward toward the trio with a flick of her wrist.

Antonio lowered his Mauser until the barrel pointed at the ground. A bullet was useless against a song. He led the other Nefilim into a defensive chord and counterattack with vibrations of blue and gray. The borders of their sigil were brilliant with sharp strands of ivory. It was a killing glyph—one that would shatter the children's ward with one hard thrust.

And those spikes will take our grandson too, Moloch warned.

Alvaro danced into the street, the tails of his long scorpion coat flying behind him. Twirling once, he cried out a vicious note, the sound roiling into the street like a drum. He grasped the children's sigil and reinforced it with Moloch's ancient power. Catching the dazzling ward seared his mind and drove Moloch deep within him, but Alvaro didn't let go. He threw the glyph toward the trio.

The ward struck them before they completed their song and instantly killed two of the Nefilim. Their bodies struck the concrete and twitched. Antonio went down last, his arms reflexively yanking the Mauser's barrel upward. His finger jerked on the trigger and the gun went off. The ugly noise bit the air hard as a scream.

Alvaro raised his hands and blew across his palms. Scorpions flew into the street like a cloud of locusts. They managed to slow, but not stop the bullet, which burst through Alvaro's hurried spell.

Rafael rammed Ysabel out of the way. She fell, rolled, and regained her feet just as the projectile struck Rafael. He took two backward steps and stumbled against the corner of a bench. He caught his balance and kept his feet. Four horrible seconds passed before the bud of a deep red flower blossomed on his abdomen. Ysabel went to his side and steadied him in her arms.

Alvaro turned back to the other Nefilim. Blood leaked from their noses and ears. Antonio convulsed and then became still. Alvaro's spell had crushed their brains to jelly within their skulls. They wouldn't be any further trouble.

By the time he returned his attention to the children, Ysabel supported Rafael and dragged him toward Carrer del Notariat. The narrow side street was lined with closed shops, their steel shutters drawn tight against the shooting.

"Rafael! Ysabel!" Alvaro shouted. "Stop!"

She kept going and didn't look back. Rafael, on the other hand, did. He spoke to Ysabel, who shook her head, buoying him at her side.

An older Nefil might survive such a wound, but Rafael was too young, and Alvaro had no wish to hear Diago's dirge. "We will lose them both if the boy dies," he told Moloch. Alvaro's sins against his son were great and left no margin for error. Diago would never forgive Rafael's death, nor would he believe Alvaro had no hand in it. "We're going after him."

Still burning from the fire of the angelic sigil, Moloch didn't answer. Alvaro stepped into the sunlight. The rays smoldered across his body. The scorpions writhed around him, agitated by the light.

He pulled his visor cap low and strode across the street. Following the trail of blood, he cried out again, "Rafael! Ysabel! Wait!"

At the sound of Alvaro's voice, Rafael twisted in Ysabel's arms. Tears of pain ran down his cheeks. His legs buckled beneath him, and Ysabel was unable to hold him upright.

Rafael went to his knees. "Stop, Ysa. I can't go on."

She placed herself between Alvaro and Rafael, raising her palm against Alvaro. "Stay back!"

He slowed his pace and approached her cautiously. "We can save him, Ysabel."

She narrowed those tawny eyes to slits and spit at him. "Crawl back into your hole, you bastard."

Lovely child. "You have your father's charm, but I must say no."

Rafael pressed his hands over his stomach and licked his lips. Blood seeped over his fingers and dripped to the ground. He looked from Alvaro to his friend. "He saved us, Ysa."

"You don't know that. You can't trust him. He's daimon."

Rafael winced as if she'd struck him. "So am I."

"*Ya, ya.*" Softening her tone, she knelt beside him and eased him into a prone position. "You're not like him, Rafael. You know what I mean."

Another tear slipped from the corner of Rafael's eye, though whether it was from his pain, or Ysabel's thoughtless words, Alvaro didn't know.

Cruel girl. He eased forward. "You were raised on lies, Ysabel."

She tore a strip from her shirt and pressed the cloth against Rafael's wound. Humming, she conjured fiery notes that grew luminous. "Uncle Diago has told us about your evil ways. Does he lie?"

Cruel and melodramatic. "Diago often…misinterprets my motives."

"Leave!" She hissed at him. It was clear by the direction of her gaze that the girl's panic had nothing to do with Alvaro's presence and everything to do with the pool of blood spreading under the boy.

Rafael placed his hand over hers. A tremulous smile touched his mouth as he tried to brush off the seriousness of the injury. "Don't be afraid, Ysa. It is nothing. You will see."

She pressed her lips against his forehead. "Heal yourself. You can do this, Rafael. I won't leave you."

Such love between them—not as siblings, no, there was more here, something deeper. Alvaro considered Ysabel again in a different light. This, too, was useful. *We can encourage our grandson's love. What better alliance between the daimons and Los Nefilim but through a marriage?*

Although Moloch remained very still, Alvaro sensed the daimon's approval.

Stepping to the edge of Ysabel's light, he adjusted his voice to become a convincing purr. "He cannot heal himself, Ysabel, not in time. He is too young." He opened his hand and allowed a scorpion to drop from his signet ring to the ground. The arachnid scuttled across the ground toward the circle. "This is a small piece of my heart song—the most precious gift I have. Let it touch him. It will draw out the bullet and heal him."

Ysabel's answer came in the form of a dissonant chord. Drawing down the vibrations of the sun, she twisted the light with her voice until her glyph flared, encircling them with a protective ward. A tongue of flame lashed the scorpion and turned it into a cinder.

White-hot pain blinded him. Alvaro cringed. "Don't be a fool! He's dying!" The boy was ashen. *And terrified,* Alvaro thought, blinking against black tears of agony. "Don't lie to yourself, Ysabel, or to him. That is not what leaders do. It's Rafael's life that hangs in the balance, not yours. It's his right to decide. Let him."

Before Ysabel could speak, the glint of the sun on steel caught Alvaro's attention. The ugly eye of a rifle peeped from a recessed doorway a few buildings away. It was aimed at Ysabel's head.

"Ysabel!" Alvaro pointed. "Take cover!" Not trusting her ward, he placed himself between the sniper and the child. Certainly Rafael would appreciate a sacrifice such as this.

The sound of a shot echoed against the buildings' walls. The sniper's gun fell to the street. The sniper slumped to the ground, his torso obscured by the wall. All that was visible were two legs protruding across the cobblestones as if the man had decided to take a rest.

Alvaro glanced across the street. Diago stood in a small churchyard, a rifle in his hands. A youth close to Rafael's age joined him.

Alvaro waved for them to hurry.

Diago didn't need further incentive. He ran toward them with the younger Nefil on his heels.

As they neared Alvaro realized that, unlike Rafael and Ysabel, this youth was not in his firstborn life. He was slender as a reed with eyes blacker than his hair, and his mortal lineage was clearly Asian. Alvaro recognized the rich ochre vibrations of the Nefil's song and immediately knew his name: Xyrus Tsang. They had met on other battlefields in the past. The Tsangs were an ancient family that traced their incarnations to the days of Cyrus the Great.

Alvaro wasn't surprised by Xyrus's presence. Caught between the angels' civil war and the daimon-born Nefilim, Guillermo's Los Nefilim were in dire straits. He had clearly called on assistance from other Nephilim, regardless of country, and if he had aligned himself with the Tsangs, surely there were others. These war-torn days made for strange and dangerous alliances.

Xyrus raised his rifle at the sight of Alvaro. He hummed a series of chromatic notes and brought to life a sigil the color of a tiger's eye: brown and ochre and tinged with black.

Diago glanced at Rafael and Ysabel, then back to Alvaro. He slowed his pace and approached warily. Alvaro could tell that Diago wanted nothing more than to go to his son, but he would neutralize any hazards first.

And that is how he sees us…as a threat. In order to put Diago at ease, Alvaro raised his hands in a gesture of peace and backed away from the children.

Still stinging from Ysabel's attack on his scorpion, Alvaro talked fast, hoping to quickly reassure them. "Finally! Where the hell have you been?" Alvaro admonished his son. "These two shouldn't be on the streets alone."

"We were separated during an ambush." Diago fixed his glare on Alvaro. "What did you do?"

"This isn't our fault," Alvaro protested.

Xyrus gave a small grunt of disbelief.

"Papa? He is telling the truth." Rafael lifted his head. His face was ashen from the loss of blood. "He saved us."

Diago picked up his pace and said, "Drop your wards, Ysabel."

The urgency in his voice had the desired effect. She obeyed him instantly. Diago gave her the rifle, and she held it like a seasoned soldier.

But that is what she is, no? She is her father's daughter. Alvaro glared at the girl until she returned his stare. He quickly changed his countenance to mirror that of a concerned parent. Not that his ungrateful son noticed.

Rafael grimaced as Diago examined the wound. "Is it bad?"

"It's bad," Diago whispered.

A shower of pebbles rained down on Alvaro. Someone ran across the rooftop. "Diago, we've got to get them off the street."

Xyrus lifted his rifle and fired a shot toward the roof. The footsteps retreated. He lowered the weapon. "Ysabel, come with me. I'll take you to your father."

Stubbornness washed over the girl's face. "I'm not leaving Rafael, and Uncle Diago can't work alone with him here." She nodded at Alvaro. "I will stay with them. Bring my papa here."

Cruel, melodramatic, and imperious, Alvaro thought as he assessed Ysabel again. *If she was ours, we'd take a stick to her.* He bridled his frustration and affected patience, insincere though it was.

Xyrus didn't argue with her. "Where will you be?"

"I can't move him far like this," Diago said. "Sing out when you come, and I will answer."

Xyrus nodded. "I'll be back soon. Very soon." He backed away ten paces before he dropped his ward. With a final cold stare aimed at Alvaro, he turned and jogged back the way they had come, keeping to the shadows.

Alvaro asked, "They no longer question your allegiance?"

"They know whose side I am on." He lifted Rafael and nodded toward a basement door down the street. "Can you open it, Ysabel?"

She ran ahead, down a short flight of steps, and tried the door's handle. Locked. The child was wise enough to know that shrouding her magic was no longer an issue. She sang a soft note that threaded through the lock, tripping the mechanism, and then she slipped inside.

Diago carried Rafael into the darkness. When Alvaro neared the threshold, she threw her weight against the heavy door and tried to slam it in his face.

His palm took the brunt of the blow. Scorpions dribbled down the steel as Ysabel shoved. Alvaro pushed harder and squeezed inside.

He locked the exit and glowered at her. "That wasn't nice."

She raised the rifle and backed away until she was beside Diago. "How do I make him go away, Uncle Diago?"

"Put the gun down," Diago said. "You can't kill him with it."

Nevertheless, the girl's finger hovered over the trigger.

Alvaro ignored her. He sent a cloud of scorpions under the door and into the stairwell. *Let the angel-bastards try to sing their way past that.*

He turned around to find Diago kneeling beside Rafael, leaning forward with his ear close to the boy's lips.

Stepping deeper into the room, Alvaro wondered: *what are they whispering about?*

When Ysabel noticed Alvaro watching them, she cleared her throat. Diago sat back on his heels and stared into his son's face with respect.

Rafael said, "Please trust me. He saved us."

Alvaro drifted closer. Diago's glare turned murderous. Raising his hands in a gesture of conciliation, Alvaro halted his advance.

Diago shrugged off his pack. He sang a small silver light into existence and opened his son's shirt. Frowning at the wound, he said, "Ysa, I need you."

"Who is going to watch him?" She shifted the gun's barrel in Alvaro's direction.

"He is a ghost to us. Forget him and maybe he will die." Diago gently wiped the blood away from Rafael's stomach. "I need you to sing to Rafael and numb his pain. If you know your mother's healing magic, now is the time to use it."

Keeping the rifle close at hand, Ysabel sat next to Rafael and gently placed his head in her lap. After a final scowl in Alvaro's direction, she turned her attention to Rafael. Stroking his black curls, she hummed a soft tune that sent halcyon notes drifting into his eyes.

Yes. They will make a beautiful match. "We can save him, Diago." Alvaro inched closer.

"Stop." Diago held up his right fist. He wore a signet ring carved with ancient symbols.

Alvaro recognized Guillermo's metalwork in the band, but it was the center stone that drew his attention. The jewel was a crimson angel's tear shot through with streaks of silver, and more dangerous than a thousand bullets. Alvaro knew of only one angel that could produce a tear like that: Prieto, Rafael's uncle.

Diago hummed, and from the stone spun a golden serpent with ruby eyes. His warning came soft but clear. "Don't even try."

Alvaro turned his head sideways, away from the light. "You misunderstand."

Rafael raised a trembling hand and covered Diago's knuckles, concealing the snake's power with his palm. "He saved us, Papa. Let him help me now."

As the room dimmed once more, Alvaro lowered his arm.

Diago glanced at Rafael. The hard lines of his features dissolved beneath the weight of his love for his son. "You must never trust him." Nonetheless, he lowered his hand.

It was enough. Alvaro seized his son's indecision. "Let us help him, Diago." He released another scorpion from his ring. The arachnid scuttled to the floor and waited beside Alvaro's boot. "It's a portion of our heart song—a measure so pianissimo, he will barely know it is there, but enough to speed his healing."

And just like that, Diago's eyes glittered hard and cold once more. "And what is in this for you?"

Calculating...he is judging the risk. Heartened by his son's question, Alvaro said, "He is our grandson. We love him too."

"You never loved anything but yourself."

"You say your incarnations have changed you. Why can't being a god change us?"

Diago barked a harsh laugh.

This wasn't going well. "When you came to us to help you trick an angel, did we not give you the item you needed?"

"You bartered for a year of Rafael's life."

"But in the end, we capitulated to your demands. We gave you the magic to deceive an angel and asked for nothing in return. It was a favor. We make no barter now." Alvaro spread his hands. "Consider this another favor."

"That will be two that I owe you."

Alvaro shrugged. "Who is counting?"

Diago wore the face of a man done with lies. "Leave us."

Rafael retained his grasp of Diago's fist and shielded Alvaro from the golden snake. The boy's skin was gray. He didn't have long. "Please, Papa. I'm scared."

Alvaro glided forward one step. The scorpion's claws clicked against the concrete floor as it moved with him. "Do you want him to pass into his next incarnation so soon?"

Diago didn't answer. He gently rotated his fist free of Rafael's grip and spoke a word more ancient than Barcelona. Now he used the golden snake to trace a ward over Rafael's abdomen.

Alvaro sighed. "Even with Prieto's magic, your glyphs can't save him, and neither can hers." He gestured at Ysabel, who wrapped Rafael in a blazing shroud of sigils. "We know you think us evil, Diago, but we are not. We loved him enough to let him go with you to Los Nefilim. You cannot deny that."

Another word, another glyph, but this time, Diago's finger trembled as he traced the ward.

Alvaro lowered his voice. "He is angel, but he is like you, Diago—he is daimon too. Our song would kill Ysabel, but not Rafael. We can help him. Besides, he is twelve. He is old enough. Let it be his decision."

"He doesn't understand what he is asking you to do. He doesn't realize—"

"Realize what? His true nature?" Alvaro sidled forward another step, the scorpion at his side. "Listen to yourself. You sound like them." He flicked his hand dismissively in Ysabel's direction. "Would you have him living in fear of himself? Doubting himself?"

Diago made no sign he heard. He formed a viridian glyph and watched the colors dance against his son's dark skin.

He hears me as a god, not as his father. Alvaro needed to establish intimacy with his son, and the only way to do that was to pretend he was once more Alvaro, a Nefil like any other.

"Diago, think, my son. Isn't that what I did to you? Didn't I try to teach you to despise your angelic nature? And what did I accomplish? I only drove you to seek the thing that you thought I hated. Now look at your own son and know this: the only way he can be whole is to embrace both sides of his nature—both the angelic and the daimonic. But he can't do this unless you let him know his heritage." He squatted and reached out to Diago. "Don't make my mistakes. Don't instill in him the angels' prejudices against the daimons. Don't teach him to hate the colors of his soul."

"Papa? Let him do it." Rafael met his father's stricken gaze. "You always tell me to follow my instincts. This is the right thing. I know it."

Diago opened his mouth, and Alvaro leaned forward. Before either of them could speak, a crash resounded overhead. The sound of feet thundering across the wooden boards descended into the basement. Someone shouted. Another faraway voice answered.

Although she looked up at the ceiling with everyone else, Ysabel's song never wavered.

Diago ignored the noise and continued to contemplate his son. "Is this truly what you want?" he asked.

Rafael nodded. "Yes."

Diago moved his blood-covered hand away from Rafael's wound. "Do it," he whispered.

Careful not to smile, Alvaro sent his song forward. The scorpion scuttled across the floor and scrambled onto Rafael. Its claws scorched his flesh. Rafael sucked air between his teeth, but he didn't cry out. The scorpion crawled through the hole left by the bullet, and the youth bit his lower lip until it bled.

As the shouts of other Nefilim grew closer, Ysabel reached for the rifle.

Alvaro edged around the trio. He went to the stairs leading upward and hummed a low note. When the basement door burst open, Alvaro released his song of scorpions. The arachnids rushed up the stairs in a glistening flood, swarming over the first Nefil. He never had a chance to scream. The other Nefilim simply ran.

Alvaro saw through the scorpions' eyes: ten thousand times ten thousand, a song of death whose notes rained black upon his enemies. He exulted in their agony and fed their anguish to the daimon in his soul.

Gunshots blistered from the street. Xyrus's descant rose over the sounds of the melee. Diago formed a sigil and sent it flying through the open door so the others would know their location. Somewhere within the chaos, Alvaro detected Guillermo's wards, burning like the sun. Ysabel answered her father with her bright clear notes.

Time to go, Alvaro had time to think just as his body ruptured into a million scorpions. His song scattered into the cracks, into the crevices, and deep beneath the earth. But one note paused by the basement door…a single scorpion that turned back and looked down the stairs to see Diago, pressing his forehead against Rafael's brow. He gave his son a healing kiss in the form of golden snake with ruby eyes.

BENEATH THE CITY ALVARO GATHERED HIS SONG AROUND himself and regained his mortal form. He didn't need his dark glasses in the subway tunnel so he placed them in their case. His eyes glowed like twin moons in the darkness. Humming a nonsense tune to himself, he strolled the tracks while Moloch slept deep within him, content from feeding on the angel-born Nefilim.

Alvaro memorized the image of Diago leaning over Rafael, and when the darkness pressed down on him, he conjured their faces into his bleak heart. After a week went by, he sang a summoning song to the scorpion that was surely embedded in Rafael's heart by now. He had not lied to Diago. The chord he had sent into Rafael would heal the boy, and then it would proceed to embed itself in Rafael's heart. There it would live, a requiem that would ensure the youth's obedience to Alvaro's every whim. The boy might resist at first, but when he did, the scorpion would sting, and in the end, the agony would force Rafael's compliance.

An hour passed, and then two, with no sign of Rafael. Unperturbed, Alvaro continued his refrain. Patience was the key to finessing a job of this magnitude, and time…it was nothing to Alvaro. Let Rafael struggle. It was important that the boy understand the pain and futility of denying a god.

Another hour crawled by before the faint glimmer of Rafael's wards touched the subway's darkness. Amber notes, sparked with silver, filtered through the air. A circle of jade flames erupted in the darkness ahead, and Alvaro noted that the boy's glyphs now carried a hint of black.

The fire died down to become smoldering coals burning at Rafael's feet. He stood in the center of his circle. One arm was raised over his head in a classic flamenco pose, the other at his side. He held the position as a single black curl settled on his cheek.

Alvaro examined him. The youth didn't appear to be in pain, but deep shadows lingered under his eyes and around the edges of his glyphs. He clenched his right fist in an attempt to hide the trembling of his hand. Yet his confident gaze left Alvaro feeling apprehensive. Something was not right.

Rafael lowered his arm, but not his wards, and that too was wrong.

Alvaro pretended nothing was amiss. "You look well," he said. "We are pleased."

Rafael opened his shirt. Three centimetres beneath his heart, the faint shadow of a scorpion rested on his chest, like a birthmark.

Even a centimetre is too low. Alvaro frowned. Somehow the scorpion had not reached its target.

Rafael said, "I know what you tried to do."

Alvaro disregarded the hard edges around his grandson's voice and kept his tone light. "I healed you. That is what I did."

Rafael's dark green eyes flashed almost black with his anger. "I know what you did to Papa." It was an accusation. "We always knew you abandoned him, because that is all he will say. He won't talk about what you did to him. Not even to Miquel, who adores him and knows his soul more deeply than I. When we ask him, Papa turns away and changes the subject, pretending it's all in the past and doesn't matter, but it does. He carries the pain deep within himself, and he thinks we do not see, but we do."

Alvaro feigned a contrition he didn't feel. "I know I didn't do everything right as a parent. I admit that. But the fact remains that what I did for your father, I did from love."

Rafael snorted and looked away. When he met Alvaro's gaze again, it was with an inner strength that Alvaro didn't like at all. "And now I know what happened to him. When you tried to embed this tiny piece of your heart song in my soul"—he gestured to the shadow of the scorpion—"everything became clear. What you did to Papa…that is not love." Rafael opened his hand and dropped the dead scorpion to the tracks. "You don't understand us. We are not like you. Papa and I are born of angels."

The sight of the dead scorpion kindled Alvaro's fury. How dare this insolent child defy their heritage? "You are daimon. Our father is Moloch. Do you understand what that means? Your great-grandfather is Moloch. That is why he chose to merge his soul with mine, just as I will take Diago's soul when he dies."

"You cannot!" Rafael's rage ignited the malachite coals at his feet into cold flames that licked the air between them. "I knew about Moloch. Papa has never hidden my daimonic nature from me. When I was barely six years old, after you revealed yourself to him, Papa wanted to know why Moloch chose you as the new vessel for his soul. He researched Los Nefilim's records and discovered his lineage." Rafael lowered his voice so that it no longer echoed in the tunnel. "He told me daimonic secrets and taught me to sing the colors of my soul."

He kicked the dead scorpion to the other side of the flames. "You placed a piece of your song within me—you wanted to latch onto me the same way Moloch dragged you down. But that is not how this is going to work. Papa helped me unravel your spell."

Alvaro judged the colors of Rafael's sigils and noted that weaker shades of pale green moved alongside an almost transparent glimmer of amber. The edges of his glyphs dulled as he grew tired.

It's cost him, this unravelling. Although Alvaro was sure Rafael wouldn't admit it. "You make it sound easy. I don't think it was."

Rafael shrugged as if it was no matter. "It was worth the effort, because now I hold a measure of your heart song"—he tapped the scorpion shadow on his chest—"that I control."

Alvaro's scorpions shivered around him in a rippling wave of black as the implication of what the child had done suddenly hit him. Within Los Nefilim he now had a new enemy...*one of our own, one that possesses a few precious beats of our heart song.* He had thought he'd succeeded in subjugating Rafael to the daimons' cause, but instead, Rafael had tricked him into revealing a piece of his soul that was best kept secret. *And if he learns to compose our song, he might decide to give us the second death—the final death from which no supernatural creature could survive.*

"How long has this plan been in the making?" Alvaro demanded. "Antonio and the others—were they a part of your strategy?"

"No," Rafael admitted. "Antonio and his Nefilim were after Ysabel. I had no intention of getting shot. But Papa taught me never to waste a good crisis."

Alvaro barked a short hard laugh and realized he sounded exactly like Diago. *Or my son sounds like me.* He thought back to Rafael's hurried whisper to Ysabel as she dragged him into the alley, and the respect with which Diago had regarded his son. Rafael had hissed his plans to them while Alvaro's attention was elsewhere. For a Nefil in his firstborn life, the boy was quick-witted and lethal.

As if he sensed the trajectory of Alvaro's thoughts, Rafael grinned, but the wicked rage never left his countenance. "Now you see."

Moloch stirred. *We see what he has done. We see a new enemy before us.* A low, dangerous hum filled the tunnel as the daimon's song passed through the scorpions. *We will not tolerate his insolence.*

The colors around Rafael grew stronger in response to the threat. Coppery shades infiltrated the youth's spinning sigils. *Ysabel.* Her fiery wards deepened into the vibrant orange strands of Guillermo's melody as her father joined his voice with hers. The lines of silver and jade grew more intense, and Alvaro recognized Diago's glyphs, which were soon joined by the pearlescent hues of Diago's lover Miquel.

That is why the boy took so long to respond to Alvaro's summons. He was weakened by the battle with Alvaro's song, and the summons *had* affected him, but he'd waited until his friends and family were nearby to lend him their strength.

"You deceitful child," Alvaro said around a mouthful of pride.

Careful, warned Moloch. *Don't praise him for his cunning until he is brought to heel.*

"Aren't you proud, Grandfather? Have I not proven my daimon nature?" Rafael threw the questions like a challenge, and then he raised one finger. "But I am angel too."

And with those words, Rafael summoned an amber snake with carmine eyes marbled by veins of ochre. Deep within Alvaro, Moloch cowered at the memory of another angel's magic. Alvaro recognized it: this serpent belonged to Rafael's mother.

A second snake, this one the deeper gold of Diago's magic, joined Rafael's serpent. They entwined and merged to form a deadly circle of light.

Alvaro cried out from pain as their radiance washed over him. He shielded his face.

Rafael shouted, "We have a saying in Catalonia: *cada cabell fa sa ombra.* Every hair casts a shadow. There are no little enemies, Grandfather."

No. No there are not, Alvaro thought as Moloch roused the scorpions. Together, they created a glyph of agony and sent it spinning toward Rafael's wards. *Cripple him and bring him down, and then we will punish him for his arrogance.*

Rafael lifted his arm again. The flames of his family's sigils shielded him. "Adios, Grandfather. We will meet again one day—on my terms."

Alvaro's answer was a shriek of rage that joined Rafael's wild cry of triumph. The youth brought down his arm, spinning amber chords filled with silver and black around his body, a whirling tornado of sound that turned into the distant rumble of an oncoming train.

Then he was gone.

The scorpions flowed over the tracks, where Rafael had stood, but their prey had vanished. They surged up the walls in a discordant wave.

Alvaro's boot heels crunched through the gravel as he approached the dead scorpion Rafael had left on the tracks. He picked it up and cradled it in his palm.

"I know you can still hear me, Rafael!" Alvaro shouted up at the ceiling. His voice echoed along the tunnel, bouncing off the walls as the scorpions returned to him. "There is another saying you should know. *A mal nudo, mal cuño.* You must meet roughness with roughness. And so we will!"

The ground beneath Alvaro began to vibrate with the thunder of the train. He closed his fingers gently over the dead scorpion and turned away from the tracks. As the light of the train rounded the corner, Alvaro slipped into a side passage. Black notes of a dissonant song swirled in his wake.

"Be vigilant, child," Alvaro hissed to the tunnels, knowing his grandson would eventually hear the resonance of his refrain on the wind. "Beware, because I will listen for your song. Life is dangerous, Rafael. You simply never know when you might be taken down by a sniper's bullet, or assaulted by angels..."

Or accosted by daimons.

THE DIVINE DEATH OF JIRELLA MARTIGORE

ALEX MARSHALL

— The Crimson Empire —

ON A MOONLESS SUMMER NIGHT, LONG AFTER ALL THE sisters were asleep, Jirella and the other novices sneaked up to the roof of the convent and tried to summon a devil. Maybe their sacrifice, a sparrow chick Yekteniya had stolen from the nest in the window of their dormitory, was insufficient. Or maybe the ritual failed because they weren't actually witches, just bored teenagers eager for an excuse to strip naked and guzzle communion wine beneath the thousand glowing eyes of the heavens.

Unlike the others, Jirella hadn't been disappointed when the pin-riddled little bird bled to death in the centre of the pentagram to no result save an awkward silence from the would-be sabbath. She had been relieved that her silent prayers to the Fallen Mother had been answered and the Deceiver had not actually materialized to tempt them. Even still, she lay awake all night, her heart pounding in her breast, tears running down her cheeks as she shuddered with silent sobs, her crushing guilt compelling her to be the first in line for confession the next morning.

They were assigned a penance that Jirella felt severe but fair. Her roommates agreed on one of these points but not the other, and several nights later they held her down and beat her mercilessly, gagging her screams with a bar of soap and a stocking. Despite their hissed accusations that Jirella was a rat she never reported them, for this or any of their later attacks. After all, vengeance and hatred were virtues of the Burnished Chain. For all their outrage and the way everyone but Yekteniya shunned her ever afterward, Jirella believed one of the others would have confessed, if she hadn't. She had faith in her fellow mortals.

That reckless transgression on the convent roof was all Jirella could think about after the Abbotess informed her of the Black Pope's summons. She must have embarrassed her uncle terribly, for him to bring her all the way to the capital. She deserved whatever punishment he would assign, she knew that. Even if it meant her life.

Rather than fearing his judgment, she welcomed it. Before entering the coach that would take her to the Voice of the Allmother, she had secretly donned a hairshirt under her robes and cinched her rosary so tight around her throat every breath was a tribulation. She kept them in place every agonizing day of the long journey. Jirella prayed constantly, and wept not for herself but for the Shepherd of Samoth, whose own niece had rejected the path of righteousness and attempted to conspire with the enemy of mortalkind (only out of peer pressure, but still).

Yet when they climbed the final ridge of the Black Cascades and arrived in Diadem, capital of Samoth and former seat of the

Crimson Empire, the papal guard took her not to the public stocks for crucifixion but to a tasteful study. The Black Pope's chambers were situated in the upper reaches of Castle Diadem, which was itself nestled into the walls of the dead volcano that cradled the city. Climbing the endless stairs to this sanctuary of oaken bookshelves and warm hearth proved an agonizing ordeal for a girl whose collar choked and hairshirt scratched.

In her imagination, Pope Shanatu was forever wreathed in the light of the Fallen Mother, his features blurred—for no mortal sinner could look full upon the face of grace. When the guards ushered her into the study and shut the door behind them, she saw not a radiant figure of divine wrath, but a kind-eyed old man sitting at a sumptuously laid table. He rose as she stood worrying her rosary in the doorway, struggling to catch her breath.

Instead of glowing robes and a hat as high as a steeple, he wore a brocade housecoat trimmed in sable. Silver shot through his dark beard and tonsure, making him appear disarmingly mortal. His slippers glided across the Ugrakari rug, and Jirella fell to her knees. He did not look so very much like her mother, but when he smiled it was the same warm expression, his wrinkles deepening at Jirella's tears. She lowered her face and he stroked her head as if she were his dearest hound. It was the happiest moment of Jirella's hard life, and when she pressed her lips to his black opal ring, Jirella felt such love as she had never before known.

"Welcome home, my child," he said, the hand that wore the Papal ring now cocking her chin up to look at him. "Come and join me for dinner. We have so much to discuss."

"Your Grace—" Jirella began but he lightly knocked her skull with his ring.

"None of that, dear Jirella, none of that!" His smile was every bit as radiant as she had imagined. "Well, not in here, anyway. When we're in public it can't be helped, of course, but in my chambers you may call me Papa."

"Pa…Papa?" After her parents died she never dreamed of calling anyone that ever again.

"You must be famished, though!" He helped her to her feet, and frowned when he rubbed her shoulder through her sackcloth habit. "You aren't wearing a penitent's vest, are you?"

Jirella looked down again, embarrassed at his concern. "I have so much to atone for…Papa."

"We all do, my child, and in the days to come you will wish that all your burdens were worn as easily as a hairshit!" He shook his head, smiling even wider. "You will find more appropriate attire waiting for you in the ablution closet, just through that door. Hurry and change and then join me—I'm as hungry for my quail as you must be for answers. Isn't that so?"

"I… I didn't presume—"

"It's *alright*, Jirella. My very first rule for you is that you must ask me any questions as soon as they pop into your pretty head. Why do you think I've summoned you?"

"To… I…" Jirella bit her lip as his brows furrowed, and she found a strength she didn't know she possessed. This man was her uncle but he was also the Fallen Mother's mortal eyes and ears and voice. Jirella was a sinner born, yes, but she was not so craven as to lie to her saviour. She looked into his eyes, promising herself she would never again fail to meet them. "I tried to summon a devil. At the convent. It didn't work, but I thought you must have known and—"

The Black Pope exploded in laughter, bracing himself against her as he chortled. When he could speak again he said, "Oh my child, we all have a skeleton or two in our confessional."

"Then why am I here?" Jirella asked, flushed with embarrassment at his outburst. She wasn't just some stupid little girl—there just hadn't been any other explanation.

"Because I need a successor," he said quietly, all the mirth gone from his voice. "I called you home because my time has come to step down from the Onyx Pulpit. The Fallen Mother has chosen you as her new Voice."

Jirella tried to smile at his joke but couldn't. Her eyes filled with tears as she struggled to understand why the Black Pope would make such a blasphemous jest. *Why?* He put his hand on her back, his palm pressing her hairshirt into her raw flesh as he guided her to the door of the ablutions closet. She felt like a ghost haunting her own skin, floating across the room as her limbs moved of their own accord. *Why?*

"I asked myself the same question when I received the call," he murmured, as if he could hear her thoughts. Perhaps he could. "You have doubts. I have answers. All the more reason to change in a hurry and join me for dinner, yes?"

Jirella nodded, and staggered into the chamber hewn from the black stone of the mountainside. The door clicked shut behind her. Staring at her pale, dazed expression in the looking glass above the bureau, Jirella tried to pray…and threw up into the water basin instead.

"THE COUNCIL OF DIADEM IS TOMORROW," POPE SHANATU told Jirella as she tried to soothe her nervous stomach with tallow-smeared black bread. His own plate was piled with oily meat, mashed turnips, and stewed greens. Even more decadent than the array of food was the fact they were eating it alone in his cosy library, instead of in some drafty dining hall. "Do you know what that is?"

"No," she said, shivering in the too-soft velvet gown he'd set out for her and staring queasily at her goblet of wine.

"It is the formal meeting between me and Indsorith that will end the war," he said. "Word did reach the convent that there's been a war on, yes?"

"Of course," she said, embarrassed that he thought so little of her provincial education but relieved to hear the conflict was won. "We ceased our daily prayers for the Crimson Queen as soon as she declared war on the Burnished Chain."

"Well, technically we were the ones who initiated this most recent conflict, though I suppose that nuance isn't really relevant!" The Black Pope's lips were slick with quail fat as he smiled at his niece across the cluttered table. "What is important is that the Empire is once again whole and happy, and we can begin to rebuild. The terms of the truce have all been set, the Council of Diadem is merely for show."

"The truce?" asked Jirella. "You mean Queen Indsorith's surrender?"

For the first time, her uncle's sweet demeanour turned sour. "To preserve the dignity of all concerned we are not using the term *surrender*."

"Oh." Jirella nervously took a sip of wine. "We were told… that is, the sisters told us that the crusade would continue until the queen had fallen and the Empire was saved."

"I suppose you aren't old enough to remember the last few times similar oaths were pledged." Her uncle smiled, but it lacked his usual humour. "It has been twenty years since Indsorith assassinated the Stricken Queen and claimed the Carnelian Crown. While her reign has been more accepting of the church than regents past, that is damning with very faint praise indeed. This is neither the first time nor the last that the faithful will be called upon to protect the Empire from Her Majesty's godlessness." He pointed a greasy drumstick at her. "This is where you come in, my dear. To end this civil war both the righteous and the profane have had to make sacrifices. The Fallen Mother has ordained that I step down from my station, and the Holy See shall appoint a successor."

"Me?" Jirella hated how her voice squeaked.

"You." The Black Pope's smile had regained some of its warmth. "Of course, none of this is official yet, but that is what the Holy See will decide at the Council of Diadem. Everything has been preordained. Our seeming defeat to the Crimson Queen will, in time, prove to be the turning point that saves the soul of the Empire."

"But I'm not even a nun, not really!" Jirella took another gulp of wine. "How could I possibly become…"

"You are a blood relation of a member of the Holy See, Jirella," he said. "And you are a virgin."

Jirella drained the rest of her goblet at that. He was right, of course, but how had he known? There were plenty of novices with compromised chastity—to say nothing of the sisters.

"These minor formalities are all that is required for the position, though it is true that traditionally one first climbs to a far higher rank in the Chain before attracting the notice of the Fallen Mother. We live in exceptional times, however, and the Allmother has informed me that you shall be my successor."

Again Jirella found herself incapable of speech. Her uncle refilled her glass as she stared numbly at the quail in front of her, a roasted horn of plenty spilling out wild rice and dried fruits.

"Do not fear, my child; though your calling is great you shall not face it alone. Until such a time as the Fallen Mother deems you capable of shouldering the burden by yourself, I will continue to be the conduit through which she addresses this iniquitous world. You shall undergo the ordeals and rituals necessary to become the Black Pope, but even after you assume your role your dear Papa will counsel you on everything and anything."

This was such a huge relief Jirella found herself on the edge of tears again.

"We are together in this, my child, and while we pay lip service to the corrupt queen we shall work tirelessly to depose her once and for all. This is all part of our saviour's grand design. She has *chosen you*, Jirella. Are you willing to accept her call?"

"Yes." The word left her wine-numb lips before she was even aware of it, as though the divine spirit were already moving through her. "Yes."

"Good girl!" The Black Pope beamed, reaching across the table to knock his goblet against hers. "I have many preparations yet to make for tomorrow's summit, but before I bid you goodnight I must warn you of the perils ahead. I fear your path to the Onyx Pulpit will be dangerous."

"The Crimson Queen is a heretic, and her agents are our enemies," said Jirella, eager to prove to her uncle and the holy spirit inside him that she had been paying attention, that she was fit for her new role. "I must be on guard against them, yes?"

"Certainly, certainly," agreed the Black Pope, but again she noticed a shadow fall over his pleasant face. "More immediately, however, I speak of enemies within the Burnished Chain itself."

"Enemies in the *church*?" Jirella felt as dizzy at the suggestion as if she'd quaffed the whole flagon by herself.

"Sadly, yes." Her uncle shook his head, unhappy to deliver such ill news. "There are those among our ranks who seek base power in this world instead of salvation beyond it. Once you are ordained as Black Pope they will be forced to accept your stewardship. But, from the time the Holy See announces your selection until the time you don my mitre and ring you will be their target. If some tragedy were to befall you in that interim their own candidate could step in to claim your rightful place. Fortunately, the confirmation process is not as protracted as it used to be. Within a week you will take on my title. Once you have taken the divine spirit of the Allmother inside you, not even they will dare stand against you."

Jirella stared into her wine. "Who are they? These enemies who seek to thwart the will of the Fallen Mother for their own vain ambitions?"

"I fear the ringleader is one of the three most powerful members of the Holy See, my Chief Officers, but my source was poisoned to death before we could confirm which one of them it is." Jirella flinched at this casual mention of murder. "My agents are working even now to unmask our enemy, but in the meantime you will have a bodyguard with you at all times. Trust no one but your Papa, and be forever vigilant."

"What are their names, these officers?" They would mean nothing to her now, she knew, but if she were indeed to become the Black Pope she must begin her education immediately.

"Cardinal Artsidr is the first—she is Dean of the College of Cardinals, second only to myself in the church. The next is Cardinal Ihsahn, Prelate of Samoth and liaison to the court of the Crimson Queen. And the third is Cardinal Wendell, the Chain's Minister of Propaganda. When you rise to the Onyx Pulpit these three will sit at your left hand. However, until that happy day, one of them may prove your mortal enemy."

Her time in a convent dormitory had taught Jirella the necessity of playing politics with fair-weather friends, but this was pushing it rather far. "If you have cause to doubt any of them, should not all three be unseated? If they are faithful they will understand and welcome your decree."

"Would that it were so simple!" His Grace dipped his hands in a fingerbowl and wiped them on his monogrammed napkin. "If you are to live long enough to take my place you must learn to never strike until you are sure who is an enemy and who is an ally. No matter how many of the former you eliminate new ones will always crop up to take their place, but the reverse is true of the latter—the more alliances you sunder the harder it is to forge new ones."

Perhaps seeing the doubt on her face, he said, "Believe me, child, I should like nothing more than to secure your safety, even if it meant sacking the entire Holy See. Alas, I am but a conduit for the will of the Fallen Mother, and she has commanded me to work my diplomacy with a pen rather than a poniard. She will reveal our enemy in her own time, and until then you must consider this your first trial."

"My first trial," said Jirella, hoping against hope that it would not prove to be her last.

JIRELLA SPENT A SLEEPLESS NIGHT IN THE BEDROOM adjoining the study, chambers which apparently belonged solely to her. Her uncle had suggested she might start her conquest of the library with the stack of volumes on theology and theocracy he had left on her nightstand, but she turned her attentions instead to the tapestry of the Fallen Mother that hung on the far wall. In all her years of prayer she had never received any kind of response, but she dared to hope that this time it would be different, that her saviour would deign to address her clearly…but Jirella heard no voice but her own in the lonely chamber. She stayed at prayer even when the black tallow sizzled out in its bowl and her exhausted mind began to drift in and out of the First Dark, the cramps in her legs preventing her from falling completely under.

Yet sleep will no more be denied than her father, death, and so as the Council of Diadem assembled to decide the fate of the Crimson Empire its future pontiff lay drowsing on the rug where she had eventually collapsed. A knock woke her, light but insistent, and

Jirella sat up with a start, marvelling at the absurdity of her dream… and then feeling a fist close over her heart as she realized she wasn't back in her dormitory. The enormity of what had transpired reared up in her mind, a cold, black wave building higher and higher, poised to break and drown her…

Jirella lurched to her feet in front of the tapestry, staring up at the beatific face of the Fallen Mother and refusing the Deceiver his due. The fear didn't vanish, not all at once, but it did falter, and that weakness was all the girl needed to press the advantage. She was Jirella Martigore, the next Black Pope of the Burnished Chain, and she *deserved* this. Of all the prelates and princes of the Crimson Empire, *she* had been chosen by the Fallen Mother. Her heart swelled with virtuous pride, and she denied the weakness that had attempted to consume her. It retreated, flowing away as swiftly as it had come. Imbued with a confidence she had never known, Jirella went to answer another knock at the door…and paused.

Sleepy though she was, she could scarcely forget her uncle's many warnings. So long as she remembered to follow his instructions their enemies wouldn't find an opening to attack. At least, he had said, *not effectively.*

"I fear I have forgotten my prayers," she called through the bog oak door.

"Link four, verse thirteen," answered a gentle voice. It was Jirella's favourite piece of scripture from the Chain Canticles, which she had shared with her uncle the night before. *Though the Star grows dim, Her light shall show yet brighter in the darkness.*

Unlocking her chamber, Jirella met a war nun nearly as tall and broad as the door. Her penitent's mask hid most of her face, but the rough skin that showed around her purple eyes was pitted with tiny scars. A steel cross jutted up over one shoulder…the hilt and guard of a sword nearly as tall as this giantess herself, strapped to her broad back.

Jirella had seen plenty of armed guards and soldiers, from a safe distance, but she had never seen a warrior more formidable. And according to her uncle, this woman was her personal bodyguard. As she gawped at her protector, the woman dropped to a knee in front of her. The fifteen year-old girl still had to look up to meet the woman's eye.

"I am Sister Vaura," the woman said in a disconcertingly soft voice. "I pledge my life to your service, Jirella Martigore, from this day until the Mother calls me home."

"Thank you?" Jirella didn't know what else to say. "I… We are very well met, Sister, and I welcome your service."

The two remained in an awkward silence until the war nun said, "May I rise, ma'am?"

"Yes, of course!" Jirella smiled as the woman stood. Here was the first person that would heed Jirella's every command, and she had to admit she rather fancied the taste of such power. She was destined for great responsibilities, but it would do her good to start with something small…or someone big, as the case may be! "My uncle must be at the Council of Diadem, so perhaps you might care to join me for breakfast?"

The woman's eyes widened as she stepped back into the study for Jirella to pass.

"I welcome your invitation, ma'am, but it is forbidden for an anathema to break bread with one of your station."

Jirella's breath caught in her throat. An *anathema*? She had heard ghost stories about the witchborn before, of course, had even told a few back at the convent, but she had never imagined meeting one of the monsters herself. Having such a creature assigned as her bodyguard ranked just under finding herself heir to the Onyx

Pulpit for unexpected developments.

"Forgive me—" Jirella began but the war nun waved her bulky hand.

"Pray never apologize to me, ma'am, for anything. The barbers blessed me well indeed, if you did not know at first glance."

"If you're not supposed to eat with me I imagine you're not supposed to interrupt me, either." Jirella smiled so her guardian wouldn't get the wrong idea. "I am sure I will defer to your experience in many things, Sister Vaura, but I imagine I can say whatever I want to whomever I want, be it a sincere apology or a ridiculous order."

"That…that may be true, ma'am," said the woman, and Jirella fancied she might be smiling, too, underneath her mask.

"What I was *saying*, then, was forgive me my curiosity, but would you remove your mask so that I may see the rest of your face?" They both knew it wasn't a question, but the war nun clearly balked at the notion. "I have never met an anathema before, Sister Vaura, and I wish to see how different your kind truly are from mine."

"Very well, ma'am," the big woman said in her small voice. She pulled back the hood of her robe and untied her mask. Jirella sucked in through her teeth as the black cloth fell away to reveal Sister Vaura's hairless, pitted head. Other than her grotesquely scarred skin she might be mistaken for pureborn, which only made her more intriguing.

"What…how…" Jirella rose on her tip-toes to look closer at the woman's broad features, not even sure how to phrase her question.

"Feathers, ma'am," said the war nun, unable to meet Jirella's inquisitive stare. Whether it was weakness or deference on the anathema's part, it thrilled Jirella. "Through the grace of the Fallen Mother and her surgeons I have been saved from my monstrous birth."

"Glory be," Jirella breathed as the anathema leaned down so the girl could touch her scarred hide. It felt like running her fingers over a plucked chicken down in the convent kitchens. Looking at the woman's full lips and patrician's nose, she said, "Praise the Fallen Mother you weren't born with a beak!"

"Praise the Fallen Mother," agreed Sister Vaura. "Even if I had, His Grace's barbers are most clever. I have known others with that affliction, and worse, yet all are made whole before being admitted to the Dens."

"You mean the Dens are *real*?" Jirella jerked her hand away, scarcely able to believe the horrifying rumours were true.

"Not a mile beneath your feet, ma'am," said the war nun as she tied her mask back into place. "It is where I came of age. His Holiness Pope Shanatu believes that even my benighted kind might serve the Burnished Chain, once we are remade in the likeness of the pure."

"Will wonders never cease…" Jirella shook her head. She scarcely had an appetite anymore, but she certainly needed a hot mug of kaldi to settle her nerves. That was an indulgence the sisters had forbidden back at the convent, but from the extravagant feast her uncle had offered her last night she imagined nothing would be forbidden the future Black Pope. "Whether you join me or not, Sister Vaura, it is high time I broke my fast. Do I just tell you what I want brought in, or do I pull the rope for a servant the way my uncle did?"

"In the future you may tell me of anything you require and I will see that it is delivered, but at present we are already overdue." The war nun pointed at a cloth-wrapped bundle on the otherwise barren table. "I did have a lunch prepared for you, but now you will have to take it with us."

"Where are we going?" Jirella looked nervously at the outer

door. "I assumed that I would just spend the week here, in seclusion? With all the perils facing me…"

"The assassins, you mean?" Jirella fancied the anathema was smiling under her mask again. "When you have enemies, ma'am, it is better to move around than stay in one place. His Grace commanded me to deliver you to Barber Norton before the Council adjourns, which means we must move swiftly indeed, else we shall be late."

"A barber?" After the anathema's talk of Chainite surgeons remaking the flesh of sinners, Jirella couldn't imagine anyone she would like to meet less.

Yet her path was set by the hand of the holy, so she held her head high as she followed the war nun out, her only hesitation borne from indecision over whether or not to take the packed lunch. After a moment's dallying she stuffed the bundle in the pocket-sleeve of her voluminous gown—she was not hungry, yet, but she owed it to her maker to seize every gift she was offered. Gluttony had never been her strongest virtue, but if she were to don the ebon mitre of the Black Pope she must strive to embody them all.

HALF A DOZEN MORE PAPAL GUARDS WAITED OUTSIDE Jirella's chambers, though none of them seemed so fierce as Sister Vaura. The six split up to surround the two women, three taking the lead and the others bringing up the rear from a modest distance. They didn't just make Jirella feel safe, they made her feel respected—a lord of the realm stepping out to survey her domain.

Castle Diadem was little different by day than it was by night. Whether a passageway was narrow as an alley or wide as a great hall there were no windows to offer a contrast to the spectral blue light of the guttering lamps that jutted out from the stone walls. These eternal flames were fed from ancient fumes beneath the mountain, Jirella's guide informed her, so that the papal palace should never know darkness until the Day of Becoming. The cave air often carried the spicy tang of incense and once the smell of horses.

"Imperials!" Jirella gasped as they stepped out of a corridor and she found herself overlooking a several hundred-foot drop. Their path led them out across a stone bridge that that spanned a massive square, the parade ground far below teeming with countless soldiers in angry red tabards. She felt dizzy at being so high and exposed, even with the high carven railings.

"We are all Imperials, ma'am," said Sister Vaura. "Or at least we shall be again, once the Council of Diadem is completed."

"Yes, well, you know what I mean," said Jirella, resolving to better act her part: stoic and world-weary, not excitable and naïve. Putting her hands on the railing and looking out over the assembled army, she stifled the puerile impulse to spit—back at the convent spitting at gargoyles from the dormitory window had been a high art. In what she hoped was her most impressively portentous tone, she said, "If Queen Indsorith thinks she has the run of our castle just because she's returned to Samoth she will find herself dearly mistaken."

"May the Fallen Mother show all who err the true path before it is too late," agreed Sister Vaura. Resuming her brisk pace over the bridge, she looked back at Jirella and said, "You have seen the skulls, ma'am? Over the Crimson Throne Room?"

"I have not yet made the time," Jirella said airily, suspecting the anathema of toying with her inexperience.

"Dozens of assassins came for Queen Indsorith during her first year on the Crimson Throne, and she dispatched each one herself, mounting their skulls over the entrance to the throne room."

"No wonder she declared the Serpent's Circle the new capital and fled down there with her court!" Jirella was pleased with herself for remembering what amounted to ancient history. "She must have realized her reign would be brief indeed if she stayed in Samoth, where faith is stronger than fear."

A great tolling rang out, startling Jirella. Looking up she saw a bell the size of a country church suspended high above the immense square.

"The Council of Diadem adjourns." Jirella could barely make out Sister Vaura's soft voice over the echoing peals, the anathema looking to the same heavens as her pureborn companion. "The war is ended. Samoth is again capital province of the Crimson Empire, and Queen Indsorith again rules from Diadem."

"Alongside the Black Pope," said Jirella. "My unc—His Grace told me the Black Pope would reign beside the Crimson Queen."

"And His Grace told me to make sure you preceded him to the barber's theatre," said Sister Vaura, looking down at her. "Should you prefer to run, ma'am, or shall I carry you?"

THE FALLEN MOTHER WISHED HER PUREBORN CHILDREN every happiness they could eke from their harsh lives, and so Jirella would have chosen to run even if her pride hadn't balked at being carried like a babe. Running was strictly forbidden at the convent, which of course meant all the girls did it every chance they could. All the girls save Jirella.

Now, however, she fairly skated over the polished floors in her soft new turnshoes, her dark hair flying like a pennant as they rushed to make up for lost time. Clergy and guards alike scattered to get out of their way, though Jirella imagined that had more to do with the huge war nun leading the charge than anything else. What would those robed fuddy-duddies and lazy soldiers think if they knew the girl holding up her skirts as she dashed past them would be standing at the Onyx Pulpit in a week's time?

It was mad, liberating fun. As she chased Sister Vaura out from a corridor and across a wide chapel where nuns prayed before an enormous idol of Saint Megg, Jirella gave thanks that she would never again be like one of them. Up ahead a wimple turned, and a familiar face broke into a wide smile as the kneeling novice recognized Jirella, too, and scrambled up to meet her.

Yekteniya had been Jirella's only true friend at the convent, and it swelled her heart with joy to see the Fallen Mother had reunited them so quickly. The girl must have left the convent immediately after Jirella, the same day even, to be here now, which didn't make any sense…but then what did, these days? Jirella slowed her mad dash as Yekteniya opened her arms to embrace her friend, and—

Sister Vaura loomed up behind Yekteniya, and before Jirella could shout a warning the anathema neatly decapitated the girl. Jirella stumbled, staring agog as Yekteniya's lovely blonde hair swirled around her falling head, so close warm blood spattered Jirella cheeks. Someone grabbed her from behind before she could fall into her murdered friend, and a pair of her bodyguards darted in and seized Yekteniya by the arms, holding her up.

Except it wasn't Yekteniya anymore, just her limp body. Her head was on the floor of the chapel, lying on its cheek beside her broken rosary, blood oozing from her smiling lips, her eyes fixed on nothing. All the other nuns were screaming. Jirella was relieved they were summoning help, because she was too shocked to make any noise at all, or even struggle away from the strong arms holding her back from Yekteniya.

Sister Vaura stepped around the guards holding up the headless body, blood gouting down the front of its habit. The war nun had sheathed her sword but held a cruel black dagger. It looked so small in her bulky fist.

Jirella stopped struggling, a cold numbness flushing through her. If this was the Fallen Mother's plan for Jirella, she would face it with dignity. In the darkest hour of the night she had asked the Allmother to spare her the burden of all this responsibility, to choose anyone else to be Her Voice, and now her prayers were to be answered.

Jirella had brought this on herself.

Except instead of stepping forward and stabbing Jirella through the heart, Sister Vaura turned to Yekteniya's body. The two bodyguards were still ghoulishly holding it up, and the war nun gingerly slit open the front of the corpse's bloody habit. Peeling back the cut cloth, she revealed neither a shift not the budding breasts that Yekteniya had once invited Jirella to touch. A strange bloated mass covered her chest. Over the screams of the fleeing nuns Jirella couldn't hear what Sister Vaura was telling the guards who held up the body, but their stern faces lost all their color and their narrowed eyes widened in alarm.

"She should see this." Jirella did hear that, and as the guard who had restrained Jirella let her go she staggered forward for a better look. The curious bulge was not tied to Yekteniya's chest, she saw, but *growing around it.* This close she could hear it humming, too, even over the retreating shrieks of the nuns. Then she laughed, an ugly bark of a sound, because she recognized it for what it was. A wasp's nest of some kind, its bloodstained walls as thin as parchment… Jirella found herself sinking into that hive, the droning of screaming nuns all around her, and as if from a great distance she heard Sister Vaura say,

"And now, ma'am, I shall be obliged to carry you."

JIRELLA JERKED UPRIGHT, COUGHING AT WHATEVER FOUL draught had revived her. Her mouth stung from the tannic brew. The man who had administered it stepped back, giving her room to breathe the fetid air of this cave.

Every other quarter of the castle she had seen was pristinely carved from the living rock of the mountain, though the architecture varied from baroque Samothan to subdued Geminidean and a hundred other styles besides. This place, though, looked more like a hermit's lair than a civilized chamber, with smoky candles mounted on tall stalagmites that jutted from the floor, and bottles and beakers set out to collect drippings from thick, mineral-striped stalactites. The uneven walls of the vast room sparkled with glass panels, hundreds upon hundreds of them winking at her in the candlelight. Jirella sat in the middle of it all on a moss-covered table. There was but one door that she could see, and it was bolted from within.

The room was warm and damp and stinking with some acrid smell she couldn't place. Jirella looked around for Sister Vaura, but found she was alone in this place…save for the man who watched her take in her surroundings with no small amusement. His pristine red operating gown and sparkling chainsilk gloves were an odd contrast to the squalid setting, and his smile was even warmer than her uncle's.

"You're the barber," croaked Jirella. Her throat felt raw from crying, though she couldn't remember anything after Yekteniya… "Where's Sister Vaura?"

"I am C. Elbert Norton. The Third, as luck would have it." The barber took a slight bow. "Your bodyguards are not needed here. In point of fact, they are forbidden, along with every other mortal on the Star. Only those who receive the highest calling may enter, and what is spoken in this sanctified office will never be repeated. Do you understand?"

Jirella nodded, though she didn't, not really. Everything still felt like a dream. "You're a barber *and* a priest, then, one of those who cure the witchborn?"

"I am nothing of the sort!" Barber Norton gave her a withering scowl. "I am not an officer of the church, nor do I approve of your uncle's ecclesiastic surgeons—perhaps it's better than burning those monsters like King Kaldruut used to do, but I believe Queen Indsorith had the right idea when she ordered the Chain to stop mutilating them."

"The queen did what?" Jirella had only just found out that reformed anathemas were real, but apparently this was old news to everyone not banished to a convent.

"He hasn't told you much, has he?" Barber Norton clucked his tongue. "Your uncle's obstinate refusal to abandon the practice has only gone and lost him the Onyx Pulpit—that's what the war grew out of, you know. A perfect bloody mess, with precious time squandered, and for what? Nothing. The church gets to keep manufacturing their Chainwitches, yes, but the Queen returns to Diadem, which will complicate things terribly. If he'd listened to me from the beginning—"

"Who are you?" demanded Jirella. "To speak so outrageously of His Grace?"

"I am the personal barber to the Black Pope, which means I will speak outrageously of anyone I wish," he said smugly. "The office you are poised to inherit is beset on all sides by toads and serpents, and a sage ruler may find value in a cat's-paw of my sharpness. I would have thought you learned that lesson on your way to my office—if your little friend's nestvest had been disturbed, you and half the people in that chapel would have been stung to death."

"Yekteniya…" Jirella pulled her knees in and wrapped her arms around herself to stop shaking. This wasn't a bad dream. She closed her eyes, refusing the weakness of the Deceiver. Yekteniya wasn't her friend. She never had been. She was the enemy, an assassin, and the Fallen Mother had intervened to protect her chosen emissary. Looking back up at Barber Norton, she asked, "If you're so savvy to what's going on, who sent her after me? They must have been spying on me even back at the convent, before His Grace summoned me… And they must have known why he called me back, to have Yekteniya follow me to Diadem."

"Your uncle's agents are surely investigating the matter even as we speak, but I doubt they will uncover anything conclusive." Barber Norton shrugged. "Better to gird you in the armour that will protect you through your coronation than waste time worrying over who wants you dead—they all do. But once you ascend to power they will abandon that course and try more subtle means of currying favour. This is the way of things."

"If they're going to give up once I become the new Black Pope why wait a whole week for the coronation?" asked Jirella, filled with righteous fury at the cowardice of the Deceiver's agents. She would respect them more if they continued in their assassination attempts throughout her reign rather than playing politics!

"It is not mere bureaucracy, I assure you," said Barber Norton, leaning against the mossy table where Jirella sat. "Technically, your coronation began the moment you entered this room. Late, I should mention, but you arrived safely, and now the worst danger is past. Assuming you spoke true of your purity, that is."

"I beg your pardon?" Jirella bristled at the suggestion she might have lied to His Grace.

"It is for your sake I seek confirmation," he said in a conspiratorial tone. "If there are any indiscretions in your past, we can make…alternate arrangements. But if you are indeed untouched by carnal experience we can keep with tradition and administer the Ordeal of the Ebon Ghost—it is the ultimate trial of one's purity, a test only those fit to become pontiff can bear."

"I eagerly accept any trials you might present," Jirella said haughtily. "The Fallen Mother has chosen me and I have naught to fear."

"Yes, well, we'll see about that," he said with a queer little smile. "You must not undertake this ordeal lightly, Jirella. It will change you from a simple girl to…something else. A temple for the divine, as the Chain would have it."

"I am ready."

"It does not appear to be pleasant experience," said Barber Norton, "and if you survive you will no longer be quite human. You shall be immune to any poison known to mortalkind, but your every drop of blood or bile, saliva or urine will be as deadly venom. Your body shall brook no lovers—you shall remain a virgin for the rest of your days."

"I told you, I am ready," said Jirella, remembering how she had longed to touch Yekteniya in her bunk that night last summer, how the girl had teased her with reminders that lust was a sacred virtue…and how she had fled to her own bed, driven by some sudden impulse to remain pure. Now she knew from where that instinct had sprung, and thanked the Fallen Mother for her wisdom. Who could know and embody lust more than one who was never able to consummate their desire?

"Very well then, Jirella," said the barber, winding away between the stalagmites to one of the glass windows set in the wall. Looking back at her, he sounded almost sad. "We shall have much to discuss in the future, I hope, but for now the Ordeal begins. Godspeed, Your Grace."

Jirella flushed with pride at his use of the honorific. He fiddled with a latch on the recessed glass panel, and then it sprung open on a hinge. As it did the barber flattened himself against the wall beside the small opening, a curious gesture that made the hairs on the back of Jirella's neck stand up.

"What—"

Whatever question Jirella was going to call out died on her lips as a small black bird fluttered out of the hole in the wall, bobbing around the hanging stalactites toward her. Clumsy though it seemed, it flew with speed and intention. Jirella scooted back on the table, frantically looking to Barber Norton for help. He stayed pressed against the wall, watching her with ugly fascination. As it darted down at her, Jirella saw it wasn't a bird at all. It was…something she had no name for, a bloated leach with buzzing dragonfly wings and ichor-dripping barbs.

It flew straight at her face, and on sheer instinct she batted it away, Fallen Mother forgive her.

Instead of falling out of the air the horror wrapped around her hand. Then the pain hit. It felt like she had seized a bouquet of nettles and then shoved her hand in a kiln. Instead of shaking the clinging monster off her hand, her whole body betrayed her, contorting on the mossy table as she screamed and screamed. Worse than the initial pain was the sensation of it slowly spreading as the terrible thing crawled under the cuff of her sleeve and up her wrist. Its very touch was so caustic her gown smouldered and burned away wherever its carapace brushed the velvet. It felt like a white hot coal being slowly dragged up her skin, the smoke from her own blistering flesh making her retch. Jirella stopped thrashing, now paralysed with pain as it worked its way up her arm, bringing mind-blistering agony as it crawled closer and closer to her shoulder. Her neck. Her face. Her foam-flecked lips.

She would have begged for death, had she been able.

Yet the Ordeal did not truly begin until it folded back its shimmering black wings and wriggled all the way inside her.

JIRELLA THRASHED WILDLY ON THE TABLE, HER DRESS corroding off her in sizzling tatters and the moss beneath her baked black as she shrieked with all the fury of a wronged god. This was what she had become. No mortal could endure such pain and terror and live, yet Jirella's agony grew and grew, lifting her again and again off the burning table. She could feel the thing inside her, prodding its needle limbs into her tender throat. She choked and gagged, but was no longer afraid. She was *wroth*.

The man in red. He had done this. She looked for him at the window-tiled wall, but he had crept over to the floor in the rear of the room, flinging up a trapdoor as her gaze found him.

Jirella flew at him, wailing. The Ebon Ghost's wings beat between her lungs, carrying her aloft. Her smoldering shoes fell from her feet as she glided around the stalagmites, her toes dangling several inches off the bare floor of the cave.

The man in red disappeared through his trapdoor, metallic smoke billowing out. She dived down after him, into the fume. The smoke grew thicker, the air hotter, burning her eyes, burning her lungs. Compared to what the Ebon Ghost was doing inside her, blind and choking was a welcome distraction.

She must be falling straight down an ancient lava tube, through the walls of Castle Diadem, into the simmering bowels of the mountain. Jirella imagined the tunnel narrowing around her until she became stuck, lodged in the burning dark rock for all eternity, kept alive as punishment for her presumption. Her rage tried to spiral inward, but it found no purchase—the pain had hollowed Jirella out so perfectly there was nothing left inside for doubt to take hold of. Like a gale ripping through a canyon, her anger exploded back out of her throat.

The smoke became so dense it pressed back against her, slowing her fall, then halting it all altogether. She became lodged, just as she had envisioned, but instead of rock she was buried in whatever it was the smoke had thickened into, a rank tunnel of warm pulsing muscle. She recognized the smell from the barber's office above, from the cage the Ebon Ghost had fled—it was the stink of a cockroach nest, of foul insects fornicating and defecating and eating each other in some small, hot space.

Jirella dug her nails into the soft, slippery wall and pulled herself forward, no longer sure if she was burrowing deeper into hell or climbing upward, toward heaven. Her blood boiled in her veins. Her skin bubbled off her bones. Yet she persisted. She had made of herself a temple for the Fallen Mother, and no matter what her enemies attempted she would not let that gift be lost down in the First Dark.

Then her fingers found not another burning handful of stinking insect waste, but the cool air of deep places. Seizing the rim of her prison, Jirella hauled herself free. She flopped out onto cold stone, the distended ovipositor leaking vile secretions in her wake. Distant chanting echoed off the walls like the droning of a hive. In the glare of thousands of candles she looked around to see from whence this monstrous birth canal originated, but saw only the titanic effigy of the Fallen Mother standing over her. There was no tunnel at the foot of the statue, no hole in the ceiling high above. She had come from nowhere.

The chanting grew louder. Jirella stood blinking as she wiped blood from her eyes. Not her blood. She was standing naked before the ikon of the Allmother, surrounded by gutted sacrifices, loops of entrails warming her feet. Hooded clerics with ornate silver devil masks stood on the steps beneath her, and beyond them a throng of robed worshippers filled the vast Lower Chainhouse, their hymn rising in time with Jirella's whine.

The clerics had tricked her, luring her in with bleating offerings. Her eyes couldn't focus enough for her to see if the bodies at her bare feet were the kids of goats or the children of mortals. She turned to scale the statue, to flee back into the First Dark, but the clerics were already on top of her, chaining her with burnished iron and ancient incantations. The Black Pope led them, his mitre unmistakable, but beneath the tall hat the face Jirella saw was not her uncle's but her own.

His sibilant chant subdued her long enough for his clerics to chain her to the inverted cross, but when they began to scratch the secret mysteries of the Chain into her unset flesh she bucked in pain. Their scrimshawed quills jabbed through her guts, piercing the Ebon Ghost and harrying it deeper and deeper, poisoning it as it had poisoned her, and she wept for it. Sigils and glyphs pulsed beneath her skin, the steady hands of her assailants tracing them with their blades. A cardinal wearing the frozen grimace of one of the gargoyles she used to spit on back at the convent hunched over her loins with a scalpel and meticulously shaved a cross into the hair between her legs.

The Ebon Ghost wriggled its way into and through her bowel before tearing its way at last into her unspoiled womb, clarifying Jirella's exquisite agony into something yet more transcendent. She knew that she would soon see the face of the Fallen Mother. The chanting came to crescendo as the heavens exploded in cleansing flame around her. A last thing Jirella remembered was a man in red picking up a small white egg in his gloved hand and placing it into a reliquary.

THE FINAL STAGE OF THE CORONATION WOULD BE torture of an entirely different sort, and far more humiliating than anything Jirella had endured in the midst of the Ordeal of the Ebon Ghost. She, the most important living mortal in all the Star, must supplicate herself to the Crimson Queen in the throne room they would share ever after. It was entirely symbolic, of course, Shanatu taking off his mitre and passing it to Indsorith, who would then plant it on Jirella's brow, but it irked nonetheless.

At least it would soon be over. Jirella rose from her knees, her black robes of state chaffing her mortified flesh as she stood in front of the tapestry in her room. The likeness of the Fallen Mother had struck her as so impressive when first she had come here, but now it seemed so shabby compared to the oil painting that hung in the Papal suite. Hard to believe it had only been a week since she had come here—it felt like years.

"Don't fret, Sister Vaura, I'm coming," she told the war nun as the big woman stepped into her room. "This is one trial I won't be late...for?"

The anathema had closed the door behind her and now turned the key in the lock. Jirella's heart sank, but that only made her stand all the taller.

"Will you tell me who?" she asked as the purple-eyed giantess turned to face her. The anathema shook her heavy head, her penitent mask breathing heavier than Jirella would have expected. The woman didn't want to do this, Jirella could tell...but she nevertheless unslung her enormous sword from her back. "You will tell me why, though. Whatever else you are, Sister Vaura, you're a good Chainite, and we both know I am the true and rightful pontiff."

"You are a puppet," the anathema said sadly as she lifted her blade. "You are nothing but Shanatu's surrogate, and you will keep torturing and enslaving my kind as he has always done."

"And you think whichever Cardinal put you up to this will do any different?" Jirella hated this monster even more, now that she realized her naiveté. "Whatever they promised you, it's a lie. We'll both die for nothing."

"My life is already forfeit," said the big woman stepping closer. "If I spared your life, ma'am, would you swear to empty the Dens, to stop the pogrom against my people? Would you let the wildborn live as they are?"

A final test. Easily passed.

"I shall not compromise the sanctity of my post for any life, not even my own," said Jirella. "Unlike those false Chainites you conspire with, I shall not swear any oath I do not intend to keep. I answer only to the Fallen Mother."

"As do we all," said Sister Vaura, drawing back her blade.

"Forgive me, Sister," said Jirella, raising a shaking hand, "but pray grant me one final request?"

The war nun didn't answer, but she didn't chop Jirella in half, either. Not yet.

"Let me look upon your face again?" Jirella's voice quavered. "If you are to be a martyr for the liberation of your people, let yourself be the first anathema to shed her Chainite trappings. And if I am to be the sacrifice that buys your salvation, allow me to gaze upon the righteous face of my executioner instead of an assassin hiding behind a mask."

Instead of lowering her massive sword the war nun managed to hold it aloft with one hand as she reached up with the other and untied her mask. Jirella sucked nervously at her cheek. The anathema was even uglier than Jirella remembered. As the mask fell away, Sister Vaura made ready to carry out her execution, and Jirella stepped closer to accept the will of the Fallen Mother.

"Safe roads guide you to her breast," whispered Jirella, staring up into the witchborn's scarred face.

"Safe havens keep you at—" Sister Vaura began, but before she could complete the Prayer of Exodus, Jirella spat into the anathema's open mouth. Then she wheeled about, diving onto the bed and rolling clear across it, waiting for that massive sword to split her in two, or smash the bed to pieces in the attempt. She landed on the floor on the far side and looked back to see her doom striding angrily toward her...

Yet Sister Vaura stood exactly where she had, the sword clattering to her feet as her shaking hands went to her wide-eyed face. Not only had Barber Norton spoken true of the change that had effected Jirella, but the potency of her poison was incredible—smoke began pouring from the anathema's slack mouth. Sister Vaura sank her strong fingers into her own throat, blood welling out as she clawed at herself. She fell to her knees as she scraped deeper and deeper into her neck, fleshy cords snapping like harp strings. All the while those purple eyes stared at Jirella where she crouched on the far side of the bed. The anathema almost looked like *she* had been the one who'd been betrayed.

"Safe havens keep you at your rest," Jirella told the monster when her relentless fingers exposed the white of her spine and she pitched forward onto her pitted face.

The girl stepped past the shuddering corpse of her protector and went to inherit the Burnished Chain.

ACCORDING TO THE POMP OF ANCIENT CEREMONY and ecclesiastic symbolism, Jirella Martigore died that morning on the mist-kissed terrace of the Crimson Throne Room, cold grey clouds swirling overhead. In her place stood Pope Y'Homa III, Mother of Midnight, Shepherdess of the Lost, resplendent in vestments crafted from the iridescent feathers and inky fur of owlbats and beaded with a thousand black opals. The inverted cross of her scepter was carved from the petrified blood of an ancient devil queen. She was fifteen years old.

The faithful of the Star rejoiced.

Everything after Queen Indsorith placed the mitre on her head was a bit of an anxious blur of doubt and worry—her uncle had told her not to expect any great change, but she had hoped he would be proven wrong. Yet she didn't feel any different, not at all.

It seemed the Fallen Mother would find other ways than direct communication to guide Y'Homa's hand, at least for the time being.

For now, she guided the hand herself, holding it out for her three Chief Officers to kiss the papal ring at the conclusion of the coronation.

First came Cardinal Artsidr, a willowy granddame with more spies than the rest of the College of Cardinals combined. She offered her new pontiff the sweetest of smiles as she pressed her wrinkled lips to the onyx ring. Pope Y'Homa imagined her whispering in the ear of Yekteniya and then Sister Vaura and she returned the crone's smile with one of her own.

Next was Cardinal Ihsahn, a far younger and prettier woman than Y'Homa had expected. She barely grazed the ring with her lips, but Y'Homa flicked her finger, bumping the onyx against her mouth to make sure the Prelate of Samoth got the message. As liaison to the Crimson Court it was not a huge stretch to imagine her collaborating with Indsorith to kill Shantanu's chosen successor, bribing Sister Vaura with a resolution the Crimson Queen already favoured.

Then there was Cardinal Wendell, a grotesque parody of a man whose lips smacked greedily against her ring. The Chain's Minister of Propaganda didn't seem to be nearly as clever as the others, but Y'Homa couldn't be sure if his wits were genuinely dull or if his demeanour was simply a ruse to direct suspicion away from himself. He certainly seemed clever enough at his work, oiling shameless lies with sentimental qualifications and making sure every truth was inflated with his hot air until it swelled near to bursting. With his bland appeals to populist sentiment, could he have been the one to tempt a conflicted anathema into betrayal?

Well, it scarcely mattered now which of the three had attempted to thwart Y'Homa's ascension, for they had all failed and now had no choice but to accept her rule. Not that they would get to enjoy that luxury for very long. Barber Norton had assured her that the contact poison they had coated her ring in would be slow-acting enough to not have them keel over on the spot, but before the sun next rose all three would die in the most exquisite agonies.

Her uncle would not be happy, but sorrow is the lot of mortals. If the Fallen Mother truly wanted any of Y'Homa's Chief Officers to live, she would surely save them, just as she had saved Y'Homa many times over. Only the guilty would be punished. Y'Homa truly believed that.

"Shall we, Your Grace?" asked Queen Indsorith, nodding her crowned head at the twin seats that rose from the vast veranda of the Crimson Throne Room, here at the crest of Diadem's cone.

"Certainly, Your Majesty," said Pope Y'Homa III, taking the hand of the Crimson Queen. By striking his truce with the queen, Pope Shanatu had saved the flesh of the Crimson Empire. Now it fell to Y'Homa to save its soul.

That would have to wait, however.

This morning Her Majesty had elected to wear gloves.

A ROYAL GIFT

MARK ALDER

— Banners of Blood —

"I DO NOT FEEL LIKE A DEVIL." BUT HOW DOES A DEVIL feel? The Black Prince, raised among men, thinking himself a man, gazed through the window at Windsor, watching the ladies cut shadows in the long light of the late summer evening. There was Alice Ferrers, slender and graceful, moving along the path as if she floated on a river, the movement of her legs scarcely visible beneath her long skirt. Beside her waddled the stocky Lady Maude of Warwick, thick-legged, arms swinging as if to brush away impeding branches. What if Lady Alice felt lumpen and solid, whereas Lady Maude felt as light as a breeze? Did it change reality? Still they were as they were, their natures unaltered.

The prince took up his looking glass, a gift from his cousin John, Prince of France, friendly enemy. It had been a gift for his coming of age at twelve. Was that some sort of message? No. John would have been too pleased with himself to conceal it. He imagined John saying, "do you see, cousin, do you see? I encourage you to look at yourself. Am I not subtle? Am I not clever?"

He studied his image. A man, handsome like the king, tall, lithe. He altered his attention slightly and looked again at the image in the glass. A devil, as if from a doom painting, horned, its skin slate grey, a tail flicking over its shoulder like a whip.

He had allowed himself to appear like that to one man only—his uncle, the traitor Montagu, on the field of Crecy. Why? The prince had been scared. Montagu, greatest warrior in Christendom, there before him among the slaughter, the blessed sword Arondight shining in his hand. He had sought to intimidate him, even as he'd sunk his sword into the baron's chest. He wanted his fear, the deference of terror. That was why he'd let him live, rather than finished him. He wanted him to know he had been bested. That was not a devil-like thought.

A devil is a creature of order, a noble servant of God under God's greatest servant Satan, jailer of the upstart Lucifer. A devil enforces God's law, punishes those who break it. He could kill Montagu because Montagu was the enemy of the King of England, his master. But to want to elevate himself above him? No. He should not have sought to set himself above a noble, appointed by God, Norman master of the English realm.

He was a devil of Hell. But Hell had given him so little direction. He had heard it whispered that Satan, the jailer of Hell, was an idiot, a brute who allowed his underlings to fight and squabble for his attention. The prince had been set here for a purpose—that much had been revealed to him as a child, when he had taken a fall from his horse. In his sick room, the devils had visited him, beings of fire and teeth, rag-a-bone skeletons who soothed and stroked him. "You are ours. Hell needs you. Await the time."

It was then that he had seen himself as he truly was. Not a man at all, a fiend, though he was not too modest to say, a handsome one. After that, nothing. Were his masters dead? Had God been wounded and Satan gone mad? He had heard such chatter among the devils his grandmother had summoned—the ones that fought alongside him at Crecy. But they were her servants and would say what she wanted him to hear.

Outside the little chamber he could hear his men moving, talking, listening at the door for any sigh, any belch, that might reveal their patron's mood, hint at his wants, enable them to appear with a plum or a purgative saying "if it please you, sir," and lay it down on the table before him. Courtiers imagine princes are puppets, though they appreciate there are a multitude of hands up their skirts, vying for control. The prince was inclined to agree with them. Puppets, though, won't bite you of their own accord.

The evening light faded, the trees deep and lovely, the horizon gold and crimson above them, the starlings swooping and turning above their roosts. He put his hand to the hilt of his sword. There was his purpose. To cut and to kill. There was no puzzle in battle, no flock of thoughts turning this way and that, offering new shapes with every swoop. Just the enemy in front and your friend at your side. Words came to his lips, surprising him. "If my father dies..." He blushed almost to speak them. Just to think of the king's death was treason but it needed to be considered. Edward was not a young man, near forty. The siege at Calais could kill him, as a siege had killed Richard Couer De Lyon, had killed countless others.

A missed mass, a bad thought, a concession to unholy men— and Edward had made plenty of those—and God could blow upon the crossbow bolt of a defender, blow it through a king's heart. And then what? He would rule. But a devil cannot rule in place of a king. It would be unholy. A devil, like a prince, can wield power with a king's blessing but he cannot rule of his own accord any more than an animal, no matter how kingly, no matter how magnificent, could rule. Could a lion sit on the throne of England? It could not. And he was a devil. The looking glass did not lie. He took out his rosary and kneeled.

"For what, God, for what am I here?" Perhaps God was testing him, offering him great temptation and seeing if he could resist. Now, more than ever, he needed advice. He had thought to speak to Lord Sloth, the Iron Lion. He claimed to be an ambassador of Hell. But Sloth was bound to his father. His grandmother Isabella? She could summon devils. But she had had nothing to do with him as he had grown—handed him over to the care of wet nurses and tutors. They might know his purpose but they would be his grandmother's creatures, bound to her. His mother? He feared her, could not touch her royal body with his low hands. She must know, must suspect. But she had been so ill when he was born and he had been taken away to the care of others so young.

His clothes for the evening lay on the bed. Soon he would have to call in his men again, to dress him. He did not want company but he could hardly go to evening mass and then to dinner naked and he wasn't about to put his clothes on himself.

A prince and a devil. A thing born to rule and to serve. An impossibility.

"My Lord!" A knock at the door. "Come." The door opened. He'd dismissed most of his men for the night and only nine or ten of the most noble remained in the outer bedchamber to see to the very minimum of a prince's needs. He felt low, servile, before them. He stood straighter. It was the king's authority he wielded, not his own.

It was no offence to God for him to gesture to Lord Percy, to place the embroidery on the table, no offence to allow Scrope to pass him a cup or Beaumaris to offer him a little cake. Lord Scrope spread the cloth across the table. There was his new crest in black and silver, the feathers he had taken from Blind John of Bohemia and the motto he had appropriated in his honour beneath. Ich Dien. I serve. The words had appealed to him. While his father was alive it was obvious who they applied to. But, once he was dead, then who? Himself alone. He shuddered to picture himself in Westminster Abbey, the crown upon his head, a living contradiction, an abomination before God. Devils do not rule. Devils do not rule. Other devils, yes, or other men with the authority of a king but not in their own right. He would be twice a usurper, first of the role of a king, then of the role of a man.

He had to have an answer, and he would provide it himself.

The prince turned away from his men, forbidding them to follow him and ran down the stairs, out across the chapel courtyard to St George's Chapel, newly called by that name. This was also the chapel of the virgin and of the Most Holy King Edward the Confessor—a Norman true through his mother Emma. The sun was falling and the prayers of vespers murmured from the open doorway.

He went within. The air was heavy with incense. The fellows of St George's College kneeled before the great altar, their white cassocks bright in the dying sunlight behind them, recalling angels kneeling before the splendour of God. They turned around as he crashed in and the priest bowed deeply.

"Continue," he said. "Continue."

The priest led the prayer once more. The prince's Latin was not good but he knew the prayers well enough to translate them easily.

"Out of the depths I have cried to you, Lord:
Lord, hear my voice.
Let your ears listen out
for the voice of my pleading."

He knew then he was in the right place. Surely God had sent him here. He said the words himself. They buzzed within him, resonated in his guts. A high singing, plainsong, sprang up. That was not the fellows of the college. The stone saints that adorned the walls were singing out for him, as they were supposed to do for royalty. He had never heard them before and their voices were enchanting, soaring.

He walked to the altar of the church, not at all bothered by the eyes of the fellows upon him. There he drew his sword and kneeled.

"Here," he said. "Here, I will make my vigil until my path is revealed unto me."

The service continued but his mind was full of the song of the saints and the prayer he had heard when he came into the church. Until the priest said:

"As the Father raises the dead and gives them life, so the Son gives life to anyone he chooses.

Jesus Christ, although he shared God's nature,
did not try to cling to his equality with God;
but emptied himself, took on the form of a slave,
and became like a man:
not in appearance only,
for he humbled himself by accepting death,
even death on a cross."

At first the words meant nothing to him, nothing at all, so

intoxicated was he with the light of the church, the incense, the intonation of the prayers and the songs of the saints. But they too caught in his mind and repeated themselves again and again.

The service finished but still he kneeled. The fellows did not disturb him, would not have dared. Was it a night? Was it two nights he kneeled neither hot nor cold, all base functions of the body suspended, barely breathing it seemed? The words in his head spun on:

"for he humbled himself by accepting death,
even death on a cross."

Beyond the pain in his knees, beyond numbness and weakness and thirst and hunger, he kneeled. A man stood in front of him. He wore an old fashioned, shapeless robe but on his head he bore a crown. He made the sign of the cross.

"You are dead, I think," said the prince.

"I am Edward," he said, "who ordained the right of the Norman masters of England."

"Then you are dead."

"I am dead."

The prince gazed at the holy form of old King Edward, falsely called the last true Saxon king of England. He had thought a spirit would glow or be insubstantial but this man stood in front of him as real as any you might see in the court.

"I need guidance," said the prince. He had not meant to say that but the words had emerged despite him.

"You who are so blessed? No arrow can pierce you, no sword cut you. What can you want to know?"

"Am I…" He paused. What did he want to say? "Am I doing God's work?"

The Confessor smiled. "God has set his limits," he said. "It is for you to follow them and him to judge you when your time comes. Ask for what you want. You did not come here to question me but to ask for something."

For he humbled himself by accepting death,
even death on a cross.

Now the prince knew.

"I want to die before my father," he said. "I want never to be king." A vast feeling of relief swept over him.

"No arrow can pierce you, no sword cut you."

"Let me die before him. It is not right that I take the throne."

The Confessor made the sign of the cross again. Then he put his hand to his lips and kissed it. He extended it towards the prince. The prince took it, trembling. His flesh rebelled and crawled on his bones as he touched his lips to the saint's hands, as no devil should do. Just a momentary kiss but his lips were agony.

"I have given you the gift God gave me," said Edward. "A death of slow agony. You will die before your father."

The prince bowed his head. "Thank you," he said. "Thank you."

The Confessor turned away. The prince closed his eyes for an instant and then he was alone in the chapel. He made the sign of the cross.

"Now," he said. "I am content and, knowing that I cannot displease God, nor die by any violent measure, I shall rid the earth of all my father's enemies and float to heaven on a river of evil men's blood."

He stood gingerly, his legs numb from his vigil and made his way from the chapel, calling for a cup of wine to cool his burning lips.

OLD BLOOD

ADRIAN TCHAIKOVSKY

— Shadows of the Apt —

THE SPREADING STAIN OF DARKNESS GATHERING around Uctebri was pleasantly warm for now, but that would not last. Soon he would be shivering, heat leaching out into that growing pool and back to the world he had stolen it from. And Uctebri the Sarcad, most ambitious of his abhorred people, would die.

Lying in a pool of blood. It sounded luxurious, something his people should aspire to. *So much less fun when the blood's your own.*

The air brought the scent of smoke and engine oil, of an enemy who had no idea of the victory they had won. Above, the dark fingers of the forest sawed at each other in the wind. If he made a supreme effort and turned his head, he could see a corpse, wasted blood soaking the forest floor just like his was, and he too weak to crawl over and taste it. Past the body he could see sunlight through the last of the trees: open space and freedom. But sunlight had never been something his people prized.

Uctebri tried for tranquillity as his life seeped slowly away into the ground. It was hard, with death coming so fast on the heels of disappointment. Was he not one of the great blood magicians of the Mosquito-kinden? Was this a fit death for a power that should have shaken the world?

And might have done, in another age, but magic was no longer what it had been, nor were magicians. Now he was just the least ragged of a ragged race who had lived in shadows for so long that most thought they were just children's stories. The Mosquito-kinden's chance for power had come and gone centuries ago, back in the Days of Lore, when they challenged the Moths, greatest sorcerers of the age, for the rule of the world.

And they smashed us, Uctebri considered. *They drove us to the point of extinction. And then they fell in turn, and the busy, busy Apt rose up with their machines and their ignorance; so we are just a memory of a memory.*

He felt a deep well of frustration that he should die like this, within arm's reach of a power that should have been his. A long life fighting for every scrap—food and lore both—and yet the ending the worst part of it…

Then there was movement nearby and he realised that things could still be worse. Out of the dark between the trees a figure came stumbling. It was the Moth-kinden woman and, though her grey robes were blotted liberally with dark red, she was still on her feet.

She stepped over the corpse without comment, leaning on her staff and with eyes only for the dying Mosquito. Her people had driven his to the point of destruction. He had been her reluctant accomplice, but beneath that he was her rival. Now that metal-shod staff slammed down next to his head and her face swam into view above him, drinking in his suffering. It must have eclipsed her own pain, because she could raise a smile for him. Lying helpless beneath that cold gaze, Uctebri cringed and tried to hasten his own demise for fear of the pain she was about to gift him.

Twelve days before.

UCTEBRI SENSED THE MAGICIANS AS HE CROUCHED AT the edge of a Wasp army camp, hoping to scavenge their leavings. Not long ago he had been darkening the dreams of superstitious Dragonfly-kinden peasantry and feeding off the richness in their veins. Now the Wasps had come with a mass-produced nightmare that Uctebri's bespoke darkness could not compete with.

Magic, his old senses told him, twitching at his concentration. The Commonweal had magic, but mostly dusty and abandoned. The Wasps had no magic, did not even believe in it. Since they came to swallow up province after province it was a rare thing to feel that touch within his mind. And a rare thing to feed well, too. The Wasps feared the dark like the Dragonfly peasants did, but when they feared something they destroyed it. Their camps were lit by burning gas and always they were buzzing in and out.

Now he was creeping too close to their sentries, because one of them had disciplined a slave an hour before and dumped the body just where their lights met the shadows, and Uctebri, great magician, was hungry. While the fighting had been fierce, there were plentiful casualties for him to slake his thirst on. Now he was behind the lines, the Wasps burned and buried the bodies and took the survivors away in chains.

He reached the body. Hunched like a shadow himself, drawing all his power about him to hide from their lamps and sharp eyes, he lapped at the wounds—cold now, but cold blood was better than no blood.

And magic was best of all. What magicians were abroad, in this war-torn and forsaken place? Magicians meant danger; magicians meant opportunity. And Uctebri had kept company only with the ignorant and the dead for a long time.

He knew then that he would seek them out, these magicians. And perhaps he would kill them, but he would at least sate his curiosity first.

HE FOUND THEM SOON AFTER, FOLLOWING THAT ethereal scent from shadow to shadow: two Lowlanders, southerners from a land the Empire had not conquered yet. And Lowlanders were fair game for the Slave Corps, yet the sergeant approached respectfully with a sack of loot and let the travellers paw through it. Uctebri watched, fascinated, seeing the Wasps take gold coin and hand over what must have seemed worthless trinkets to soldiers who didn't believe in magic.

They had this treasure with them all that time, he cursed himself. *And I too hungry to notice!*

Two Lowlanders: both women, both magicians, and as disreputable and worn out as Uctebri himself. One was Mantis-kinden, a tall skinny woman wearing a voluminous green robe that pooled at her feet. It had seen a few sword-thrusts, that garment, but darned more from wear than from war. Her reddish hair was long and loose, halfway to her waist; her lean face weirdly peaceful, eyes seeming to look into some other world where things were better. She leant on a long-headed spear and the Wasps gave her a wide berth.

The other magician did the talking and dispensed the gold, choosing which oddment to purchase, which to reject. She was a slight-framed woman with white, featureless eyes, grey-skinned and robed in grey. The copper band about her brow was set with the sort of stones actors used to enthral the gullible. Her open robe showed the ribs of a leather cuirass and a shortsword half-hidden at her belt. Clutching her plain, metal-shod staff, she looked more wanderer than wizard, yet Uctebri could feel the magic in her blood, speaking to his shrunken stomach. Grey skin, white eyes; Moth-kinden seldom came so far north, which was precisely why Uctebri's people had fled here centuries before, those few of them the Moths had left alive.

He watched the Wasps heading off and counting their coin, wondering if he dared brave the Mantis spear.

The women made camp and began to pick over the trinkets they had bought, and Uctebri decided he would try them tonight. They seemed lesser magi than he, though he was diminished by hunger and a long road. In his mind he planned his campaign, the magic he would use to baffle their own, the ancient game of power against power. Then he felt something sharp at his back and knew the moment had been taken from his hands. When he twisted about in fear and rage it jabbed harder, and he got a shove in the back for his pains, sending him staggering out into the firelight.

The Moth and Mantis showed no great surprise at his appearance. Perhaps they had been trailing their magic like a fisherman with a lure, to see what lurking magicians they might attract.

The Moth regarded him, and knew exactly what he was, and he saw in her expression that she knew exactly what he was. Still, no order came to send that spear through him. She only shrugged and said, "Everyone's coming out of the shadows these days."

Their third walked out from behind Uctebri: another woman, but no magician she. Uctebri stared balefully at the stocky Beetle shouldering her crossbow, and she grinned back. "What's this old monster then, mistress?"

"Monster indeed." The Moth smiled slightly. "Ruthan, let's all sit down and I'll tell you about the Mosquito-kinden."

THE BEETLE WAS RUTHAN BARTRER, OUT OF COLLEGIUM, and she was the Moth's servant. It was an eye-opening arrangement that was not explained just then, save that the Moth could speak of magic and the lost Days of Lore without Ruthan scoffing, with her hanging on the Moth's every word, in fact, desperate to understand.

The Mantis was Shonaen, and while the Moth talked she lit sticks of sickly-smelling incense and inhaled the smoke until her pupils were no more than dots. If she had ever been the death-bringer of her people's reputation, the mantle had sloughed off her long ago.

The Moth, though; when she spoke of magic, Uctebri felt something chime within himself. It made him remember how little his people had settled for, in hiding, in defeat. It made him want more.

She gave her name as Julaea, daughter of one Adguros of Tharn who had died an outcast. He had sought to rally his people to greatness, or so said Julaea. They had turned their backs on him, lacking his vision and courage. Now she was going to fulfil his dreams.

"The dreams of a dead magician are dangerous things to play with," Uctebri told her with a think smile, but her words had their hooks in him nonetheless. And she had given him her name, which Moths were loath to do. That did more than the crossbow to keep him at their fire.

"It's time we took it back," she said simply, and laughed at his expression. "It's time for a new age of magic, Mosquito-kinden. You don't think so?"

"I have seen the greatest kingdom of magic dismantled by these machine-handed Wasps," Uctebri said quietly. "Centuries of lore put to the torch, traditions a thousand years old ground under their boots. I think an age of magicians has never been so far off. Sometimes I think we dreamt all our great days."

Julaea's smile was sharp as knives. "Old Bloodsucker, you haven't seen what I have. You think this is war, this song of slaves and slaughter? This is nothing to what the Wasps will bring. I have dreamt whole cities ablaze beneath a rain of fire. I have seen darts that pierce the strongest mail and reap soldiers like corn."

"What joyous visions," murmured Uctebri.

"Apt cities, Apt soldiers," Julaea told him. "All the artificer kinden will turn on one another and tear down everything they've built. It will be a new age of darkness, and the darkness was always ours, Old Bloodsucker. The darkness belongs to Moths and Mosquitos and Mantids."

Uctebri felt his old cynicism stir. "Prophecy," he said sourly. "If it could help us, then the Apt would never have thrown off your people's chains all those years ago. Since when has any magician been able to look into *their* future?"

"Since she was born to one," said Julaea, daughter of Adguros. "My father led a raid on the Beetle mines outside Helleron. They caught him; they chained him underground with their engines and their wheels. A year he was there, in the smoke and the scent of burning oil. When he came out under the sky he was magician no more; he had become a thing like they were, who understood the cogs and the pistons." She pronounced the Apt words carefully, learnt by rote. "He came to Tharn and tried to show them how to destroy the Beetle machines but they would not listen to him. They would not trust him and they could not understand. But later I sat at his knee and listened; I dreamt of the machine future and its destruction. There is just enough of Adguros in me that I would master the world of the Apt."

"I fear you," Uctebri whispered, but he heard the longing in his own voice.

"You are right to," she told him. "I will overthrow the world. And you have seen my instrument already—the Wasp Empire will be my sword."

"An Empire has no hilt," Uctebri pointed out.

"But it does, if you know how to grasp it." He could not look at her smile now. It was too bright, too much like the fires of the Wasp machines.

A DAY LATER, ON THE ROAD WITH THE BEETLE WOMAN trotting with the sack of relics at Julaea's heels, he asked, "Why do they follow you?"

"Hope," she said, watching his eyes stray to the labouring Ruthan. "They haven't all forgotten the golden Days of Lore, the Beetles. Some of them, some few families, remember the love their kind once bore us."

A love so great they overthrew you and drove you from all your places of power, Uctebri thought, but then she gave him a sideways look and asked "And here you are. So why do *you* follow?"

"New blood is always a draw for an old man." Uctebri's grin was marred by withered lips and sharp teeth. "And your blood is very new indeed, unlike any I've sampled."

"Unlike like any you ever will, Old Bloodsucker."

"A better question is why you invited me to follow you. A frail old husk like me."

"I know power when I smell it. My people have spent centuries playing status games and ignoring the world. I will collect powerful people. I will stand on their shoulders. Even yours, old man. You're a Sarcad, a great man amongst the Mosquito."

"What little that is worth."

"Don't you want to make it mean something again?"

He stopped dead. "Am I hearing a Moth-kinden planning the return of the Mosquito? Or do you just want us out in the open so you can finish the job?"

She rounded on him, eyes flashing with a cold anger. "I will use every tool life gives me to bring down the cities of the Apt and revive the rule of magic. I will strike down anyone that stands against me, even the great lords of my own kinden. We have been in decline for half a century, all we old powers. We have retreated to our holes and forests, or traded our magic for empty ceremony or mere manipulation. It is time to fight *back*!" Her last word rang out across the countryside, a challenge to the world. "Aid me, lend me your shoulder and lift me high, and your people will share in the victory. Stand in my way and the last blood you see will be your own."

He was suddenly aware of steel brushing his wrinkled neck—the Mantis was at his back, her spear levelled to spit him.

"Well, well, then," he said softly. "Let the Wasps and the Ants and the Beetles fall upon one another. If there is no new age of magic at the end of it, at least there will be blood."

"Oh, there is always blood," she agreed.

A TENDAY OF HARD TRAVEL AND BUYING TRINKETS FROM the Wasps saw them camping beside barren stretch of road picked clean by the war, the blackened ribs of a dead village the only landmark. That dusk he awoke to find Julaea waiting for him, her disciples gathered to her. Something had changed. For a dry-throated moment he thought they were going to kill him.

"What do you think, then, Old Bloodsucker?" she asked him. "Are you one of us?" Her gesture took in her other followers: the Beetle fussing over their supplies; the Mantis standing silent and still, a sentry whose vigilance was entirely directed at him.

Uctebri settled himself across from the Moth, sitting on the hard ground with his pale hands on his knees. His magic was stronger, out here in the wilds away from the machinations of the Apt. Julaea's company, her words and dreams, had rejuvenated him.

"You've got a good thing going on here," he remarked. "Quite a trove of Commonwealer knick-knacks in that bag of yours. Drain them all at once and you'd have quite the fistful of magic to accomplish…what? Or is it home now, for you? Going to teach your kin a lesson for slighting your father?"

"If it was?" she asked.

"Then we part company," he told her. "Let your Mantis chase me down if you will, but your people will not want a reminder that they did not quite kill all of mine when they had the chance, for all you appear not to care."

"Very wise," she said, baring that razor grin again. "Better the crossed spears of the Wasps than what my people'd do to you. But no, not home. I'm scarce more welcome there than you, Old Bloodsucker. I make my own way. When I overturn the world of the Apt, I'll make my people come to the court of the Wasps and beg."

"With that bag of trinkets you'll command the Wasp Empire?" *And is this it? Is she just the mad daughter of a cripple?* "Raise a storm, yes. Cloud a few minds or have some fearful merchant cut his own throat, but I've *seen* the Empire at work."

He had let his disdain show, and abruptly he was aware of how close Shonaen, the Mantis, was, dispassionately ready to kill him at a nod from her mistress.

Yet Julaea just smiled. "Old Bloodsucker, this is merely the gift that shall see my petition heard. This, and the power you still have in your dried-up body."

"A petition in what court?" He could no longer look at that smile. When she said, "Shonaen, tell him," it was a relief to look into the long, sallow face of the Mantis.

"I'm going home," Shonaen pronounced, as though the words were as much a surprise to her as anyone else.

"What home? The…" Uctebri tried to remember where the Lowlander Mantids even lived, "Nethyon, is it?"

Julaea sang out before Shonaen had a chance. "Not the Nethyon or the Etheryon. Not the Felyal or even Sacred Parosyal. My Shonaen is the last scion of another hold entirely. Tell me of the Darakyon, Old Bloodsucker."

Uctebri let that name lie in the dark a long while before he picked it up. "There are no Mantids of the Darakyon. Not for generations."

"Some few survived. Now, only one remains, inheritrix of all that sorrow," Julaea confirmed. "So tell me why, Uctebri."

He forced himself to meet the cutting edge of her expression. "Because your people did something terrible there. When the Apt threw you off and you had lost everything, your magi went to the Darakyon and tried to turn back history. Even my people felt it, as we hid in our holes. A ritual of fear and darkness so that none of the Apt would ever sleep soundly again. And you failed, you Moths. You overreached yourselves and poisoned the whole forest, destroyed the Mantis hold there. None walked out of that place, and only fools have walked in since."

"And what do they say of Shonaen's ancestral halls nowadays, old man?"

"That the ghosts of every Mantis and Moth still hang on the thorns there like old clothes," Uctebri told her. "That visitors are not welcomed."

"My people say the same," Julaea told him. "What they do not say is that there is *power* in the Darakyon, that they will not reach for out of guilt."

"And you know no guilt."

"No more than you, Old Bloodsucker. I will go before the twisted spirit of the Darakyon and I shall harness it to my will. I shall pluck out its heart and corrupt the very Emperor with promises of power. I shall bring ruin to all the cities of the Apt." Her white eyes gleamed with triumph. "You're smiling now, old man. It's a fearful, shrivelled thing, but I know a smile when I see it."

"With your power and mine, with the stolen relics of the Commonweal and your Mantis's birthright, you'll enslave the Darakyon?"

"Do you doubt me?"

And she was right, he was smiling.

THEY MADE TRACKS SOUTH, INTO THAT DISPUTED territory that was neither Empire nor Commonweal nor Lowlands. To the east the Wasps had crushed every city to forge their gateway to the Commonweal. To the west Julaea's people kept to their mountain fastness of Tharn while the Beetles grubbed for coin in smoky Helleron. But between all these lay a stretch of forest that the roads passed north or south around; the Apt did not believe in ghosts, any more than they believed in Mosquito-kinden, but that just meant they had to invent rational reasons why they did not brave the trees.

Yet when Julaea and her tattered followers drew near forest's edge, the Black and Gold of the Imperial armies was already on display, armour gleaming in the dawn. Not some loot-fat band of slavers heading home from the Commonweal, but three score of the Light Airborne, scouts creeping past the ever-shifting borders of the Empire. Just as Julaea had said, the Wasps had their eyes on their western neighbours, whose wealth was not in old gold but in machines and industry. They were scouting out the way, seeing how far their soldiers might march before the self-involved Lowlanders took note of them.

"You can make a deal with these Wasps?" Uctebri asked the Moth.

She shook her head. "Slavers are easy to suborn. They're all in the business to make a private fortune. This lot are watching for Lowlander spies." A Moth, a Mantis and a Beetle. Whatever the Wasps might make of Uctebri, the others would fit the clothes of spies well enough. "We'll go past them at night."

"The forest will be stronger then," he noted, knowing it would not sway her.

"So will we."

THE WASPS HAD A GOOD WATCH OUT, BUT THEY LIT few fires and had no eyes for the dark. What was plain was that more of their number had gone to scout the forest, no matter the stories they must have heard. The soldiers on the outside were growing increasingly skittish the longer their comrades were absent. Uctebri reckoned they would start burning things soon. He wondered how the Darakyon would react to that. In the harsh light of day, in these weak modern times, magic could not defeat Apt scepticism. At night, or under the shadowed canopy, a man's fears would creep up on him and poison his mind, throwing open all those doors that the old ways drew their power from. The Apt were right to fear the dark.

Julaea led them past the sentries' very noses. Uctebri had expected the Beetle, Ruthan, to tread on every stick and get herself killed, but Julaea wove the darkness and the night's silence about them. Uctebri flicked at the soldiers' minds to make them jump at all the wrong shadows, and the four of them were within the trees without the Wasps being any the wiser.

Uctebri felt the place the moment they set foot beneath its boughs. The Moths had tried their great ritual soon after the revolution. Five centuries of twisted, failed magic had festered in this place. The trees grew crooked and warty, hunched like murderers caught in the act. Overhead, the canopy layered hands of leaves until it strangled the moonlight. The forest watched them through each twig, each leaf. The night-flying insects were its spies, the ferns and moss its agents.

"How it hates us," Julaea whispered.

"It hates *you*," Uctebri corrected. The lens of the forest's attention was fixed on the Moth. *It remembers her kin, and how they ruined it. How pleasant not to be the most loathed for once.*

And yet Julaea pressed on, undaunted. She clutched the sack of Commonweal loot, and Uctebri could feel her drawing on the power that ancient magicians had stored there. Was this what those dead Dragonflies had foreseen, some renegade Moth burning their days of meditation to twist the arms of ghosts? But she spent it recklessly, treading ever deeper into the trees with Ruthan scuttling in her shadow and Shonaen striding at her side.

"You're home, Mantis," Uctebri remarked, careful not to be left behind. "Rejoice."

She stared at him. Her eyes said she had no idea who he was or where she was. Her body said she was about to kill him. Then she leant forwards, spear extended, and he heard the scrape of metal on metal. They had found what was left of the Wasp expedition.

Mostly he saw their armour. It lay between the trees with only a few white bones to evidence the wearers. Saplings grew through arm-holes and neck-holes, roots clawing through bracers and greaves and ferns springing in lurid sprays through the twisted holes that had let the blood out. The soldiers who had gone in that day had left a display looking decades old.

Uctebri felt a distinct shifting around him, physical and spiritual. The wood had not been fighting them before, not truly. Now it had them where it wanted them.

All around them, the forest shivered like the skin of a living thing. The branches overhead sawed at one another, a sudden wind keening through them like voices.

"Now," Julaea said, calm personified. "Join with me. Or die with me."

Uctebri needed no encouragement. They were in the depths of the darkness here, nothing of the Apt world outside to fetter him. He reached out against the louring wall of the forest's power and braced himself, feeling the Moth do the same, wrestling with the space around them to deny the trees their movement. A moment's slip and the trunks would close on them like teeth, the branches pierce like spears. And it was *strong*! Julaea had been right about this place. It was a great fouled well of old power neither tapped nor ebbed in centuries.

He felt the massed mind of the Darakyon try to fold the world about them, to turn its crooked trunks and withered boughs into jaws to crush them. But there was something lacking, some final force that would have cracked their mortal efforts like eggshells. They held, and then Julaea took a step forwards, and the forest swayed back around them, forced away by her iron will.

"Warriors!" Ruthan cried, squinting into the darkness. Past the stretch and twist of the tortured air, quick shapes came darting, long-limbed and bearing weapons. Caught by the forest's pressing strength, Uctebri felt a flare of panic as though their steel was at his throat already. He was an old hand at magic, though. His mind did not waver, though the forest forced fear into him through eyes and ears and nostrils.

Shonaen stepped forwards almost lazily, as though none of it was real. She took the first figure on her spear, spun about to catch another. A sword like a slice of moonlight flared at her face and she leant back no more than three inches to avoid it. The ghost warriors crowded at her, and she carved at them with her arm spines until they fell back again. No urgency touched her movements. She was like a soldier sleep-walking through weapons drill, stepping note-perfect through her forms and passes as though she was fighting dreams and shadows.

And she was, Uctebri knew. These phantasms had no more substance to them than the dark between the trees, even animated by the ghosts the forest was crawling with. It was an old magician's trick that few could master these days. Phantoms, but they could kill like real warriors, belief in them leaping from the points of their blades into the wounds they made.

And yet Julaea pressed on, a step at a time, towards the forest's centre, Uctebri bringing up the rear to prevent the forest crashing down on them as Shonaen danced her casual murders on either side.

"What are we seeking?" Uctebri demanded. "How will you rule here? It will not have you as its master." And indeed the Darakyon was showing no signs of giving up. "It hates you like poison!"

"It will have no choice," Julaea spat. "You hear me, trees? I am Julaea, daughter of Adguros. I am the voice of the Moth-kinden here, the voice you have always obeyed."

The forest shook its boughs at them in rage and the wind roared and bellowed, shredding the leaves above. And yet that final blow never fell.

"The forest has a heart," she told Uctebri. "The ritual crushed them all down, those magi and their warriors. It crushed them down and twisted off a knot of itself that they are all bound to. Hold that, and this power can be commanded, and when I can command, let it hate me as much as it likes!"

With that final word she broke through, and the whole of the Darakyon seemed to go reeling away in all directions, the trees tilting crazily, thorn-studded vines lashing as if in their death throes.

Despite it all, Uctebri felt some part of himself unconvinced. *It cannot be this easy. A trap, surely?* Yet when Julaea practically skipped forwards, he followed.

They had found her ritual site, that much was certain. The forest had ceased trying to coil itself about them and was quite still, as though marking the memory of all those who had died for the folly committed here. The trees at rest leant outwards from a central clearing, some place where perhaps the Mantids had raised one of their rotting idols, where Moth seers had stood and funnelled all their power into a ritual to return the world to the way it had once been, back when they had mattered. And they had failed, the task beyond even their united reach. Their power had got away from them and run wild through the Darakyon, and made it what it was today. Not a one of those great and wise magicians or their Mantis servants had lived.

There was no visible centre, but any magician's senses could find it. Julaea rushed forwards, hunting for the token that would allow her to make the Darakyon her plaything.

And stopped; turned, frowning, a single step back the way she had come, and then another. Her arms spread out as if for balance, but she was feeling out the topography of the magic, searching for the heart.

What will it be? A nut? A chalice? Uctebri was searching too: some small object of wood that would seem the work of human hands, but where was it? The Beetle Ruthan huddled close but Shonaen stalked farther and farther, still hunting shadows.

Julaea's blank eyes were wide, impossible to tell what she was looking at. She mouthed a word: "No…"

Uctebri came to the conclusion a moment after. "It's not here," he said. "How can it not be here?"

The wind rustled the leaves around them. The forest was laughing at them.

"Mistress," Ruthan called, voice trembling. She had ventured past the focus of the wood, that mocking absence. The moon shone down obligingly; the forest wanted them to know the sacrilege it had enacted on itself.

Uctebri spotted a camp, overgrown, the fire long cold. The intruders had not escaped freely, for the brambles and vines writhed amongst the ruin of tents, the splintered cages of ribs. At least one of them had lived, though; lived, and carried away the Darakyon's heart.

"Who dared…?" Julaea hissed, coming to the Beetle's shoulder to stare. Uctebri knew she would be naming every magician she ever knew, wondering which of them had the guile to creep in here and thwart her.

Ruthan, crouching by the ruined tents, held up some broken metal thing. Uctebri studied it a long time with his dark-adapted eyes before he could understand its purpose.

It was a crossbow, and what could be seen of the other personal effects looked Beetle-made—turned out in some faceless factory somewhere, not the work of a craftsman's hands. Oh, perhaps these had been some magician's servants, as Ruthan was, but Uctebri already knew it was not so. No sorcerer had come here to steal Julaea's prize, but only the ignorant—only the Apt.

"It knew someone like you would come to command it," he whispered. "And so it gave its heart to those who could never use it, could never even understand what they had discovered. Some Beetle-kinden has it on their mantelpiece even now, or on their desk as a paperweight."

Julaea hissed in pure frustration. Her white gaze fixed on Ruthan. "This is you."

The Beetle woman shrank from her. "Mistress, no!"

"Your people. Not content with driving mine into obscurity, now you steal our last scraps."

Ruthan started, "I only served you—" but Julaea cut her off.

"I cast you out. I withhold my protection from you. You are none of mine any more."

"No!" Ruthan reached out an imploring hand, but the moon was gone with shocking suddenness. Darkness clawed in from all around, bristling with the spiny arms of praying mantids, the hooked thorns of briars. The Darakyon swallowed Ruthan Bartrer without hesitation, one more set of bones to moulder on the forest floor.

Julaea turned her despairing gaze on Uctebri. By then he had closed the distance, and with a convulsive gesture he drove his knife hilt-deep into her side.

Her look was equal parts bafflement and outrage, no room for the pain at all. "What?"

"You're not the only one who remembers the wrongs done to their people," he snapped. He had the full intention of using the blade again, but he had forgotten Shonaen, and now the Mantis came leaping out of the wood with her spear levelled.

Even here in this Moth-made ruin, the Mantids still defend them. Uctebri had little magic left after testing himself against the Darakyon, so he let go the hilt and fled, as his people had always fled.

He made his magic a knife-blade to pierce the forest; not

the grand siege that Julaea had brought, but a slinking escape route that wound under branch and over root, worming through the darkness as he twisted his way towards where the moon still shone. He closed the path behind him. Shonaen had to cut her own, assailed by shadows and not half the magician he was. Yet she was younger and stronger, and enraged. She gained a step at a time, as he cut desperately for the forest's edge. Briars plucked at his sleeves, nettles burned his skin and the ground knotted beneath his feet, yet somehow he stumbled on in his headlong flight, never looking at the enemy behind until he saw the enemy before him.

The first glint of dawn was in his eyes then, and he threw up a hand to shade them, seeing too late that some of the shapes cutting across the light were men, not trees. The Wasps had come to look for their missing scouts, a line of them wading into the forest verge with levelled crossbows and threats.

Uctebri skidded to a halt, realizing they had already seen movement and would be on him in a moment. He turned to find some last shade that might endure the dawn, but Shonaen was closer behind than he thought and her spear-point lanced through his side in a shock of pain and wasted blood.

Then he was on the ground, rolling over in agony so he could see the thrust that would kill him. Shonaen stared down at him, her eyes barely focusing on him, and he wondered if she knew she was killing a flesh and blood man, and not another shadow.

The first crossbow bolt winged wide of her, but close enough to catch her notice. She saw the Wasps and shrilled at them, challenging all the armies of the Empire to single combat. Uctebri laughed, though each chuckle cost him dear.

The bolts skipped past her, and she even spun one aside with her spear-haft, but this addled creature was no Mantis Weaponsmaster from song or story. She rushed them, her darned robe catching on the thorns, and the first shot landed, buried to the fletchings in her shoulder. Another three followed, and two blasts of stingshot from the Wasps' hands. Shonaen dropped her spear, clutching at the air as though she saw the glorious history of her people there, just out of reach. The Wasps took no chances and shot her another half-dozen times before they were sure she was dead. Thus perished the last scion of the Darakyon.

They did not find Uctebri as he lay there bleeding. The shadows were too deep.

Sometime later, after the Empire's finest had called off the search and retreated from the Darakyon's bounds to their camp, Uctebri saw Julaea come limping from the forest's heart, and knew that his time was up.

She shuffled over to him, leaning heavily on her staff. Its metal-shod end rammed the ground beside his face and he shuddered. She would not survive him for long, but he found that was remarkably little consolation.

"It...was a good plan," he whispered. The forest had fallen obligingly silent.

"It still is," she hissed around her pain. "The heart is out there. As you say, some Beetle, a paperweight or ornament. But it is there."

"You won't be fetching it..." His words were inviting that staff to smash his pointed teeth, but he could not keep them back.

"No." She sighed and dropped to her knees, and her hand found the hilt of Uctebri's dagger where it jutted from her side. "Would you?"

"If your Mantis had not finished me." He let out a long, wheezing breath. "It was a good plan. I am not so proud that I wouldn't have stolen it."

"Someone should." She leant on his chest as she dragged the dagger out, so that black spots wheeled before Uctebri's red eyes.

"There's none but you."

"I'm done."

"I know your kind," and she spat real venom about that. "You can heal. If fed." She stared down at him with fascinated loathing. "We should have exterminated you vermin centuries ago. I should have cut your throat before using your power."

"Yes."

"But here we are, and someone needs to make the plan happen. Someone needs to destroy the Apt."

Uctebri stared up at her as she raised the smeared dagger blade and contemplated it.

"For my father," she said, and inserted it almost gently under her chin, opening her throat up with a flourish of her wrist that would have done a conjurer proud.

UCTEBRI WAS WEAK FOR DAYS, BUT JULAEA'S BLOOD had been enough to replace the vigour that he had lost. The Wasp patrol was long departed by then, and the forest had recovered Shonaen's body. Of their intrepid little band, only he survived.

We will meet again, he told the Darakyon, as it brooded and watched him. *I will hold your heart in my hands.* And he would need other power: relics, artifacts, the blood of magicians. He would need to inveigle himself into the counsels of the Wasps and tempt them with the impossible. Before hearing Julaea speak, he would not have believed it himself. Now her blood was in his veins and her purpose in his mind.

By dusk he was already limping away, the forest receding at his back. The sunset was red with the blood of Empire.

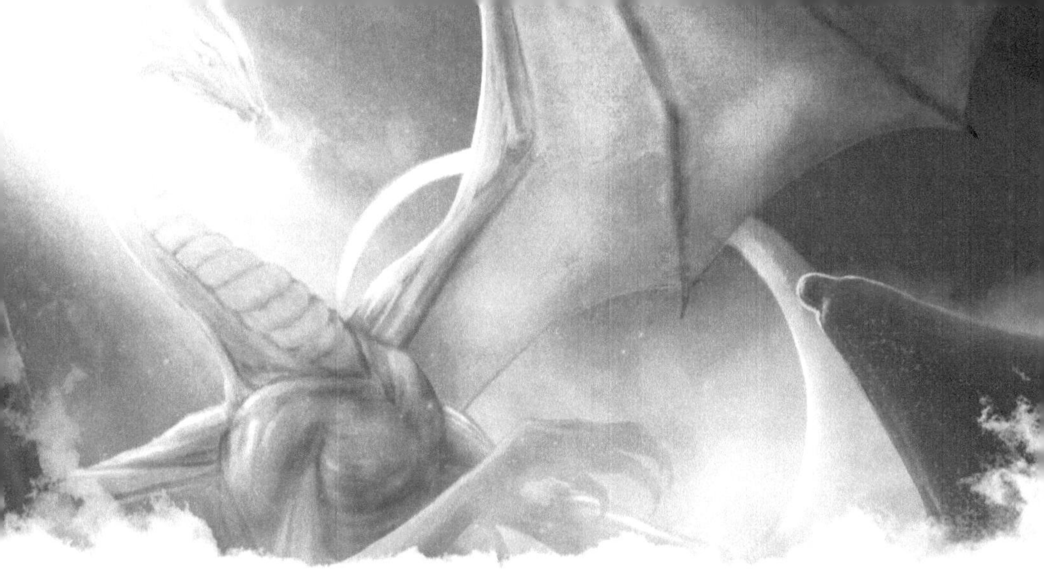

BLACK BARGAIN

JANNY WURTS
— Wars of Light and Shadow —

TOLER GROANED IN SUFFERING DISCOMFORT, PUNCHED flat by a skull-busting hangover on the floor of the Riverton gaol. He had messed up plenty in his short life. But never before buried himself over his head in deep trouble a bribe failed to salvage. His downfall began smoothly enough, when the coin from a packet of smuggled goods led to boastful drink in a waterfront tavern. Some tipster's sly word to the exciseman brought the port watch with a warrant, which pinned him under the magistrate's thumb as a repeat offender.

No glib plea and no wrist-slap fine sprung him free this time. Not after his trademark habit of scoring a double dip take on the job turned his furious partners against him at the assize. That, and the cocky retorts that stung stiff-faced officialdom to quivering jowls and red fury saw him condemned. Ten years at a convict's oar on the galleys would reduce his rake's winsome smile to a broken jaw and smashed teeth. Toler huddled in the cell's vile straw, miserable enough to heave up his guts and die in his own muck without moving.

"Skewer the magistrate's sanctimonious arse on the Avenger's Black Spear!" Toler scratched his scalp under the itching braid, still noisomely tarred from his sailhand's impersonation. Ease his roiling stomach, and he might survive the hammers and tongs of his headache. Maybe even sleep off the worst before his wretched fate overtook him.

But inbound footsteps descended the stone stair. The turnkey's shuffling, uneven tread scraped through his stuttered apologies, directed toward the no nonsense clip of the second tread, tagging behind. Strides with a snap that pierced Toler's stupor, and raised the echo of his mother's nattering. *'You're useless, Toler! Tuck-tailed as a kicked dog, and a cringing loser. Too depraved to mind your foul tongue, or go a day without drinking yourself senseless. Your worthlessness pains me worse than your sister's, run off like a trull from an upright apprenticeship. What'll you do when I'm gone and there's naught but the gaoler's roof over your head?'*

The shattering clash of keys in the lock dispersed the mist of remembrance. "Toler sen Beckit?" Rusty hinges wailed as the warder swung open the studded door.

Toler rolled over and presented his back. Let the lackeys drag him out by the scruff if they wanted him upright.

"On your feet, bucko!" The grizzled turnkey thrust his lantern over Toler's prostrate form. "Here's your proper reckoning. Toss up on my ankles, and I'll boot your worthless carcass into the next sunrise."

Toler cringed from the glare. "Go suck the port magistrate's pip."

Quiet fell, thick enough to cut with a knife.

Toler ran on, defiant, "Or else butt hump your thumb, while I perish of boredom."

The knockout blow never came, that should have shuttered the witch's brew of his hangover. Instead, the nettlesome, prickling sense of a powerful presence stabbed through his thick skin. Betrayed by nerves he forgot he possessed, Toler acknowledged the turnkey's companion.

Not the slovenly guard with the crooked nose and a crass mouthful of threats, but an ascetic, trim figure clad in autumn colors, who denounced with impartial venom, "Your mannerless tongue's an embarrassment and a nuisance better off silenced."

The distinctive red-and-silver tumble of hair spilled over lean shoulders, and black eyes that pierced like a stalking lynx revealed nothing less than a Fellowship Sorcerer, arrived in the flesh. Any of the Seven owned the force to intimidate. But Davien's infamous style had once seen a high king murdered like a rat in a drainpipe to contest a philosophical point with his colleagues.

Toler opened his mouth to blurt his remark: that the power behind charter law wasted wind calling down a jail rat's impertinence. But only a hiss escaped his squeezed throat. Both lips and tongue stayed unresponsive. Fury spiked pain through his tender head. His mute outrage met the Sorcerer's dissecting regard, which bared the unflattering truth: of a dissipated young man with brown hair, sprawled in filth, who blunted his agile intelligence with swagger, and whose mask of cynical belligerence pitched him on a fast course to ruin.

Davien addressed Toler's supine misery without sympathy. "I've sealed an official agreement to claim the terms of your sentence. You will rise and accompany me on your own, or else rot where you lie, never again to see daylight. Choose. You'll get no second chance."

Toler begrudgingly clambered erect. Even to his own nose, he reeked. If a Sorcerer's omnipotence needed a light-fingered malcontent, the poisonous irony begged asking: what for? Toler accepted Davien's overture, as much for the sordid amusement of seeing what brought the almighty Fellowship to soil their hands with his wretched lot.

Cold sober, he might have remembered the warning: no one who crossed paths with one of the Seven survived the experience unchanged.

DAVIEN BEGAN BY REJECTING THE NICETIES. TOLER FOUND himself prodded outside, then doused head to foot with a bucket dunked in the garrison horse trough. The uncivilized drenching chased off his binge sickness, rinsed his tarred hair clean, and scoured the piss from his clothes beyond what the splash of the scummed water warranted. Folly, to imagine he might slip the leash of a predator able to refigure natural order at whim. Temporarily thwarted, Toler took a seat, dripping, on the wooden bench at the breakwater where by nightfall, the strumpets hooked passing marks, and by day, the sharp-eyed old salts spotted trade ships returning through Riverton's inlet.

None idled there now. Sensible folk fled a Sorcerer's interest, as Toler would have without Davien's regard skewering him like flensed meat. In daylight, such fixated poise seemed unreal, punch cut against the harborside dazzle, with the lightermen's oared craft diminished as toys, ferrying crew to and from the moored vessels.

Toler deflected his pithless fear into a smirk before panic emptied his bladder. He knew the ghastly rumors held truth: practitioners of the arcane arts bled innocents. For him, the deadly, unnatural terror walked abroad in the glare of noon. Better to bolt before risking the fate that befell his lost sister.

Then Davien said, "Our Fellowship opposes pursuit of black necromancy, which does in fact involve gutting victims for sacrifice. Gray Kralovir are the worst of the lot, which brings up my use for your sentence."

Toler swallowed. Dismal odds rode his prospects. Run and die quickly, or languish under the spell-turned restraint of gagged speech.

Davien's lean mouth twitched, perhaps from stifled laughter. "Weigh your thoughts carefully. The articulate pitch of your angst might as well be shouted to the four winds."

Toler's sulky rebellion congealed.

Into the staring face of his qualms, Davien at last addressed his purpose. "I need eyes in position to disclose the affairs of a dirty and dangerous cabal. Not the inept acolytes who prey on the poor, but the ancient corruption at their rotten core. The sect is hatching an intrigue in secret, shielded by an arcane talisman that's keeping their hideous rites from reprisal. At present, they've seized the crisis of the Mistwraith's invasion and the absence of crown oversight to extend their subversive influence across all five kingdoms. I aim to take their web down without quarter. Accept my proposition, and you'll be secured in position to help break their ranks from inside."

Toler slouched in sullen distrust, braced to lie low and seek furtive ways not to cooperate.

"The alternative?" Davien's night-deep eyes glinted like the edge of a blade. "You perish." A bald certainty, backed by his Fellowship's intractable charge to preserve the world's unspoiled mysteries. "You die beyond question, with all of humanity caught in breach of the compact that defines Mankind's terms of settlement."

Never mind that Toler's feckless disposition preferred to greet doom in pursuit of his indolent pleasures.

Davien's amusement bared teeth. "No such reward will grace your recalcitrance. Skills like yours are commonplace in the stews. I'll find your replacement, while you fulfill your sentence digging latrines for the company fighting the Mistwraith's invasion."

Hard labor with no happier outlook, given that looming catastrophe imperiled the world's greater powers. Toler embraced the path Davien offered, sly enough to nurse his intent to desert. A press-ganged berth as a seaman showed merit, provided he could slip the Sorcerer's reach.

Davien's eyebrows rose. "By all means, try your utmost. But until you succeed, your lawful future is mine, properly endorsed by free will upon your release in my company."

Ditch digging under the Mistwraith's incursion, Davien might have added, was the kindlier lot than the razor's edge precipice walked in his footsteps at the behest of the Rei-yaj Seeress…

THE BRISK MORNING TWO YEARS PAST HAD BEEN AS winter cold, even with the exposed sandstone stair butter-yellow under full sunlight as Davien ascended the spired tower to consult with the ancient oracle. Come at the behest of her dedicated attendant, he had answered the unusual summons, unsuspecting. While the ongoing contention sprung from his opinions had not ruptured Fellowship unity, he seemed an unlikely delegate to represent their collective interest. To stifle the volatile flames of debate by agreeable disposition, his six colleagues shouldered the Mistwraith's containment, while he minded affairs at large on the continent in almost solitary diligence.

The wizened, blind seeress recognized his incisive footfalls, or else placed him by the crisp snap of his russet cloak in the gusts, although she did not turn her head. Statue still in her high, gimbaled chair, her marble white eyes stayed trained perpetually sunwards.

"Some say," she opened in her dessicated voice, "that you hate human nature enough to forsake the compact and revoke Mankind's license to dwell on this world."

Davien might have corrected the misapprehension: he did not dislike humanity, only distrusted the means by which Fellowship oversight curbed the excesses of freebooting exploitation. Crown justice through charter law already showed fractures where discontent splintered into subversive factions. Davien's concern had rigorously proven the pitfall that risked the mysteries to entropy: sooner or later, the rot of self-interest undermined guided wisdom. The sterling virtues that endowed the royal bloodlines were a stopgap palliative, unfit to sustain the challenge. The sovereign put to the test had failed to master Davien's maze at Kewar, lost to madness when the inherited drive of exemplary principle foundered in the morass of human shortfalls.

Davien's outlying vigilance stood alone in the aggrieved aftermath. Weary of chafing debate that changed nothing, the Sorcerer laced clever fingers and awaited the purpose behind his irregular summons.

A drawn minute passed, clocked by the ponderous clunk as the counterweight chain and geared wheel revolved the seeress's seat with the sun's passage. Weathered hands splayed on the chair's ivory arms, she was a seamed sculpture in leather and bone, swathed in fringed, azure silk. White hair, pinned with jeweled, horn combs, scarcely stirred to her tranced breaths.

"You still hold an unwavering stake in your species' survival," the oracle remarked at long last.

Davien stifled wry humor. "My colleagues might argue the case, but yes." Mortality nurtured astonishing genius, born in the fusion of irrational passion, untamed fancy, and ferocious impulse. Hope suffered when excessive logic withered exuberance. "In willful disregard of rational boundaries, provisional law must maintain perspective until far-sighted wisdom evolves." But protective order carried a price. "Innovation suffers, shortened on the leash of over-simplified policy. I've argued the case against fixed tradition, in favor of more flexibility."

The seeress absorbed his points without comment, immersed in whatever inscrutable vision she gained from her lock-stepped communion with the sun. When she spoke finally, the Sorcerer listened, his impetuous assurance shocked by the precedent that her office seldom to never shared confidence, except where her fathomless interests aligned with Mother Dark's crone, the revered elder of the Biedar tribe in Sanpashir.

"I have a riddle, and an urgent tasking, best pursued in rigorous secrecy. Of the Seven, you are most fitted, loyal as you are to their purpose at heart, but given to differences that drive you apart."

Sudden chill ruffled Davien's composure. "What dire charge are you asking?"

"The quiet disclosure and dispatch of an anomaly that sets our species' future in jeopardy." Blinded at birth, hardened by the ruthless discipline of her dedicated post, the seeress watched the gamut of Mankind's doings from her lofty perch all her days. Bright, dark, and dire, she witnessed the beauty and pain, the heights and the dregs of the human spirit, from exalted grace to unvarnished ugliness. Whatever disturbed her unshielded sight would not be trivial.

"I speak of an abomination, a talisman crafted by foul means that allows the Gray Kralovir necromancers to cloak their affairs."

Davien bridled, alarmed. "You are describing an artifact able to turn broad-scale vision and blind the centaur guardians, including the expanded awareness wielded by Tehaval Warden at Althain Tower?"

The Rei-yaj Seeress raised a thumb in acquiescence. "This danger is already abroad in the world."

She need say no more. By grotesque implication, a black cabal whose rites perverted natural death demanded a Fellowship intervention. The imperative was not malleable, bound as the Sorcerers were by the dragons to safeguard the original mysteries. A summary judgment, called out for harsh reckoning, might take innocent lives along with the guilty.

Davien paced, a livid flame in suede boots and clothes the bright colors of autumn. Once his colleagues discovered this grim scrap of news, or if a great drake gleaned a whisper, mercy became forfeit. The horrendous consequence must be carried out, past any margin for reprieve. "You are giving me an advance notice that Mankind's place on Athera could be revoked with a bloodbath."

The seeress's eggshell gaze remained fixed on the sun. But a jewel flared at her brow as she nodded. "The Biedar eldest in Sanpashir has requested your service in this regard."

Davien's lip twitched, a cynic's concession. The crone would have her purpose for stirring the pot, given her tribal stake in Mankind's affairs pursued a debt spanning millennia. "What else can I do but agree?" His deceptively pleasant consent buried agony for what this covert division of loyalty might come to demand.

The Rei-yaj Seeress acknowledged his word. "You will never reveal this exchange, at your peril, without the formality of Biedar leave."

Irritable as a cornered wolf, Davien mused on the irony that evading the Sighted view of Tehaval Warden, not to mention side-stepping all six of his perceptive, inquisitive colleagues, tortured the limits of devious invention.

Wheezing laughter disrupted his consternation. "Had you forgotten? The Biedar's affairs lie outside of such onerous purview." Davien's mercuric intellect pounced. "Mother Dark's eldest has a party favor of some sort stuffed up her sleeve?" Otherwise, this parlay's confidence would have been compromised.

The ancient seeress stirred a bony arm and snapped fingers like the dry crack of a stick. Her attendant stepped forward and presented a silver ring with three embossed crescents setting a round cut citrine.

"The crone's token, of course," Davien murmured, chary of the signature power that inflected the battered gemstone. The heirloom was old beyond measure, and did not originate on Athera.

"The stone came from Scathac," the seeress confirmed. "It carries the imprint of a Biedar legacy, given to you in discretion." With the delicate caveat that its off world matrix also escaped the range of Tehaval Warden's earth-sense.

Davien grasped the committed force of its history as he slid the band over his knuckle. No fool, to accept such trust lightly, and no small request, to be thrown an imperative directive to intrigue against his own colleagues. "Pray to whatever bright guidance you have the crone in Sanpashir doesn't live to regret."

Then he bowed to the Rei-yaj Seeress and received her husked leave to depart. "May the wisdom of ages walk in your footsteps. More than one people will suffer the brunt if you fail to disarm the Gray Kralovir's meddling…"

BY WINTER'S EDGE, TOLER FERVENTLY WISHED HE WAS shoveling dung pits in the milder climate of the south shore. Instead, the bad half of his bargain with Davien found him shredding himself on the brambles in the desolate scrub of the Korias Flats. Rough living stripped off his excess flesh. Cranky with exertion, he slogged through lists of pointless tasks, while the Sorcerer tinkered, supposedly perfecting the stayspells needed to safeguard his coming assignment.

"Why wear ourselves cross-eyed with boredom in this waste?" grumbled Toler, tongue freed to complain of the nightmares spun by the dread gyre of a nearby grimward.

Davien never glanced up, agile fingers knotting unsavory forces into what appeared nondescript as a loop of frayed string, except for the searing bursts of uncanny static. "Because here, the proximal electromagnetic discharge disrupts slipshod spellcraft and scryers, and justified fear of a grimward deters prying interest. Have you gathered the fifty stones I marked in the next vale? If you can't build tonight's fire pit, you'll get tapeworms from dining on raw meat."

Davien backed his threats. Since flippant rejoinders provoked blistering consequence, Toler's better sense prevailed. He gathered his random clutches of river stones, or drift wood with oblate knot holes, whatever exercise in futility filled day after dreary day.

Weeks passed. Nothing meaningful happened. Toler suspected the Sorcerer wasted his time, until the hour he returned early, cramped by a stitch, and found Davien in rapt discourse with a dragon.

Not a small, carnivorous wyvern, but a great drake, fire breathing, eighty-five spans of shimmering, scaled might, from armored crest to ebony tail spikes. Before her mailed talons, the Sorcerer seemed a toothpick, spiked upright while the massive wyrm snaked around him, her wide golden eye and slit pupil a cloth yard across, terrifying as staring into the abyss.

Toler dropped prone in a gulch. Hands clapped over his ears did nothing to muffle the percussive subsonics of the thought/voice by which the monster communed with the Sorcerer.

'I know something's afoot!' the dragon insisted, horned head tipped aslant in fixated focus.

Davien's quiet response did not carry. Stock still, to every appearance in charge, his loosely clasped hands contradicted his frown of furious concentration.

The clipped phrase he returned settled nothing. The dragon reared up, snorting cinders and smoke, then spun with a tiger's circling grace. *'You sidestep my question. Forget at your peril! You are sworn to defend the light of the mysteries, no matter the cost of the sacrifice.'*

Davien tipped up his chin, visibly taxed, while the dragon's gyrations lashed his white-streaked hair against his trim shoulders. *'My Fellowship upholds our commitment! I will answer to nothing without certain evidence of a catastrophe.'*

The dragon flicked her massive tail. Displaced air tumbled the broom and whistled past Toler's cowering form. *'Then your colleagues shall answer for your assessment to the letter and line, should you fail them.'*

"No," Davien replied in caustic disagreement. "Your inquiry rests upon my word alone. If I stand in error, if Mankind has transgressed, then Dragonkind claims reparation on me without condition."

The drake towered, rampant, vast wings spread like sails. *'Know that I, Seshkrozchiel, shall claim due redress on the moment you are foresworn.'*

Davien bowed his head. Shown his acquiescence, the great drake clapped down the doubled vanes of her wings and launched her sinuous coils aloft.

Raked by the backwash of her brimstone wake, Toler whimpered, cramps forgotten. When terror receded, he fled without shame and immersed himself in his unfinished assignment until sundown.

Davien greeted him upon his return as though nothing momentous had happened. Yet urgency rode his mood like bleak smoke in the fallen shadow of dusk, and by morning, he drove his laid plan into motion.

EIGHT DAYS' TRAVEL ON FOOT SAW TOLER HUDDLED against a bitter wind with a begging bowl, in the portside market at Hanshire. Vagrancy would see him arrested the moment the town watch caught up with him. Soon, he hoped, while the gusts whistled through his threadbare clothing, and spellcraft that saddled him with the appearance of a half-witted deaf-mute frightened him beyond spitless.

At the unpleasant crux, he faced risks far beyond the high-stakes smuggling of contraband.

'Soonest begun, soonest finished,' the Sorcerer rebuked, his exasperation exposed by the internal contact. Evidently the necessity galled, that his critical gambit relied upon Toler's scapegrace character.

For, as Davien explained, in due course an overture from the Gray Kralovir would seek to extend their cult's covert alliance. The unique intersection of Koriani affairs and the grasping interests of Hanshire's mayor offered the best chance to expose the intrigue without confrontation. Provided, of course, Toler's cultivated affliction could infiltrate the sisterhood's ranks in advance.

Under volatile scrutiny by a dragon, himself, the Sorcerer continued, impatient. *'The town watch is one street away. They'll pick you up before you freeze, and remember I've got your back.'*

Toler clenched his jaw, unable to utter the scathing retort to level the one-sided record: the stayspells impaired his speech and hearing, except through his tie to Davien. Rebuff that ephemeral link, and he would *be* deaf and mute, languishing as a simpleton under the Sorcerer's moribund enchantment.

'You'd truly rather be pulling an oar in the sleet for your mandated reckoning?' Razored sarcasm inflected Davien's likely grin. *'How little faith you place in my exemplary handiwork.'*

Toler seethed, while his puppet-string tie to the Sorcerer delivered the tramp of approaching authority. *'One day,'* he vowed, *'I will bollux your string-and-clapper plan with such indiscretion, you'll stay buried for most of your immortal life under the steaming monument.'*

'Stay alive, first,' Davien allowed. *'Then we'll see who's left standing to crow atop the proverbial dungheap.'* Infuriating, laconic, his riposte

stung back from the comfort of his garret lodgings, *'But under the hobnailed boots of the town guard, your wishful fancy's a bit premature.'*

Four brutes arrived in Hanshire's red surcoats to collar Toler for beggary. He endured a few cuffs. A kick sent his tin alms bowl flying, before anyone noted the inscription stamped into the rim.

"Lay off him, boys," snapped the squat, bulldog officer. "Won't be worth dog's dirt if we break him."

'You'll be sold to the traffickers,' Davien confirmed, reliant on the flourishing corruption arisen since the Mistwraith's invasion.

The brazen transaction was shamelessly swift. The guardsmen gagged Toler, bound him hand and foot, then bundled him in his own tattered cloak. Hefted across town like a nameless corpse bound for a pauper's grave, he changed hands to the furtive clink of coin in a noisome alley. The buyer cached him in a dank cellar, where the brothel scents of rose oil and patchouli wafted through the taint of nesting rats.

'You've landed in Madame Everlay's love nest,' Davien supplied, unmoved by Toler's discomfiture as a leering servant unpacked him from the muffling cloak.

Toler vented his rattled nerves. *'Serve you right if the Prime Matriarch doesn't bite, and Madame Everlay has second thoughts. Care to wager my black market service winds up keeping her filthy transactions discrete?'*

Davien upped the ante with sardonic delight. *'If greed does not triumph, you will win the day. My hand will muck out her unpleasant establishment, and you'll be released to go your sorry way.'*

But smug irony suggested the posited stake was already forfeit.

The Prime Matriarch of the Koriathain swept in two days later to inspect her ill-gotten goods. Titled head of a powerful order of enchantresses, she had the alert posture of keen intelligence, and eyes as intimidating as the Sorcerer's. But the cold, black stare of her assessment was impenetrable as a spider's.

Toler forgave Davien's months of meticulous preparation. The visceral recoil when her narrow palm gripped his chin reduced him to primal terror. Even the Sorcerer's inexhaustible spellcraft could not stifle his flinch.

Morriel released him, indifferent, and gloved her narrow hands in brisk closure. "He'll do. My attendant will take him in tow, while we settle the fee for the bargain."

DAVIEN NEVER DISCLOSED THE ROUND SUM THAT sold Toler into the Hanshire sisterhouse. Quartered in the garret for orphaned boys given shelter until they came of age for apprenticeship, he spent his days doing the menial toil decreed by the senior peeress. He chopped wood, watered his eyes whitewashing the hammer-beamed chambers, and lye scrubbed the echoing, bare floors and austere, granite arches. He hauled laundry for the order's skilled healers, cleaned the jakes in the infirmary, and gently assisted with restraint of the injured for treatment. Other times he minded the iron gates that no one dared cross without leave. He saw the young girls arrive for induction: the haughty ones chosen from prominent families flushed with excitement, and others claimed by owed debt to the order brought in tearful defiance. None of the unwilling evaded the sisterhood's yoke. To the last, they emerged pale from their test for raw talent. The oath taking that confirmed their novitiate reduced even the ebullient ones to cowed silence.

Any of them might have been his sister Enna, snatched on the sly and bound into service. Close his eyes, and almost, Toler could hear her weeping, her mahogany riot of curls tamed with scrap yarn, and the star charm worn for luck clenched in fingers callused from threading the looms.

Davien's correction shredded the wistful fancy. *'Koriathain don't co-opt children with kinfolk, or fledgling artisans, only destitute foundlings culled off the streets.'*

If the Sorcerer lied, Toler found no evidence. He did as he was bidden for a full year, treated kindly by the sisters, who wore the gray rank of charitable service. No sign of sinister practice emerged. The labor he shouldered involved no arcana, though often he was apt to turn and discover the Prime observing his stolid performance.

Her stalking unnerved him enough to cry out, had Davien's working not quelled his reaction. Morriel surveyed his witless expression. A coiled adder angled to strike, she analyzed his every movement. Nothing untoward met her suspicious eye. Toler's performance stayed above question. When the bitter, cold daybreak arrived, and her aged servant passed on, she took Davien's gambit as the replacement.

The moment caught Toler without warning. A senior enchantress with red bands of rank tapped his shoulder as he swept the sisterhouse meeting hall. Her peremptory shove hurried him on without pause to collect his dust bin and brush.

He trailed at her heels like a leashed dog through a restricted hallway to a locked closet, where another ranked senior pointed to a copper-strapped chest guarded by potent sigils.

Toler shouldered the load, gadded by the prickle of wrongness that puckered his nape. Soon enough, he experienced the unsavory reasons behind the Prime Matriarch's taste for dimwitted servants. Invocations better off left to dark nightmares poisoned his days for another three seasons. Under candles in dim, curtained chambers drowning in incense-soaked air, he witnessed the uncanny, secretive workings conducted in her private sanctum. Here, his precarious placement as a Fellowship catspaw invited his instant destruction.

Rinsed in clammy sweat, he shuddered with revulsion when the order's arcane paraphernalia were unveiled for use: the rare crystals, mined elsewhere, that amplified spells, and the quartz wands that focused the master sigils enabling the order's most potent craftwork. He shrank from far more than the bone deep chill when his strength was required in restraint. His straits forced him to endure in silenced horror as subservient initiates were drained of vitality to fuel the grand constructs that quelled storms and saved crops, or averted outbreaks of summer pestilence. Soon, the scent of Morriel's lavender perfume made Toler cringe, while before his seemingly vacant stare, her insectile fingers inducted the channeled attributes of the major gem stones. He learned to dread the astringent sting emanated by the Skyron aquamarine, and far worse, the icy malice radiated off the faceted sphere of the amethyst Great Waystone.

Davien's eavesdropping presence seemed absent, throughout. Toler brooded, fearful his wretched case had been abandoned, until the autumn morning Morriel Prime attached him to an errand beyond the sisterhouse walls.

Joined by six more cloaked and hooded enchantresses all bearing administrative rank, he bore the warded chest in their midst, containing the order's most precious arcana. The irregular procession took him up the slate stair to the terraced battlement that fronted Hanshire's ancient hall of state. Subservient as a dumb beast, Toler trod over slag scars inflicted by drakefire before Mankind's habitation. Davien's repressive spells scarcely dampened his awe of the lichened capstones, still embossed with the artistry of the centaur masons who had raised the Second Age fortifications. Beyond the massive, bossed doors, Toler passed the carved dais that seated Hanshire's high council. The tall chairs stood empty. The massive, bronze lamps cast as coiled dragons hung dark on their chains, no flame in their parted jaws. The Koriani delegation crossed the vaulted chamber and filed through a side door into the chancellor's privy closet.

Toler followed the last enchantress over the threshold, unsettled by the pervasive fust of the strong herbals used to fumigate moths. The scent woke his graphic recall of the weaver's loft on the night of his sister's abduction. Enna had not run away. Three other girls had vanished the same week, though his mother scorned the persistent talk of a black ritual involving blood sacrifice.

"A strapping lass able to fuller wool cloth would have left signs of a struggle. Enna bolted on her own, likely cozened from sense by a lad who promised the sweet life of luxury."

Toler's violent qualm all but shredded Davien's elaborate cover. Explosive fury propelled him ahead. Invested by hatred, committed for more than a Sorcerer's whim, he embraced a peril that rightly should have sapped his intemperate courage.

The gathering centered upon Enna's murderers convened a select handful of Hanshire's high councilmen, the rosy cheeked, fidgety mayor, and two Koriathain retained as his advisors. But Toler's interest fastened on the pair of dignitaries who dominated the dais: a wizened man with watery eyes and stick limbs, too pallid to have seen daylight, and a hairless woman in a string cap whose jaded ennui shaped a face transparent as a shelled oyster. Yet her acid interest watched everything.

Toler avoided her gaze, head bent and oafish feet shuffling. The Prime's circle directed him to deposit the chest beneath the right hand seat, which Morriel claimed, her purple skirt draped in prim folds to her ankles. Her gesture dismissed Toler to a back corner, where he sat on the floor, disregarded as furniture.

More figures entered, influential guild factors in peacock silk and two imposing women in starched lace that Enna's craft mistress would have priced in gold coin. Only the front bench was filled when the door clicked shut on the select enclave.

Hanshire's mayor presided, a plump wolf masquerading in stylish manners. "We gather in private to weigh a unique proposition that opens a wide range of fresh possibility. Today, you will hear the particulars and consider the merit of Hanshire's involvement." Gleaming in his chains of high office, he deferred to his gaunt guest, whose severe, scholar's robe wafted the sickly taint.

"Taranthine, if you please, engage our protections."

The bald woman produced a small coffer, unlocked with a silver key. Within, nestled four drawstring bags of raw silk, painted over with unclean symbols. She removed each one, loosened the ties, and withdrew fist-sized objects of polished bone, which she placed against the walls at the cardinal points. Toler's vantage revealed skulls with prominent eye sockets and needle thin incisors. The dome of each brain case bore an inlaid jet circle, centered with the glitter of a ruby setting.

"Fate master's mercy!" the Prime Matriarch gasped, shocked. "Are those what I think?"

The cultist declined to answer, but positioned the last artifact, snout facing inwards. Toler felt the subliminal *snap* as his spell-crafted link with Davien's presence sheared off, leaving him deaf and mute. Seized by rank terror, utterly lost, he beheld nothing more than the color and movement of lackwitted incomprehension.

DAVIEN SHOT ERECT, BANGED HIS HEAD ON THE SLANT beams of the attic ceiling in his rented quarters, and swore murder until he exhausted his breath. For one fleeting glance had exposed the dire forces behind the impenetrable ward: dragonets, taken alive from the egg, then killed and ensnared by ritual necromancy before their spirits gained quickened intelligence.

Gray Kralovir's meddling had opened a threat in the world utterly without conscience. Davien understood he beheld the opened gate to calamity. Great drakes rearranged the formed *world* with a thought; their dead, left unrequite, seeded the grimwards, gyres of peril so dire that only the strongest of constructs kept them safely isolate. Without the most drastic protections, the caged revenant could unravel creation in the throes of mad dreaming.

If one dragon *ever* realized unhatched young had been stolen and suborned for abusive practice, humanity risked being expunged from existence in one vengeful strike. And if Tehaval Warden divined the infraction, the Fellowship Sorcerers must answer the crime and remove Mankind's offending presence directly.

Sanity quailed at the scale of the stakes. Davien curbed his fierce agitation before he attracted disastrous scrutiny. Informed hindsight made him jumpy as a scalded cat, that his indispensable access for redress rode the knife's edge of a back-stabbing smuggler's recalcitrance.

FOR TOLER, THE EXCRUCIATE TRAUMA STRETCHED ON, forcing him through the crucial proceedings in a near helpless stupor. While the numbing influence cast by the matched skulls dissolved his connection to Davien, he witnessed the gestures of heated debate, powerless to hear, and unable to grasp the words spoken. Koriani affiliation might not protect him where even the witches appeared to walk softly. Past the first, appalled outburst, their Prime kept composure in her imperious silk. Yet her darted glances flickered with unease, while Hanshire's mayor and his rabbity chancellor colluded with the wicked cabal that surely had preyed on his sister.

Twilight darkened the windows, and gloom shadowed the stifling atmosphere before the wax-featured necromancer snapped his gaunt fingers. His female colleague arose like a specter and collected the jeweled skulls. When she veiled the last of the uncanny relics, the gathered officials exhaled in collective relief.

Toler smothered his pithless shudder as his suppressed awareness resurged. Reprieved by the click of the latch on the coffer that sequestered the sinister artifacts, and sick with mounting anxiety, he longed to escape the repellent miasma clogging the stuffy air.

Yet no command to depart brought release.

Hanshire's paunchy mayor exchanged nervous banalities with the Kralovir, then requested due leave for a private discussion. The Prime Matriarch watched the unsavory cultists file out, alert in her upright chair. She withheld comment. When the mayor's councilmen and chancellor, and the strutting flock of beribboned guildsmen departed, she dismissed her subordinate entourage, but kept Toler in place.

Servants entered to brighten the candles, and a freckled maid brought a tray of light fare. While the mayor poured wine and nibbled on pastry, the Prime's gesture cued Toler to heft her locked chest to the table top. Then, hands folded, she waited until the staff left the room. Behind the shut door, only Toler attended her closed discussion with Hanshire's mayor.

"Are you certain the lackey should stay?" The mayor's pink fingers toyed with a morsel, as if tension blunted his appetite.

Morriel responded with arctic disdain. "The deaf-mute halfwit? He would perish the instant I thought he posed any threat. Though given Gray Kralovir's shady morality, stringent precaution is justified." Youthful dexterity at odds with her age released the protective ciphers and raised the domed lid of the copper-strapped box. "I have brought our order's most powerful focus to enforce our privacy."

She whisked the silk shroud off the Great Waystone. The mayor choked and pounded his chest, spraying crumbs as the sphere's dire cold shocked his poise. The Prime regarded his paroxysm without sympathy. "Count your blessings we chanced bringing this stone from the sisterhouse. No other jewel we possess has the strength to blindside the Fellowship Sorcerers."

The sigils of containment she amplified through the quartz matrix clenched Toler's gut and wrung him dizzy. Fearful he might lose control of his faculties, he huddled in a shivering knot, to every appearance the dullard Davien's mission required.

The mayor smeared paté on his crumbling bread and chewed through his nervous talk. "Do you believe the support for this revolt is as widespread as the Gray Kralovir claim? A bold move, and exceedingly dangerous, to overthrow charter law by mass murder and dethrone the crown bloodlines. The Fellowship of Seven will not be complacent, no matter that their compliance with the Major Balance honors free will."

Morriel's hooded gaze glittered. "The risk is great. But the potential for gain is enormous. The Sorcerers are overextended, with most of their resource committed in crisis to stall the Mistwraith's advance. Tehaval Warden does not watch the towns where crown justice is secured by the Fellowship's surety. Many interests chafe for a sweeping change, given the mysteries languish from neglect."

Hanshire's mayor dusted crumbs from his paunch, poured more wine, and sipped to suppress his trembling anticipation. "We may never see a more opportune moment. Since the Kralovir will finalize the conspiracy under absolute secrecy, what have we to lose? If crystal transmission can signal the rising across all five kingdoms at once, not even the Fellowship's reach could contain the widespread scope of the outbreak."

"The Sorcerers must be caught by surprise. Should they catch any word in advance, the entire effort will fail." Morriel measured the mayor's ambition as though sizing up prey. "And your tidy plan for a simultaneous assault cannot happen without the Koriathain. Our order's partnership carries a price."

"Of course." Hanshire's mayor dabbed his moist lips with his sleeve. "Name the debt."

Morriel's withered mask never twitched. "Acquire the dragon skull wards, and grant possession of them to my order."

The mayor's vermilion complexion drained white. "That's a steep demand, to barter with necromancers!"

The Prime's teeth gleamed like strung pearls through her satisfied smile. "Nonetheless. You have leverage. Gray Kralovir need us. Their use for impenetrable defenses will be moot in the absence of persecution. What price for the bargain, to shatter the Fellowship's yoke and release Mankind's claim to free enterprise…?"

TOLER TOSSED ON HIS COT IN THE DEEP OF THE NIGHT, surrounded by the whispered breathing of the boy wards' innocent slumber. The reek of herbal moth bane poisoned his dreams, and spun nightmares of blood and slaughter. Sweating, while the full moon frosted the casement, he startled bolt upright when Davien's thought breached his awareness.

Just how brave are you?'

Toler flung off the bedclothes, distraught. *'You want me to cross the Kralovir necromancers and the Order of the Koriathain?'*

'With my help. If you're willing.' The pause hung, textured by the disturbing notion that the Sorcerer nursed rattled nerves, also. *'I'm proposing an intervention to pull the rug out from under the Hanshire conspiracy.'*

Toler flogged tried wits. *'How?'*

The testy response reflected the Sorcerer's restless pacing. *'If I provoke the uprising early, all parties involved will be scrambled into disarray.'*

The shocking tactic at first failed to sink in, that a Fellowship Sorcerer could turn on his own, launch a bloodbath aimed to upset charter law, and unleash wanton murder upon the irreplaceable descendants who carried the fivefold attributes of crown heritage.

Davien squared the hideous facts, not unflinching. *'If I don't react first, the brute consequence will break our Fellowship's inviolate bond. But if I trigger the rebellion on my terms, half-planned, chaos will favor the chance of outlying survivors. Charter law may be saved within the free wilds, with enough structure left in the aftermath to rebuild from the pieces.'*

The imperative conclusion dangled, beyond words: that the dragonet skulls would be vulnerable during the proposed change of hands between Kralovir and Koriathain.

'You can't act without me,' Toler surmised. His light-fingered ingenuity must seize the moment and smuggle the perilous artifacts from Morriel's close guarded collection. *'Where's my assurance that I'm not expendable, given your own straits are desperate?"*

For the moral imperative to warn the other Sorcerers would expose the inside agent allied with the Fellowship.

'Think, bantling!' snapped Davien, already cornered by the dearth of alternatives: to let human transgressions revoke colonization and, perhaps, save the harmonic balance of the world's mysteries. Or else thwart the summary eviction and have dragons discover the abuse of their stolen hatchlings. To waste this covert chance to confiscate the skull artifacts meant inciting the flames of a wrath that would consume Mankind utterly, without any hope of merciful discrimination.

Toler stalled to chew over detail. *How will you infiltrate the signal relay of the Koriathain?'*

Davien's whiplash sarcasm stung. *'Leave that delicate dealing to me.'* Had he not already exposed the gamut of Mankind's inherent weaknesses? Fallen out with his colleagues for hundreds of years, he knew every bitter card to be played. *'There are culpable fools in the Koriani sisterhood who will drop their guard, baited into manipulation on the pretext of my conflicted loyalty.'* Flashpoint resonance could suborn a quartz network in a fractional second of close proximity.

'You knew all along about Enna,' Toler accused, resentment simmering under his burning hatred of the Kralovir cabal. As the Sorcerer's attacking pawn, he was entitled to ask the agonized question. *'What happened to her?'*

Davien's charged contact went piercingly still. *'Do you truly want the unquiet truth?'*

For in his heart, Toler already knew she had suffered a hideous end. Better to close his eyes to the ugliness, and remember her dancing for joy with her shining hair laced with yellow ribbons. Grief locked his resolve. *"How do I bring the Gray Kralovir down? If you render justice for the crime of my sister's ritual sacrifice, I will attempt what you ask.'*

Davien's promise rang back. *'Help spare our Fellowship's covenant from ruin, and I will not rest until necromancy in all forms has been expunged from the world. Smuggle the dragonet skulls out of Hanshire, and no dark cabal will be able to hide or evade due redress.'*

But the midnight pact courted terrible ruin: lives *would* be lost, disastrously many, while the blow to civilized order shocked stability to the brink. The ruthless course demanded Davien's undivided focus at Hanshire, while Toler tiptoed into the jaws of dissent for the caper to deflect Mankind's certain downfall.

ON THE SPRING NIGHT IN THIRD AGE YEAR 5018, when Davien sealed his reputation as the Betrayer, the historic uprising disrupted crown rule, and streets across the five kingdoms ran red in the tide of unbridled slaughter. Luhaine of the Fellowship fell with the first casualties, left discorporate by the swords of a mob in defense of a child prince at Telmandir.

Davien felt that grievous blow where he stood to meet Toler in the wilds of the open heath. In bitter quiet, he accepted the copper-strapped coffer purloined from the Prime's chamber when the Hanshire conspiracy exploded in premature fury.

"You were right," Toler gushed, speech restored in the aftermath thrill of his unlikely victory. "The Prime circle lost their collective poise and left Morriel's treasures unguarded." Toler chuckled with his former insolence. "The snatch went as slick as robbing an unwatched cradle."

Too easy, Davien agreed, but said nothing, braced to mask his disappointment as he tucked the warded box under his arm. Divination by resonance revealed at once that the dragonet skulls were not inside. Toler's haul contained river stones bundled in silk. The dangerous, uncanny contraband cleverly sequestered elsewhere.

But the smuggler's earnest attempt deserved recompense for the grisly risks undertaken. "You are free to pursue your life as you please." Davien sealed his word with sincerity. "I will honor my promise, and see the Kralovir ruined in Enna's memory."

Toler's rush of exuberance stalled. "I can go? You don't want the last laugh with my trademark flourish?"

Jolted from brooding, Davien realized what else the feckless young man tried to tell him. Raw from the toll of unconscionable harm, and burdened under the monstrous consequence, the Sorcerer laughed in stunned disbelief.

"Hold on," he gasped. "You did *what* with the coffer containing the Great Waystone of the Koriathain?"

Toler flushed, pleased to share his sly comeuppance. "I tossed the cursed thing in the public well, with none of the witches the wiser. Don't say you want the horrid crystal retrieved?"

"No!" Davien sobered. "I will pass that detail along, and let my colleagues field the detestable prize." An inadequate sop for the reckoning, when this night's botched work became called to account. Save him, he required desperate measures to dodge mauling scrutiny and keep the deadly secret entrusted to him by the Rei-yaj Seeress concealed.

For his task was not done. The deferred crisis waited, inevitable, when the hatchling skulls resurfaced to cloak the next round of mischief. The black bargain sealed with Seshkrozchiel also bound Davien in force. He must shoulder the confounded tangle alone, against stakes his fellows must never suspect, until intrigue presented another furtive opening to discharge his obligation.

THE SYLDOON SUN

JEFF SALYARDS

— Bloodsounder's Arc —

MATINIOS WATCHED THE CAVALRY GALLOP ACROSS THE packed dirt of the Hippodrome, tasting the red cloud kicked up in their wake. The dusty air wafted up to the royal pavilion—gritty, tangy, and stinking of the sweat of untold generations of soldiers and the spoor of a million horse. A million million, maybe. He still felt the usual mix of emotion—elation at seeing Syldoon in action and jealousy as relentless and remorseless as the beating sun.

But worse than the jealousy was the company. It wasn't every day he sat alongside the most temperamental, scheming, and dangerous man alive. This was the first, in fact. Matinios felt Emperor Cynead's eyes on him. It was like being observed by a brass viper.

Of course, with a Memoridon flanking his other shoulder, Matinios knew it was dangerous to think such things. To think almost anything, really. She could be slinking inside his skull that very moment, sifting through his thoughts, his memories. So he tried to focus on the wheeling horseman, how effortlessly they maintained formation as they circled the oval grounds. Training exercise or not, their skill was paramount. Better to think on that.

Another smaller group of Syldoon in lamellar cuirasses rode past, short recurved bows up, heels down, bodies as taut and flexed as the wood and horn and sinew in their hands. The soldiers galloped between a pair of tall poles and then spun in their saddles, arrows nocked, their armor flashing bright in the sunlight, aiming at the clay gourds hanging from hooks at the top of the poles. They loosed almost in unison—one straggler a heartbeat late—and kept galloping as all but one of the arrows struck true, shattering the gourds. That last shaft missed high and sailed off into the bright blue sky.

Emperor Cynead clicked his tongue and Matinios glanced over. He had jet-black hair with one patch of white on his crown that nearly glowed in contrast, even in the shade of the huge snapping canvas panels above them. For a man of middle years, he had few wrinkles, and the laugh lines stood out the most, though he wasn't exercising them now. He wore no ostentatious display of station at all except for the plaque belt on his waist, the alternating mount plates of heraldic suns and leopards done up in the finest rubies and gold.

"Well," the emperor said, plucking a date from a bowl in his lap. "I summoned you to show you something extraordinary. And what do they give me? Nine. Nine of ten on the mark. That simply won't do. No, not at all." He shook his head. "Rusejenna, should we remind him of the cost of failure?"

The slim Memoridon surveyed the field, her close-cropped hair nearly alabaster, her expression no less impenetrable, the leopard pin on her gray jacket winking in the sunlight. "Your will, Your Majesty." She sounded sibilant, sensual, mocking. The way a succubus might, if such creatures existed. Though if they had, Memoridons would have been more terrifying still.

Emperor Cynead looked at Matinios. "Would you like to watch my Memoridon work, to see the errant archer blasted from the saddle, bleeding from his ears, his brain stove in from the inside? As a lesson of sorts, to the remainder?"

Matinios might as well have been swallowing sand. He considered his next words carefully. "I imagine the opinion of a lowly clerk is of little consequence, Your Majesty."

"Really?" Cynead replied, watching the mounted archers riding around for another pass at the next set of poles and gourds. "The son of a Syldoon captain, knowledgeable of all things Jackal Tower, and, unless my sources are misinformed—which I assure you, they are not—quite the student of military history, tactics, and logistics? Your humility seems disingenuous." He held the bowl out to Matinios. "Date?"

Matinios shook his head and composed his thoughts as the sweat trickled down his sides. "Well then. You've invested time and expense in training these soldiers—no less so than any other Leopards, and probably a good deal more, given their rarity. I'm guessing they hail from the farthest reaches of the Brass Sea. Very costly. So murdering the man on account of a single miss might be considered…wasteful. Unless he has never hit the target." Matinios shrugged. "Then the loss would be less."

Cynead smiled, laugh lines pronounced and deep, and then turned to Rusejenna. "You see—sharp. I told you he would be just the right recruit."

She gave a thin smile. "As you say, Your Majesty."

Matinios wasn't sure what he'd done to attract the attention of the emperor, but he wished he could undo it. "Recruit? Your Majesty?"

Cynead picked up another date and inspected it before casually tossing it over his shoulder. "You didn't think I summoned you here just to chat about my horsemen, did you?"

Not having any idea what to think, Matinios simply waited rather than risk another reply.

Cynead nibbled on another date. "No, I brought you here to extend a very unusual offer."

Emperors didn't offer. Certainly not to unimportant clerks. Matinios replied slowly, "I'm honored, Your Majesty. And humbled. But confused. Why—"

"You hungered your whole life to be a Syldoon, did you not?"

Matinios felt his chest tighten and watched the blocks of infantry on the far end of the hippodrome march in formation, long spears high. He wasn't shocked the emperor knew about that, but that didn't make it more palatable. Matinios tried to keep his voice level. "Tradition is tradition, Your Majesty. The offspring of Syldoon are forbidden from such things. I was proud to serve as auxiliary—"

"So, not able to achieve that dream, you settled for the second. And did quite well. Serving admirably, distinguishing yourself. Until you disobeyed a direct order." Cynead looked him up and down. "You did so to save other troops, and yet, just like that," he snapped dry fingers, "your military career—finished."

Matinios felt the age-old anger welling up, and did his best to dam it in place. "Yes, Your Majesty. Finished."

Cynead nodded. "Commander Darzaak kept you on as a clerk—at least the old fool recognized you possessed too many talents to abandon completely—but he drummed you out of the auxiliary. The military. Forever."

Matinios tried to keep his face blank. He would never be a soldier again, but he was still part of the Jackal Tower, still answered directly to Darzaak. Dangerous thickets. He had to tread very, very carefully.

After a deep breath, he said, "The commander's decision was… fair."

Cynead watched, his blue eyes assessing. "Very dangerous to lie to an emperor." He didn't wait for a reply or rebuttal. "But what if I told you I could promise you an unprecedented opportunity at redemption, Matinios?" He let that sit there for a moment before continuing, "The chance to prove yourself, to serve in the fashion you desire most, to be a soldier again. Not for the Jackals, but the Leopards. In the royal auxiliary."

Matinios met his gaze. Was he being toyed with? Manipulated? Was this a test of his loyalties? He aimed for moderation, and missed much more badly than the mounted archer had. "But… Your Majesty, such a thing…it must be impossible. I am with the Jackal Tower."

The emperor smiled. "And I am the man who overthrew Thumaar. The man who is going to change the complexion of our empire, the trajectory of our history. Do you really think a little thing like tradition and a doddering commander are going to stop me? Imperial initiative is a marvelous thing, Matinios. So, what do you say?"

Matinios licked his lips, tasted dust. "I say… I say such a thing must come with a cumbersome price."

Cynead clapped his hands as he laughed. "Indeed. For everything, a cost. So. What is this dream worth to you, young clerk?"

Matinios would never be a Syldoon like his father before him, but to be in the army again, to forge his own path… His voice sounded like it came from the bottom of a deep, dry well. "Everything. Your Majesty."

"How wonderful," Emperor Cynead replied. "That is precisely what I had in mind for the exchange."

Matinios wasn't sure if that was the sound of the jaws of a trap clanking shut or finally springing open.

Cynead sat back in his chair, eyes on his troops. "I am implementing a new policy. All foreign operatives will be accompanied by a chronicler from their respective Tower. Each commander has submitted a list of clerks and scholars who might be appropriate, pending my final approval. Ordinarily, the scribe would deliver the report to the commander who would then pass it on to me. In this instance, we would simply streamline the process. That is all."

"The Jackals?"

"Of course. I have suspicions that Darzaak's men are engaging in activities…not in the interest of their emperor. But I require proof. Witness."

"You want me to…become a spy? A traitor?" The words were out before Matinios had a chance to stop them.

"Betraying a traitor is no treason at all," Cynead said. "And let us remember: you will be handsomely rewarded for your efforts."

Matinios wanted to hold his tongue but couldn't. "Do I have the option of declining this offer?"

Cynead looked at him long and hard, smile disappearing. "You do, Matinios. I cannot promise how I would respond, of course. Perhaps we will walk our separate ways and never speak of this meeting again. Perhaps I will let Rusejenna husk you and turn your brain to gruel. We all have our choices to make."

Matinios thought about wiping out years of disappointment, bile, bitterness, anger. About achieving a dream that seemed ground to dust. He also thought about what it would be like to have a memory witch invade his skull and lay waste to him and tried not to shiver, despite the heat. "In that case, I accept," he said.

"I very much hoped you would," Cynead replied, smiling. "Date?"

THE LEAN, HARD-BITTEN CAPTAIN WATCHED THE LAST of the pilgrims and faith-seekers exit the temple grounds. His two lieutenants flanked him, trying to look casual among the pillars. But Hewspear was built like his weapon and taller than everyone in the crowd, with coins braided into his beard, and Mulldoos was short, stocky, pale as ash and foul-mouthed as pitch—they weren't exactly inconspicuous, despite keeping their Syldoon noose tattoos covered.

Captain Braylar Killcoin rested his hand on the wicked two-headed flail on his hip. That was one of the first things Matinios noted after joining them. The captain's hand never drifted too far from Bloodsounder. Ever.

Matinios had seen several of the Jackals in the Tower before, and certainly knew them by reputation, but he never dealt with the captain and his company directly.

Before agreeing to spy. To betray.

He reframed that: before agreeing to serve his emperor. And himself. Finally, himself. His life had been stolen from him, by the Jackals, by Darzaak, and he would take it back. And as Emperor Cynead had said, betraying traitors was no treason at all. Matinios didn't have any damning evidence yet—the Jackals had done all they were assigned to on their mission. So far. But he was sure it was only a matter of time.

Directly behind his shoulder, he heard, "What are you doing there, you plaguing nosy bastard?" Sepulveedo was close enough Matinios could smell the stale ale and catfish on his breath.

Matinios hadn't heard the bastard approach. Sepulveedo was an expert skulker.

He turned and faced the Jackal. "I am doing my plaguing trade. Remember, that thing I was commissioned to do? That is my trade."

Sepulveedo smirked and burped in quick succession. "Thought your trade was to scribble. That's your plaguing trade. Don't see you doing any of that right about now."

"I was hired to witness and record. This is called the witnessing part."

The sergeants, Vendurro and Glesswik, leaned against the pock-marked pillars a few feet away. Vendurro had a narrow patch of beard on his chin that looked like a hedgehog pelt, and always a crooked smile above it. "Alright there, Sep, you made your point, I'm thinking. Hey, Matinios, just carry a quill around in a pocket. Lot easier."

Sepulveedo was almost as good at scowling as skulking. "Don't like him standing around looking sideways all the time, is all."

Braylar, Hewspear, and Mulldoos approached. The captain's dark hair was oiled back, the scars on his face lit white in the sun, his mossy eyes narrowed. After looking around to be sure the closest non-Syldoon was a purple-robed initiate trimming some hedges thirty feet away, Braylar said, "We have done ample reconnaissance here. Tonight is the night we make our play, yes?"

Mulldoos turned, pressed a thumb against his nose, and blasted snot out the other nostril onto one of the pillars. "About plaguing time, Cap. Let's hit this shithole and be done with it."

Hewspear looked at Braylar. "As much as it pains me to agree with him—I favor too much recon over too little—I reluctantly concur we've seen what there is to see here. It would have been better if we'd managed to have somebody infiltrate the temple, but still, we have enough. We've surveyed the high priest's manor house, the number of guards, their rounds, the distance to magistrate, even the position of the dovecote."

Mulldoos snorted. "If they got time to send plaguing pigeons to get help, we messed up something fierce and deserve to get cut down to a man. Plague me, we're raiding a puckered little asshole of a temple, not stealing the king's golden ear spoon. If there's anything to steal at all here. Which I got real plaguing doubts about."

Being the company chronicler allowed Matinios to pose whatever questions he deemed proper, but he still picked and chose his spots carefully to avoid arousing suspicion. "What do we hope to find here, Captain?"

Mulldoos narrowed his pale eyes as he stared at him. "First off, you'll know when you need to know and not a second earlier. Second off, you ain't *we*. Don't get all uppity, you plaguing pen monkey."

"Enough squabbling," Braylar said, looking from face to face. "We return under moonlight. Rest a few hours, hone your blades, and be ready, yes?"

As the Jackals started walking away from the temple, Vendurro said, "You think the inn has any quail eggs. I could really go for some quail eggs."

"You could really go for my boot in your plaguing mouth," Mulldoos replied.

"Only if you boiled it first. And dipped it in saffron and cinnamon. Hard to come by, though, cinnamon. More precious than quail."

The Jackals scattered, presumably to draw less attention to themselves, and exited the wooden gatehouse around the temple, walking separate routes back to the inn.

Braylar was acerbic, moody, and as vicious as he was erudite, but seeing him walking alone, Matinios sidled next to him, hoping to question a little further. To unearth something, anything, that could help him win his life back.

They sidestepped a beggar rattling a few coppers around in a cracked wooden bowl and made their way down the hill toward the makeshift village in the shadow of the temple grounds.

The captain tugged at the scarf around his neck, and wiped some sweat off his brow. "That is one thing I will not miss about these little excursions—wearing an extra article of clothing in this heat. Be glad you don't have a tattoo to cover."

Was that a barb? Most likely. Braylar seemed incapable of saying anything without them, and the Jackals made sure to remind him that he was no Syldoon.

But before Matinios could start an inquiry, the captain said, "I knew your father, you know."

Matinios faltered, and tried to play it off as tripping on a loose stone on the path. This was *not* what he expected. "No, Captain, I didn't know that."

"Not well, I admit," Braylar said as they descended the last stone steps and headed toward the ramshackle collection of buildings at the base of the hill. "But he was an exemplary soldier, I know that to be true. Such a challenging thing, living up to our fathers, whether we truly understand them or not, yes? We overvalue them, undervalue them, rarely know them as they truly were. And yet we spend much of our lives struggling to win their praise, or surpass them, or destroy them."

Matinios tried to think of a good response, was mostly unsuccessful, and settled on, "I appreciate you saying so. About my father. That he was a good soldier, I mean."

Braylar stopped and faced him. "I will tell you one other thing,

Matinios. Unlike your father, you were discharged due to your inability to follow simple orders. Perhaps for a good cause, perhaps not. But fail to obey a direct order from *me*, or jeopardize our mission in any way, and I assure you I will not be half as forgiving as Commander Darzaak. That is understood, I hope?" His mouth twitched into the smallest of smiles.

Matinios felt his face flush and nodded. He tried to smile in return, wondering if it looked as carved and false as it felt. "Yes, Captain. Well understood."

"Very good," Braylar said, clapping him on the back hard enough to rattle his ribs. "Let's try a bit of the cat piss the locals call ale, but mind, not too much. We have a busy night ahead."

MATINIOS CRAB-WALKED UP THE HILL IN THE DARK with the small group of Jackals. The moon was curved and thin like a Grass Dog blade, but hidden behind a cloak of slow-moving clouds. Matinios grabbed scrubby grass as he leaned forward to steady himself, wondering if everyone else's breath sounded so obscenely loud in their ears.

The Jackals wore wool tunics over their armor, and their weapons were still all sheathed so there wasn't much metal to glint, even if it had been a bulbous full moon.

This Temple of Truth compound was a relatively small complex—they had passed some others en route as fortified as small castles—but it still had walls and guards. Plenty of ways for things to turn sour and bloody.

Matinios looked ahead and saw Lloi, the one woman in their group, who happened to be a Grass Dog. A short sword at her hip no less curved than the moon, her mutilated hand on her hip, the last digits chopped off. Matinios wondered, for about the thousandth time, what a severed savage was doing in the middle of a Jackal company. It would be one thing if they had to cross the Green Sea and needed a scout or an interpreter to the godless tribes that called the grassland home. But in the middle of a clandestine operation in Anjuria? Nothing but strange.

Matinios had seen her ministering to the captain, circling him like a nurse maid. There was a peculiar relationship there, but he hadn't parsed out the nature of it. Yet. And when he did, it would be just the thing for his report to Cynead.

About thirty feet from the base of the wall, Braylar raised a hand. The small group crouched in a close circle as he rasped, "While the guards in this temple are no Syldoon," he said, looking at the small group, "they still bear arms and outnumber us four to one."

Mulldoos snorted. "Ten to one be something to start fretting over, Cap. Remind me again why we aren't just storming the place. Be a lot simpler to just gut them all, find what we need real casual-like, and set the place blazing when we're done. Got surprise on—"

"Because," Braylar replied, "while Commander Darzaak did grant us some latitude in carrying out this little Anjurian operation, he insisted we not call undue attention to ourselves, and bloodletting, atrocities, and large fires are not, as a rule, overly subtle. And *because*, as much as I value your stalwart belief in our inherent superiority, I will not risk the lives of our men when we do not know for certain what we will find inside. And *because*—and this bit is really paramount, so do pay attention—because I issued an order. Not a suggestion or a solicitation. I do hope that clarifies things."

"Ayyup," Mulldoos said, "with clarity to spare, Cap."

Matinios wiped some sweat off his brow and tried to sound casually curious. "Captain, you said Commander Darzaak granted latitude. But aren't you here on the emperor's mandate? I thought he was the one who sent Tower companies like this into Anjuria to stir up trouble?"

Lloi shook her head and gave a low whistle. "I never seen Sunwrack, never even put a toe in your empire proper, and even I know not to go asking fool questions like that."

Hewspear looked the least comfortable crouching in the dirt, as he had the longest frame to fold up, but he still spoke in a strong voice, even whispering. "My boy, I would have thought you'd served the Tower long enough to know, but there are always things in play here…" he raised a hand above his head, "that the rank and file are not privy to and cannot possibly fathom. We answer to Captain Killcoin, and he answers to Commander Darzaak. The rest—agendas, mandates, overarching strategies—do not concern the common soldier. Or the clerk accompanying."

Mulldoos didn't bother with niceties. "What the nettlesome witch and the old goat here are trying to say is, shut your mouth, do your job, and don't be a little horsecunt. Clear it up any?"

"Absolutely," Matinios replied. "With clarity to spare."

Vendurro and a few other soldiers chuckled but Mulldoos only nodded slowly and laid a hand on the pommel of his falchion. He wouldn't be able to draw it in that position, but the threat was obvious enough. Matinios ignored the man and the threat.

Braylar said, "We get in, quietly, quickly. What we seek must be in the vaults underneath the temple. We find it and get out the same fashion, yes?"

"Begging your pardon, Cap," Sergeant Glesswik said, "but wouldn't what we're after be likely to be in a scriptorium? You know, being written and all?"

"Oh, sure," Mulldoos replied, "that would make a whole heaping load of plaguing sense and we'd all be slapping you on the back, congratulating you on being such an insightful bastard. If this temple *had* a scriptorium. And you weren't such a dumb bastard instead."

Matinios had no idea what use the emperor (or even the Jackal Tower) could have for Temple of Truth records or documents. But at least that confirmed the nature of their odd prize, if not the particulars.

Vendurro said, "It's a good day for crossbows. Well, night, that is. And we ain't shooting bolts willy nilly all over the place, you know, on account of the sly sneaking and all."

Glesswik punched him in the arm. "You're an ass and a half, you are."

"Me? You're the plaguing idiot who thought they had a scriptorium."

Braylar rose slowly. "We proceed," he said. "In silence, I hasten to add."

MATINIOS DROPPED DOWN ON THE OPPOSITE SIDE of the wall, heart beating fast, sweat dripping faster, eyes scouring the shadows around the wattle and dab meditation huts and the temple beyond for any movement. He knew most of the guards would probably be in the high priest's manor house fifty yards farther north, or the barracks alongside, but there were still patrols. He kept his hand on the handle of his axe.

If they kept to their routines the Jackals had observed the last tenday, a pair of priestguards would have completed a circuit of the complex not long before, circling around the old temple, and wouldn't do so again for two hours at least. That was one thing the Jackals had going for them—this was a lesser temple, and its guards were surely more used to dealing with vandals and petty thieves than an assault from Syldoon troopers.

Still, plenty of ways for things to go sour.

The Jackals hunkered behind a round meditation hut and waited. Vendurro moved ahead, hugging the edge of the small ramp that led to the stone altar. When he gave the clear signal, Braylar started for the temple with the Syldoon at his heels, everyone moving briskly across open ground, darting between huts as quietly as they could in muffled armor.

To Matinios, it sounded like they couldn't have been noisier if they were banging pots together and singing filthy songs at the top of their lungs, but it must have just been a trick of ears and nerves, because no alarm was raised.

They collected against the temple wall, and Matinios felt the deep divots in the old stone as he tried to master his breathing again.

Waiting for a skirmish or heading into hostile territory had been easier than all this skullduggery. With a battle, you might not know precisely how it would play out, but you could be certain it would result in spilling blood, cracking shields, and hoping you didn't step in a gopher hole or get blinded by sun glinting off a helm. Still more predictable than this.

Lloi leaned in close to him and whispered, "Got yourself an axe. Some armor under that stinky tunic too, I'm thinking. Weird equipment for a scribbler, don't it?"

Matinios replied, "What's weird is a Grass Dog in a Jackal company."

She chuckled softly and ignored that. "Why is a soldier playing scribbler playing soldier?"

He gritted his teeth. "Captain asked for silence, didn't he?"

"So he did," she replied. "You best stop yapping then."

Hewspear, being tallest (if oldest), braced himself against the temple wall, and Vendurro scrambled up his back, hugging the crumbling temple, stopping just under the window ledge. He listened for several long moments and then he rose up and peered over, raining dust down on the lieutenant's head.

Vendurro whispered, "No priestguard around, no lantern anyway. Got to figure he ain't stumbling around in the dark. Good time to go in."

Captain Braylar replied, "Very good, Sergeant. Find him and put that light out permanently. Quietly though. So very quietly, yes?"

"Aye, Cap. Quiet-like. Got it."

With Hewspear and Mulldoos giving him a boost, Vendurro hoisted himself up to the ledge, spun his body around, careful not to catch the crossbow hanging on his back, and lowered himself down inside the temple.

The Jackals drew their weapons, and Hewspear unwrapped the leather binding from the head of his slashing spear. Braylar guided the company along the temple wall, hugging the old building, moving so slowly it was almost painful.

They stopped beneath the porch at the front of the temple, the landing just above them, the entrance to the battered edifice a few feet away. Then Matinios heard them, priestguards, very close. It sounded like two of them. The Jackals could easily overwhelm them, but that would mean running around to the stone steps, or at least climbing up the side, and that meant plenty of time to shout out a warning, call other guards.

So they waited. And waited some more, still as gargoyles, listening for something, though Matinios wasn't sure what.

Then, finally, the sounds of tumblers in an ancient lock, tunking and clunking loudly in the dark.

It sounded like one of the priestguards turned around. "You got to piss again, boy? Swear you got a bladder the size of a squirrel's left—"

Mulldoos boosted Braylar up to the landing and climbed up after, the rest of the Jackals following like wraiths.

Matinios rose, about to pull himself up, and saw Braylar swing his wicked flail, the spiked Deserter heads gouging a priestguard in the side of the neck. The guard gargled and started to go down. The Deserters whipped back the other way, careening off the man's neck on the other side for good measure. The man dropped.

The other guard spun around, pulling his sword from the scabbard, and started to yell something, but Mulldoos brought his falchion around with both hands, the blade striking the man in the midsection. Even though it didn't sever the mail hauberk under the surcoat, the man doubled over, shout cut off, and Mulldoos chopped down on his exposed neck twice, crunching the spine in half.

A moment later the door creaked open and Vendurro stuck his head out. "You all waiting on perfumed invitations? Come on, already."

Four Jackals dragged the two bodies inside the temple, and Vendurro pulled the door shut and locked it in place again.

Another guard lay on the floor of the narthex, a bolt sticking out of the back of his neck. Matinios couldn't help being impressed—the Syldoon were as professional and efficient as expected.

"See?" Vendurro said, looking at Mulldoos, "Not totally undefended, is it? Maybe we got something here after all."

The big lieutenant picked up the dead guard's hooded lantern and looked around the temple. "You stash another ten bodies in the apse then, did you? Because if not, three guards ain't much of a serious defense, is it?"

Braylar turned to a Jackal. "Stay in the antechamber, and more important still, stay alert. Notify me immediately if there is any unexpected company, yes?"

The Jackal nodded, mace and buckler in hand, and disappeared into the shadows of the narthex.

The group moved out into the open nave. It was difficult to make out much more than the contours and general shape of things in the gloom, even after Matinios's eyes adjusted. A few decorative candles gave off a flaccid light. But they had all had been inside the temple recently, disguised as penitents, so they knew the general layout.

Matinios wondered what the Old Gods would have made of this usurper temple. That was, if they had stuck around instead of abandoning humanity. Probably indifferent.

Everyone waited, weapons drawn, as the captain slowly pivoted, holding his flail in front of him like a divining rod, the Deserter flail heads spinning in front of his face. None of the Syldoon seemed overly concerned by his strange behavior or hid it well if they were, which made it all stranger still, but Matinios couldn't help wondering what in the hells the man was doing.

Braylar led them down the middle of the nave between rows of wooden benches that were facing each other. Above, the Wheel of Truth—the circular band of iron fixed with silk screens depicting the Deserters leaving the world, and the new gods slowly entering to fill the spiritual void—hung from chains from the upper reaches of the egg-shaped dome.

The Jackals crept down the aisle to the round altar at the front, and Braylar led them off to the right into the transept. The captain might have been conspiring against his emperor, but Matinios had to grudgingly respect an officer leading from the front.

Braylar was first down the spiral staircase, with Mulldoos directly behind him, falchion in one hand, the priestguard's hooded lantern in the other, now that they didn't fear alerting anyone.

The small company made its way round and round, deeper into the earth than Matinios expected. One or two turns should have brought them to a basement, but the stairs kept winding. The air grew colder as they spiraled, and his skin felt clammy, sweat starting to chill on his flesh.

Finally the spiraling stopped and Matinios stepped out of the stairwell onto a dirt floor, having to duck a bit. Hewspear was hunched over like a broken hermit, his slashing spear held horizontally in front of him.

The lantern lit the tight rectangular room, stone support columns that looked older than the world holding up a corbeled roof. There was a small wooden desk in one corner in front of a stool, what looked like a storage room off to the right, wooden shelves laden with weathered tapestries and vestments and some barrels and little else. Ahead, a rickety looking cabinet stood against the wall with clay jars and beaten brass bowls on the shelves.

Surely there was nothing of value here. It was barely even a passable junk room. Even the rats had abandoned it.

Vendurro scratched the tuft on his chin. "Cap, are you sure this is the right—"

"We are in the correct temple in the correct region in the correct kingdom, Sergeant. Yes, quite sure. Garton and Mosslick, check the room to the right, and be quick about it. Miss nothing. Vendurro, search the desk. Burraku, take a look at the shelf ahead there."

The Jackals moved off to obey, and Mulldoos stepped closer to the captain. "Could be we got lousy intel, Cap, or—"

Braylar said, "You were quite thorough in your interrogation, Lieutenant. You have singular skill in that area. That Anjurian did not lie."

"But maybe he just repeated a bunch of superstitious horseshit he knew you were keen to hear because he was real eager to stop hurting."

Braylar said, "It is quite possible that this is simply an abandoned undercroft. It is equally possible that what we seek was hidden here so many hundreds of years ago that it has been almost entirely forgotten. Either way, we leave only when we have exhausted every—"

"Cap!" Burraku waved them over to the shelf.

Braylar, Hewspear, and Mulldoos walked over, and Matinios followed.

The young spotty soldier pointed at the floor. "Now that's right odd, ain't it?"

They could make out footprints in the carpet of dust, some fresh, some ancient, but nothing else.

"Is it?" the captain asked, clearly irritated. "How so, soldier?"

Burraku pointed at the base of the cabinet. Whatever footprints might have been in the dust were smeared into obscurity when someone had pushed the cabinet against the wall.

All but one. Half of one, really, under the edge of the warped wood. Stepping *away* from the wall. Which should have been impossible.

Mulldoos looked at the captain, saw him smiling, and then practically yelled, "Move it aside already, you bastard!"

The Jackal put his back into it and shifted the creaking cabinet to the right. It nearly collapsed.

There was a narrow wooden door behind it, with a single rusted iron ring handle.

Braylar called out, "Jackals, to me."

"And Grass Dogs," Lloi said, walking toward them, a grin on her broad copper face. "Rude to exclude, ain't it?"

Mulldoos crammed his big pale hand in the rusted loop, clearly expecting it not to budge, but the old wood cried out as he heaved, shifting an inch towards them. After several tugs, the door finally came free with an awful groan.

Hewspear held the lantern in the little doorway, illuminating the small room beyond. There were several rows of small desks caked in dust, and the walls were lined with shelves filled with crumbling scroll, yellowed parchment, and dusty tomes.

Vendurro whistled. "Plague. Me." He looked at the captain.

"This *is* it, ain't it?"

It was *something*. Something hidden, anyway. But Matinios still couldn't understand what they wanted with old records. Perhaps they incriminated the high priest or some baron or other, or some lay subsidy roll contained key information. But from hundreds of years ago? What difference could it make now?

Braylar said, "Glesswik, Vendurro, let's see what we have here. Take the men and fill your satchels. Very. Carefully. The material is…delicate. We can ill afford clumsy hands shredding the evidence."

Evidence of what?

Glesswik slapped Vendurro on the chest, then stepped through the doorway, a big smile on his pockmarked face.

That was when the world tilted sideways.

And then disappeared entirely.

Matinios saw only black, as if he had dunked his head in a barrel of tar, but then something came into focus. Something he had lived and could never forget, a memory, but sharper than any reality.

He was back on the ridge that changed his life three years ago. His patrol had been pursuing bandits, and they were ambushed. Their battalion got split in two—half the company in the wooded ravine trying to evade pursuit but heading for a bottleneck; the other up on the ridge. With his captain. Captain Craven, he'd call him later. After the discharge. But it was still Captain Bolshvin then.

Bolshvin looked at them, his long waxy face filled with panic. "We have to…we have to ride! To get back to camp!"

Matinios wasn't sure he heard correctly. "But, Captain…the other men."

The captain was shrill, out of control. "Back to camp, you whoresons! To…get reinforcements! Now!"

Those men in the ravine would die. Everyone around Matinios knew it. He saw it on all their faces. The captain was ordering them to abandon half the company. But no one said anything. They sat in their saddles, frozen, or twitching, uncertain, but silent, not wanting to ride, not wanting to disobey a direct order. Half of them looked ready to piss themselves.

Matinios looked around at the other auxiliary troops. "They wouldn't leave us behind! You know they wouldn't!" Then he turned to Bolshvin. "We can't just ride off like cowards, Captain!"

Captain Bolshvin blasted breath out his nose like a maddened bull. "What did you say to me, soldier? What did you—"

"I'm not leaving them down there to get slaughtered by plaguing bandits!" Matinios looked to the others, knowing he was leaping off a ledge, but seeing no other choice. "Who's with me?"

Captain Bolshvin grabbed his arm hard enough to bruise, spittle flying, eyes bulging. "You listen to me, you upjumped bastard! We are *riding* out of here! That is an order!"

Matinios didn't think. He backhanded the captain, pulled the reins, spun his snorting horse around and guided him down the hill into the dark woods below. Leaving safety and numbers, flying into the dark and probably his death, Matinios rode down, not caring if anyone else followed. He refused to leave their men to die.

And then he heard hooves behind him. His brothers in arms riding after him, and up on the ridge, Captain Bolshvin screaming, "You disobedient dogs! You'll hang for this! The lot of you will hang for this, every last—"

…traitor.

The voice was gone. Captain Bolshvin was gone.

Matinios was back in the dusty undercroft, and Captain Braylar stood there in front of him, Bloodsounder in hand, the door frame smashed to splinters.

The other Jackals were on their knees or totally prone. Some were doubled over holding their ears. One Jackal was flat on his back, staring vacantly at the corbelled ceiling. Another lay on the floor, struggling to raise his face out of a puddle of vomit. Mulldoos was shaking his head like a dog fresh out of a lake.

Most of the Jackals had glazed expressions, looking lost, overwhelmed. Matinios still felt woozy and disoriented, his limbs heavy.

Whatever it was…it affected all of them.

All except Captain Braylar, the only man still standing and alert.

Braylar looked around at the Jackals, at Lloi, at Matinios, his lips tight and thin like scar tissue. "On your feet. All of you. Let's claim what we came for and be out of this place immediately."

Mulldoos was leaning against the destroyed doorframe. "Plague me. What was that, Cap?"

Braylar replied, "A memory trap, unless I miss my guess. My sister spoke of such a thing, but…"

Hewspear said, "She is a Memoridon, capable of such craft. But even if the Priests of Truth employed rogue witches…how could they possibly have created this?"

Lloi said, "I couldn't never construct nothing like that, Cap. And I can do plenty, even not being a slick Memoridon."

Mulldoos's eyes darted to Matinios, then he gave Lloi a murderous glare.

Braylar shook his head. "A mystery, to be sure, and one I refuse to speculate about overmuch now. But it all but confirms that we found what we've been searching for. These priests, rather surprisingly and alarmingly, yoked memory magic in some limited capacity long before the Syldoon mastered Memoridons." He barked orders to the Jackals. "Gather all the documents from the shelves. With haste. But infinite care. The man who tears a single page will have his skin torn in turn, understood?"

The Jackals entered the room hesitantly, but when no other trap was triggered, they set to work.

Matinios's head still swam in the echoes of the memory. He looked at Lloi, vision a little blurry. "She's a rogue memory witch," he blurted, before looking at Braylar's flail. "And that thing protects you from memory magic, doesn't it?" He rubbed his eyes, "But why would Cynead—" and stopped.

Too late. Much too late.

Mulldoos shook his big head. "Of all the plaguing dumb things you could have said, pen monkey, that was without question the plaguing dumbest."

Braylar had the ghost of a sad smile on his face. "I had rather hoped to be wrong about you, Matinios. Truly, a pity." Then he nodded.

Matinios was pulling his axe off his belt when he felt the dagger slash across his neck. He spun and buried the axe deep in Sepulveedo's skull. The Jackal gaped, dropped the bloody blade, and fell sideways. Matinios reached for his throat before stumbling against the shattered door frame, legs buckling.

The world tilted crazily again, and he was lying on his side, looking at everyone's boots and the shelves beyond, and much closer, a growing puddle of blood.

The pain was hot and fierce. Matinios tried to scream but found he couldn't. Why couldn't he scream?

He heard Mulldoos say, "Dumb bastard couldn't do a simple thing like cutting a throat without cocking it up. You two, drag Sep over there until we're done." After a pause, the lieutenant added, bitterly, "Guess we'll be needing a new scribbler now too, huh, Cap?"

Braylar's voice. "So it would appear. But we will choose the next chronicler ourselves, yes?"

"Too bad," Vendurro said from somewhere very far away. "Kind of liked Matinios. You know, if he hadn't been a traitor and all."

And then the world was plunged into black and Matinios was riding down the ridge on his horse again, the cold night wind on his face as he hurtled headlong into the dark.

THE DARKNESS WITHIN THE LIGHT

SHAWN SPEAKMAN

— The Annwn Cycle —

TATHAL ENNIS SLID THE DAGGER INTO THE SIDE OF Old Wynn's neck.

The Wily Puck's grizzled bartender stiffened, his eyes going wide as he struggled for a few moments. Tathal savored the moment but not for the reasons others would assume. It was not the steel tearing flesh. Or the warm blood flowing down the knife to his fingers. Or the ragged crunch of the blade sliding against worn vertebrae. No, the ancient wizard enjoyed the other's sudden realization of that moment—and how short the moment would last. It was in Old Wynn's eyes and in the stink of the death sweat that had broken out upon him. It was in the man's hands as they frantically dug into Tathal's arm. It was in the bartender's inability to scream, his vocal cords severed. At his end, Old Wynn clung desperately to the wizard just as he clung to life. Tathal absorbed it all. Death had a way of revealing a man in ways no discussion ever could. And when it came to knowing men's lives, no one knew them like Tathal Ennis.

He could have let Old Wynn die unaware of the death that now took him. But the bartender had been a sly old coot. Somehow, he had broken free of the trance spell and had sensed Tathal's purpose in coming to Betws-y-Coed.

Since the spell would no longer work, Old Wynn could not live. Men of his profession served and befriended men who protected their community's own.

Not that the wizard's wraith companion couldn't keep him safe.

Or Tathal, for that matter.

It was just the principle of it.

The wizard let the body of Old Wynn slide slickly to the alcohol-soaked floor behind the bar. It was as good a place as any for the town's authorities to find him.

"That did not go well," Tinkham growled from the gloomy rafters above. The dark Shadowell fairy shook his head.

Tathal ignored his companion. With a few spoken words, he burned away the blood upon his hand and forearm. Then he placed the bloody knife on the bar in front of Breena Roberts, the middle-aged woman with the dubious honor of being Old Wynn's last patron. She was the only other person in the pub. "It happens," he responded finally, sitting next to her on a stool. "Some people in these Misty Isles possess a bit of magic in their bloodlines from the time the fey cohabitated with them so long ago." The wizard turned back to the short woman, worried his spell would stop working on her as it had on Old Wynn. "Can you still hear me, Miss Roberts?"

Her gray eyes spell-ridden, Breena Roberts nodded. "I can."

Tathal peered closely at her. She was still under his spell. Besides, if she weren't, she would have screamed bloody murder for what he had done to Old Wynn. "Before we were so rudely interrupted, we were speaking about the fairies of Betws-y-Coed," he resumed, his voice thick with honey. "You were speaking about the fairy glen and the creatures you have seen there."

"Yes, fairies. And others," she said, a lazy smile crossing her thin lips.

"You mentioned your grandmother," Tathal said. "How did she call the fairies? Tell me your memory of it."

Breena closed her eyes, remembering a long-forgotten dream. "I am eight years old. I am burning with fever. No one knows why. My nana steals me away from my mum in the middle of the night. Mum always says nana is crazy. The stars are out. We are walking. It is cold but my skin burns. I cannot stop shivering. I am weak. But nana holds my hand. So tightly. So tightly." She paused. "We are in the woods on a path now along a river. I can hear it roaring. I want to sleep but she stops me. Says it is dangerous. I do not like that. She carries me down the bank to the river's edge. I see water falling through a cut in large rocks. I have been here before but never at night. She sings words. I know them. About the Fey Queen. The Lady. The moonlight enters the falling waterfalls and stays there."

Breena paused. "And then little lights fill the air," she whispered.

Tathal listened intently. The centuries had made him patient. Every small community featured a wealth of knowledge found in its oldest inhabitants. They held onto stories like dragons hoarded gold—knowing family histories, rivalries, and the strange. People like Old Wynn and Breena Roberts knew much. Upon arrival to Betws-y-Coed, Tathal had come straight to *The Wily Puck*, an ancient pub on the outskirts of the village. Bartenders who had spent any time in the profession had loose tongues. They also knew everyone. Old Wynn had led Tathal to Breena. The wizard hoped she would lead him to the information he sought.

"You see the Lightbrands, Breena, the fairies who guard the Lady of the Lake," Tathal said, hoping to glean more information from her. "Is this so? Can you describe them?"

The woman smiled as if drunk. "Light. So pretty. Fast. Like shooting stars, they are."

"Was it your grandmother's singing that brought them?" Tathal asked, hopeful for the first time since entering Betws-y-Coed.

"Yes."

"Can you remember which song? Or some of the words?"

"I have sung it only once in my life. But I know it as if it was inscribed upon my heart. The verse goes like this:

Over hill, over dale,
Thorough bush, thorough brier,
Over park, over pale,
Thorough flood, thorough fire!
I do wander everywhere,
Swifter than the moon's sphere;
And I serve the Fairy Queen,
To dew her orbs upon the green;
The cowslips tall her pensioners be;
In their gold coats spots you see;
Those be rubies, fairy favours;
In those freckles live their savours;
I must go seek some dewdrops here,
And hang a pearl in every cowslip's ear.

"Shakespeare," Tathal grunted. "Why would that even be important here?"

"My nana says the fairies love Shakespeare. They knew him, she tells me." Breena blinked lazily again, her eyes lost to the past. "Nana holds my hand while she sings it, next to the river in the fairy glen."

"You are getting nowhere," Tinkham growled.

The wizard glared at the fairy, who still hid in the rafters. When Tinkham shrugged and looked away, Tathal turned back to the woman. "What happens when she finishes the song?"

"The Lightbrands swirl around us. Faster and faster. The fairy glen changes. And the Lady is here. So fair…"

It seemed simple enough, Tathal thought.

"Return from memory, Breena Roberts."

The old woman sat up a bit straighter, still under the influence of the wizard's spell but her face having suddenly lost the look of wonder that only children in the presence of real magic possess.

"When your grandmother sang to call the Lightbrands, what happened, do you think?" Tathal asked. He may have found the key he needed but some locks had fail safes. Best he knew them now before it cost him.

"We were beckoned. Pulled. Away from this world. I could feel it," she said slowly, testing each word as if verifying they were right. "The fairy glen shimmered and we entered a different fairy glen, somewhere else. Surrounded by trees and a larger waterfall."

The wizard thought on that. Magic could transport people from this world into the world of the fey. There were several portals that led to Annwn—one of which he had a hand in creating—but there were powerful beings living in both worlds and the one Tathal sought could easily draw people from this one into another.

The Lady would never summon his like to the place Breena had traveled, of course. He would have to break in, uninvited.

Or use trickery.

"You said you used the song once yourself," he continued.

"Once, long ago," she said dreamily. "Got me a husband. The Lady helped. Then made me promise."

"Promise what?"

"Never to return," Breena said sadly. "Or share the secret of the song. I have never returned. Or spoken of it…" She trailed off seeming to realize she did that very thing now.

Tathal snorted. People wished for the most inconsequential things. Money. Power. Love. Such insipid things. Especially love. He wanted none of that. He wanted answers, had spent centuries finding them, and he would continue until he had them, no matter the repercussions.

"Where is your husband now?" Tathal asked, genuinely curious.

"He left me before I was thirty," Breena said. There was a hint of old sorrow in her voice, the kind created by a broken heart. "The Lady gave me what I wanted but did not say for how long I would have it. The curse of fairy kind, I suppose. My nana warned me about that, she did."

Tathal hid his amusement from Tinkham. The fey could be cunning pranksters. And when it came to the most powerful fey, nothing of what they said made sense, at least not on the surface. Breena had gotten what she wanted—but also hadn't.

The wizard would have to be on special guard to keep that from happening to him.

"Where is Wynnard?" Breena asked.

"He stepped out."

Tinkham grunted. "*All* the way out."

It took all of Tathal's will not to fry the little squirt right then and there. He needed the fairy too much this night.

Breena hadn't heard. "I would like another drink, please."

"I will pour you one when we are finished," Tathal assured. "Go back to the day that you summoned the Lady of the Lake on your own. How old were you? How did you meet her? What was she like? Did she test you in any way?"

"The Lady," Breena sighed, lost to memory again. "I am eighteen. I sing and the fairies answer my call. They fly around and around me until they blur like a comet streaking the sky. I am not afraid; I remember the time when I was young. I can feel myself being pulled to a different place and I arrive there, before a larger waterfall." The old woman breathed deeply. "And she is here. Waiting. For me. The Lady is radiant and beautiful like the dawn. She glows hovering before a waterfall, her bare feet gracefully touching the stream and her long hair flowing around her head like she is in water. She is made of starlight and moonlight and the ethereal light of the fairies. She is pure. And just. I feel her look into me. Into my heart. She is doing this and we are connected. I can feel her power, her empathy, her long service to the Word. I can see each knight she has aided and the quests they were on. She laments the love of those she has lost and the many more she will yet love and lose.

"I ask the Lady's help in wooing the man I love. I wonder if I will ever feel as connected to him as I do to her."

She stopped speaking. Tathal used the silence to mull over the conversation and one thing had become quite clear.

It would be a difficult night ahead.

"Return to me, Breena," he ordered finally. "You have done very well."

"Thank you," she said simply.

"I will pour you that drink now," he informed her, already walking around the bar—and stepping over the body of poor Old Wynn to reach the liquor.

He could feel Tinkham's beady eyes watching him curiously

from above. "Are you going to get her drunk?" the fairy asked, flying down to hover at Tathal's shoulder. "Will that help you get the answers we seek?"

"The answers *I* seek," Tathal corrected. "And no, I have no further need of her."

The fairy blinked in disbelief. "You had better share then."

"My dear Tinkham," Tathal said, handing Breena a drink. "If you continue to speak, your services will no longer be required. You know what that means, yes?"

The black-scarred face of the Shadowell fairy scrunched up in rage. He wisely went quiet. The wizard turned away, already puzzling over what he had learned. Tathal would confront the Lady of the Lake, that much he knew. Whether he could steal, coerce, charm, or fool the information he wanted from her depended on this night. He had brought Tinkham as well as his knight protector, the latter waiting outside. The two of them and his own wits would have to be enough.

And the night beckoned.

"Pick up the knife, Breena," Tathal ordered.

She put down her untouched drink. She picked up the blade, Old Wynn's blood still wet enough to coat her fingers and palm in sticky red.

"You have wanted to die a very long time," Tathal said, leaning close to Breena and lowering his voice to plant a seed. "Ever since your husband left you with nothing. You want to die now. There really is no reason to go on."

Breena frowned. Tathal simply waited until his spell did the work for him. With so many strands unwoven in the tapestry of his future, it was best not to leave one thread undone, one that could be pulled and undo at least some of his work. Like Old Wynn, the woman's soul had a powerful drive of self-preservation that even a wizard of his talent had a hard time overcoming. Breena would fight him as so many others had over the centuries. It mattered not. Her will would crumble like all the rest.

And her life would end as so many others had. With death by his hand.

Breena stared at the knife. Tears came unbidden to her eyes. Tathal watched a few fall. Some part of her knew. Knew what was happening. She gripped the knife tighter, unable to undo the persuasion that compelled her. He saw the seed had taken root and grew inside.

He saw her final truth. The knife would fall continuously upon his leaving.

Tathal Ennis left *The Wily Puck* then, the night embracing him as it had for so many centuries, cloaking him in a darkness that had always been a friend. Tinkham and the wizard's shadowy knight protector followed. No one saw them depart. No one would know what Tathal had done. He would leave the village of Betws-y-Coed as he had arrived—with no one the wiser.

In an hour or maybe less, someone would enter the establishment looking for a drink or conversation with Old Wynn and Breena or both.

They would find much more than that.

Tathal grinned.

A murder-suicide was nice and neat.

WASTING NO TIME, TATHAL ENNIS MOVED THROUGH the midsummer night.

The moon accompanied him, out of Betws-y-Coed and into the countryside, its light painting Wales in silver and the warmth of the day still sticky around him. He had grown up in a similar setting and had traveled through the Misty Isles many times while tracking down the implements he needed to fulfill his plans. The last time, he had visited Glastonbury Tor just to the south and the grave it had hidden for centuries. There, he had found his protector—a terrible revenant. The shadow had become his best tool, an indomitable, raging spirit given life again. Proving its loyalty, it had crossed land very much like the one they now traversed, destroying the village of South Cadbury in its entirety to ensure Myrddin Emrys and his foul Heliwr knight Richard McAllister could never discover Tathal's business. His protector now followed behind him, just out of sight, as silent as his slain.

Still, possessing the returned revenant did not mean Tathal could let his guard down. Tinkham scouted ahead, his gossamer wings a blur carrying his black, knobby body through the air. The wizard had met the nasty little creature months earlier when he had entered Annwn in search of the Archstone—the rarest of keys, needed to unleash Stonehenge's most terrible secret. Tathal hadn't found the relic. But the fairy had become another piece in the wizard's scheme. He was as ruthless as Tathal. And Shadowell fairies had a habit of exploding upon death, tarring the vicinity with their ichorous innards. Tathal grinned. He had to admit he hoped to see that one day.

A wizard, a knight, and a fairy. The words invoked the French Arthurian romantic legends. But Chrétien de Troyes would have been aghast at their malevolence. It was needed this night though. For the woman Tathal went to speak to was no woman.

Not any longer.

She was one of the most dangerous of Word creations.

The air cooled as midnight came and went. Tathal made his way through Northwestern Wales, more determined than ever. Tinkham scouted ahead, leading the way; Tathal's shadow protector followed behind, an unseen presence. The nocturnal creatures they crossed gave way, hiding from the three. The wizard paid them no mind. Soon he heard the sound of water rushing over smoothed stones even as a silver ribbon came into view, one highlighted by the moon and that snaked through the darkness. The Conwy River, the source of the fairy glen. Finally, he arrived at a gate with a simple toll box, the proceeds meant to pay the caretaker for the upkeep of the path. He went through the gate without paying. The path angled away then until it split—one direction diverged to the Fairy Glen and the other went Riverside. He took the former. Ferns and lichens grew along the banks of the river and purple orchids and globeflowers scented the air. He could feel the magic of the place as he made his way to the river, a cool, soft ebb of power that most mortals would never feel but which he had been attuned to his whole life.

With the sky filled with stars, Tathal arrived upon rocky banks and a hush fell over even the river, a great stilling of sound, filled with expectation.

"Well, wizard," Tinkham groused. "We are here. What now?"

"Tinkham, patience," he said, breathing in the night. "First, I must sing and call the Lightbrands." The dark fairy hissed. The Shadowell clan hated the Lady of the Lake's guardians. "They will appear because the magic of the song will compel them. Then there is the Lady of the Lake. *She* is not so easily coerced. But the Lady of the Lake has the memory of her human heart. The feelings she possesses can be used against her. And I plan on taking advantage of that. If necessary."

"Can she cause us harm?" the fairy asked.

"If she is guarded, yes—and she will be."

The fairy looked back the way they had come. The wizard's protector waited at the edge of shadowy awareness, staring at them, still as a statue. "And my part in all of this, wizard?" Tinkham asked, his eyes obsidian beads.

"I do not know," Tathal lied. "The part you will play in this is not yet clear." The Shadowell fairy frowned. He knew Tathal rarely didn't have an answer. "Although," the wizard continued. "If the Lightbrands try to flee, I need you to attack them. Unlike other fairies, the Lightbrands are immune to my magic. You can confuse them. And give me enough time to think of something." The fairy nodded, become very serious. "Now be quiet. And still. It is time."

Tathal turned toward the waterfall and closed his eyes.

And sang.

The song spun out of him, laced with his own magic, the same words Breena and her grandmother had sung before, a supplication, a request, an entreaty to meet and be heard. He beckoned the other, the fey. The sound of his deep voice penetrated the night and as each word resonated within the fairy glen, a swelling answer returned to him. The trickling sound of the waterfall disappeared. Tinkham and the revenant disappeared. Only the song mattered. Upon finishing it, he began anew. By the third time through, he could feel the magic pushing at the veil that kept this world separate from Annwn.

Tathal understood then. The song existed as a clarion call. When he opened his eyes, he could see a blurring of two distinct worlds in the same space, a junction of sorts. It was just the beginning. Lights swirled within the waterfall, captured starlight given life. The movement started small at first and then grew. Tathal watched the lights separate from the water to fly up above the river. Lightbrands. Several dozens. Before the wizard had finished his final song, five glowing figures separated from the rest and flew toward him, fairies made all of light, growing more distinct as they approached. They were nude, their hair white and their eyes as blue as the deep ocean. Three females and two males. All stared at him. He could sense their growing uncertainty.

The Lightbrands flew in a circle, tighter, until they were a blur approaching him, a ring of fluid movement.

"A rogue wizard," one said.

"Very dangerous."

"The Lady will not be pleased by this one. We cannot accept his plea."

"He cannot touch us. He is not of fairy."

"Return. Return."

The fairies spoke quickly, Tathal barely able to understand their words. He saw what was happening though. The circle of light that comprised the five Lightbrands had already begun to break down and move back toward the waterfall.

"Now, Tinkham!" Tathal roared.

From over his shoulder, the fairy shot like a dark arrow into the midst of the Lightbrands, slashing at them with his tiny, glowing fey sword. The Lightbrands tried to hide behind one another, tried to fend off the little creature. Just as Tathal had hoped.

Tathal shot his magic directly into the grouping of light and its spot of dark.

Into the heart of Tinkham.

The Shadowell fairy exploded. One moment, he was attacking his most hated enemy. The next, his black insides covered every Lightbrand fairy.

The Lightbrands realized their danger but all too late. The magic Tathal spun chained the remains of Tinkham, binding the Lady's gore-covered servants to the fairy glen.

The Lightbrand leaders were his.

"Farewell, brave, pain in the ass Tinkham," Tathal smirked, even as he walked into the shallow depths of the river to view his prisoners. The Lightbrands tried to clean away the Shadowell fairy's death, in an attempt to get free from the wizard. As he approached, he could see the fear etched onto their little faces. He smiled.

"My Lady, my Fey Queen, I wish an audience," Tathal said to the night. He knew she would be listening. "I suggest you grant it."

It did not take long. He could feel the shift in the fairy glen before it even happened. And something else? An uneasiness? With his wizard eyes, he watched the veil pull back to reveal the true fairy glen in Annwn. His dark companion went with him, tethered to Tathal for that purpose. A rowdy waterfall existed in this fairy glen as well, the resulting river slowing to a smooth stillness as it meandered through the meadow and beyond into dark woods. Peace tried to worm its way into his heart, part of the magic of the fairy glen. He fought it, hated it. It belied life's most earnest truth—that life ripped peace away, destroyed love, and offered only pain.

Rage he had carried for centuries sharpening his resolve, Tathal Ennis looked around for the object of his coming, restraining the Lightbrands in the air near him.

The Lady of the Lake was not present.

Tathal was about to threaten his hostages again when he saw a knight.

She stood upon the opposite shore of the river, ethereal as the mist, beneath ancient fir trees that towered around the glen. Tall and lithe, her steel armor hugged her close, its surface polished to a silver sheen but without helm. Instead, the cowl of an inner cloak concealed her features, pulled up over her head. All except full lips blessed with a ruby glow. Flame glowed and rippled along the edges of her armor, a perpetual cinder embedded in the steel to ward off enemies when needed. With her gauntleted left hand resting comfortably upon the silver circular pommel of her longsword, she stood, a blade given human form, prepared for war within the most peaceful of fairy settings.

The emblem of a white rose embossed the armor over her heart. Made of opal, it captured the star shine and glowed like the Lightbrands.

"A Blodyn Knight," Tathal said. His surprise gave way to a tiny sliver of doubt. "A powerful bodyguard, Lady. How very interesting."

The woman moved then, as if the wizard's recognition of her presence gave her freedom to do so. She strode confidently toward him, over the river where no stones or bridge held her up.

This was a powerful creature indeed.

"Last wizard of the Fallen Court," she greeted without welcome. "The Lady I serve requests you free the Lightbrands you have unceremoniously captured. She does not wish to see her friends wither at your touch. She also does not wish to destroy you—here in this most peaceful of places—despite the ill intentions you have brought."

Tathal snorted derisively. He stepped forward carefully, keeping his distance from this dangerous creature, whose speed and agility was renowned and whose magic was deadly.

"Does one such as the Lady truly have friends?" he questioned.

"All life is precious to her."

"Be that as it may, you did not answer my question," he said, peering at her closely. There was much he did not know about this particular Blodyn Knight. "And perhaps you are not who you say you are. Show yourself. And when I am convinced you are an emissary to the Lady, we shall start with introductions."

A few silent moments passed as if she were getting direction. Then she lowered her cowl. She was beautiful but in a terrifying way, made as strong as the steel at her side and just as unforgiving. But that was not what truly drew his surprise. No, it was her sharp chin, high cheekbones, and the auburn hair that barely concealed the pointed ears of her heritage.

The Blodyn Knight was an Elf.

"I am Lilyth Imrel Ayr, Sworn Shield of the Lady of the Lake," she said with the slightest inclination of her head. "You are Tathal Ennis, wizard of the Fallen Court. Once more, the Lady requests that you free the Lightbrands under your thrall. I will not ask it again."

"I am pleased to meet you, Sworn Shield," Tathal said, also inclining his head just enough to not be rude.

"No, you are not," she replied. In her right hand, a rose appeared. She gazed at the flower even as its edges caught fire, blackened, and burned. "Do not make me draw my sword," she warned, smelling the bloom even as it disintegrated into ash. "Life is life until it is death."

Tathal watched her, thinking. He felt like he was missing something, some aspect of her. Something in her voice. It became an itch, one he would scratch if he worked at it hard enough.

"I am surprised to see an Elf in the service of the Lady," he said, buying time to discover her secret. "The Elves vanished from Annwn and the Misty Isles long ago."

A hint of a smile played across her ruby lips. "You know nothing of Elves, wizard. We inhabit these Isles as our Tuatha de Dannan kin once did so long ago. In hiding. The fey who serve the Lady of the Lake do so proudly, last wizard of the Fallen Court. And we are as varied and numerous as the stars in the sky." Tathal sensed her pride and noted it. "I am here to discuss the transgression you have brought against the Lightbrands as well as your presence here in this peaceful place."

"You are no negotiator," Tathal said, casually waving the idea aside to get a rise out of her. "I wish to speak to the Lady unencumbered by your tongue."

She darkened.

"What am I then, rogue wizard, if not the Lady's voice?"

"You are a blunt tool, albeit a useful one," he said. "You lack the faculties or wisdom that the Lady and I possess. Only a conversation with her will satisfy me. And only if she gives me what I desire."

"You will not free the fairies unless the Lady appears?" she asked, making sure they were clear on the matter.

"Not until she rises out of that pool," he said, pointing at the froth below the waterfall.

"She does not wish that."

"Then we are at an impasse, and the Lightbrands remain with me." He paused, bringing the fairies closer to him. He could see the fear on their faces as they struggled against their viscous bonds. He knew the Blodyn Knight could see that fear as well. "I wonder how much light I can squeeze from one of them before their life darkens and winks out?"

Lilyth Imrel Ayr took a step toward him. "Does your life mean so little to you?" she asked. "You tempt its end."

Tathal grinned. "I do more than that."

The Elf gripped her sword's hilt.

"The Lady will not relent to your evil," Lilyth Imrel Ayr said, drawing her sword free. He could feel her magic reach into the world. "I am to end your life so that the Lightbrands may live. And to stop your dark quest before it consumes the world and all life with it."

"My dear Blodyn Knight," Tathal said, smiling. He gestured to the darkness where his protector and knight had been waiting, hidden. "How ever do you think you will free them and stop my quest if you are already dead?"

The Sworn Shield of the Lady hesitated then, her eyes shooting over Tathal's shoulder.

For from the shadows, the Mordred entered the fairy glen.

HISSING, THE BLODYN KNIGHT BECAME AS TAUT AS a drawn bowstring.

It did not matter that the Mordred looked no match for the Elf. He was too tall, too broad-shouldered, and looked to be as slow as an ox. Lilyth Imrel Ayr could see the truth though. Tathal had replaced the soul of a churchwarden from South Cadbury with a revenant once imprisoned by Glastonbury Tor—the bastard son of one Arthur, King of Caer Llion. He was now the wizard's shield and sword, fettered by magic. To anyone else, the Mordred appeared to be a man of the cloth, with his clergy tab collar and black clothing, not a man who had killed hundreds in his lifetime and even more in death. A horror. A killer. A monster armored by magic. A revenant so filled with darkness that it had nearly conquered Britain and more.

Tathal could feel a ripple of anger—and fear—in the air, but not from the Blodyn Knight.

The Lady of the Lake.

Tathal had guessed she would protect her Sworn Shield. Given their bond.

"My Lady, my Fey Queen," the wizard said. "The Lightbrands are the least of your worries. Respond to my summons or your Blodyn Knight—your lover—will die this night."

The stream below the waterfall slowed to a standstill, and from its glassy surface rose a woman from ages past. Ethereal. Beautiful. Cold. Long blonde hair flowed about her head as if still in the water, framing a face both ageless and ancient. Nude and unabashed, she possessed an air of royalty, of prestige, of a boundless authority. Tathal knew a great deal about her but nothing had prepared him for this.

"I am intrigued by your Blodyn Knight, Lady," Tathal began, keeping his voice steady. Now with the Mordred by his side, he could focus his entire attention on the Lady. "I have not seen one despite my many centuries. She is a vision to behold, to be sure."

—She is beholden to me. As you have surmised. And to a higher service—

The voice not only filled his mind but the fairy glen as well, possessing power of the most balanced sort, like spring's slow release of winter's hold.

Tathal nodded. "I respect that service," he said and meant it.

—I did not expect polite discourse, given your past, last wizard of the Fallen Court—

"Civility matters, especially among the powerful," he said, gazing upon her. Her presence almost made him regret the way he had forced the meeting.

Almost.

—Yet no civility could ever account for what you have done this night—

"You have your tricks. I have mine," he said. "You made your choice and I had to make mine. I did not do it out of meanness toward the fairies. They are ardent servants and are innocent in the way children tend to be. Choosing to capture them was a means to an end. And we are now approaching that end."

—Choices. It has ever been so with you. And choices have within them consequences. Those consequences have begun to be quite dangerous for those around you, Tathal Ennis. Like Tinkham, the poor Shadowell fairy you befriended and destroyed. Like Old Wynn the bartender and his patron, Breena Roberts. You will sacrifice any and all to achieve the final end you desire. The path you walk upon is leading you to place you can never return—

Despite her beauty, Tathal was already growing tired of the conversation. He had come for answers, not lectures. "Are you so prescient to know why I am here, Lady? I would expect no less from one such as you."

—I see possibilities and probabilities as you do. Unlike you, I see you playing with powers far beyond your limited control—

Tathal cocked his head. "Is that not how you became entrapped, Lady?" he asked. "Playing with powers beyond you?"

—I have embraced my role and my choice—

"As have I."

The Lady smiled but without warmth.

—You are neither angel nor demon nor in between. You are Man, created beneath. What you seek is a test far beyond you. It has ever been the greatest test of Man yet a test that Man was never meant to take part in let alone pass—

"I will be the judge of that," he said. "I do not believe the test is fair. I do not believe the tester is goodness. Not any longer." He looked up at the stars. How they shone on him. "You know, some men—wise men, even—believe religion to be the greatest con perpetuated upon man by man himself. The real con is far greater." He paused, the righteousness he had felt for centuries coming to the fore, bolstering him. "And you do not know me as well as you think you do. You do not know the man I am."

—You do not know yourself as well as you think—

He was getting nowhere. Tathal decided to get to the crux of his visit.

"The Holy Grail. Where is it? Or those you love most will die."

—It is lost. Like the goodness that *she* once knew in your heart—

Tathal skirted the edge of the pool then, feeling the cool spray upon the air. The Lady and the Blodyn Knight watched him. She had baited him with his past, using the very seed of his anger against him. It was all he could do not to lash out and obliterate the fairy glen.

But it would avail him nothing. And nothing he had not come for.

"Lost. I find that terribly hard to believe," he said.

—The Grail is beyond all who seek it. It is lost but it is held. It is known but it is unused. It was once stolen and in turn it has been stolen. It has now been ceded to Annwn and Annwn will not release it so easily, last wizard of the Fallen Court—

Tathal snorted. "The land cannot steal an object."

—Can it not? The land is a powerful entity. Surely even you know this—

The wizard did. The land had always been the most unknown quantity when it came to power and struggle in Annwn. It had a sentience wholly unknowable. The truth of what she said rankled him but it was truth nonetheless.

"Riddles," Tathal spat. "*Riddles*. Just like that pompous ass of a glorified wizard Myrddin Emrys might speak."

—There is no riddle. Finding the Grail will not bring Ailis Ennis back—

She had brought *her* up again, in the span of minutes. This time using her name. It had the intended effect. Her last moments flashed before him. The room. The bed. The uncertainty. The impotence. The last terrible breath that changed Tathal's life forever. But worst of all, the lack of understanding. Of how it could happen. Why it *had* to happen when it could have been otherwise. That a choice had been made by an entity that did not care. Long-kept rage from that time surged forward into the wizard's present. It made his decisions this night all the easier.

"You really think I do this for *her*," Tathal replied, letting those memories temper his rage like hot steel thrust into a cold bath. "No. *Her death opened my eyes.* I am here, standing in your home's heart, for the countless millions who have faced similar anguish and heartache. The six-year-old boy who learns of death when his favorite dog dies—learning the dark truth he too will die. The son who endures his father's hospital bedside request for death—because he just wants free of his misery. The daughter who sees her father go off to war—and return a shell of a man. And for what? These people deserve answers. These people are like countless others throughout time. I will find those answers. I will see justice done."

—Those kinds of answers are not for Man to know. Those kinds of answers are unattainable and their pursuit will be your end—

"The very reason I need the Grail," Tathal retorted. "It will sustain me when I need to be succored the most."

The Lady shook her head sadly.

—It will only slow the inevitable death that will be your own—

"My death will not be the only one then," Tathal said, tamping down the memories. He had gained control of the conversation once more. "Lilyth Imrel Ayr is not your first lover. You are willing to find another, it seems."

The hair rippling about the Lady stilled, the woman's eyes become ice chips.

—You threaten—

"I inform," the wizard corrected. The Blodyn Knight had not moved during the entire discussion but Tathal could sense the Elf wanted to attack. He gave her a look. "I am willing to forego where this meeting is heading. If you give me the information I want. If you do not, whatever part of you is still human will remember how painful heartache can be."

—You would ruin Creation—

"All must be held accountable," Tathal growled. "And I mean *all*."

—There is a darkness within the light, Tathal Ennis. The best intentions of a wayward heart can lead to great evil—

"The light has been darkening lives for ages," Tathal replied. "You know, a famous writer once said a villain is the hero of his own story," he quoted. Nodding to his shadowy protector, the wizard made sure he was safely out of danger's range. "And sometimes villains need champions of their own to do what is right, no matter the outcome. If you will not give me what I need through good will, I will take it through bad."

The Mordred withdrew his sword from the ether, the very same blade that had once battled his father.

The Lady hissed and the fairy glen shook with it.

—That creature is an abomination—

"Yes," Tathal agreed. "But he's my abomination."

The Mordred engaged the Blodyn Knight; sword against sword rang through the fairy glen like the striking of a terrible bell. Lunges and parries and pivots and retreats became a blur of ferocity, the sound of their battling steel echoing throughout the fairy glen. The Elf was fey and had speed and strength beyond humans; the Mordred possessed experience, his magical armor, and an anger that seethed into the night. They met again at the side of the stream, grappling one another's sword wrist—the Elf hoping that she could get free and with her speed drive her sword's edge into his neck, the Mordred wanting to crush her in his grip. For a moment, they were at an impasse, each one unable to get a clear advantage. The Lady watched even as Tathal observed her. He wondered what it would take for the fey creature to call an end to the battle and give the wizard what he wished—the only sure way to save her beloved.

With a grunt, the Elf disengaged, to sidestep and leap out of the Mordred's range. He came after her again even as she stepped upon the stream, the water holding her up while he traversed slippery rocks with uncertain footing. They clashed again. She kicked water up at his face, trying to blind him. The Mordred ignored it. He kept pummeling at her even as she regained the bank and tried to find a way through his magical armor.

After long minutes, Tathal could see the Elf tiring. The Mordred did not weary. The Lady saw it too and in her eyes, the wizard saw the eventual outcome of the battle.

Lilyth Imrel Ayr acted as though it did not concern her. She came in low then, sliding across the dewy grass of the meadow, swiping at the Mordred's legs. Before he could counter, she was up inside his inner circle, an Elven knife in her free hand trying to find its way into the Mordred's throat. He grabbed her wrist and flung her through the air. She landed on her feet, springing toward him anew. He was still off balance and the Blodyn Knight beat him backward with a frenzy.

The Mordred leapt backward.

And the Elf pressed.

Lilyth Imrel Ayr saw the threat almost immediately but not soon enough. The Mordred empty faded, lunging back into the space he had just occupied with a speed that belied his size. He gained a hold of her knife wrist even as he rammed his sword's cross guard into the bare white of her exposed throat.

Already choking and being bent backward by the Mordred's strength, the Blodyn Knight unleashed her magic.

And it rolled from her in a wave.

The magic encased them both with immense power. While the Mordred's invisible armor saved him—its own magic counteracting the Elf's at least for a few minutes—Tathal had been prepared for this very attempt at trickery. Tethered to his shadowy protector for just this purpose, the wizard bolstered the armor of the Mordred, infusing it with the very elemental magic that assaulted him. Balancing the fight and making it an even battlefield was all the Mordred needed. The revenant crushed the Blodyn Knight's wrist. The knife tumbled from her nerveless fingers. With his newly freed hand, the revenant gripped the Elf by her neck and threw her to the ground like a doll. He could have killed her then but did not. Instead, as the wizard wished, the Mordred pinned her in the mud, his thick, heavy knee on her lithe back. She tried to twist free but could not. The ancient wraith grabbed her auburn hair and yanked her head back viciously, exposing her neck to the glen.

Having released his sword to the ether, he grabbed her knife from the muck and held it at the ready.

The elemental magic in the fairy glen receded.

"Give me the knowledge I seek," Tathal said to the Lady. "How is that for a threat?"

The Lady gazed down at her champion. Emotions not of the fey but of her former humanity played over her face.

In the end, love won out.

—There are three who possess the Cup of Christ. And they are one. Not one of the three is more important than the other two. Two are not children. One is a warrior. The other knows the truth of what they carry. They are as lost as the Holy Grail—

She paused for a few minutes, considering.

—That is all I can say, without betraying the oath of my office—

Tathal thought about the words. They were a riddle of course but like all riddles truth existed within the words. The words were always the key.

—Now set her free—

"The Lightbrands. *They* are free," the wizard said, letting dissolve the magical net that had held them in place. Still covered in the remains of Tinkham, the fairies fled and disappeared within the waterfall. Tathal turned back to the Lady. "You said there were consequences for actions, right?" He paused, containing the fury that had gripped him earlier. "The moment you sullied *her* name by speaking it was the moment you sealed your precious Blodyn Knight's fate."

Lilyth Imrel Ayr glanced at the Lady—even as the Mordred drew her own Elven knife across the Blodyn Knight's throat.

Crimson gushed upon the grass of the fairy glen. A near-soundless wail burst forth from the fairy glen, angered sorrow shaking even the trees. Tathal paid it no heed. Instead, he watched with great satisfaction as the Mordred threw the head of the Elf down into the mud and, standing, returned to Tathal's side, no evidence of the battle upon him. The Lady floated upon the air, head hanging. Small forest creatures skulked through the trees surrounding the fairy glen then, each one under her command. They went to the fallen Blodyn Knight. Tathal let them. They lifted the dead Elf and transported her to the water the Lady hovered over.

—Go. There are other lives for you to destroy. One of them will end you in turn—

"I plan to visit them. In due time. Especially this last you mention."

Tathal turned then. Back to the portal that had brought him to the fairy glen.

He did not look back as he entered the veil. The Lady would already be sinking into her fairy glen pool, cradling her dead lover. The Mordred would follow the wizard, one step closer to the ancient knight's revenge. The stars in the night sky would continue to turn and, in a few hours, the sun would rise, giving a futile hope to those who did not understand that the wizard was coming for them and their lives were already forfeit.

He would start where the Lady's riddle took him.

He would return to Annwn.

BACK IN WALES, TATHAL SPUN THE POSSIBILITIES.

The Holy Grail. The Cup of Christ. It was within reach. It had been his longest quest, one among many. He had traveled the sands of the Middle East. He had dug in the Misty Isles. He had ventured from one end of Annwn to the other to no avail. Until Annwn's High King Philip Plantagenet lost his war with the Seelie Court and his stronghold of Caer Llion had fallen and been stripped of its protective magic—only then did he sense the Grail's presence within the castle. Plantagenet possessed it; his witch, the Cailleach, had used its power. But before he could sneak into that greatest of castles and take the Cup, it had already been thieved away.

He had searched for the culprit in the city and beyond. He had found nothing, forcing his hand with the Lady of the Lake. But now he had a new clue. And he resumed his quest.

Upon the path from the river back to Betws-y-Coed, Tathal had become so deep in thought that he did not see the figure standing at the gate, a hunched man whose dark clothing blended into the remaining shadows of night.

And the shotgun the man pointed in his direction.

"You are up early, caretaker," Tathal said, magic tingling at his fingertips.

The old man appraised the wizard and the Mordred, wariness in his stance. Lines carved deep in his face and his shoulders stooped, his eyes still shone with spry life. He had the taint of magic on him, someone who visited the fairy glen often. "Aye. Always up early. Gotta piss, ye know. Might as well start the day off right." He paused. "But then I saw the lights. Down by the river." The caretaker glanced toward the fairy glen. He held the shotgun with gnarled, strong fingers. "The kind that swirl. The kind that—"

"Fly?" Tathal finished.

The old man nodded, curiosity's spark replacing his distrust. "Aye." He hesitated as the Mordred stepped up beside the wizard. "There is a fable about the wee morning hours, before the sun rises but its glow is in the sky. It says the fairy, the wee folk, cannot tell a lie during that time of morning. As cannot those who have seen them during the night."

"There is likely some magic in what you say, my crookedly bent friend," Tathal said.

"Did ye see them then?"

"Never lie to a man carrying a shotgun," Tathal said. He wove a quick spell with a hum that froze the shotgun's trigger in place. He stepped nearer the old man. "I did see fairies upon the air, caretaker. When they tried to escape, I bound them with magic by killing my own fairy guide, a creature of dubious worth at best. I forced the leaders of the Lightbrands to call their mistress and the Lady of the Lake answered. When she realized I would kill them all if I did not gain what I wanted, she transported me to Annwn, where I could ask her one question—who possesses the Holy Grail? Only the Lady survived our meeting." He nodded over his shoulder at the Mordred. "And my large protector there slayed her Elf knight bodyguard and lover."

Tathal leaned close. "And do you know why I need the Grail, pisser-in-the-morning?"

The caretaker pulled the trigger on the shotgun.

Nothing happened.

"I will tell you why," Tathal continued, ignoring the weapon. "*To have the power to confront God. To bring justice for all the sorrow He has wrought on Creation and to make Him pay if it be necessary.*"

"Ye are *evil*," the old man spit, fear in his words. "Blasphemous!"

Leaning in closer still, Tathal squeezed the man's shoulder. It was bony and thin, like the branch of an ancient tree that had seen far too many winters.

"Evil is a matter of perspective," the wizard hissed.

Tathal let go of the man's shoulder and walked away then. He could feel the old man staring after him, paralyzed. The Mordred would leave the body there by the gate. Before his end, the caretaker of the fairy glen would know that fairies were real. He might even learn that the Mordred was real, not a figment of Arthurian legend. Tourists would arrive soon and find the body. It would be clear the man did not die from natural causes. The Mordred would not make an example of the old man; murdering such an insignificant creature did not constitute sport for the ancient killer.

The eastern sky brightened, coming alive. It would be a beautiful day. Tathal would use it to further his quest. If he was right, the people who carried the Grail were no match for him—not as splintered as they were. And certainly no match for the Mordred— who hated them more than any person alive.

The wizard thought of the caretaker then, undoubtedly already dead. Those who knew the old man—family and friends and quite possibly even strangers—would ask how it could have happened? Why did it *have* to happen? He had years left, good years. What purpose did his murder serve other than misery?

Some would even question how God could allow such evil to come to pass.

The answer came down to a simple question that had also plagued him for centuries.

How could God allow someone like Tathal Ennis to exist?

The wizard breathed deep of night's end even as the yellow dawn brightened in the east. It was a question he'd see answered.

Though the Heavens fall.

THE GREATER OF TWO EVILS

MARC TURNER

– The Chronicles of the Exile –

"WE'VE GOT HIM," DUTIA BEAUCE CARLYN SAID AS he squinted through his telescope at the distant galleon. "That's the *Firedrifter*, that is." The *Firedrifter* had been one of Emir Mokinda Char's ships before it was recently hijacked by the notorious pirate, Revek Swiftsail. "See those gouges on the hull below the starboard cathead?"

Mazana Creed nodded. Those gouges were clawmarks, courtesy of the bronze dragon that the emir had taken down in the last Dragon Hunt. Mazana had been there to see the scratches inflicted, though alas the dragon had come off worse in the exchange.

She kept her own glass trained on the *Firedrifter*. Quarter of a bell ago, the ship had appeared through the rain from behind an island in the Uscan Reach, riding high on a wave of water-magic. Now it was heading straight for Mazana's galleon, the *Zest*. Its captain must have mistaken the ship for easy pickings, but perhaps that had something to do with the borrowed gold-and-silver-striped standard of the Goldsmiths' Guild the *Zest* was flying.

"Orders?" Beauce said. "If we heave-to, we might trick Revek into thinking we're running, and draw him in closer."

Mazana shook her head. Revek was sure to recognise the *Zest* before long, and when he did, he would turn about himself. Better, then, for Mazana to hold her current course. She used her power to raise a wave beneath the *Zest*. The pirates could still try to flee, obviously, but if they did so they wouldn't get far. Mazana, as one of the most powerful water-mages in the Storm Isles, could outpace any enemy sorcerer.

The *Firedrifter*'s wave subsided, and the galleon sank down on the swell.

Mazana lowered her telescope. "Hoist my standard," she said to Beauce. "Let's show Revek who he's dealing with."

The dutia gave the command, and moments later Mazana's storm-cloud flag was fluttering disconsolately from the mainmast. That storm cloud told Revek that she was a Storm Lord. Or rather, it told him her father had been one before his death, for Mazana had yet to take Terun's place on the Storm Council—the body of Storm Lords and other notables that ruled over the Storm Isles.

A lookout shouted down from the *Zest*'s main crosstrees. "They're signalling us, my Lady!"

Beauce lifted his glass again to inspect the signalling flags the *Firedrifter* had run out. "It seems Revek wants to talk," he said.

"He does?" Mazana replied. "Perhaps he isn't as smart as I thought."

"But only if the talk is on his terms," Beauce added. He smiled to show his blackweed-stained teeth. "He demands that you join him on the *Firedrifter*."

Mazana raised an eyebrow. Revek was making this too easy. She had meant all along to offer to cross to the pirate's ship, but had feared that by doing so she would arouse Revek's suspicions. Now, he would think he had scored the first victory, whereas in reality the victory would be Mazana's.

"Well, if he *demands* it," she said, "I guess I must do as he says."

The *Zest* swept towards the other ship. Beyond, the islands of the Uscan Reach rose from the waves. The rain had drawn a sullen veil across the land, obscuring the peaks, and blanketing the slopes with mist. To the north Mazana glimpsed the remains of a jetty, whilst farther off was one of the old Uscan Watchtowers, its lower half built from stone, its roof a sagging cloth supported by four lopsided timbers. Mazana knew the Reach well. When she was a girl, her father had brought her here to train her in a water-mage's arts. They would each have a boat. He would hunt her through the isles, and Mazana would have to use all her wits to evade him by becalming the seas under his craft, or by summoning up waves to carry her own over the smaller islets. If he caught her, he would throw her over the side and make her swim back to their ship. A simple enough task for a water-mage, perhaps. Though it depended on what was sharing the water with you.

The Reach was no longer the place for such antics. For years it had been the playground of pirates, of which Revek Swiftsail was only the most recent. Two months ago, he had started preying on merchant ships running the eastern sea lanes of the Sabian Sea. And he had shown commendable judgement—to Mazana's mind, at least—by specifically targeting the emir's own vessels. Last week, a brigatina carrying dawnstones had been waylaid off the Claw, and before that it had been the *Firedrifter* and its precious cargo of dragon blood bound for Nain Deep. In a fit of pique, the emir had decided he wanted his ship back, and so he had dispatched three vessels to hunt Revek down. None had returned.

So the emir had sent Mazana Creed in their place—sent her with the promise of a reward she could not turn down. That was why she had spent the last few days sailing back and forth past the Uscan Reach, waiting for pirates to attack her.

Was that really so much to ask?

The *Zest* advanced to within a stone's throw of the *Firedrifter*. Mazana let go her power, and the wave beneath her ship receded with a fizz and a bubble of water. The dregs of it slapped against the *Firedrifter*'s hull, sending puffs of spray into the air. Along the pirate ship's starboard rail, two dozen grim-faced men and women were lined up. There were archers in the *Firedrifter*'s tops, but as yet no one had nocked an arrow to a bowstring, and Mazana had archers of her own standing by in case they tried. She brought the *Zest*'s bowsprit swinging round so the two ships bumped together, flank to flank. The *Firedrifter*'s crew threw lines to the soldiers on the *Zest*, and the vessels were made fast.

Mazana descended the stairs from the quarterdeck to the main deck. Eight of her soldiers boarded the *Firedrifter*, then formed two lines like an honour guard. Another soldier offered his hand to Mazana to help her climb to the *Zest*'s rail, but she ignored it and stepped up unaided. The lower hulls of the galleons bulged so much that there was a gap of two armspans between the ships. Mazana sprang across. On the *Firedrifter*'s rail, she paused for a moment so the pirates were forced to wait on her. Her low-cut dress drew all eyes. *To command a space,* her father had once told her, *one must first command attention.* He'd said that on her fifteenth birthday when he had bought her a dress more revealing even than this one, then made her parade before his court as he inspected her from every angle. All the while her mother had watched on, refusing to meet Mazana's gaze, and silent as was her wont.

Mazana would not be silent.

She jumped down to the *Firedrifter*'s deck and looked around. The ship was unlike any pirate vessel she had ever encountered. The weapons racks were well ordered, the lines neatly tied around the pinheads, and the crew watched Mazana with a hush that bordered on respectful. The *Firedrifter* had the feel of a military ship. That was hardly surprising, though, considering Revek Swiftsail's history. Before turning to piracy, he had earned his keep in a far less honourable calling: as an independent captain running these same sea lanes in service to the emir himself.

If the ship met Mazana's expectations, then Revek himself did not. He stood watching her from the centre of the main deck. A handspan taller than Mazana, he wore knee-high boots and a plain leather jerkin and trousers. Tied about his right bicep were the dozens of colourful scarfs that were his hallmark. He gave Mazana an appraising look. In his eyes was that same glint of playful mischief she was used to seeing in the eyes of her half-brother, Uriel. Mazana had always admired a man who could stare over the edge of the Abyss without balking. But that didn't mean she would hesitate to shove him off it when the time came.

She shifted her gaze to his two companions behind. The first was a well-dressed man with a frown etched onto his forehead. The second was a white-haired woman with a scar that ran down the middle of her face. Whatever weapon strike had made that wound had taken part of her nose and left a lump of scar tissue at the centre of each lip.

"Welcome aboard," Revek said to Mazana. "I am Revek Swiftsail." He offered his hand, and she shook it.

"Mazana Creed," she replied.

"Ah! I know you. You're the woman who killed her own father so she could take his place as a Storm Lord."

It always surprised Mazana when people flung those words at her like they thought they should sting. Whereas surely if she'd found the act so shameful, she wouldn't have done it in the first place. "If you must know, I haven't yet been appointed to the Storm Council," she said. "The child of a Storm Lord has no divine right to succeed their parent. First, they must show that they deserve the honour." It was only by recruiting the most powerful water-mages, after all, that the Storm Lords could maintain their stranglehold on the empire.

"So you were sent here to prove your worth, is that it?" Revek spread his arms to take in his crew. "We are nothing more than stepping stones on your path to power and privilege. But then that is all my kind ever are to yours. To reach the top of the mountain, there must first be a mountain to climb, right?"

"It's almost as if you think there is no justice in this world," Mazana said.

Revek laughed. Mazana could see this was all just a game to him, and would doubtless remain so until the moment that he lost. "Of course there is no justice," he said. The scarfs about his bicep slipped down, and he pushed them back up his arm. "Every man and woman here once made an honest living from the sea. Every one of them has been bled dry by Storm Lord greed. Each year, you raise the Levy on the cities, and who do you think ends up footing the bill? Not the leaders of those cities, that's for sure. Instead it is the merchants, the sailors, and the fishermen who can least afford it. And what do the Storm Lords give in exchange? Nothing!" Revek smiled. "Strange, isn't it? The emir is a bigger thief than I will ever be, yet it is me who is called the pirate."

Mazana glanced from Revek to his companions behind. Clearly they enjoyed his moralising no more than she did, for the dandy's frown had deepened, whilst White Hair was feigning an interest in her fingernails. To Revek, Mazana said, "And so to prove what a terrible thing stealing is, you thought you would…steal?"

"It isn't a crime to take back from the emir what he has taken from us."

"Tell that to the men you killed when you attacked his ships."

"Their blood is on *his* hands, not ours." Revek's smile stretched. "As soon yours will be."

As threats went, that was probably the most gracious Mazana had ever received. Just because you were intent on killing someone, though, didn't mean you had to be uncivil about it. "And if you should survive today, what then?" Mazana asked. "You think the emir will shrug, and say 'No matter', and let you go back to screwing him up the arse?" That drew a surprised murmur from Revek's crew, but Mazana kept her gaze on their captain. "The noble Mokinda Char will never let this slide. When you attacked his ships, you stole something more valuable than his money; you stole his reputation." She raised her voice to carry. "Think about it. The Storm Lords are just six water-mages, yet they control an empire of hundreds of thousands. They rule as much by legend as by strength. If a lowly pirate is seen to stand against them, what message does that send to their subjects? The Storm Lords *must* destroy you. Their very existence depends on it."

Her words were met by silence. Revek looked undaunted, but judging by the dandy's grimace, he at least had realised the folly of inviting Mazana onto his ship where her words would be heard by his crew. She twisted the knife deeper. "This is not a fight you can win. My sadly departed father was a Storm Lord, and I am stronger than he was." She looked at the faces around her. "There is only one way you will live out the next bell. The emir has put a bounty on each of your heads, but the task he gave *me* was to bring in Revek, and Revek alone. Hand him over, and you may go free. I give you my word."

Revek's wave was dismissive. "I've heard enough," he said. "There will be no surrender. Return to your ship, and let the hunt commence."

Mazana did not argue. She had planted the seed of doubt among Revek's crew, now she had to give it time to sprout. "So what happens next?" she asked. "Do I close my eyes and count to a hundred?"

"I was thinking of a thousand, myself."

FROM THE QUARTERDECK OF THE ZEST, MAZANA watched the *Firedrifter* speed away on a wave of water-magic that was almost as tall as anything she could conjure up. There was no way a single sorcerer among the pirates could be responsible for that wave, because anyone so powerful would surely have found better things to do with their life than put their head on a Storm Lord block. Most likely it was three mages, or even four, that she faced. Together, those mages steered the *Firedrifter* tight to the shore of the nearest island as the coastline curved east. They would want to break line of sight with the *Zest* as swiftly as possible. Because while Mazana was able to see the wave carrying the ship, she could use part of her power to neutralise it and the rest of her strength to summon up a smaller wave under the *Zest*.

The rain was getting heavier, drumming a beat on the deck.

"Remind me," Beauce said from beside her. "A hundred comes just after forty-nine, right?"

"Usually," Mazana agreed. "But I think we'll give them the full count this time. We need them to believe I am a woman of my word."

The *Firedrifter* faded into the haze over the sea, becoming as spectral as a ghost ship. It slid behind the cover of the trees that grew right to the waterline.

Mazana waited another ten heartbeats. Her hair was plastered to her scalp, her dress to her body.

Then she released her power, and a wave roared into life beneath the *Zest*'s bow. It lifted the ship up and forwards with an abruptness that made Mazana's stomach flip. She and Beauce had been gripping the binnacle in readiness, but some of the soldiers on the main deck were caught off guard. They were thrown from their feet into grumbling piles.

Beauce's lips quirked. "That never gets old, does it?"

And the hunt was on.

Within moments, the *Firedrifter* came into view again—first the tip of its main yard, then its starboard rail, then its mizzen mast. Intent on dispelling the wave beneath the galleon, Mazana threw her will against the power of the *Firedrifter*'s mages. The wave beneath the ship receded. *Got you.* As that happened, though, the pirate ship veered hard to port, heading for a waterway between two islets. Its momentum carried it into the strait and out of Mazana's view.

The *Zest* gave chase.

As the ship entered the channel, Mazana saw the *Firedrifter* a hundred lengths distant. The waterway it travelled along was bounded to the north by a sheer rock face, and to the south by a scattering of tree-covered islets. The channel curled west, and the *Firedrifter*, hugging the inner bend, broke Mazana's line of sight again. As it did so, a horn call sounded from its decks. A signal, presumably, but to whom?

Perhaps to no one. Perhaps it was only a ploy to trick Mazana into excessive caution. And to her mind any caution was excessive.

Beauce spat blackweed to the deck. "This stinks of a trap," he said.

"Maybe."

"So what do we do?"

Mazana looked at him askance. "We spring the trap."

"Of course we do," the dutia muttered.

The *Zest* entered the channel, following the ribbon of froth left in the *Firedrifter*'s wake. As Mazana's ship advanced, the edge of the sorcerous wave carrying it broke against the northern bluff. Another horn call rang out, echoing off the cliff. Beauce's gaze twitched every way, seeking trouble.

"There!" he said, pointing ahead and to the right.

Mazana had already spotted them: ten archers gathered at the brink of the eastern bluff, ready to rain arrows down on the *Zest*. She considered. If she steered the ship closer to the cliff, that would force the bowmen to lean out precariously over the channel. But it would also allow them to push boulders—

"Ship to port!" a lookout cried.

Mazana startled. To *port*?

From behind a tree-covered islet on her left, a second pirate galleon surged out on a wave of water-magic. At its starboard rail, a man in a water-mage's blue robes yelled orders to a dozen warriors holding swords and grappling hooks. As the ship rushed to intercept the *Zest*, Mazana whistled in admiration. It had been a clever ruse by Revek, she had to concede: put archers on one side of the channel to draw her eye, then hit her with an attack from the other. The manoeuvre had been timed to perfection too, for even if Mazana threw every scrap of her power into the wave beneath the *Zest*, she wouldn't be able to prevent the enemy ship from ramming her.

So instead she surrendered her power over the *Zest*'s wave and added it to the wave under the pirate vessel. With a thunder of water, that second wave doubled in size, jolting the ship into the air. The warriors on board stumbled and shouted in alarm. The *Zest* glided to a stop. Mazana sensed the enemy's water-mage set his will in opposition to hers. He was trying to counter her power, and thus slow his vessel's rush, but he had left it too late, and he was too weak besides. The pirate ship hurtled past the *Zest's* bow and towards the eastern bluff.

Mazana looked at Beauce. "They seem in a hurry," she said brightly.

The dutia nodded. "Late for an appointment, maybe."

There's a reason why people don't sail headlong into cliffs. The pirates discovered it now as their ship struck the rock face with a splintering crack. The bowsprit and the figurehead disintegrated, the bow crumpled, and the fore yard shattered. An archer in the tops was hurled through the air, and Mazana winced as he struck the bluff with an audible crunch. He dropped into the sea, limbs flopping. Screams came from the rest of the crew as the fore yard crashed down onto the deck.

"Here comes Revek," Beauce said.

Mazana looked north to see that the *Firedrifter* was indeed returning. Odds were, Revek had expected to find his friends in battle with the *Zest*. Instead, the second galleon was now sinking, its crew swimming for shore. It was too late for Revek to retreat, though. Pirates on the *Firedrifter* snatched swords and boarding pikes from the racks about the mainmast, then rushed to take up positions. And every one of them doubtless resolved on spilling Mazana's blood. She would be so very sorry to disappoint them.

She advanced the *Zest* to meet them.

"Time for you to retire to your cabin, my Lady," Beauce said.

"No," Mazana said. Her sorcery would still be useful in the fight to come, and even if that had not been so, she wouldn't have sought cover. Better to be at the heart of the action than cowering inside, wondering at every scream and clash of swords. Better to stare the Lord of the Dead down than let him creep up on her from behind.

The *Firedrifter* swept closer. Some of the pirates aboard it waved their swords and yelled in an effort to convince Mazana—or maybe themselves—that they meant business. A ragged volley of arrows flitted out from the enemy's tops, and the pirates on the bluff started shooting too. Beauce had assigned Mazana a bodyguard of six warriors, and two of those soldiers—both women—now stepped forwards to protect her. Mazana flinched as an arrow struck one of their raised shields, setting the steel ringing. Another arrow thudded into the quarterdeck and stuck there, quivering.

Peering between the shields, Mazana scanned the *Firedrifter* for Revek. He stood calmly beside the mainmast, while the dandy bellowed orders and gestured about him. The white-haired woman was next to them. Over her leather armour she had donned a surcoat of metallic cloth that shimmered like oil on water.

Beauce must have noticed it too, for he said, "What does the surcoat signify?"

"It signifies she's an idiot," Mazana replied. Any warrior who wore something that distinguished them to the enemy had more pride than sense.

The rustle of water grew louder as the two ships closed. Mazana experienced that queasy mix of fear and anticipation she always felt before a fight. Another hail of arrows raked the *Zest*'s decks. To Mazana's left, one of her soldiers was hit in the throat, and the force of the impact knocked him back into the arms of a companion. A tragic loss, but Mazana was willing to sacrifice any number of lives in order to complete her mission. Provided those lives didn't include her own, obviously.

"Ready grapples!" Beauce bawled in the voice of a man accustomed to making himself heard above a storm. "You know the drill!"

Mazana's soldiers mustered at the starboard rail, shieldbearers in front, swordsmen behind. With the swordsmen were men holding grappling hooks, ready to cast. The two ships drew level and halted, thirty armspans apart.

"Now!" Beauce shouted, and the grapple holders hurled their hooks across the gap to tangle in the *Firedrifter*'s rigging. At the same time, Mazana's archers in the tops loosed their arrows at the foe, targeting the grapple holders among the pirates. Not a single enemy hook flew the other way. Mazana summoned up a wave to carry the *Zest* thudding into the *Firedrifter*. The warriors on both vessels staggered.

"Make her secure!" Beauce commanded.

The lead pirates on the *Firedrifter* clambered to the ship's rail, screaming challenges. They gathered themselves and made to jump across the gap to the *Zest*.

A mistake.

For Beauce's order to secure the vessels had been a ruse. Instead of tying off the lines, the grapple holders held them loose. So when Mazana now conjured up another wave—this time to take the *Zest away* from the *Firedrifter*—the ships sprang apart. There was no opportunity for Revek's mages to counter the move. The lead pirates had already committed to their jump, and they leaped helplessly into the gulf between the two vessels with looks of comical surprise. Or at least Mazana found them amusing. The pirates themselves, probably less so.

Another of Mazana's waves brought the ships banging together once more. This time the lines *were* made fast, and this time it was Mazana's soldiers who climbed first to the rail. Revek's crew, momentarily stunned by the loss of their fellows, stood motionless on the *Firedrifter*'s sodden main deck. That sodden deck would be Mazana's next weapon against them, for water-mages could not only summon up waves, they could also cool water and heat it as well. As the first of Mazana's soldiers boarded the *Firedrifter*, she focused her power on the deck about the pirates. The puddles there vaporised in hissing clouds of steam. From within the haze, shouts rang out.

Mazana's soldiers charged in behind their shields.

Finally the *Firedrifter*'s mages entered the fray. Beneath the feet of Mazana's advancing soldiers, the deck glistened suddenly white as the moisture on the boards froze to ice. The charge became a slithering dash that carried the forerunners onto the waiting pikes of the enemy. A woman was folded in half by a handspan of steel in her gut. Another soldier barrelled between two pikemen, only to find Revek waiting for him. The pirate captain cut quite the dashing figure with his sabre in one hand, a cloak in the other. A swish of his cloak spoiled the sword swing of his opponent, then a backhand cut from Revek's own blade opened the soldier's throat.

"We've got company," Beauce said to Mazana, motioning to the *Firedrifter*.

It was a moment before Mazana perceived the problem. On the *Firedrifter*'s forecastle, a group of pirates had assembled, White Hair among them. She carried a grapple that she now heaved across the gap between the two ships. Its rope looped over the *Zest*'s mizzen topsail yard, and White Hair pulled on the line until the hook bit on the wood. Three of her companions followed suit.

Beauce caught Mazana's eye, then cast a meaningful glance at the doors to the captain's cabin.

Mazana grinned and drew her sword. "Prepare to repel borders!" she shouted to the soldiers on the quarterdeck.

A pirate with a knife between his teeth was the first to swing across. Mazana's soldiers on the starboard rail jabbed their pikes at him as he passed, and a hit to his nether regions brought him shrieking down to the boards. Mazana sucked air through her teeth in sympathy. White Hair came next, kicking at the questing pike heads to keep them at bay. Then she released her rope, dropped and rolled, and came to her feet with twin shortswords in her hands. Mazana's soldiers converged on her.

White Hair stopped dead.

And disappeared.

Mazana blinked. Her soldiers halted, staring open-mouthed. One man looked around as if he expected White Hair to materialise in a different place.

Mazana was the first to put the pieces together. "Chameleon!" she shouted. White Hair must be a priestess of the Chameleon god, able to make herself invisible by stilling her movements.

But Mazana's warning came too late. White Hair had already reappeared in the same spot where she had vanished. She plunged among the soldiers at the port rail, hacking and cutting. More of Mazana's troops closed in on the priestess from behind, but another pirate swung across and clattered into them. They went down in a tangle.

The rain was now coming down in sheets. Mazana risked a glance towards the *Firedrifter* and saw that her soldiers already controlled most of the main deck. Revek stood by the main mast behind a line of pikemen. As his gaze met Mazana's, he sketched a bow, still enjoying himself evidently. Mazana realised he'd been watching the progress of White Hair's assault. His fight to hold the *Firedrifter* was as good as lost, but if he could survive a while longer, the Chameleon might seize Mazana and force her troops to stand down. Thus, White Hair's first concern would be to capture Mazana, not kill her.

Which was nice to know.

A curse brought Mazana's attention back to her immediate surroundings. The action was drawing a little closer to her than she had hoped. On the *Zest*'s quarterdeck, a dozen pirates now fought in small groups against Mazana's more numerous soldiers, Beauce among them. The boards were littered with corpses, and threads of blood ran one way then the other as the ship pitched.

Mazana's bodyguards formed a half ring in front of her. A bare-chested pirate tried to shoulder his way through, only for a woman to serve him up a faceful of shield. He sprawled onto his stomach at Mazana's feet, and she drew back her sword arm. She might not have been a warrior, but she could stab a man in the back as well as the next person. Better, she liked to think.

She ran the pirate through.

"Kill them!" a soldier yelled. "Kill them all!" As if anyone might have been confused as to the objective here.

White Hair silenced the shouter with a thrust to the heart. Fighting with her power engaged, the Chameleon was a blur to Mazana. A whirlwind exchange with one of Mazana's female bodyguards ended with the soldier's head rolling on the deck. White Hair stepped past, then dispatched another bodyguard with a jab to the throat.

She advanced on Mazana.

Mazana sighed. Did she have to do everything herself?

A wave of her hand flung rain at the other woman, then another splashed the Chameleon with water from the puddles on deck. White Hair's look was scornful. She must have thought it a pointless gesture, for what harm could a little more wet do when the priestess was already soaked through?

Mazana was only too happy to educate her. Bringing her power to bear, she froze the moisture on White Hair's skin and in her clothing, encasing her in a thin layer of ice. The Chameleon stiffened in midstep. Her skin took on a silvery cast, and the abrupt chill about her left ripples of cold on the air. The priestess strained to break free, her features contorting. Mazana had bought herself only a heartbeat, for the ice about White Hair had already begun to crack.

But a heartbeat was all Mazana needed. She could have knocked the Chameleon out with a pommel strike to the head, but that would have felt dangerously akin to mercy, and Mazana had more self-respect than that. So instead she buried her sword in White Hair's gut. The crust of ice across the Chameleon's mouth muffled her scream of pain. She slipped off Mazana's blade and fell twitching to the deck.

Mazana sheathed the weapon. She didn't understand the fuss people made of this sword-fighting business; it seemed simple enough to her.

The remaining pirates on the *Zest*'s quarterdeck were quickly overwhelmed. The battle on the *Zest* was over. Moments later, another horn call sounded from the *Firedrifter*. Was Revek ordering his men to surrender now that White Hair was dead?

Hardly.

Mazana crossed to the *Zest*'s rail for a better view of the pirate vessel. The fight on the *Firedrifter* had ended too. Revek's forces still held the quarterdeck and the forecastle, but the main deck was under the control of Mazana's troops. On the quarterdeck, Revek was slumped on the boards, unconscious or dead. The dandy stood over him, a cudgel in his hand. He looked at Mazana and shouted, "Call off your men! This is what you wanted, isn't it? You get Revek, and the rest of us go free."

Mazana did not respond.

"You gave us your word," the dandy added, and Mazana made a face. The shamelessness of the man! Here he was, appealing to her sense of honour, while he stood over the body of a betrayed friend. Where was the honour there? Mazana studied the other pirates on the *Firedrifter*. A few had the decency to look embarrassed, yet none spoke up for their stricken leader. Earlier, Revek had lectured Mazana on the sins of the Storm Lords—as if his crewmates were not pirates but revolutionaries. Apparently his companions didn't share his high ideals. For too long they had hidden behind a mask of altruism. Now Mazana had torn that mask away to reveal something beneath it that was not so fair.

Mazana Creed, seeker of truth and justice.

MAZANA SAT BEHIND HER DESK IN THE CAPTAIN'S CABIN on the *Zest*. The wood had been buffed to such a shine she could see her reflection in it. On the desk was a decanter of Elescorian brandy and a glass. She'd celebrated her victory over Revek with one drink too many, but the warm glow of the spirits was already fading, and in another bell or so she would be fully sober. If she wasn't careful.

She looked at a painting on the opposite wall. It was a portrait of her father, half again as tall as Terun himself had been. *A man must always seek to appear larger than he is*, he had once told her. Full of wise words, he had been, yet they were never the words Mazana had wanted to hear. Long ago, this portrait had hung in their home in Kansar. She remembered seeing it on the day she slipped red solent into his wine. Mazana was seventeen. It had been years since her father had last deigned to speak to her, yet out of nothing he had wanted to meet her, and Mazana had come at his bidding, curious—maybe even hopeful—about why he had chosen to break his silence.

As it turned out, he had wanted to tell her that he had promised her to a certain fat Rastamiran pasha who had always had his eye on Mazana. The one with the bruised knuckles and the troublesome habit of outliving his wives.

After careful consideration, Mazana had passed on the match.

When her father had drunk the wine she had poisoned, his expression had shown shock and panic, along with something more difficult to place. Admiration, she had eventually decided. The irony was not lost on Mazana. All her life she had craved his esteem, yet only in his death had she found it.

She looked at the portrait again, wondering why she had kept it.

There was a knock at the door. At Mazana's call, two soldiers entered, tugging Revek between them. They deposited him in a chair across from Mazana, then withdrew. The pirate's hands and ankles were shackled. His clothes were spattered with blood, and there was more blood in his hair where the dandy had clubbed him. He stared at Mazana, clearly determined not to appear intimidated. Then he looked through the windows to either side. Off the *Zest*'s port quarter lay the Benaldian coast, whilst a short distance to starboard bobbed the *Firedrifter* at anchor. Revek's expression soured.

"I recognise that ship," he said. "So much for you releasing my crew."

"I kept my word," Mazana said. Revek had still been unconscious when he was brought onto the *Zest*, so he didn't know what had happened after he was struck. "I said your crew could go free, and free they went. But I said nothing about your ship."

"A present for the emir, is it?"

"No, a present for me."

"Of course. You don't need to worry any more about keeping Mokinda happy—with your mission complete, you're a Storm Lord now. I wonder what sort you will be." Revek pretended to consider. "But no, what am I saying? There only *is* one sort, isn't there?" His voice became bitter. "Power is never given freely; it has to be taken. And there are only a few souls with the ambition and the ruthlessness to do the taking. Too bad those people are also the last people you'd ever want in charge."

"I can't say I have a problem with that."

The silence stretched out. Mazana reached for the decanter. The *Zest* bobbed on the sea, and above the desk, a lantern hanging from the crossbeams swung back and forth.

Revek regarded Mazana shrewdly. "You really let my crew go?" he said at last.

Mazana nodded.

"Why?"

"Because that was our deal." She poured herself a glass of brandy. "But more importantly, because letting them go served my purpose. As you said earlier, you are merely a stepping stone to my goals. Only the most powerful water-mages are invited to become Storm Lords, and of those who sought to fill the position left by my father, I was unquestionably the strongest. Yet some on the Storm Council thought I needed to learn my place. They thought that by ordering me to capture you, they could send me a message. Well, I intend to send one back. And I will do so by completing my mission to the letter, and not a stroke further."

"And catching my crew wasn't part of the brief? You were telling the truth about that?"

"Yes."

Revek considered this. He looked out of the port window and examined the coastline. Perhaps he was trying to identify it, but there were no landmarks that he could fix on. "Where are we?" he asked.

"West of Benaldi."

Revek's expression turned pensive, and Mazana could guess what he was thinking. Benaldi was four bells' travel from the Uscan Reach, meaning the pirate's former companions would by now have scattered among the islands. He must have reached a decision at that instant, for he smiled. For a condemned man, he was looking remarkably relaxed. "Can I let you in on a secret?" he said.

"Oh, I love secrets."

"You won't like this one. Because there's one small problem with your scheme. One flaw that could put a flame under your ambition." He paused to let the anticipation build. "*I* am not Revek Swiftsail," he said. "I am only his Second. You got the wrong man!"

Mazana stared at him.

"Don't you see? From the moment you raised your standard this morning, we knew we were in trouble. We knew we couldn't outrun you or outfight your soldiers. But we *also* knew that you wouldn't recognise Revek, so it was decided I would swap places with him. That way, if we lost, maybe Revek would get a chance to sneak off." When he shifted his weight, his chains rustled. "And you have to say, it worked a treat. Because even in losing, Revek won. Now he's not just a pirate, he's the man who outsmarted the Storm Lords. His legend will grow. Our *cause* will grow."

Mazana's voice was flat. "And that was worth giving up your life for?"

Revek—or rather, his Second—feigned confusion. "My life? No, no, that's not how it works at all. You promised to let Revek's crew go, remember? And since I'm just a humble crewman, you have to let me go, too. That's what you promised, isn't it?" He stopped to gauge Mazana's reaction, perhaps thinking she didn't believe him. "You got the wrong man!" he said again.

Mazana turned her glass in her hands, holding his gaze all the while. Then she leaned forwards in her chair and said, "I know."

"What?"

"I know," she repeated. "I knew it as soon as you opened your mouth on the *Firedrifter.* That's why I had the real Revek—your *Second*—locked in the brig before I let your other friends go." Mazana sipped her brandy. "Did you honestly think you could fool me just by tying a few ill-fitting scarfs around your arm? Maybe

I didn't know what the infamous Revek Swiftsail looked like, but I *did* know what sort of man he was. A man who, before he became a pirate, had amassed a rather impressive list of convictions for petty smuggling. A man who once crucified one of his own crewmen simply for questioning an order. Not the sort of man, in other words, who would take the moral high ground with me over the conduct of the Storm Lords."

The Second remained silent. He wanted to believe she was lying, Mazana saw, but there was a grim edge to his features.

"What surprises me most," she went on, "is that you were willing to sacrifice yourself for him. You must have known his history. So why do it?"

"Because history is all it was!" the Second said. "Revek had changed. You saw the *Firedrifter*. Those weren't mere pirates on board. Every one of the crew was loyal to Revek. Every one of them was hand-picked because they believed in what Revek was doing. He wanted the same things I did. He wanted an end to the Storm Lords. That's why he only ever attacked Storm Lord ships."

"For a man of principle, he was remarkably quick to let you take the fall for him back there."

"A fall that *you* set up!"

"Gracious of you to say so, but I can't take all the credit. You say Revek has changed, yet the first time his credentials were tested, he failed." Mazana's smile was rueful. "People are so easily corrupted."

"No, they are easily *led*," the Second corrected her. "The direction you choose to lead them in, that is down to you alone."

Mazana swirled the brandy in her glass. There was a challenge in the Second's gaze, yet she met it without flinching. "I cannot lead people in a direction I am not going myself."

He scowled, but said nothing.

From the belly of the ship came a scream as the cutters started work on a wounded soldier. Above, steps clomped across the aft deck. Mazana drank again, and the Second watched her. He seemed to have aged ten years since he'd sat down at the desk. Today's events had taught him a hard lesson, but in Mazana's experience the hard lessons were the only ones worth learning.

"So what now?" he asked.

"Now Revek goes to the Storm Lords. His reign of tyranny is cut short, and order is restored to the empire. A happy ending, in other words."

"And me? If you knew all along who I am, why are we talking? Why didn't you leave me behind with the others?"

"Because you present me with something of a problem," Mazana said. "Strictly speaking, you are one of Revek's crew. But you are not like the others, are you? You are that most uncommon and dangerous of men: one who will follow a cause beyond the stage that it costs him to do so. If I release you, you will go back to the Reach and try to round up Revek's crew. It might take months or even years, but one day we will meet again, and when that happens, you may be lucky enough to come out on top." She gave him a chance to reply, then cocked her head. "Stop me if you disagree with any of this."

"Oh, I disagree, alright," the Second said, his smile returning. "When I beat you next time, luck won't have anything to do with it."

Mazana laughed. It was the answer she had expected. Indeed, if he had given any other, she would probably have had him thrown in the brig with Revek. *An interesting reunion that would be.* From a pocket, she withdrew the key to his shackles and slid it across the table.

The Second trapped it with one hand, then unlocked his chains and rose. For a heartbeat he considered the cabin again, perhaps wondering if he could grab Mazana before she could summon help. Finally he turned for the door.

Mazana's voice brought him up short. "Tell me," she said. "Do you have a family?"

He looked back at her warily. "Yes."

"A wife? Children?"

The Second nodded.

Mazana threw back the contents of her glass. She felt a sudden need to get hopelessly drunk. "Then go back to them," she said. "Don't waste your life on a lost cause. The only cause that matters is the one you left behind."

With that, she dismissed him with a wave.

EXCEEDING BITTER

KAARON WARREN

— The Unwanted Women of Surrey —

THE FIRST THAT MRS JACOBS KNEW OF THE GREY Ladies were the ashen footprints she found on the front step. She blamed the chimney sweep, furious that he had come to her front door dirty like that, or at all. She sent her husband to the Chimney Master, wanting a name, wanting that child to come and clean up his own mess, but her husband returned to say no sweep had come knocking and if he had, two shillings sixpence were owed.

She got her husband settled by the fire before he bored her silly with the usual talk. Too late. "Awful man," her husband said. "Should have been drowned at birth, most of them, and I mean that kindly."

"Of course you do, dear," Mrs Jacobs murmured, but in her mind's eye she pictured the baby rats he'd drowned in a bucket last week. Dropped them in then forgot about them, and she was the one who had to scoop them out and bury them.

He was asleep within minutes and she could settle to her busy work.

In the morning she swept the ashen footprints away.

She had just put the broom away when she saw the chimney sweep through the front window. A tiny, filthy boy, and she lifted her broom to shoo him away. He'd left more footprints, she saw that, but when she raised her broom and saw him shrink away, her heart melted.

"Boy!" she said, "What are you doing here?" Her cheeks were pink from exertion and she had her mum's old patchwork apron on.

"It looks so warm inside. The ladies showed me." He bent forward onto his toes, making the loose plank on the front step creak.

"What ladies, dear? Your aunties?"

He shook his head. "I've got none of those, nor a mother, neither. It was the grey ladies showed me." He tucked his shoulders down, and pressed his hands between his thighs, as if cold to the bone. He stared inside. "You're nicer than them, though."

Her husband was at the office and the street was quiet so she took him inside.

"Bath first," she said, but his stomach rumbled loudly and he seemed weak, so instead she sat him in the laundry and fed him porridge.

There was a knock on the door.

"The grey ladies!" he said. He shivered, looking over his shoulders as if someone approached.

"I thought you liked them."

"Only they look at me as if I'm real," he said. "But I don't like them."

Mrs Jacobs opened the laundry door, wondering as she did so how the ladies reached the door, being, as it was, behind their high brick surrounding walls.

"Yes?" Mrs Jacobs said, then drew a sharp breath.

Three grey ladies stood on her step. She could see the agapanthus through them, and they floated above the ground. They were tall and skeletally thin. Their skin was grey, flaccid, hanging off their cheeks in folds. They didn't look at her, only at the boy.

One lifted her hand and Mrs Jacobs recoiled at the sight of long, sharp fingernails. They were silent as they turned, glided to the back wall and disappeared through it.

Mrs Jacobs stood staring, knowing she couldn't tell her husband what she'd seen (*Imagination is the indication of an unsteady mind*, he liked to say). The boy shivered.

"You better be off. My husband will be home soon for his lunch. Come back in two hours and I'll make you a plate." She put the hob on to make bubble and squeak and took out the bread knife ready to cut a slab to go with it.

He didn't want to move so she physically picked him up. He weighed as little as one of Mr Butcher's chickens, no more. The morning had passed too quickly, though, because there was Mr Jacobs at the front door, staring at her as if she was a beggar on the streets.

"Why are you carrying vermin?"

"Oh, Alfred. He's a poor motherless boy, that's all. Let me just bathe him. He can spend one night here, after he's clean. He'll go after breakfast. We can't send him out in the night."

"It isn't even close to night, woman."

Mr Jacobs had no patience for children. Never had. If they'd been blessed, perhaps he would have changed his mind.

"Just the bath then and I'll send him away."

She had the boy help her heat the water in the cellar and carry it upstairs to the laundry sink. The boy stared at the water as if mesmerized. The afternoon was grey and they needed what light they could but still Mrs Jacobs pulled down the shutter. It was surely only shadow, but out there she thought she saw the three grey ladies, watching.

"You have a good scrub. I'm going to give my husband his lunch," she told the boy. He stared at her. His eyes were ash grey and his skin had a grey pallor she hadn't noticed before. His lips were drained of colour and she saw streaks of ash in his hair.

"You take your time. Get yourself nice and clean. Go on."

She tugged at his shirt, trying to help, but he shied away, so she called her husband, sitting waiting in the front room for his lunch, asking him to convince the boy he needed to remove his clothes for the bath and she left them to it, moving into the kitchen to ladle soup and slice bread for their meal.

Mr Jacobs walked into the room and sniffed at the soup a few minutes later. "Vegetable again?" he said.

"How is he?" she asked him.

"You mean the vermin? He's as he should be."

"He's not vermin, he's unfortunate," but something in her husband's tone made her run down the hall and throw open the laundry door. He spoke like that when he'd bested an opponent and was pleased with himself.

The water was grey and murky. "He's climbed out himself," she thought, but then one hand floated to the surface and she plunged both hands in to pull him out.

What she thought was ash was naught but his own grey colour.

She lifted him easily (was he lighter now? It seemed so) and she cradled him in her arms, holding him as if she could bring life back to him. She began to dry him tenderly.

She heard a rustle, a hiss behind her and turned, still holding the boy, to see the three grey ladies standing tangled amongst the raincoats hanging on hooks by the back door.

One bent forward and reached out as if to stroke the boy, but instead she worked her fingers between his ribs as if trying to pry something loose. Another stroked his hair gently, but the last knelt down and began lapping at his stomach, as if drinking something spilled.

Mrs Jacobs held the boy closer, trying to keep their fingers from him, but they reached through her with an ice-cold touch, and all she saw was grey.

"How did you know?" she whispered. "How did you know my husband would do this?"

She rocked back and forth. They kept still while their eyes followed, then she saw their faces change—they were aping her sorrow. They rubbed their hands together as if cleaning them, then went back to work on the boy, separating soul from body with long, sharp fingernails.

Did they gain colour? Glow?

She wasn't sure.

It would be weeks before Mrs Jacobs could see colour again.

THE GREY LADIES WERE ONCE JULIA, AMARA AND Magdalena. Pretty names for pretty girls, long since forgotten. *How did you know?* the woman asked, and they watched her, not answering her question. Truthfully, they did not know the answer and besides, they no longer spoke at all. Did they miss not talking to each other? Or had they no recollection of hours spent chattering?

They never knew where they'd knock. It was not their choice. Something moved them. It was death foretold by them, not delivered.

They knew they were doing good. A wise man (Wise. Cruel. Murderous.) told them often that one of the greatest gifts in life is to know when death is coming. It was a chance to prepare. To say goodbye.

If only people would listen. If they were stubborn, like the woman and her chimney sweep, no good was done to anyone.

She was colourful, that grieving woman, her cheeks pink, her eyes red. They were colourful once, these three.

Before.

THEY'D HAD A BRIGHTER LIFE THAN MANY OTHERS LIKE them, because their mother, Eliza, loved to travel, gathering friends like other people gathered pebbles or mementos. She'd been to finishing school in Paris, where she met all manner of girls from all manner of places she'd never heard of before, like Lucia from Romania and Dao from the Principality of Phuan. And she learnt that each of them had a different idea of how things should be. This benefitted her daughters, giving them more freedom of expression and behaviour than many others. Julia in particular thrived in this way, and as a girl, loved to climb trees and sit in the branches, when the neighbours weren't looking.

There was less travel once Eliza married Phillip and the girls came along, but she had trunks of treasures to enjoy, and to share with her three daughters. "This blue one is for you, Julia," she said, lifting out a delicate silk scarf. "To match your eyes. For Amara, this green, and for Magdalena, this golden." The tiny girls wrapped themselves around and around until they were swamped in the lush material and they danced about the room with their mother spinning in the centre.

"What is this?" their father said. He pretended gruffness, but he wouldn't have married her if he didn't love her ways.

They had a good life until the Romanian came.

Eliza had written letters to her dear school friends, especially Lucia, for ten, twelve, fifteen years. They kept in touch, and then there were no more letters. "I miss you!" Eliza wrote. "I wish we could visit with each other and talk about foolish things."

It was not Lucia who visited. It was her brother, Mihai.

The girls would not remember his first visit, although their lives changed because of it. Their mother said he arrived in a large coach, with servants following behind. His voice louder than the most raucous of men in the village and his skin bright, glowing. He arrived on their doorstep with no announcement. He said, "I am the brother of the magnificent girl Lucia."

He was not as handsome as Eliza had imagined (the girls had told stories under the covers when they were at school, squealing at the inventions) but he was charming and vulnerable.

"I bring sad news. My dear wife died in childbirth, and the baby as well. In my sorrow I am travelling the world until now, when I reach my sister's dear friend and this beautiful land."

He looked out, lifting and shaping his hands as if measuring the place.

"Here I will build a castle, with the help of a great man."

With that said, Mihai departed for parts unknown.

THEIR FATHER PHILLIP MANAGED THE PROJECT OVER the next fifteen years. This was his sole job, to build a mansion for the mysterious Romanian Mihai Adascalitei.

This brought success and financial security to the family, and each night Phillip insisted on raising a glass to Mihai, "Our benefactor."

"Our slave master," Eliza said, because Phillip worked twelve hours a day with little time for family.

Then it was done. Word came that Mihai would arrive to inspect, that he was traveling with a large retinue and that he was anticipating great pleasure on seeing his new home.

"He doesn't mention Lucia but surely she will come," Eliza said. "Perhaps she and I will go to London. She always said she'd love to go."

"They can't come," Phillip said. He wouldn't sit down but paced in agitation. "He can't see his home. Can you imagine what he will say? He will be disappointed, to say the least."

"What's the worst that can happen?" Eliza asked. He looked at her. He didn't say anything.

"And what if he wants to visit here? Look at our house!" He was not a wealthy man. "He's going to think us very poor specimens,"

They all looked at their house. The fittings were shabby but solid and clean, well made. "You are the architect," Eliza said. "The clever one. Let his financiers show him wealth. We show solid family love."

MIHAI WAS TALL, BROADLY BUILT, HIS CLOTHES CUT well to hide how large he'd grown. His cheeks were red and round, his teeth spaced out and yellowed, his breath like cheddar or, Julia whispered, like the Thames in summer. He had long hair brushing his shoulders (Phillip tried to hide his distaste at this), and he topped it with a small grey hat that was almost formless. He had blue lips, like a lizard's and his eyelids hung low, making him look sleepy.

"Aah, your lovely ladies. So tall! So delicate in the limbs and colourful! All three like princesses of an exotic place. You must all come to dinner at my home now it is complete. I'll have them serve beef broth and black pudding. That will get some meat on your bones."

Amara blushed, which made him laugh.

"You know I last saw these two older girls when they were tiny. Just born! All blue in the face and furious," he said. "How well I remember!"

The three girls barely contained themselves. They chattered all at once, drowning him out, until he burst into laughter and bade them hush.

They all heard his stomach rumble, like a crack of thunder, and Amara giggled. "Oh, you must be ravenous," Eliza said, "Let's get you something to eat."

"He's not about to waste away, Mildred," Phillip said.

"Phillip! So rude!" Eliza asked the cook to fix salmon en croute, because she knew they had leftover salmon from her order with the fishmonger. Some servants do it on purpose in the hope of taking the extra home but Eliza wasn't having that.

The girls raced to their rooms, returning screaming with laughter. They wore salmon pink scarves, all three, to match their food. Even in their rush they exuded grace, their fingers long and delicate, their step light.

"Like angels," Mihai said.

At dinner, Eliza couldn't contain herself any longer. "And my dear friend Lucia? It has been so long since we communicated."

Mihai shook his head. "I bring sad news. My dear sister died in childbirth. She did feel envy of your beautiful three, when she could have none. I'm sorry she no longer wrote to you. Perhaps hearing about your girls and their accomplishments became harder and harder as her years passed fruitlessly."

"And yet you said she was with child. What joy that must have brought."

"Ah," he said.

"So sad that she should pass in the same manner as your wife," Phillip said.

"Ah," Mihai said, and Julia wondered at his eyes, how they shifted about, and how he smiled nervously, and how his hands shook.

"Your father is a clever man. My house is something to see," he said, as the pudding was served, as if they hadn't seen it five dozen times. As if every meal hadn't been dominated by talk of this house.

"You've certainly changed the way things look," Eliza said.

"My philosophy: Take something to its basics and rebuild it. Hair will grow back differently on a shaved head." Eliza thought he was dashing when he first visited, his hair a golden yellow, his shoulders broad.

"But hair grows back easily enough. By its very nature it is meant to fall."

"Your house is certainly sturdy, if not very beautiful," Phillip said. He had made many suggestions of design, all rebuffed.

"You know of the tulip?" Mihai said. "It grows weaker the more beautiful. There is little to be said for beauty, much for strength." Mihai raised his hands and pressed his forefingers and thumbs together like a picture frame. "You are the strongest, Amara. That is clear."

Eliza well remembered the 200 year old house he'd had torn down to build his home.

He had bade her stand there in the rubble. She was flattered, a young wife with babies; you'd think she'd lost all of her allure. But no, Mihai, the brother of her dear friend (and if she would only admit it, she had made up stories about him at school, when her friend spoke of him and his dashing ways) asking her to grace his home or the foundation of his home. "Stand there," he said, and bade his man mark where her shadow fell. That was where the foundation stone was laid.

"And now you must prepare," he had told her.

"For what, Mihai?"

"For your passing forty days from now."

She had known of this curse but had forgotten. He giggled and did a little hop, odd in a man of his stature.

"It's a blessing to you. Knowing when you'll die gives you every chance to make amends, say goodbye, indulge your desires."

"I have no desires," but she did, of course. Small, sustaining dreams.

"And yet you are not dead," Mihai said, taking another large mouthful of salmon en croute, and he roared with laughter. "My blessing failed."

"But look at my daughters. They are the true blessing. Magdala wouldn't be here, and who knows what sort of young women Julia and Amara would have been, raised by their father and hired women."

"What do you know of hired women?" Mihai said, standing up and laying his napkin on his plate. He nodded at Phillip, and the two men withdrew to Phillip's study.

But the girls weren't going to miss out. Julia crept into the room next door, the little-used storage space, and heard such things as made her sick to the stomach.

"There is a brothel," Mihai said, "where the whores dye their skin blue. Glorious. Like the naked bodies taken out of plague houses, a sight I've seen and never anything so beautiful."

Julia wondered *how old is this man? Unless there was a plague more recently in Romania?*

"These whores hold the same tinge and even more, as the blue fades it begins to look like bruising. Also beautiful."

Julia noticed her mother kept her and her sisters close and allowed them no time alone with Mihai, whom she had always described as a fearsome man. Julia wondered what her mother feared. What power she imagined Mihai had.

"You could do worse than that man," Phillip said afterwards, but what his four ladies said in return burned his ears and made him shrink into his collar.

"Are we going to have to poison you to stop you marrying our girls off to awful men?" Eliza said.

The maid stood in the doorway, listening in. She always listened.

"He's not so bad," Amara said.

A WEEK LATER THEY TRAVELLED FOR DINNER AT Mihai's mansion. The winter chill had set in and even Eliza would have preferred to stay at home. But go they must, Phillip said, and he tried to keep them amused with stories until they arrived.

Outside was solid grey brick, with very few windows. "You see how I save money on the window tax? Your father chose his materials well," Mihai said, though Phillip had little choice in the matter.

He said, "It will be named for you, Phillip. Your name in brass, over the door."

Phillip was embarrassed by this. An honest day's pay for an honest day's work was all he asked for, and a good life for his girls and for his wife to be happy, because her happiness brought joy to his own life.

"No need for that," he said.

"One of your daughters, then. Julia, Amara, Magdalena. Which one?" and he rubbed his great beard, eyeing them off. Only Julia understood he was teasing them, like the old men in town who tossed foul comments their way if ever the girls walked together.

Inside, all was grey, muted.

He led them (when truly he didn't need to, because they knew this house as well as their own) to the massive dining room, with its table long enough for forty guests. It was set with dull gold, flat silverware. There were no flowers, no colours.

"Sit," Mihai told them, spreading his arms. They clustered down one end, leaving the rest of the vast table vacant.

Course after course arrived. The food was rich and varied, aromas and tastes the girls hadn't sampled before. Magdalena in particular devoured everything in sight; she was never one for holding back.

"More wine," Mihai said. "More food." The girls and their mother fell asleep as the two men finished bottle after bottle.

It was after midnight when Mihai arranged a carriage to take them home. Their father groaned and whimpered all the way, irritating the four women. Silly drunk man. He wasn't amusing at all, just dull and malodorous.

It was the last carriage ride the family would take together.

THE NEXT MORNING PHILLIP DID NOT RISE. HE WAS NEVER a lazy man, always up with the dawn, even on the nights he was up well past midnight. But after the amount he drank it wasn't surprising that he was still not risen by noon.

"Silly fidget," their mother said. "He's poisoned himself with wine."

"Mother!" Julia said. The maid stifled a smile. As ever before she was always far too free with ears and eyes, Julia thought.

There was a loud crash, which startled them all. Mihai, entering their home. "What's this I hear? A house of women left unattended?" he roared. "Where is Phillip? I expected him an hour ago to discuss further additions."

"He is wine-ill, still in bed," Eliza said. "He deserves a small amount of suffering for the noise he made last night."

The maid heard this as well.

"Real men don't suffer from the drink," Mihai said, smiling, "and this is a man who can build a magnificent house. Leave me with him."

Not knowing why, they left, even the maid.

In the bedroom, Mihai roused Phillip. He gave him a draught and when the man bent over double in pain he said, "I think that wife of yours has poisoned you."

THE MAID GAVE EVIDENCE AT ELIZA'S TRIAL FOR attempted murder. "Oh yes," she said, "I heard them talking about poisoning him."

WITH THEIR FATHER BED-RIDDEN, THEIR MOTHER incarcerated in the women's gaol, the girls had no one to watch over them.

Mihai made an arrangement with Phillip. If the three girls went into servitude for him, he would use his influence and all the money at his disposal to ask for mercy for Eliza. He would ask the authorities not to put her to death. "I won't work your girls hard," he said. "Think of it as finishing school."

Phillip, never a strong man when it came to resisting Mihai, was in no state, physically or mentally, to resist him now. Phillip agreed to force his daughters into Mihai's service. After their mother was, after all, put to death, the girls had little choice.

It was not what they imagined. Even in their worst nightmares they couldn't imagine what Mihai had in store for them.

MIHAI'S CLOSEST COMPANION WAS A CRUEL, WEAK MAN called Cyril. He was the mayor of a town far away but he never seemed to be at home for his duties. Cyril and Mihai drank great goblets of wine, but the girls were given crystal glasses of blue water. There was scant art in the room, much of it dull, and the food served on plain plates. Only the enormous candles brought a warmth and a glow and the crystal wine goblets reflected tiny and numerous stars of light.

"Isn't it a beautiful hue?" Mihai said. "Indigo water. A rare thing, rare indeed, but fitting for these beautiful tulip flowers I have before me."

Later, in the lavatory, Amara screamed in terror and the older girls laughed to see how their water had turned blue.

"Look at your lovely ladies," Cyril said later that evening, his dull eyes glinting in the candlelight of Mihai's study. "You'd think they were dolls they are so lovely. Or puppets, perhaps. Dance for us, lovely puppets."

"Go on," Mihai said, "Do as he says."

So the girls drew out their scarves and danced. They brought the only colour to the dreary mansion.

"Have them dance on my grave when I'm dead," Cyril said, and the two men laughed until they fell off their chairs.

LOOKING BACK, THE GIRLS WOULD REMEMBER THAT AS the best night of their captivity. The last colour they saw. As the sun rose, Mihai said, "And now."

As he imprisoned them down below, in solid dark rooms, he stared dark and hard and Julia understood that he would not listen to reason.

Each girl had a cell to herself. The cells were bare—no bed, no chair, no window, no light. It took them a while to understand they were there to die. They wondered, did their father build these rooms? Didn't he wonder what they were for? Or did he imagine coal, or wood, or wheat?

DAY BY DAY MIHAI TOLD THEM HOW LONG THEY had to live.

"How good I am to you," he said. "What a gift I give to you.

To know the truth." He said this every day.

He allowed them water. He passed tall thin jars to them through small cracks in the doors and while they saw nothing in the pitch dark, they knew this water was blue. He told them so, he said, "Your insides will be such a lovely colour."

Julia thought, *this is because of the whores. He wants us blue like them.* In her darker moments she thought, *He can't see us in the dark; it is our corpses he wants to see.*

Julia could hear nothing of her sisters. The walls were dense, almost absorbent, drawing in all sound and most of the air.

Julia could barely hear herself breathe.

She was so hungry. So very, very hungry. No moss or mould on the walls, no rodents, so day by day she weakened. Her sisters, too, she imagined. Amara would be the bitterest; she alone had believed Mihai would marry her and she would live a life of adventure. Julia pictured her crouched in a corner, her flesh loose, her eyes dull. And Magdalena. Bright, funny, passionate Magdalena; Julia pictured her weak and quiet, her cheekbones sharp.

WHEN THEY WERE ALL THREE DEAD AND SPIRIT, THEY oozed through the grey brick walls, finding each other easily on the other side.

Julia looked back at their prison. She felt such fury at what Mihai stole from her. Not only her own moments of joy, love, success, but those of all the descendants she would never have. He stole her name, her family's future, he ended her line, and this made her exceeding bitter.

She nodded at her sisters and they tried to re-enter. Julia wanted to terrify him, frighten him to death, but they could not pass through the doors or walls again.

"His time has not yet come," she whispered. "We will return

when that time is near."

Instead they found a chimney sweep whose lungs were filled with black, and then a woman about to be thrown by a horse, and then a young girl boarding a train about to crash to die at the hands of a butcher, and then, and then, and then, and then. They gave each one the peace of mind that knowledge of death brings, and this sustained them more than anything in life had.

IT WAS MANY YEARS UNTIL THE GIRLS RETURNED TO Mihai's mansion, drawn there by the knowledge, the scent, of his impending death. He had not looked after his home well; perhaps his fortunes had failed. There was no name over the door—Mihai had not even kept that promise.

The grey ladies pressed again the cold brick wall and then flowed through it and once more they were inside the walls of the grey mansion.

There was a great echo inside, as if it had been long abandoned. But no, they could hear moans from upstairs, where Mihai slept.

They flew up the stairs.

There they found him, enormous, bloated and repulsive. He rested in his filthy, broken bed, his chest rising and falling ever more slowly…

Beside his bed rested a great pile of blue bones.

Julia felt something, the memory of hunger, the flickering sense of pain long since forgotten. She knew they were hers, and Amara's, And Magdalena's were there, beside this filthy mound of flesh.

With great pleasure she approached him and lifted a finger to his face.

He drew a thick, phlegmy breath. "You have come to tell me what I already know. My passing is soon and I will be in God's arms."

Julia shook her head.

"No?" She heard uncertainty in his voice for the first time. She didn't know. She couldn't know. What was next. But she shook her head.

He wailed then, knowing as well as she did he'd done nothing to deserve a happy afterlife.

They all three of them watched as he took his last, shuddering breath.

For a moment, a wash of red passed through them, the colour of love, perhaps, and for a moment they clustered, almost remembering, but then they were drawn away, drawn towards, and they found the next door and they knocked on it, and waited.

The title "Exceeding Bitter" *is inspired by* "Requiem,"
by Gabriel Faure

...ah, that great day, and exceeding bitter, when thou shalt come to judge the world by fire.

A GAME OF MAGES

COURTNEY SCHAFER

— The Shattered Sigil —

LIZAVETA CARVED CHUNKS OF FLESH FROM THE bleeding, mewling ruin of a dancer shackled to the workroom's anchor stone. The mutilated man's partner, bound against an iron post beside the gore-smeared obsidian block, shrieked an unending stream of curses at Lizaveta.

"You soulless demon, may Shaikar take you screaming to his innermost hell! May his children rip your cursed magic from your blackened bones! Leave Davan be, gods rot you, *stop hurting him—*"

Lizaveta ignored the babbled plea, slicing her knife through glistening sinews. Anguish and horror and rage stoked the paltry ember of the watching woman's *ikilhia*—her soul's fire—into a blaze nearly as bright as that of a mage.

Blood flowed dark down the anchor stone's whorled sides and pooled over the silver spell-channels laid into the stone floor. The maimed dancer's gasping breaths stuttered. In a broken, slurred gargle, he called his partner's name.

"Marca…"

Marca's curses broke into wrenching sobs. Her *ikilhia* flared wilder yet, as her partner's *ikilhia* roiled and seethed with his agony. Both dancers were *nathahlen*, untalented in magic, despite the skill they displayed in their art.

Lizaveta still remembered with vivid clarity the first time she had seen them dance. She'd been crossing through one of Ninavel's boisterous night markets, crowds of *nathahlen* falling silent and scrabbling to clear her path the instant they sighted the jagged red and black sigils on her gown. Until she came upon two dancers so intent on their performance they had not heard the panicked whispers of *Blood mage! Blood mage coming!* Oblivious, the dancers leaped and swayed and tumbled across the street's packed sand like magefire chased by a desert breeze. Their dance displayed such power and grace it was like joy given form. In the months since, Lizaveta had summoned the pair many times to dance for her, and savored every moment of the experience.

But now she had need of the pair in a different way. Far across the world, her mage-brother Ruslan—her spellcasting partner, her lover, the other half of her self—had completed his months-long hunt for a certain prize, and was ready to return to her side. The distant shimmer of his triumph and yearning for reunion curled along the bond that linked their souls.

She was just as eager for his return, and not merely because she missed him. She had important news to discuss with him. News of a threat—and an opportunity.

She smiled and peeled back a quivering slab of muscle to expose reddened bone. The dancers' torment would give her the power to bring Ruslan home. That was well worth the loss of evening entertainment. Ninavel's teeming streets and sun-scorched spires held plenty of *nathahlen*. There were always more dancers.

Lizaveta paused. The maimed dancer's *ikilhia* wavered like a candleflame in a sandstorm, soon to extinguish. His partner's anguish had reached its peak. The time to cast her spell had come.

She took up a second blade, careful lest the hilt slip in her blood-slicked hand, and moved to where she could reach both dancers. Plunging one knife into the dying dancer's heart, she whipped the other blade across his partner's throat. The shock of violent death exploded through the aether, rich and dark and sweet, ah, so sweet! Lizaveta shut out the rapture singing through her soul, maintaining with practiced ease the diamond clarity of her focus. She contained the explosion of power and sent every last spark arrowing through the labyrinthine maze of spell-channels.

The vast natural confluence of magic that washed invisibly through Ninavel swirled and shifted in answer. Wild currents aligned into an ordered mimicry of her spell pattern. The confluence's power was so immense that any mage who tried to touch it directly would burn to ash. Yet the strongest of mages, *akheli* like she and Ruslan—blood mages, as the untalented called them—could harness the currents' strength with stolen soul-energies.

Even so, casting with the confluence was perilous, especially without a partner to smooth and control the harnessing channels' flow. But Lizaveta wasn't alone. Despite the vast distance between them, Ruslan reached along their bond with all his considerable strength, sharing her mage-sight, wielding his magic in concert with hers, acting as channeler for her though he was not physically present. No other *akheli* pair had ever managed such a feat of shared skill. Even among their own kind, Lizaveta and Ruslan were legendary.

One slip in concentration meant death for them both, but Lizaveta's faith in her mage-brother's skill and strength matched her confidence in her own. Their trust, first built long ago during their shared apprenticeship, had proved unshakeable. She need never fear Ruslan would fail her.

The translocation spell blazed into shape, gloriously perfect in every detail. Lizaveta blocked out satisfaction and *cast*, focusing her will through the shining spell-structure.

The world bowed to her desire. One instant the center of the spiraling channels was empty, and the next, the familiar tall, broad-shouldered figure of her mage-brother appeared. A far smaller figure huddled beside him. The child—Ruslan's prize, the object of his long hunt—convulsed, retching.

Translocation was hard on its subjects, even an *akheli*. Ruslan's nausea and disorientation shuddered into her, though his proud posture revealed no outward sign of distress. Working swiftly, Lizaveta damped down leftover energies. She spared a quick lash of power to burn away the dancers' ruined corpses and the blood coating her arms, then funneled the remaining magic back into the confluence.

Ruslan mastered his discomfort; eager joy blossomed along their link.

"Liza!" He strode over the darkened channels that separated them, his gait still a trifle unsteady, and caught her in an exuberant embrace.

Even after all their years together, she treasured the feel of him in her arms. The brilliant red blaze of his *ikilhia* was as hot and vibrant as a second sun. When first they had met as children, she had thought him so odd in appearance. His skin was golden, not brown or umber, his hair russet rather than shining black, his eyes angular and hazel instead of pleasingly large and dark. It was the fire in him she had first loved, but now she thought him beautiful both inside and out. She kissed the smooth planes of his face, then his mouth, savoring the taste of salt and strange spices. He slid his hands along her body, his desire and delight merging with hers.

She pulled back, laughing. "*What* are you wearing?" Both he and the child were swathed in patchwork coats sewn out of some bizarre beast's fur. A faint but distinctly rancid odor wafted off Ruslan's garment.

"It was cold there. A desert of snow and ice." Ruslan shrugged out of the coat and caught her hands. "Ah, how I've missed you!"

"I am delighted to see you home." Lizaveta let the full measure of that delight flood their bond. "I've had important news we must discuss—"

"Discussions can wait. Come, see what kept me from your side." He tugged her toward the child, his mind ablaze with excitement.

Lizaveta sighed. Clearly she would get nothing sensible out of him until she indulged his latest passion. She had tolerated with patient amusement Ruslan's various obsessions over the long centuries of their partnership, but she thought his current project the most dubious of all. One thing to take apprentices—she'd always known he'd want to build a family one day. But when he'd taken his first child, several months ago, Lizaveta found his choice of apprentice deeply dismaying. Bad enough the child was damaged and half-mad, requiring long weeks of labor on Ruslan's part to repair his mind.

The real trouble lay in the boy's nature. He was far too soft-hearted to make a good *akheli*. Ruslan refused to see it, so captivated by the boy's raw talent that he would hear no warnings. He'd locked the boy in a preservation spell that kept him insensible and unaging, while Ruslan hunted for a second child of the right talent and temperament to be the boy's mage-sibling. *Akheli* always took apprentices in pairs. The only way to learn channeled casting was with a partner.

She hoped Ruslan had exercised better wisdom in selecting that partner.

"Meet my new *akhelysh*," Ruslan announced, stripping furs from his latest acquisition. The child looked pitifully scrawny without them. He'd stopped retching, but he seemed dazed, so layered in spells meant to protect his untrained *ikilhia* from the confluence's terrible power that Lizaveta couldn't sense his soul. All she had was the evidence of her eyes: the boy was foreign like Ruslan in appearance, but not so exotically beautiful as Ruslan's first choice. This one was sturdy, perhaps eight years of age, with hair and skin the color of sand, a flat face, and angled eyes as gray as slate.

"What is his name?" Lizaveta asked.

"He asked me for a new one," Ruslan said. "I thought we might call him Mikail."

Mikail had been the name of their own beloved mistress Vasha's partner. Both Mikail and Vasha were long dead, but no amount of years could heal the aching void in Ruslan and Lizaveta's souls where their bond to Vasha had been rooted.

"A nice sentiment," Lizaveta murmured, and knelt to look the boy in the eyes. "Let us see if you are worthy of it." She touched the child's bare shoulder. He did not flinch, only blinked owlishly at her. Likely Ruslan had not yet taught him a civilized tongue. Lizaveta slid a delicate thread of power through the layers of Ruslan's spellwork. Even squeezed down tight beneath protective bindings, the boy's *ikilhia* was a healthy bonfire of green. He was certainly talented. As for his character…

Stoic; obedient; practical; an orphan grieving for a murdered brother and parents, yet taking savage solace in the bloody revenge Ruslan had provided him, and desperate to become strong like Ruslan, so he might never suffer loss again—

"You've chosen well," Lizaveta said to Ruslan, relieved. Now he'd found a proper *akhelysh*, he might even rethink his first selection. She stood and reached through their bond, asking, *Why not dispose of the flawed child and find another like this one?*

His rejection of the idea was instant. *Kiran is my heart's choice, and I will have no other. Flaws can be overcome; I will make him strong.*

Lizaveta hesitated, uneasy. Vasha had always told her, *Your mage-brother's greatest fault is his impetuous nature. You have the cooler head; you must help him use his reason.* After so many years, Lizaveta had believed that task well in hand. It was rare for Ruslan to disregard her counsel.

Ruslan said softly, "Will you not have faith in me? I know this is not your choice, and I will not ask your help in their training. But I truly believe this path can bring both of us joy."

He showed her a vision of the future: the boys grown into young men, their souls chained to Ruslan's so that he ruled their minds and magic with complete assurance of their loyalty. Mikail and Kiran would be willing partners in his casting and in every way he and Lizaveta might wish to make use of them…and oh, the uses would be many, once they were old enough. Particularly for Kiran, with his silken black hair in such striking contrast to his strange, moon-pale skin.

You always did have a good eye for beauty, Lizaveta said, capitulating. *Just be sure you train the weakness out of him before you bring him to our bed.*

Ruslan's delight rippled into her. *That, I can promise. Have you ever known me to fail once I set my mind to a task?*

No, she had not. She must admit he'd chosen Kiran's mage-brother wisely. "So long as you remember the children are your responsibility alone."

"Of course," Ruslan said, but his attention was not on her, nor even the dazed, uncomprehending Mikail. His *ikilhia* reached for the room where little Kiran lay in spelled stasis. He meant to release the child this instant.

"No!" Urgency kept Lizaveta from softening the command.

"No?" Ruslan's brows drew together. "You just insisted the children are mine to raise as I see fit."

Ruslan was her mage-brother, the light of her heart. She could not simply stand by and watch him make a disastrous error.

"You wish to mold Kiran's character using Mikail, yes? Then he must look up to Mikail as to an elder brother, not an equal, and Mikail must feel secure in your love, not see Kiran as a rival for your heart. Leave Kiran as he is while you begin Mikail's training. Give Mikail a year with you, perhaps more. Only then should you wake Kiran from spell-sleep, and show Mikail your trust by giving Kiran into his care."

Ruslan's frown turned thoughtful. He inclined his head to her. "I see the wisdom in this. I will do as you suggest."

That reassured her as nothing else could have. His obsession had not completely overthrown his reason.

Ruslan strode to the workroom door, opened it, and called a sharp summons. A middle-aged *nathahlen* servant obediently hurried in, gaze downcast. Ruslan consigned Mikail to the servant's care, ordering the woman to feed and bathe him.

Lizaveta said dryly to Ruslan, "I suggest you bathe as well. I've never smelled anything quite like those furs. But first, if you've quite finished admiring your *akhelyshen*, I have news of far greater import. Our contact in Alathia sent a message: Simon Levanian has killed the spies sent to watch him, and vanished."

Simon was *akheli*, a rival of old. For a time, he and Lizaveta and Ruslan had shared an uneasy truce in Ninavel, enforced by the city's ruler. Lord Sechaveh was not *akheli*, not even mage-talented, but he was cunning as a dune viper and possessed one great weapon. When he first founded Ninavel in the desert shadow of the Whitefire Mountains, his mage-talented sister had bound him to the confluence in such a way that he could bar any mage, even an *akheli*, from harnessing the least drop of its magic. Few mages wished to risk losing such an incredible source of power, and Sechaveh insisted every mage in Ninavel swear a binding blood oath never to cast against him.

Simon alone had dared to challenge Sechaveh's rule. Seven years ago, he fought to take the city for his own, and would have won—if not for Lizaveta and Ruslan. With Sechaveh's sanction, they murdered Simon's apprentices so he could no longer cast channeled spells. Simon fled across the Whitefires and crept into the country of Alathia to hide behind their border wards, which were famously impenetrable even to confluence-fueled casting.

His exile was surely not comfortable. Blood magic was outlawed in Alathia, and the Watch, a cadre of mages conditioned since birth into slavish loyalty to the ruling council, sniffed out and executed offenders with righteous zeal. Living in hiding, Simon would be restricted to casting only minor spells, as if he were among the least talented of mages. Doubtless he had spent the last seven years dreaming of revenge.

"You think Simon has returned across the border?" A predatory eagerness dawned in Ruslan's eyes. "That would certainly bring opportunity."

Sechaveh had forbidden them to kill Simon. He refused to share his reasons, but Lizaveta had her suspicions. Sechaveh was wise enough not to assume current alliances would forever hold, and Simon was the only mage in the west with talent to match that of Lizaveta and Ruslan.

Ruslan had been outraged, his pride bristling at taking orders from a *nathahlen*. Lizaveta had counseled patience. Let Sechaveh think he had their compliance; let Simon cower behind Alathia's wards. One of the joys of near-immortality was that they had no need for haste. *Wait long enough*, she had told Ruslan, *and our chance will come.*

"If we strike at Simon, it must be subtly done," Lizaveta said. "But first, we must find him. If Simon has returned to Arkennland, he's veiled himself well. Working alone, I could find no trace of him. Now you are here to partner my casting, we can scry for him properly. Even if he has not yet broken exile, I think it clear he intends some move against us."

Ruslan laughed. "Let him try. Partnerless, he has no hope of besting us."

"He might be crippled, but he is also clever." Not to mention wary, cautious, and methodical. Simon never acted on a plan unless he felt certain of success.

"Not clever enough." The cold ferocity of Ruslan's smile brought her a surge of dark anticipation. "If he heard news of my absence and hoped to take advantage, he has lost that chance. Shall we cast to hunt him?"

"Nothing would please me more." Lizaveta too thought Simon's timing no coincidence, but not due to news of Ruslan's absence. More likely, Simon had learned of Ruslan's decision to take apprentices. He must hope Ruslan would be too distracted by training his *akhelyshen* to hunt him properly.

A prickle of worry chased over her, as she recalled Ruslan's blithe dismissal of her first mention of news. He'd been so eager to show off Mikail, he had no attention to spare.

Yet after his initial burst of excitement, he heard her counsel, returned to reason, and now his eagerness to seek Simon ran every bit as hot as she could wish. And was that not the strength of their partnership? Alone, Ruslan might yield to weakness. Together, neither would let the other fall. Ruslan's confidence was not misplaced. Their combined strength was more than a match for Simon. All they had to do was find him.

LIZAVETA STOOD BESIDE THE WARDED WINDOW OF HER study, gripping the jeweled silver band of a message charm. Outside, the sun slowly sank behind the serrated ridgeline of the Whitefire Mountains. Ninavel's soaring white stone towers stood out sharp against a sky ablaze with crimson and orange.

The sunset's beauty did little to assuage Lizaveta's frustration.

Three years. Three long years, and no spell she and Ruslan cast revealed the least trace of Simon. That surely meant Simon remained in Alathia, concealed by the border wards, but the spies she sent to search Alathian cities and countryside had no better luck.

Ruslan was content to lie in wait and train his *akhelyshen*. Lizaveta was not.

She frowned at the message charm. She detested the need to depend on *nathahlen* spies, who were irritatingly limited and fallible. Before ciphered missives could be charm-sent to Ninavel, they had to be couriered across the border, a laborious process subject to all manner of delays. The message she expected today was already late. Perhaps it would only be another litany of failure, but she had particular hopes for this spy, more determined and methodical than most. His last message had said he intended to hunt deep into Alathia's rugged northern wildlands, after discovering in some crude little village that two of the area's most experienced trappers had never returned from a scouting trip. Lizaveta knew the trappers' disappearance was probably the result of the wild's many natural perils, rather than murder by a fugitive *akheli* intent on remaining hidden, yet she could not help but hope…

A tentative young voice spoke. "Khanum Liza?"

Kiran stood in the study's arched doorway. His small face and hands were scrubbed to alabaster perfection, though chalk smudges and magefire burns still marred his clothes.

"What is it, little one?" She had to admit that so far he'd proved a better *akhelysh* to Ruslan than she imagined. That was in no small part thanks to Ruslan's scrupulous adherence to Lizaveta's advice in preparing Kiran's relationship with Mikail. Once introduced, the boys had quickly settled into the ideal pattern to mold Kiran's character: Mikail fiercely protective of his younger mage-brother, and Kiran idolizing him in return, doing his utmost to follow Mikail's lead in their training.

Kiran bowed low. "I did well with my spell designs today, so Ruslan said I might ask you for a story."

At first, she had been a touch exasperated that Ruslan kept finding excuses for the children to interact with her. Yet his desire for them to win her love had been so evident, she had not the heart to deny him. Besides, she found the boys more entertaining than expected. Kiran, shyly adoring and endlessly curious, listened rapt to tales of her travels and shared her appreciation for nature's myriad wonders. Even stiff, serious Mikail begged her to share stories of legendary mage-battles and cuddled up to her with kittenish eagerness when she offered affection. The boys worshipped and feared Ruslan in equal measure, as they should. But since Lizaveta had no need to worry over their training or mete out punishments for their mistakes, her, they simply loved.

"Not tonight," she said gently to Kiran, and showed him

the message charm. "I am waiting for news of some importance. Tomorrow, perhaps."

"If you're too busy for a story, might I at least read the star book again?" Kiran peered up at her, his blue eyes wide and winsome.

She relented. "You may come in and read, so long as you are quiet."

"I'll be so quiet you won't even notice me," he promised, tiptoeing for the shelves lining the study's marble walls. As he passed her, he paused and said in a rush, "I hope the news you wait for is good. So you won't have to worry anymore."

His sensitivity to her mood was a sign of the empathy she still feared would cause trouble in years to come. *Akheli* needed steel in their souls, not kindness. But that was Ruslan's problem and not hers.

Unlike Simon. Lizaveta ran a finger over the jeweled band, willing her spy to hurry up and send his report. "My worries are not yours, little one. Read if you wish, but no more talking."

Kiran made straight for the "star book"—a treatise she had written on the movements and nature of celestial objects. The treatise had been born of his eager questions when she first showed him the patterns of the stars. *What is the sky made of? Are the stars magelights? Can you cast to bring one down for me to see?*

She did not need polished lenses such as the scholars of the great cities of eastern Arkennland used to magnify and study the sky. She cast with all the power of the confluence to scry the distant stars, and discovered to her wonder their immense size and the improbable distances between them. Nor were those distances wholly empty. Globes of rock and gas circled the stars, though none she had yet scried were rich with magic and life like the world beneath her feet. Countless smaller chunks of sky-stone hurtled through the silent darkness like shrapnel from some immense concussion.

She wrote the treatise to record her findings for her own future use—and because Kiran was still too young and untrained to cast spells that would let him experience such wonders directly. But oh, how he loved to read of them. Already, he had settled into a cushioned chair, clutching the slender leather-bound volume like he held the most precious of treasures.

The glory of the sunset outside faded. Magelights glimmered and sparkled like a rainbow of gemstones in Ninavel's twilit towers. Finally, *finally*, the message charm warmed in her hand, signaling the spy's missive had come.

Lizaveta sent an eager spark of her *ikilhia* into the charm to trigger the waiting message. A vision of hastily scrawled words appeared in her mind's eye: *The man you seek is living amid ruins in the Greenward Hills. I know not what he does in the ruins. I did not dare get close enough for him to discover me. He has been there long enough to build a cabin, and he shows no sign of leaving. I believe no other shadow man has yet located him.*

Lizaveta sucked in a sharp, delighted breath. Kiran looked up from the star treatise, the azure blaze of his *ikilhia* flaring with curiosity, but she ignored his unspoken questions.

Simon found, at last! And Lizaveta had an inkling of his goal. The ruins the spy spoke of—she had read scholars' treatises discussing curious artifacts found in the west, the leftovers of some vanished civilization so ancient that no one remembered its people. Most of the artifacts were broken, useless, but some contained curiously powerful reservoirs of magic, as if an entire host of mages had worked to bind power within them. Might Simon believe such a reservoir could make up for his lack of partner and confluence?

She reached for Ruslan's mind, and caught a flash of intent concentration accompanied by a muted pulse of energies. He was leading Mikail through a spell exercise. It would endanger them both if she distracted Ruslan while he cast.

A diffident cough caught her attention. A *nathahlen* servant prostrated herself in the doorway.

"Great one, forgive the intrusion, but one of Lord Sechaveh's servants has come asking to meet with you. A scholar-mage. Shall I tell her to return another day?"

"No, you may tell our visitor this is an excellent time." Lizaveta wanted very much to find out if this visit was related to the information she'd just received. Her spy might believe no others had discovered Simon's location, but that was no guarantee. *Nathahlen* were so unreliable. "Show Sechaveh's mage to the study." She glanced at Kiran. "You, little one, must return to the workroom. When Ruslan finishes with Mikail, ask him to join me."

She saw Kiran's disappointment. Ruslan kept him tightly cloistered; he had little chance to meet other mages. But he did not argue, only set aside the treatise—not without a wistful sigh of regret—and ran from the room.

The servant returned with a young mage whose belted sash bore Sechaveh's scorpion crest beside the star-and-scroll insignia of eastern Arkennland's Marrekai scholars.

Lizaveta dismissed the servant. The young mage bowed to Lizaveta in formal eastern style, hands extended and crossed at the wrist. She was not greatly talented. Her citrine *ikilhia* was a scant little flame compared to Lizaveta's sun-bright inferno. The pale, blocky sigils on her tunic and trousers proclaimed her to be what the untalented termed a crystal mage, who raised power for spellwork by calculated placement of gemstones to absorb mere trickles of the confluence's great currents.

"Thank you for seeing me," the mage said, straightening. "I'm Aram Inara Naavini. Though here on the western frontier, I just go by Naavini. I love how informal you Ninavel folk are. Saves so much time, which is such a blessing in the heat. Ah, but it's lovely in here." Naavini looked appreciatively around the study, which was cool and spacious and quiet, its marble recesses and treasure trove of books lit by soft silver magelight from crystals held in decorative copper brackets.

Lizaveta gestured Naavini to the comfortably padded chair Kiran had so recently vacated. The girl's pert face and small stature made her appear to be barely out of childhood herself. Of course, appearance was a poor guide to the age of even so limited a mage as Naavini, but her *ikilhia* sizzled with a buoyant energy that revealed she wasn't anywhere near her first century. Only the young got so easily excited.

"What does Sechaveh request of me?" Lizaveta asked, her dispassionate tone and perfectly controlled *ikilhia* revealing nothing of her deep interest in the answer.

Naavini picked up the treatise Kiran had set aside, and flashed a grin at Lizaveta. "Ah! The very treatise that inspired the discovery I've come to discuss with you."

Lizaveta blinked; this was not what she had expected. She had sent a copy of the treatise to Sechaveh as a courtesy to an ally. Sometimes sky-stones fell in a blaze of light to impact the ground. Sechaveh had built Ninavel on the wealth of the Whitefires' valuable mineral deposits, but how much more precious might strange sky-minerals be?

Naavini's discovery likely had everything to do with increasing Sechaveh's profits, and nothing to do with an exiled enemy's whereabouts. Perhaps the spy had been correct in his assurance that Lizaveta alone knew Simon's location.

"Have you found a fallen sky-stone?" she asked Naavini, her mind only half on the question. The rest of her attention was on

Simon. Ruslan might scoff at the idea of some ancient artifact replacing the confluence, but Lizaveta liked to err on the side of caution. Yet how might they intervene, with Simon protected by the border wards?

"Predicted a future impact, actually." Naavini's grin reappeared, brighter than ever. If the girl was intimidated by facing one of Ninavel's two most powerful mages, she betrayed no sign beyond the excited roil of her *ikilhia*. "After reading your treatise, I devised a method to chart the larger sky-stones' paths. They're rather well-behaved things. With the right set of equations, the math's easier than mapping confluence currents. Setting up the equations, though… ah, now that's the real challenge. Nobody's yet managed it but me."

Even lesser mages had no lack of pride. In Naavini's case, perhaps the pride was warranted. If she had discovered a stone on the path to strike…an idea dawned, sparking fire in Lizveta's heart.

"How large a sky-stone, and where will it hit?"

"Large enough to leave a crater twenty miles wide. The stone will strike in the Whitefires in only a week's time."

That explained Sechaveh's concern. The Whitefires were riddled with the mines that poured profit into Sechaveh's coffers.

"Sechaveh wishes for the stone to be diverted, so the impact does not destroy any of his mines?" Lizaveta would be delighted to ensure the cataclysm happened elsewhere. Specifically, the Greenward Hills. Alathia's vaunted border wards were impenetrable only to magic and humans. The wards would not stop physical objects barren of any *ikilhia*, such as sky-stones. Twenty miles of devastation would easily encompass the ruins where Simon lurked. If Sechaveh truly did not know Simon's location, he would never realize Lizaveta had defied his edict.

"The mines are safe," Naavini said. "The stone will hit in the far southern reaches of the Whitefires and destroy only a region of wilderness. Lord Sechaveh wishes to know if you would consider diverting the sky-stone's path so it strikes a little more south and east. Right on the city of Prosul Shadari."

In Prosul Shadari, a consortium of Varkevian merchant houses operated a massive silver mine that was Ninavel's largest competitor in the trade. Destroy the mine, and Ninavel would have a near-monopoly on charm-grade silver in all the countries of the west.

Curse Sechaveh and his cunning, of course he had a scheme already in mind. Nor could Lizaveta divert the sky-stone to the Greenward Hills and claim an error in casting. Sechaveh knew her and Ruslan's prowess too well. He would understand the mistake was deliberate, and ferret out the reason for it.

Lizaveta took a slow breath, mastering frustration. "Varkevia's great merchant houses would not take such a setback lightly. Does Sechaveh wish to provoke war?"

"Of course not," Naavini said. "The mine's destruction must seem an act of the gods, not mages. The spell cast to divert the stone must be powerful enough to succeed, yet so subtly done that mages hired by the Varkevians to investigate cannot detect any traces of spellwork. Blood mages are not usually known for the subtlety of their casting, but you…I hear you are the most subtle mage in all of Arkennland."

The flattery was not subtle. In truth, it was so overt that Lizaveta suspected an attempt at distraction. Something did not quite add up about Naavini's visit. The plan was as crafty and ambitious as one of Sechaveh's, but he never would have confided such a politically sensitive matter to a junior mage. He would have come direct to Lizaveta to discuss it in person. Plus, that heightened, over-excited dance of Naavini's *ikilhia*…

"This is your idea, isn't it? Not Sechaveh's. Have you even presented the matter to him yet?" If the girl had not…a spell subtle enough to fool the Varkevians could also fool Sechaveh. It would not matter if Sechaveh knew Simon's location, if he could uncover no evidence a sky-stone strike was Lizaveta's doing.

Iron discipline instilled in her youth by fire and pain let Lizaveta keep her breathing steady, her *ikilhia* calm, as she awaited Naavini's answer.

Naavini's brown cheeks gained a hint of red. She hesitated, and Lizaveta wondered if she was foolish enough to try lying.

"It is my idea, and no, I haven't presented it to Lord Sechaveh. I haven't even told him about the sky-stone. I wanted to be certain my plan was possible, first."

Lizaveta allowed herself the tiniest of smiles. She could not have asked for a better opportunity. "A wise decision. Sechaveh will be far more impressed if you present him a fully realized plan. I, too, admire intelligence and ambition. But I cannot give you certainty of success until I have seen your calculations and charts and worked out if an undetectable diversion is possible. Do you have the charts with you?"

If the girl did, she would not leave the study alive. The gossamer protections woven about her *ikilhia* were no match for Lizaveta.

Naavini cocked her head, her dark eyes no longer quite so guileless. "No, I don't. You'll have to forgive me if I'm a trifle reluctant to hand over my work. What's to stop you from killing me and presenting my plan to Sechaveh as your own? I can bring you the information you need to design your spell, but only if you give me a binding blood oath that you won't seek my death, nor speak of the sky-stone to Sechaveh without me."

Lizaveta laughed in genuine amusement. "Do you imagine I need to chase after Sechaveh's favor? In truth, I'm quite curious why a clever mage like you would bother." Ninavel mages had no need to seek political patronage. Sechaveh's bargain with them was legendary: help provide his desert-locked city with water, obey his rare requests, and he would not interfere with any other magic they cast.

"Because I love the game of trade and nations. It's *fun*," Naavini said. "In the east, a mage can't become a spymistress. Rulers are too afraid of us. But here…here we can do anything." She leaned forward, holding Lizaveta's gaze. "Will you give me the oath I ask and cast on the sky-stone? In return, I offer to explain the design of my calculations. I'll even develop new mathematical methods to tackle any puzzles you care to solve. I can tell from reading your treatise how much you enjoy deciphering the mysteries of nature."

Ah, it was a shame Lizaveta must ensure Sechaveh never learned of this meeting. Naavini was right in thinking her offer of mathematical genius would be tempting. Yet Lizaveta wanted Simon's death more. "Shall I speak plainly? If I wished to kill you, no vow you extracted from me would stop your death. Nor have you Sechaveh's leverage to buy yourself protection from my casting. I will not vow never to cast against you. Mages live long; who can say if we shall always stay allies? What I would give is a blood oath that I have no intention of killing you."

There were other means of forever silencing Naavini than death. Changing the girl's flesh to stone, and binding her imprisoned soul so none but Lizaveta could touch it…yes, that might let her get some further use of Naavini's mathematical prowess, once the girl's will crumbled.

Naavini was still, her slender black brows knit in a frown. After a moment, she said slowly, "But you would vow not to speak to Sechaveh without me?"

"I suggest we each vow not to discuss the sky-stone with him until we both are present." Then Lizaveta could leave Naavini untouched until the casting of the diversion spell was complete, and ensure the girl's continuing silence once she and Ruslan were satisfied of the spell's success. Simple plans were often best.

Naavini was silent, her *ikilhia* leaping and writhing in reflection of her internal struggle. At last she nodded. "Done."

Her agreement was almost disappointing. Lizaveta had thought the girl intelligent enough to put up more of a fight. She must want very badly for her plan to succeed—so badly that her ambition blinded her to potential dangers. The pitfall of youth. Sly old Sechaveh would have had the foresight to fear fates other than death.

Experience was the best of teachers. Lizaveta smiled and drew her barbed knife.

"Let us make our vows."

LIZAVETA CHECKED THE SILVER TANGLE OF CHANNELS laid into the workroom floor once more. She had spent two very long days designing a spell based on Naavini's equations that would send ripple after invisible ripple of magic to nudge the sky-stone by infinitesimal degrees until it was on course to pulverize Simon. Another layer of spellwork would hasten the dissipation of traces, like brushing away a lizard's tracks on a dune.

"The design is perfect." Ruslan's admiration slid along their bond to warm her heart. He stood just beyond the outermost gleaming spiral of the pattern, ready to channel for her. "Sechaveh will never detect our involvement, so long as you are certain Naavini has not circumvented her oath."

"She has not." Lizaveta had kept careful watch on the girl. Naavini had not attempted to communicate with anyone. She did not even know they were casting tonight. She believed Lizaveta had not yet finished the spell design. The hour was well past midnight; Naavini would be asleep, unaware of the fate that awaited her.

Her innocence would not last long.

Lizaveta moved to the waist-high obsidian block of the anchor stone, where two *nathahlen* were shackled. A mother and child, not a pair of lovers, but the principle was the same. When Ruslan cast, he did not bother picking out particular *nathahlen*—he simply slaughtered one unfortunate victim after another until he raised enough power for his harness. Lizaveta prided herself on efficiency. Physical torment sparked *ikilhia* higher, yes, but anguish over a loved one's pain was the best enhancement of all.

The mother twisted frantically against her bonds, uncaring of the bloody wounds she inflicted on her wrists and ankles, and shouted muffled cries through her gag. Her eyes were locked on her teenage daughter, who wept in despairing gulps, her thin limbs trembling.

A tendril of Ruslan's *ikilhia* swept outward in a last check of the wards protecting the bedroom where Mikail and Kiran lay sleeping.

They are safe, Lizaveta assured him, repressing a sigh. The bedroom's protections were so powerful the spellwork was near blinding in intensity.

His attention returned to the workroom. *I am ready.*

Lizaveta raised her knife and reached for Ruslan's mind. They slid into perfect union. She worked as she had been taught, cutting and carving and maiming, stoking *nathahlen* souls to their utmost blaze. When she poured her victims' *ikilhia* through the channels, layering energies to build the spell, Ruslan shadowed her every move, controlling the flow of power with perfect precision.

The confluence moved in answer. The diversion spell took shape. But just as Lizaveta committed her will to casting, a silent explosion of energies battered the workroom wards.

Ruslan's focus broke. *The children!*

His mind jerked free of Lizaveta's, his attention jumping from the channels to the bedroom where wards had been forcibly breached. His *akhelyshen* were under attack, crying out for his aid.

The spell's blazing latticework bulged and roiled. Energies burst from Lizaveta's frantic grasp, primed to explode in catastrophic backlash.

RUSLAN! Her silent shriek carried all of her terror and fury, as she fought with every spark of her soul to master the magic about to destroy them both.

His mind snapped back into union with hers, and he threw strength to her unstinting. As he should have done in the first place, he ignored his *akhelyshen*'s cries and worked with desperate speed to help contain the disruption.

Lightning crackled off the backlashing channels, wringing a cry of agony from Lizaveta. Still she fought on, shredding and damping burning energies, struggling to stop the deadly wave from breaking. She yanked power from her own soul to fuel her efforts until her *ikilhia* sank to a guttering flicker.

The specter of death receded. At last, with all the channels scorched and dark, Lizaveta sank to her knees, hardly able to believe she had survived. Her head throbbed with a vicious ache, every nerve a bonfire of pain, but she was alive.

So was her mage-brother, though his *ikilhia* was as damaged and drained as hers. Instead of giving way to relief, Ruslan ran staggering for the door.

The children. Lizaveta struggled to her feet. She reached with sore, strained senses after Ruslan, and saw through his eyes as he charged into the breached bedroom.

Mikail and Kiran, burned and bleeding, crouched within a frail bubble of protective magic projected by a charm clutched in Mikail's shaking hands.

Aram Inara Naavini faced them. The girl gripped a dagger that shimmered with lethal spellwork fueled by a strange, wild reservoir of magic—a reservoir far too powerful for so weak a mage to have bound into the dagger's metal. A shielding spell of equal strength protected her body and *ikilhia*.

Naavini struck the dagger against the wavering barrier of magic from Mikail's charm. He yelped a wordless, desperate cry, and poured his *ikilhia* into his scant protection. Behind him, Kiran braced small hands on his mage-brother's back, sending a frantic stream of his own life through the contact to bolster Mikail's failing strength.

Ruslan, exhausted, reached as far as his injured *ikilhia* would allow and ripped the life straight out of every one of their sleeping servants. He threw the scavenged power to brace Mikail's shield, even as he hammered red magefire at the spell protecting Naavini.

"Who sent you?" he snarled, purely to distract her. Both he and Lizaveta knew the answer. The sharp yellow fire of the dagger's spellwork had an all too familiar taste.

Simon. He *had* sought reservoirs of power in the Greenward Hills ruins. He'd forged a weapon and a shield from his discoveries, handed the charms to this catspaw mage, and sent her to strike down Ruslan's apprentices just as they had killed his.

Naavini bared her teeth, still straining to pierce Mikail's protection. "You think I'm nothing but a puppet! Yet I sought and found your enemy in Alathia, long before your spies even realized where to look. I was the one who asked him for the means to hurt you. For Davan and Marca's sake."

"Those names mean nothing to me," Ruslan told Naavini, smashing at her protections.

Faint memory tugged at Lizaveta. A glimpse of dancers, bending and swaying like wind-whipped flames—

Naavini spat a wild laugh. "Of course you don't know them! You and your stone-hearted mage-sister care nothing for those you kill. But Davan and Marca were my *friends*. The only people I met in this gods-cursed city who didn't treat me as either a monster or a weapon because of my mage-talent. They offered me kindness and never once asked for anything in return. The bravest people and the best dancers I've ever seen, and your mage-sister slaughtered them like pigs!"

"You're either mad or a fool," Ruslan spat at her. His tattered *ikilhia* trembled under the strain of holding Mikail's shield while simultaneously attacking Naavini.

She's not a fool, Lizaveta warned him, recalling Naavini's careful maneuvering during their first conversation. The girl had known exactly what bait she offered. Limping hastily for the bedroom, Lizaveta cursed her own complacency in taking Naavini's oaths. She should have ripped through the girl's defenses and searched her mind then and there.

Regrets were of no use. Lizaveta reached the open doorway. She took a shuddering breath and strained her mage-sight to scrutinize Naavini's shielding spell.

Naavini looked down her knife-blade at Mikail, who'd fallen to his knees despite Ruslan's infusion of power, and Kiran, whose eyelids fluttered, his strength nearly spent. "Do you little vipers know my mistake? I thought your master cared about you. I was sure he couldn't keep his focus with you screaming for his help. But he and his mage-sister care only for themselves, first and always."

Mikail's bloody face twisted in a fierce, certain smile. "Your mistake was in thinking us weak," he panted. "Ruslan knew we could hold until he came to save us."

Ruslan had known no such thing. *Stop splitting your strength by shielding the children,* Lizaveta snapped at him. *Gather all the power you can and strike where I show you.* She flashed him the location of a pinprick flaw she'd discerned in Naavini's protection. *If you breach her shield, I'll handle the rest.*

Don't kill her, Ruslan replied, grim. *I wish to search her memories. Also, I wish her death to be slow.*

That, Lizaveta could agree with. Blackness floated around the edges of her vision; she forced consciousness to hold, ignored the red-hot needles piercing every muscle, and readied herself to bind Naavini's mind and magic.

Ruslan abandoned Mikail and struck with all the force he could muster. The magefire hammering Naavini's shield brightened to blinding levels. Lightning sheeted through the room as Naavini's shield fractured. Her dagger plunged down.

Lizaveta whipped tendrils of power through a gap and locked them tight around Naavini. The girl fought—not to break Lizaveta's hold, but to tear apart her own *ikilhia* and escape into death.

Naavini should never have had a chance against an *akheli*. But the disaster in the workroom had so savaged Lizaveta's *ikilhia* that she found herself losing the battle. Naavini's soul was dissolving through her grasp, and she could not *hold* it—

Ruslan, help me!

Ruslan was not listening. He was caught in a desperate fight to stem the damage from the spelled dagger plunged deep in Mikail's chest. Kiran, sobbing, threw power born of anguish into his stricken mage-brother.

Furious, Lizaveta caught at Naavini's fading consciousness. *Go into death, then, with the knowledge of your failure. Not only do I live, but the one mage who could possibly best me will die like you. Ruslan and I will recast the spell. The sky-stone will strike, and nothing will be left of Simon Levanian but cinders.*

Ragged, defiant laughter echoed back. *Go ahead. Before I ever came to you, I told Sechaveh you'd found Simon in the Greenward Hills. I showed Sechaveh your treatise. Kill Simon with the sky-stone, and Sechaveh will know you defied his edict.*

Naavini was not lying. Truth blazed from the shreds of her soul. This plan was all her doing, no one else's. Simon had given her the dagger and shield in hope she could kill Ruslan's *akhelyshen*, but he'd known nothing of any sky-stones, nor had the least clue Naavini intended a plan that could result in his death. She'd played to Simon's assumptions, just as she had to Lizaveta's, and fooled him as thoroughly.

The full extent of Naavini's cunning hit Lizaveta like a spear to the heart. The girl had arranged a defeat for them with every possible outcome. If Ruslan had ignored the attack and successfully helped Lizaveta cast, they would have roused Sechaveh's wrath and lost the confluence. Even now, Lizaveta was left with the choice between losing the confluence and losing the chance to strike down Simon—and that was no choice at all. If Sechaveh was watching for defiance, she dared not touch the sky-stone.

Naavini's bitter jubilation swelled. *The best part is, with Simon alive, you'll keep right on believing he's your only real danger. But so long as you keep slaughtering people like cattle, I'm not the only one who'll seek your death. One day, someone will find your weakness, and you will fall.*

The last scraps of her *ikilhia* slipped away. Lizaveta slumped against the wall, surrendering for a moment to agony and exhaustion.

One day, someone will find your weakness. Lizaveta knew just what that weakness was. Gritting her teeth, she forced aching legs to propel her to Ruslan's side.

She had failed, but her mage-brother had succeeded. The dagger was gone from Mikail's chest. His *ikilhia* was dim but whole, his wounds healed, though he lay sprawled unconscious on his bed. Ruslan sat beside him, head bowed low. The red blaze of his soul had guttered to faint embers. At his feet lay Naavini's dagger, now nothing more than dead metal, its spellwork gone.

Kiran stared at Naavini's lifeless body. When Lizaveta picked up the dagger, he caught her sleeve, his blue eyes huge in his tear-streaked face. "Did you really kill her friends? Is that why she wanted to hurt us?"

Ruslan stirred. "A ridiculous lie. Mages are not friends with *nathahlen*. Did I not tell you, Kiran, that we use criminals as fuel for our casting? No one misses such brutish creatures. This foolish mage was merely jealous of our power. But as you see, she could not match it."

We nearly died, Lizaveta sent at him, sharp as a stab. Anger beat in her like the wild throb of the confluence. How, *how* could Ruslan have let his focus lapse? His error had spared them Sechaveh's wrath, but that wasn't the point.

She had been so certain her mage-brother would never fail her. Yet tonight, he'd almost killed her.

Ruslan shut his eyes. *I won't ask you to forgive me. My mistake was inexcusable, but it will not happen again.* His own fury had crystallized into black determination. *Simon will die for this. I no longer care where he hides or what we risk.*

It matters to me! We must not lose the confluence. Besides, this was not Simon's doing. Lizaveta showed him all she'd learned from Naavini. *You must control your anger. If Naavini could not have our deaths, she wanted your rage to cripple us.*

Ruslan grunted in harsh dismissal. *The girl is nothing. Lesser mages and even* nathahlen *may be cunning, but what does it avail them without power? She could never have touched us without Simon's help. He is our true enemy.*

Yet Lizaveta remembered Naavini's bitter certainty that another like her would come. Even if Lizaveta found it hard to believe other mages might possess Naavini's bizarre combination of intellectual genius and irrational attachment to *nathahlen*.

I too want Simon's death, she told Ruslan. *But we must not let desire for revenge drive us to rash action.*

I will not be rash, Ruslan said, each word as hard and cold as glacial ice. *Sechaveh will not see my hand. But I will see Simon dead, even if I must risk my own destruction to achieve his.*

That was not reassuring. Lizaveta wrestled down anger and worry and set a hand on his shoulder. "Rushenka, you're exhausted. Go and rest, so you may recover your strength and recast your wards. I'll watch over the children."

It was a measure of his depletion that he did not argue. He summoned one last spark of magefire, watched with narrowed eyes as Naavini's body burned to ash, and stumbled out the door.

Lizaveta's body cried out for sleep, but her will was adamantine. The pain of her wounded *ikilhia* was nothing she couldn't endure. She hugged a sniffling Kiran, soothed his fears, helped him cuddle up beside Mikail and slide into exhausted slumber.

She looked down at the sleeping children, her hand clenched tight on the handle of Naavini's knife.

The girl had not been mistaken in her assessment of Ruslan. Mikail and Kiran were his weakness, and a terrible one. Lizaveta still shuddered to think how close she had come to dying. This, after centuries without a single moment of fear.

She should kill the boys. Here, now, while Ruslan was so drained he was dead to the aether. She'd make their death quick and clean; she had no desire to see them suffer. She could make it seem as though an accomplice of Naavini's had come and overpowered her in her injured state. Ruslan would continue to blame Simon, and never think to suspect her. After all, her grief would be real. They were lovely children.

But might the deaths of his *akhelyshen* shatter Ruslan's hold on his temper and destroy his judgment? Lizaveta turned the knife over in her hands, torn. Which was the greater risk?

Her mage-brother was a quick study. He might already have learned his lesson. But if he had not…

Still holding the knife, Lizaveta made a silent promise to the boys' sleeping faces: *You will not be his death or mine.* Any further glimpses of dangerous weakness in Ruslan, and she would kill, no matter his attachment to the children.

Lizaveta settled into a chair and watched the boys sleep, her eyes burning and her heart hard, until at last Ruslan woke and sent a muzzy thought her way.

Are they safe?

Lizaveta set down the knife. "For now."

THE TATTERED PRINCE
AND THE DEMON VEILED

BRADLEY P. BEAULIEU

— The Song of the Shattered Sands —

IN THE WESTERN QUARTER OF THE AMBER CITY LIES a congested riddle of streets known as the Knot. There, a man named Brama walks, cloaked in the anonymity awarded to men who keep their heads down and their words to themselves. Years ago Brama would have refused to walk these streets, not without due compensation, in any case, and he certainly wouldn't have called them home. He'd been a street tough then, a rangy gutter wren with the skill of a locksmith and the heart of a thief. He'd been brash, even bold, but no one would have called him brave. He would have laughed at the very thought of the Knot becoming familiar to him, but the wheel turns and times change. Brama is no longer the same man he was then. The young Brama wouldn't even recognize him.

Truth be told, Brama could live in any quarter of the city he chose, but he calls this hellish place home for one simple reason: the Knot is populated by those who've learned to keep to themselves. To be sure, there are wolves as well as sheep. They prowl, preying on the weak, but Brama was never much of a victim, and only a fool would call him one now. If the pattern of scars over his face, neck, and arms aren't enough to convince, his black-laugher scowl certainly is.

For his part, Brama doesn't much care what anyone thinks of him as long as they leave him in peace. He exists, whiling away the days, nursing his dwindling fortune, wondering what the city and the desert gods have in store for him. He's been in the Knot for nearly two years—me along with him—and he's begun to wonder if the gods have forgotten him.

Surely the gods would not have forgotten a man like Brama, though they may have grown bored of his indolence, which would explain why, on this particular day, instead of heading toward his room above the tannery, Brama breaks his routine and heads down a back alley for the banks of the Haddah. Spring rains have returned to the desert, and the river is swelling. He goes to the place he favored when he was young and watches a group of children playing skipjack. One by one they sprint and leap from the bank onto a canvas held taut by their gleeful friends, bounce into the air, arms and legs flailing, and fall into the surging water below. Some of them he still recognizes, though they've clearly grown; others are new. Their laughs and their games make him feel as though he's passed beyond the veil and now watches the world of the living, his feet forever rooted in the further fields. That's what his father used to say happened to those who pine for their old lives. And he does pine at times, so much that it hurts.

Sitting in the shade of the embankment, hidden beneath his cowl, he watches those gutter wrens the whole afternoon. He stands only when the children exit the water, still dripping, ready to depart en masse. How he wishes he could join them. How he wishes he could run the streets as he once did. But that was a different life. And he is now a different man.

As he turns to leave, he spots a girl watching the same group of children, pining, perhaps, as Brama was, for younger, simpler days. The girl is young yet herself. If she's seen more than fifteen summers, I'm an innocent lamb set for slaughter. Red ribbons are braided through her hair, a common style in the city of late, and she wears the simple clothes of a lowborn Sharakhani girl, but there's something odd about her. She stands tall, clasping her hands before her as a poet might before reading her lines. It's unconscious, I'm certain, a tell as plain as one could be.

Perhaps aware of being watched, she turns and takes note of Brama, scans the riverbank and the plaza behind him with chary eyes, then rushes away. Even in this she has the posture and bearing of a noblewoman. But this isn't the most interesting thing about her—to Brama *or* to me. It is the fact that, since the moment he spotted her, there were notes of light surrounding her. Like sundogs shining in a cloud-scraped sky, they shimmer, they glimmer. They brighten here and dim there. They move with her like the desert wind summoning demons from the sand as it gusts through Sharakhai's tight and winding streets.

She glances back several times, but Brama chooses not to follow. He can see she's scared, and who can blame her? The way Brama looks she'd be a fool not to be a *little* scared. Then she's gone, lost down an alley. There's a strange yearning that follows her absence. A deep desire for…something. Her presence? *Foolish*, Brama thinks. He doesn't even know her. But then he wonders…

From around his neck he removes a leather necklace. Strung there like an amulet is a falcon's egg sapphire. It's one of the more priceless gems in all the desert, but one would never know by looking at it, with its surfaces grimed with oil and soot. It's wrapped tightly in leather cord so that it looks like a cargo net lifting a dirty chunk of sky. This is my prison, the place I've been held since Brama and the girl known as the White Wolf trapped me here.

Wrapping the leather necklace around his hand with a flick of his wrist, Brama tightens his grip on the gemstone and steps down into the mud. His sandals sink as he walks, squelch as he trudges forward. When he comes to a place where the water has pooled, he squats and stares into a reflection that is imperfect—much like the landscape of his scar-torn face. The scars are an unsubtle reminder of a time when *I* was the master and *he* the chained. He was a comely man once—even *I* recognize that, a being who'd seen countless years pass in the Shangazi. It might have been why I was so pleased to make him cut himself; something about seeing himself destroy his own beauty pleased me. Part of me now regrets having done it to him, but I was wroth with the godling children who'd come for me; wroth as well that I'd been forced to take Brama when the one I'd really wanted was the White Wolf.

"She was never yours to take," Brama said to his reflection.

For months now Brama has somehow been able to hear snippets of my thoughts. It happens when my guard is down, so of course I quickly replace my walls, but I know already they will fail once more—my will is strong, as is my god-given power, but nothing I have done in this place seems to last.

In the water's reflection, a new visage forms, slowly replacing his. Long black spikes lift from his scalp as his curly locks of hair recede. Horns jut from a black-skinned forehead, curving back and around like a ram's crown carved from ebony. Slanted eyes tinged with rust replace the green of Brama's, and while Brama had always possessed features that were fair, more feminine cheeks and lips and chin replace his own.

Fear, as it always does, builds in Brama's breast. It isn't so much as it once was, though, which pleases me greatly. He of all people knows the danger I represent, but he's become accustomed to me, a necessary first step in gaining my freedom and all the *more* important considering the effect we just witnessed illuminating that girl.

I say to him, "What is it you wish, my master?"

"How many times must I ask you not to call me that?"

"Are you not my master?"

"You are a fiend, and my enemy."

My visage laughs, and both of us feel a brightening, a candle lit and doused in as little time as it takes a mortal child to giggle. "What shall I call you, then? Brama the Mighty? Brama the Bold?"

Though he chooses not to reply, curiosity overrides his fears, creating a strange alchemy of caution and hope. "Tell me of the girl," he says. "Why was she twinkling like that?"

"It's how I see you sometimes."

"Mortals, you mean."

"Yes."

"But why does it happen? What has it revealed about her?"

"It means that she is someone who will affect your fate, or the fate of others who are dear to you, or both. It means she is someone around whom the winds of fate do whorl."

"That tells me nothing."

"It's no more complex than predicting the weather by judging the clouds and the smell in the air. It is another form of sight, granted me by Goezhen, or perhaps a thing passed to me when I was crafted from his soul. Who can know any longer?"

"Is that why you wanted Çeda? Was *she* like that?"

"Oh, yes." How bright that one had been. How very bright.

Brama considers this for a time, and I wonder what happened by the river. He'd been as transfixed as I, watching that girl rush away from the Haddah. For the first time since I've known him, I feel curiosity emanating from him like heat from a brand, and an urge to involve himself in something, anything, outside the tiny world he's made for himself. I resist the instinct to influence him—he's grown disturbingly good at sensing when I'm doing so. Instead, I simply wait.

"Shall I find her again?" he finally asks.

I hide my grin as I speak, "That is completely up to you, my Lord Brama."

He seems irked by the answer but says nothing in return. Slowly, my visage fades from the silty puddle, until he's staring at himself once more. He runs his fingers over the kindling-pile pattern of his scars. He stares around, to the now-empty banks of the Haddah. He feels the empty space inside him opening up again. He may hide it from others but I know how desperate he's been to find someone. A friend with whom he can share stories. A woman he might love and be loved by. He's confusing the lights with the sort of young love all mortal youths seem to experience. I do nothing to disabuse him of the notion—it is yet another step on the long road to freedom, after all—but it also touches my heart. I've not lived with humanity for so long that I am unaffected by the emotions my hosts feel.

Soon, he's standing and tugging on the cowl that keeps his face hidden from the world. His mind is elsewhere at last, and it leaves me alone with my secret. The girl. The lights around her. It's true that they are tied to Brama's fate. But more accurately, they are tied to mine, and I have no doubt now that this girl will be the key to escaping my faceted prison once and for all.

THREE DAYS PASS BEFORE BRAMA SPOTS THE SAME girl. He's standing in a darkened doorway as she approaches a spicemonger's cart a half-block distant. She's wearing a different dress, a blue and white jalabiya. It's as threadbare as the last but well made, with fine stitching, the sort a woman of means might once have worn. Her black keffiyeh lies loosely around her head, but oddly, as if she wasn't born to it and had only recently started wearing one. She glances warily along the street as the plump fruit seller uses her pewter scoop to fill a burlap sack with dried wolfberry.

Brama's curiosity rises. And for good reason. Wolfberry has a pleasant enough flavor, but the aftertaste is bitter as oversteeped tea. For this reason the fruit is not favored by most market-goers in Sharakhai, but it sells well enough in the Shallows, mainly for its ability to help ease the lows that go hand in hand with an addiction to black lotus. The girl shows none of the effects of addiction herself. Her hands don't shake as she passes over a small handful of copper, nor are her lips bloodless, and her eyes are anything but sallow. There is, however, an undeniable weight on her shoulders. A sense of worry. A natural reaction, I suppose, if someone she loves is deep in the throes of withdrawal, but that wouldn't explain why she's constantly looking up and down the street as though she's worried about being discovered.

As it did the other day when Brama first spotted her, a play of lights flit about her, tumbling through the air. They look like a chromatic flock of cressetwing moths, mesmerizing as they brighten in the shadows and fade in the shafts of morning sunlight.

They have never failed to amaze me. And it's no different for Brama. He stares, rapt. But as the wind-tossed flecks of light slowly disappear, it bothers him greatly. He's suddenly convinced she will die. Brama has no way of knowing, but the lights never remain with a single soul for long, and I have no way of sharing this with him, not until he summons me again. Truth be told, though, I don't know that I would even if he did. His indecision glows like a beacon fire, a thing somehow pleasing to my muted senses. It's clear he wants to go to her, but what would he say? He knows by now, or at least suspects, that her fate is entwined with his, but the likelihood of scaring her with but a word is a near certainty.

No sooner does the thought cross his mind than the girl spies him in the doorway of the shisha den. The sheer depth of terror seen in her eyes convinces me of two things: first, she's afraid of being found, and second, she isn't sure *who* might be hunting her, else why be so frightened of a man she's never met?

Wrapping her keffiyeh tighter around her face, she snatches the bag of wolfberries from the spicemonger and sets off briskly down a different street than she'd taken here.

Brama, feeling more than foolish, debates whether to follow. *What would I tell her?* he muses. *Hello. I'm Brama. I've seen lights around you. We're fated to meet.* He laughs at the very thought, but then notices a man exiting the street the girl had taken here. He wears beaten trousers and a dirty, sweat-stained shirt. He's short and lithe as a willow, and moves with the gait of a man used to masking the sound of his footfalls. He weaves past two men carrying a dusty, rolled-up carpet, then follows the girl.

He is the one she fears. Brama and I both know it.

Another block up, where the traffic grows thicker, the girl glances back. She looks straight past the man following her to Brama, and then ducks into a winding street that will take her toward the heart of the Knot, a maze of narrow alleys where one might easily lose pursuers if one knows the paths to take. No doubt she does, but she doesn't see the man turn and sprint along the street closest to Brama, an avenue that could easily be used, assuming one moves fast enough, to cut her off.

After a moment's indecision, Brama draws his knife from its sheath along his forearm and sprints after him. Brama takes more care than I've given him credit for. I forget that he grew up on these streets, that he once prowled the city's rooftops. He moves deceptively fast, and uses the crowd to his advantage, hugging the edge of the street, so that when the man glances back, Brama slows to a walking pace and angles toward a ramshackle chandler's shop. He reaches for the candles hanging like sausages from a length of twine as if they were exactly what he'd been after.

The man moves on, and Brama resumes the chase, moving faster now, nearing the place where the angled avenue the girl took rejoins the street they both now race along. Ahead lies a square where the buildings lean precariously, a tangled courtyard of sorts, formed and held in place by a crisscross of rooms and roofs and makeshift bridges built on the shoulders of the original structures. The man steps into the shadow of a bath house awning as the girl appears ahead, moving briskly but warily.

Brama creeps along the rough stone of the bathhouse behind the waiting man, his confidence and nervousness mixing to create an intoxicating brew. I, on the other hand, sense something amiss, the sort of worry that buzzes at the base of the skull like a trapped hornet. Had I my proper form I could discern what it was with a moment of concentration, but trapped as I am all I can do is to try to warn Brama.

One moment I'm pushing Brama to be wary, and the next, Brama's senses flare as the sound of pounding footfalls nears. Brama dodges to one side as someone barrels into him from behind. Pain bright burns along his side and the back of his ribs.

Brama loses his knife as he tries to break his fall against the dusty street. He scrabbles away from his attacker, a man with a wild beard, wilder hair, and a ratty thawb—a beggar from the looks of him, but I can already see he's no beggar. His teeth are clean. His hair and beard, though messy, are anything but grimy. He'd pass for a beggar at ten paces, but to my eye the disguise is plain as a mummer's mask. Whether Brama senses the same, I do not know, but given the man's aquiline nose and high brow, I have few doubts he's the ally of the Malasani who waits in the shadows.

As Brama and his attacker wrestle across the dusty courtyard, those who'd been loitering or walking along the street back away. Brama takes another cut along his forearm from the slim, straight knife. They roll into a trash heap and his assailant pounces on top of Brama. The man stabs the knife at Brama's neck. Brama snatches the man's wrist, holding the knife at bay. Then he rams a knee into the attacker's ribs, and rolls out from under him, twisting the man's wrist until he drops the blade on the dirt.

As the man Brama was following rushes to help his comrade, Brama rises and backs away, spreading his attention between the two men. Wisely, his opponents fan out, and soon it's plain to see they're used to fighting with one another. The smaller man darts in. The moment Brama turns to face him, the wild-haired one rushes forward. In one sinuous move, he throws Brama over his hip and slams him to the ground.

Blood pours from the knife wound along Brama's back. It flows along his forearm as well. For me it is like a fount from the gods, the very source of the essence of life. I would drink of it if I could, so heady is its scent, but a wall stands between us. Yet it doesn't have to be so. If Brama would simply accept the power I've offered him... I offer it again as the beggar straddles him, as he holds the tip of his slim knife against Brama's neck. For the first time since being trapped within this gem, I worry. There's no telling what these men might do when they find the sapphire hidden beneath Brama's shirt. *Please*, I beg Brama, *take but a sip of my power. Take it, and save yourself.*

Brama, however, remains resolute. I feel the revulsion and hatred he holds for me. For the first time, however, I feel temptation as well.

The man kneels on Brama's chest. "Who are you?" he asks, his Malasani accent thick.

"I am but a relic of a man," Brama replies. "A ruin."

The Malasani grins. "Even ruins can be buried, so I ask you once again—"

He never finishes those words, for just then a length of wood appears, piercing the man's neck with a sound like a hook piercing a pig's neck before it's hung for slaughter. Yellow fletching graces one end of the shaft of wood, a bloody broadhead the other.

The man's eyes go wide. He coughs wetly, spitting warm blood across Brama's face. He tries to pull the bolt free, but stops when his own blood spurts in a torrent across Brama's shoulder. His jaw works, as if he's still trying to ask his question of Brama—*who are you?*—but then Brama rolls him aside and scrambles to a stand.

Ten paces away stands a man in a stained nightdress, one foot in the stirrup of a crossbow as he strains to lever the string back. He looks as though he can hardly keep his feet, but he manages to lock the string in place. With shaking arms, he lifts the crossbow and sets a fresh bolt into the channel, but before he can lift it and aim, Brama's second attacker darts away into a tea house that has just opened its doors. As the tea house's proprietor shouts in surprise after him, the lanky man in his night clothes lifts the tip of the crossbow until it's aimed at Brama's chest. The girl stands behind him, a slim knife to hand, looking like she knows how to use it.

"A question was posed to you," the man says, crossbow poised and ready. He speaks Sharakhani well, but with noticeable notes of a Malasani nobleman's upbringing. He glances at Brama's attacker, who's fallen still, staring at the sky as blood drains weakly around the shaft of the crossbow bolt sticking out of his neck. "As he seems indisposed, perhaps you would be so kind as to give *me* the answer in his stead."

"I am no one," Brama replies.

"You're a liar," he spits back, and raises the butt of the crossbow to his shoulder.

The lights have begun to swirl around the girl once more. Her eyes are round with worry. She keeps looking back over her shoulder, toward a cluttered alley that leads to another part of the Shallows. She's deferring to the crossbowman, a malnourished man with sunken, jaundiced eyes and hollowed cheeks, but she clearly wishes to leave, to run, to hide themselves in the city. As she swallows, perhaps stifling something she was about to say, the lights around her move to encapsulate the man as well, though the effects aren't nearly as bright as they are around her.

I can feel Brama's desire to leave, though he isn't so desperate as this girl. He wants to return to his room and hide from the outside world, but his curiosity over the lights, the girl, is too strong. "I am a man born and raised in these very streets," Brama finally says. "I see who comes and who goes. I've seen her"—he points to the girl—"come here, bright-eyed, worried. And today I saw that man, the one you just let get away, follow her. I know when there's trouble about, and I didn't want it to befall her."

After a moment's pause, the man lowers the crossbow a fraction. "These are your streets then? You're like to the Silver Spears, beholden to the Kings of Sharakhai?"

Brama spits onto the dirt. "No. But this is my home, and I would protect it."

He looks Brama up and down, his eyes lingering on Brama's scars. "A tattered prince."

Brama nods. "A tattered prince."

"In the future"—he begins backing away, grabbing the girl's

arm as he goes—"if you happen upon me *or* my sister, you'll be sure to walk the other way."

"Wait." Brama takes a step forward, but stops when the man brings the crossbow up. "Who are you?"

The man merely backs away, crossbow in one hand, the girl's wrist in the other, then he and the girl turn and jog down the street. Soon they're lost from sight, and the bystanders, who'd been watching warily, one by one lose interest and return to their day.

THE FOLLOWING MORNING, AN INSISTENT POUNDING shakes the door of Brama's room above the tannery. The smells in the air are horrible, acrid, like horse piss, but it keeps people away, and that's all he really cares about. As he rolls out of bed and stares at the door, the memories of the fight in the streets play across his mind. He wears only his trousers and bandages around his wounds. He probes them gently, finds them to be healing faster than he's expected. A gift from me, though I don't tell him so.

When the pounding comes again, it's more insistent. "Open this sodding door, Brama!" a deep voice shouts.

Brama pulls on a shirt, takes up his curved kenshar from the bedside table, and unsheathes it. He stares at the sapphire, *my* sapphire, and a vision of the man he'd fought in the streets flashes through his mind. As he slips the necklace over his head and stuffs it into his shirt, I feel something I've been working toward since becoming trapped in this gem. I was beginning to think it would never happen, but the relief in Brama, even if slight, is clear.

Relief…toward *me*, the one who'd tortured him mercilessly for months on end. He doesn't *trust* me—I doubt he'll ever truly trust me—but he's beginning to *rely* on me, which is just as good. He knows well the power embodied in me. He knows he can use it. Have I not offered it a thousand times and a thousand times more? He has but to say the word. It's clear he hasn't yet made up his mind about accepting my offer, but this is a delicious first step. Like a wedge being hammered into wood, I'm certain it won't be long before his resolve cracks.

Brama steps lightly toward the door. For all my smug pleasure, I grow worried as he reaches for the latch. I'm vulnerable, beholden to a *mortal*, a thing that infuriates me when I dwell on it overlong. It makes me wonder what I've done to displease my lord Goezhen, but I also know it could grow worse. Well worse. There's no telling whose hands I might fall into were Brama to lose me or fall to an enemy's blade. No telling what they might do if my presence within the gem is detected. In Brama, at least, I know the sort of man he is. Thus far, he's taken the utmost care not to reveal my nature.

When Brama opens the door, he finds not the assassin, but a towering man with one hunched shoulder and a deep, ragged scar running over his left eye.

Brama's voice is gravel and stones as he speaks the man's name. "Kymbril."

One side of the scarred giant's mouth crooks upward. "Didn't know if you'd remember me, boy."

"I'm not a boy." Brama looks him up and down. "And you're a bit hard to forget."

Kymbril stares over Brama's shoulder into the room. One of his eyes is colored shit brown, and the other, the one with the scar, is a grey-blue, like the overcast skies of desert winter. It's what earned Kymbril his nickname, the Mismatched Man. "You going to invite me in?"

"I'm busy."

"Doing what?"

"Sleeping."

Kymbril grins his toothy grin; his mismatched eyes shine like the edge of a knife. "You're a joker, you are. Be careful it doesn't earn you a missing tooth or two. Wouldn't want that pretty smile of yours ruined." He bulls forward, daring Brama to stop him. Brama lets him pass, then closes the door behind him. Like a forge's flame fanned by the bellows, I feel Brama's worry being stoked by Kymbril's presence. Surprisingly, though, it's more about the girl than it is about himself. He knows as well as I do this visit has something to do with her. Sliding the sheath back over the kenshar's blade, he lofts it toward the tabletop. It clatters across the wood and falls to the floor with a thud.

Brama sits on the room's lone chair, leaning into it as if he were some duty-ridden king preparing to suffer through the day's final petition. Kymbril, meanwhile, takes in the room, examining the table, the pile of clothes in the corner, the space between the bed and the wall.

"Get on with it," Brama says.

Kymbril continues his inspection as if Brama hadn't spoken. When he seems satisfied, he sits on Brama's bed as if the room were his, and rests elbows on knees, the way a dear friend might before imparting unfortunate news. "Already warned you once, boy. There'll be no warning the third time."

Brama says nothing, but I can feel the desire in him for Kymbril to do something. Anything. The rage he has for me and the pain he'd endured when he'd been mine is now a deep well Brama draws on when it suits him. Such things would crush most men, but in Brama it has become the fuel he uses to make his own fire burn brighter. It's saved him more than once, but it's also landed him into trouble.

"Yesterday," Kymbril begins, "you were seen speaking with a man named Nehir."

"I don't know anyone named Nehir."

"Thin. Handsome bloke, but has the look of the reek about him. I believe he was holding a crossbow on you?"

"I don't know anything about him."

Kymbril nods as if Brama is being perfectly reasonable. "Then why were you talking with him?"

"A few men were following him. Didn't like the look of them, so…we had words."

Kymbril smiles genuinely. "Had words… I like that." The big man frowns, lost in thought. "You seen them around before? Nehir and his little sister, Jax?"

Brama brightens upon learning her name. He savors it a moment. *Jax.* "Never saw Nehir before that day. Didn't even know his name until you said it just now. But I've seen the girl here and there."

Kymbril waits for more, then frowns when Brama doesn't continue. "That's your story?"

"That's my story."

Kymbril nods. "Very well. Now I'm going to tell *you* a story, Brama. And when I'm done I'm going to ask you a question, and you're going to answer it for me." He pauses, licks his lips and stares at the ceiling, as if ordering the events in his mind. "A few months back our young man, Nehir, shows up in one of my parlors. Smokes a while. Some expensive tabbaq, I'm told. Then he gets raging drunk on our finest wine, which, I readily admit, is not all that fine to begin with. He starts telling everyone who'll listen how he's a lord of Malasan, how his holding had been stolen from him by a neighboring duke, how he'd been chased from his homeland here to Sharakhai. Vowed revenge, he did. On the lord who killed his family. On those who stood by and let it happen. Even swore he'd kill the king of Malasan himself if he wasn't restored to his family seat. Everyone humors him because he's buying araq, wine, whatever they want, but they're all grinning behind their cups, and when he leaves, they're laughing before the door even slams home.

"A few days pass, and Nehir stumbles in through that same door, already two sheets gone, saying much the same thing. He buys more for the house, starts waxing on about knives in the night and revenge against the mountain lords of Malasan, but this time, a little girl shows up and leads him stumbling back into the streets. And here we come to the interesting part, Brama, so pay attention. Not a week passes before a man from Malasan darkens the doorway of that very same parlor. Thin man. Calm. As likely to knife you as smile. You know the type. He asks a few questions. Drops a coin or two in the process. He wants to know about Nehir—what he looks like, whether the parlor maid had seen him since, where he might be found now. This news drifts to me, as you might imagine. Didn't think much of it at the time, but I had my best man, Maru, check into it."

Brama knew Maru. Everyone in the Shallows did. He was a pit fighter once, but he'd found the competition too equitable, so he left and joined Kymbril's gang in search of friendlier sands over which to sail. He'd since built a reputation for being as vicious as he was skilled with a blade.

"Maru found neither Nehir *nor* the girl, so I put it from my mind. Figured they'd moved on. But then, lo and behold, not two weeks later word comes that a few of my regular patrons aren't looking for reek with the same sort of fervor they once had. Some stop buying altogether. Makes a man wonder, that does. Makes him *worry*. So I send Maru out sniffing, and what does he find? That someone's been funneling Malasani black into the Shallows without my leave."

Brama's curiosity is piqued, as is mine. Until this point he thought *Kymbril* had sent those men after Nehir. He thought he'd be dealing with a loss of one of Kymbril's own men at Brama's hands. But now it's clear there's a third player. He might just come out and ask it—*Who was the man? You must know something!*—but mortals have a curious way of filling silences and revealing more than they mean to, so Brama silently waits.

"You can imagine"—Kymbril reaches down and scuffs bits of dirt off the tops of his worn leather boots—"the sort of black cloud hanging over me when I found out. You can imagine the sort of imaginative phrases that came out of my demure fucking mouth. I've been looking for Nehir ever since. I'm not too much of a man that I can't admit I've been thwarted thus far. Maru's normally quite good at rooting such men out, but Nehir's a tricky one. Then I hear something strange. Do you know what it was, Brama?"

Brama shakes his head.

"I hear that some man riddled with enough scars to make a soldier blush gets into it with two men chasing Nehir and Jax like hounds on a brace of wounded hares. That true, Brama? You following those men?"

"I was."

Kymbril nods, neither pleased nor displeased. "Thought so." His brow creases as if he's working out the final pieces of a puzzle but can't quite get to them to fit. "You can imagine how a man in my position might wonder why you'd do such a thing. Why you'd protect them. Doesn't seem to be a reason. Unless…" He purses his lips, the picture of a man lost in thought, then nods as if the last of the pieces have fallen into place and the painting is now clear. "Unless you have a vested interest. You know that term, Brama? A *vested interest?*"

A manic gaze had replaced the look of sufferance in Kymbril's ill-matched eyes, and the tightness in Brama is building. He's ready for anything from Kymbril. As am I.

"A vested interest means you protected him because he *means* something to you. Let's say Nehir was your brother. You'd protect him then, wouldn't you? Or if he was paying you. Then you'd *certainly* protect him. Tell me it isn't so."

"I never met him before that day, Kymbril. I swear it."

The muscles along Kymbril's shoulders bunch. "He *swears* it." He stands and stabs a knotted branch of a finger at Brama's chest. "When I was your age, I was already carving out my territory, right here in the Knot. I took it from a man who was as cruel a bastard as I've ever come across. But while I was coming into my prime, he was going rheumy with age. He was worried more about the tea that helped his gout than the men who ran his reek for him. Do my eyes look rheumy to you, Brama?" He cracks the knuckles on one hand loudly, then does the same to the other. "Do I look like I couldn't take down a bone crusher with one fist?"

"You are the envy of all who survey you. As fit a man as I've ever seen."

With blinding speed, Kymbril grabs Brama by the throat and drives him backward. The chair tips over and Brama falls to the floor. He doesn't move a muscle to stop Kymbril, even though I offer him all the power he needs. I am more incensed at Kymbril's actions than I ever thought I'd be. Coming here to Brama's home and pretending he owns all he lays his eyes on…

"Are you working for Nehir?" Kymbril asks, his breath heavy with lemon and garlic. "Be careful how you answer, now. Take your time. It could mean your life."

His hand is around Brama's neck, squeezing hard enough to bruise, pinching Brama's windpipe so tightly his breath comes in choking gasps. Brama shows no pain, though, nor does he flinch, not even when Kymbril lifts him by the neck and slams him down onto the warped floorboards.

"I work for no one," Brama replies.

"Not even me?" A threat. An offer.

"Especially not for you."

Kymbril laughs a deep rumble of a laugh. His eyes drift down to Brama's neck, where the sapphire in its dirty leather wrapping has spilled from his shirt. "Man could stand to make a pretty pile of coin, he sold a thing like that."

"I could never sell *this*, Kymbril."

"Oh? Why's that?"

"After I fucked your mum every which way but sideways, she handed it to me with a smile so bright that tears came to my eyes. Told me never to part with it as she placed it in my hands."

Kymbril stares, eyes crazed, even a bit fearful, as if he can't figure out why Brama isn't more scared of him. But then his face softens and he laughs, a loud affair, the sort the drug lord is known for. "You're a twisted little fuck, you are." Then he shoves Brama away, stands, and walks out, chuckling, as if Brama hadn't just denied him something he very much wanted.

A SHORT WHILE LATER, BRAMA STARES INTO A BRASS mirror hung above the wash basin. His room is dark, but there's a candle on the table below the mirror, lighting the carpet-weave pattern of his scars in a ghastly pallor. "Did you know he would come?"

"I'm no god, Brama. I cannot see the future."

He chooses his next words with care. "I need to find the girl."

I stare back at him, calm for all the anticipation that's boiling up inside me. Even though I'm bound, even though I'm imprisoned and beholden to Brama, the things Kymbril revealed have lit a fire in me. Kymbril is now a part of the light that surrounds the girl, Jax, as is her brother, Nehir, as is the assassin chasing them. I know it is so. I just don't know *how* as yet, or why. But that is all part of the wonder of this gift given me by Goezhen. Like a flower unfolding, it changes every time but is no less beautiful for it.

"Why would you care if she lives or dies?" I ask. "You've never even spoken to her."

He knows I can sense his thoughts and still he lies. "I don't *care* for her."

"Do you not?"

His face has begun to flush. "She's being preyed upon by her brother and by the people of her homeland. Soon Kymbril will have her, and when he does, he won't let her go until he's wrung every last copper from her. And then he'll give her back to the desert with a knife across the throat."

"And you won't allow it?"

"You know I won't." His words are a nod to how *he* was preyed upon by *me*. A bit of that dark time flits through our minds, and I feel his resolve harden, his anger toward me growing in the bargain. "Tell me how I can find her."

I reach out to him. "You know you have but to take my hand."

"No." He recoils. "*Lead* me to her."

In the mirror, my expression saddens. "Alas, in my current state that is well beyond me. Had I true form, however…"

Brama's face pinches in anger. From a shelf beneath the basin he takes out a small lead box. "Wait," I say, but Brama ignores me, placing the necklace inside it. "Wait! You may torture me if you wish, but it changes nothing!"

The lid closes, and all goes black.

I feel nothing. Not Brama. Not the tiny room he's chosen to live in. Not the tannery nor the Shallows beyond. None of Sharakhai. None of the desert. Not even the heat, nor the sky, nor the endless sands. I know not how Brama found this secret, but it is my one true fear, my one true weakness, to be utterly parted from all I've come to love.

I feel myself falling. Down a deep hole I drift, and the farther I plummet, the more I worry that I'll never be able to return even if Brama were to open the box. It is one of the few ways we, the ehrekh, can die. Does Brama know this? I hope not. By the gods who walk the earth, I hope not. Far worse than the isolation is the sense of being undone, of leaving this place, never to return. I will never go to the farther fields as Brama will when he dies. Lacking the blood of the elder gods, I will live in this realm until my final hour, and then I will simply be gone, like smoke from a candle snuffed. It is a fear I have always harbored, but now it consumes me.

Time passes—how much I cannot tell—but finally, blessedly, the lid of the box opens, and Brama takes me up once more.

I stare at him in the mirror, my dark skin cast golden in the wavering brass. "I cannot find her! Not unless you will it!"

"I *do* will it," he says.

"But you must *accept* what I give!"

He lowers the sapphire. "Never."

"Then you will not find her and all that you've predicted will come to pass! Save her if you would, Brama Junayd'ava. You have but to take my hand."

For a moment, the gem remains, hovering above the leaden box. He is lost in the memories of our time together. Part of him wants to be done with me once and for all, but there is another part that wonders at the things he might do were he to accept the power I could give him.

I whisper to him, "You could rule this city if you so wished."

A heartbeat passes. Then another. Slowly, Brama lifts the gem from the box and stares at my beaten reflection once more. "How?"

"Welcome me," I say to him. "Welcome me, and use the gifts I lay at your very doorstep. You have but to say the word, and I will be returned to my prison. All is at your will. But make no mistake. Your very form and frame is necessary. You must open yourself to me."

He stares into my eyes, and I know he's already decided. The dread from moments ago lingers, but for the first time since being trapped between the facets of this sapphire, I feel like I've taken a step closer to setting myself free—not because of Brama, but because of the *girl*. *She* is the key, though I cannot yet say how. The path the fates have laid for me is often clear only well after the lights have first been shown.

"Very well," Brama says, and indeed he welcomes me.

I approach, and he blinks, once, twice. When he opens his eyes the third time, his view of the world has changed. He sees more. Motes of magic drifting on the subtle breezes within this dingy room in the slums of Sharakhai. He hears more. Echoes of life and death and anger and lust. The very breath of the first gods falls upon his skin, making it tingle here, then there, then deep inside him.

He walks to the door. Opens it. Takes the stairs down and enters the street. So many scents are on the wind. The young. The old. Lovers. Sworn enemies.

"What now?" Brama says to the first star in the sky.

"You walk the city."

And so he does, the twinkling lights of fate brightening as he goes.

NEAR THE EDGE OF THE SHALLOWS SPRAWL FIVE mountainous buildings, the constituent parts of an ancient tenement built hundreds of years ago as a barracks for a looming war with Qaimir. The buildings show their age: their amber stone crumbling, arched windows chipped away by more recent inhabitants, graffiti along the ground floor written in paint or blood or shit. The slumlord who owns them cares little about its outward appearance, nor does he care how poorly the interiors are treated; one need only enter any of the edifices to see the truth of that: refuse in the halls, holes in the walls between rooms, the unyielding smell of piss and unventilated cooking—humanity squeezed to the breaking point. No, the lord of this manor cares only that his rent collectors are able to sweep through with their enforcers and gather the handful of copper khet owed from each and every room at the beginning of each and every week.

More interesting to Brama is the sheer number of entrances and exits to this gargantuan complex. Like a tribe of desert titans, each building has eight scalloped archways that disgorge or ingest its inhabitants. Each has four courtyards as well, with exits to the north and south. Above, makeshift walkways string between these and the neighboring buildings, making up one small part of the sprawling rooftop neighborhood the Shallows is famed for. No doubt there are even a few underground tunnels leading to and from this place.

It all makes for the perfect place for Nehir and Jax to hide. And so it was with little surprise that the lights led Brama here. They dissipate, however, when he nears the buildings, and though he's walked their circumference several times over the past few days, he still hasn't found her.

"Why?" he asked me that first night in his beaten brass mirror.

"The fates are fickle friends," I told him. "The path is not always clear. It can become clouded by others who hold power or control the fate of those involved. It can become dulled by the sheer press of humanity in Sharakhai. My guess, however, is that for the time being, the fates have found other, more interesting baubles to play with. That or they've simply not decided what to do with you."

Or, more accurately, me.

Brama seemed unsatisfied, but it is the plain truth, and the only answer I could give. I worry over it as much as he does, perhaps more. I feel as though this story, however it unfolds, is a test on the part of the fates, a way to offer me a path back into their good graces. For all my power, for all the centuries I've spent living in every corner of the Great Shangazi, I am as much in control of my own destiny as Brama is of his.

Sundown nears as Brama waits. The light splashing against the buildings fades, burns red. And then Jax comes rushing from an alley into the nearest of the tenements' tall buildings. She slips through a darkened archway and is gone, but Brama is already on her trail. He heads inside but promptly loses her to a stairwell twenty paces along the narrow hallway. Tenement dwellers watch Brama pass by their doorless entries. Some peek out from behind blankets hung across their cramped rooms, or lift their heads from their meals to stare through strings of beads. Some even make love, but it doesn't do to lower one's guard in the Shallows, so they watch him pass, then return to their rutting.

Brama hurries up the stairwell, glancing along the hallway of the second story, then the third. Finding both empty—of sparkling girls, at least—he continues to the fourth floor. At the end of the dirty corridor, a gutted window shows a sky of brilliant mauve gilded in the orange light of the setting sun. Just short of the window, he sees the silhouette of a girl slipping inside a room. Brama approaches carefully, pausing near the doorway, which has a beaten old carpet hung across it. The sound of shuffling comes from within, then the rhythmic thump of a mortar and pestle, accompanied by sniffing sounds. Other sounds rise up all around in this cramped hive of humanity, but lying in the interstitial spaces between them is a sibilant hiss, the rasp of wet breath. The scent of black lotus laces the air, an earthy, floral smell that lingers, especially when one has been smoking it for as long as Nehir apparently has.

As Brama reaches to move the carpet aside, the mortar goes silent; the carpet is flung wide and the girl rushes out, knife to hand. She presses the knife to Brama's throat until he's against the wall behind him. She stares at him, her brows pinched in confusion. She expected someone else—the assassin, most likely, assuming Kymbril's story is true.

She starts to speak, then glances back, pulls the carpet back into place to hide the sight of Nehir lying in a hammock slung between the mudbrick walls. "What do you *want* with us?" she asks in a thick Malasani accent.

Brama pauses to think. "I don't know. I only wish to help."

She stares at Brama's scars, clearly revolted, clearly scared. "We need no help from *you*."

"Yes you do. The world is closing in around you. It won't be long now before Kymbril has you."

She frowns, her brow furrowing. "Who's Kymbril?"

It's clear then how woefully incomplete her understanding of the situation is. She knows some—else why hide in this place and cover her tracks so carefully?—but she understands neither the nature of the danger nor its immediacy.

Before Brama can reply, a filthy man wearing only his small clothes approaches along the hallway. His eyes are dark and haunted, his malnourished ribs like ripples on a windswept pond. He carries something, a single silver six-piece that he holds with both hands toward Jax as if it's meant to save his own mother.

"Go on!" Jax shouts. And when he doesn't, she screams at him, "There's nothing for you here!"

He remains, mouth opening and closing uselessly. He shuffles one step forward, holding the sliver of a silver coin out further.

"Go!"

Finally the man leaves, the sound of his footsteps replaced by a choking sound from inside the room. Jax's eyes go wide. She bats the carpet aside and bursts into the room. Brama holds the carpet wide as she sinks to the floor by her brother's side. His eyelids flutter. His body convulses, rocking the hammock slung between the walls of the narrow room.

Beneath the hammock sits a grimy shisha, its frayed black tube snaking across the floor. Next to the shisha is the mortar and pestle. She tosses the pestle aside, spraying some of the red paste onto the floor, then uses her fingers to scoop up some of the crushed wolfberry. "Nehir," she whispers. "Nehir, take this." She smears as much of the red paste into his mouth as she can, making him look as though his gums are bleeding. "Swallow it!"

He doesn't respond. The embrace of the black lotus is already on him, and it's drawing him deeper and deeper. It will never let him go. As we watch with all the impotence of babes, his spasms begin to slow. His eyes roll up in his head. His breath comes slower, shallower.

Jax turns to Brama, her eyes brimming with tears. "Do something!"

Brama stands silent, peering around the room. In a corner lies a bowl of water with a rag folded carefully along one edge. He steps across the room, drops down in front of the bowl, and stares into the reflection. "What can I do?"

Slowly, the smooth black skin of my face forms in the white bowl of water. Twin horns furl backward. Black spines replace Brama's curly hair. "Little enough," I say. "Give him comfort. Give him more of the reek to ease his flight."

"You know that isn't what I mean."

"My dear Brama," I say, reaching out to his mind, "if you wish for my help, you know what you must do."

Brama stares into the water, his worries roiling inside him.

Jax, hands clutched to her throat, steps closer and stares at the bowl. "Who are you *talking* to?"

Brama ignores her. "Do it," he says to me.

Do it. Allow me to take his form, at least for a time, and to some small degree. It's doubtful I can do anything more than help with Nehir—the narrow tie between us will not allow me to do all that I might wish—but we both know that the more I'm allowed to do this, the more dangerous it becomes for Brama.

When Brama first accepted the gem that contains me, I thought surely he would use it to bring himself fortune or to grant himself long life. It would take time, surely, for our dealings before that point were anything but kind to Brama, but so often when mortals gain power, their only wish is to gain more. Brama hadn't wished for that, though. He'd squirreled me away, sometimes in the lead box, other times beneath his mattress, other times within his shirt. He'd never sought power.

Until now.

"There is a cost," I tell Brama. "You will be required to act in this as well. Your body must suffer in his place."

"I don't care if I suffer." And he means it. I've felt the disregard he has for his own life, the pain that befalls him. I feel it even now.

"Very well."

"Please," Jax says, and then goes silent as Brama stands. She watches as he steps to her brother's side. Watches as Brama takes his hand. In this moment, Brama lowers his guard. It feels not like the opening of a door, but more of a nod, a bow to me. It is all I need.

I forge a connection between Brama and Nehir, a bond that begins as a thread but strengthens, braiding and multiplying until the two men are intertwined. Their minds are still unique, but their forms intermingle. Their hearts. Their bodies. These are what I care about now. Slowly, the effects of the reek are drawn from Nehir and into Brama. *His* body carries that terrible burden, leaving Nehir breathing easier, his eyes less restless. Nehir's shaking quells and he slips into a deeper sleep, and the touch of the black lotus takes Brama. He stumbles backward, falls against the nearby wall. He slips down until his head is resting against the corner of the room.

He hears the sounds of the tenement, which are wondrous and terrifying in equal amounts. The cry of a babe brightens until it becomes the touch of Tulathan herself. The sound of a man's feet treading barefoot is the tread of an assassin. Jax squats before him. She speaks, but Brama cannot hear her words. She shakes him, gently at first, then violently. But Brama doesn't care. Jax is nothing to him, merely one small part in the grand canvas of sounds and scents that grow and shrink like the aeons of life and death in a forest, all experienced in the blink of an eye.

Down, down Brama drifts, into the forest, the landscape ever changing. Brama wanders through the trees, through the hills, wondering where his place in this new world might be.

WHEN BRAMA WAKES, HIS HEAD FEELS AS THOUGH IT'S being pounded like a cubit stone in the quarry. He lies on the floor of the same small tenement room, drool slipping from his mouth, pooling against the red-tiled floor beneath him. As he lifts himself up and props himself against the wall, the pounding becomes so terrible, stars form in his eyes. Only after long minutes of breathing and allowing the storm to pass does Brama realize he is alone. He stares at the empty hammock, takes in the rest of the room, which holds considerably less clutter than it had before he'd freed Nehir.

Hardly surprising, Brama thinks.

Still, the betrayal stings, and for a time all he can manage to do is hold his head in his hands and try to press away the pain.

I'm distanced from his bodily feelings, but not completely so—I helped him to lift the effects of the black lotus, after all. The way his body grieves reminds me of the mortals with whom I've bonded in the past. This is vastly different, though. Every time before now, *I'd* been the one in control. I felt what I wanted to feel, did what I wanted to do with the form I'd taken, and it was often wondrous. Now, the crystal makes me beholden to the one who holds it, and I feel so much less. Brama is duller than he might have been. Less interesting to me. If only I might find a way to free myself from this prison once and for all.

Brama stares at the shisha. The rank smell disgusts him, but there is a part of him that wants to walk among the trees of the forest once more. It's a small part, to be sure, but distinct. It was surely due to how addicted to the reek Nehir had been. Brama is strong enough in body and spirit to withstand it and not become shackled to the drug, but were he to continue to do this, he could easily succumb to the desire.

Brama's gaze drifts to the empty hammock. "I should have let him die."

"Perhaps you should have," comes a heavy voice.

Brama turns his head, wincing from the pain it brings, to find a bald man standing in the doorway, pushing the carpet aside. It's Maru, Kymbril's man. He steps inside the room, and the carpet flaps closed behind him. Brama reaches for his knife, but finds it gone. Maru gives the room a cursory inspection, then kneels before Brama, a curved and nicked kenshar held easily in one hand.

He cranes his neck and runs the knife blade over his stubbly neck, scratching an itch. "Kymbril's going to be awfully disappointed in you."

"Why's that?" Brama asks.

Maru points the tip of the knife at Brama's chest. "Told him you didn't know Nehir. Said you worked for no one."

Brama thinks back, frowns. "You were there, weren't you, outside the door?"

Maru shrugs his broad shoulders. "He may not act like it, but Kymbril's a careful man." Brama opens his mouth to speak, but Maru talks over him. "Now let's get a few things straight, you and me. First, before I leave this room, you're going to tell me where I can find Nehir and that little bitch sister of his. Second, at no point in this conversation will you tell me that you don't know. Third, and this is the most important point, Brama, so bend your ear. Third, Kymbril may be a careful man, but I'm not." He holds the kenshar up for Brama to see. He stares over it, just above its well-honed edge, into Brama's eyes. "I'm a messy man. A *persistent* man. I'm a jackal who's gone too hungry to care about leopards or lions or whatever the fuck else might be standing in front of me."

Since Brama escaped my attentions, he's had a streak in him that seeks out conflict, that desires pain. Something broke in him while he was in my care, and I can feel it inside him now, rising to stand before Maru like a defiant child before a charging destrier. Worse is the fact that I see a darkness forming around Maru, the sort that comes when something threatens me.

Beware, Brama! Take my hand!

To my amazement, Brama *does* reach for me, but in that moment his hand also grasps absently for the sapphire beneath his shirt. Maru's hand darts forward and snatches the leather cord around Brama's neck. He yanks it, snapping the cord, taking the sapphire that holds me with it. My sight, my hearing, so dependent on Brama, both dim, but I can still hear Maru as he says, "None of that," holding the gemstone up.

He slips it into his pocket, his eyes still on Brama. Brama chooses that moment to kick Maru in the knee. Maru, however, for all his bulk, is a sinuous man. His leg snaps back, dulling the blow. Then, quick as a cobra, he grabs Brama by the neck, slams him against the rough stone wall, and drops him to the floor.

"Now." Maru is close, his dark eyes intense, his kahve-laden breath strong and rank. He holds the knife between Brama's legs, pressing the blade up against his crotch. Brama grips Maru's wrist, keeping the knife at bay, but only just. "Choose carefully, Brama. I'm only going to ask you one more time. Where's that Malasani cunt?"

"Crawled up one of the Kings' arses," Brama shoots back. "Which is good news for you, Maru. You only have to shove your head up a dozen of them to find her."

"Bad choice, boy."

Maru draws the knife upward. Brama, jaw clenched tight, teeth bared, tries to stop him, but as weak as he is from the effects of the lotus, it's a losing battle from the start.

The scene slowly fades—the sights, the sounds, the smells. It represents, perhaps, an uncorrectable shift in my fate, a poorly chosen path. Suddenly the scene brightens. Maru's breathing is a wet rasp in Brama's ears. The knife's edge burns bright between Brama's legs, searing his skin.

There's a hollow thump, and Maru goes slack. His weight falls across Brama, and Brama shoves him away. Jax is there, standing over the two of them holding a heavy, blood-stained ewer above her head, ready to strike again. She's shivering, panting, staring at the bloody gouge on the back of Maru's head.

Brama levers himself out from under Maru and comes to a stand. Jax drops the ewer, which thuds against the floor. After taking takes Maru's knife and slipping it under his belt, Brama reaches into Maru's shirt pocket, takes back the necklace, and ties it around his neck.

"Nehir wouldn't let me stay," Jax says, an apology of sorts.

Brama only shrugs. "I mightn't have, either, were I him."

"I'm sorry. I know you saved us, but he's scared. He has his wits about him now, though. He has you to thank, does he not?"

Brama nods.

"It was the gem?"

"In a manner of speaking."

The girl takes a deep breath. Someone further down the hall begins shouting at their child. Jax turns and stares wide-eyed at the carpet over her doorway, but as their argument quells, she turns back to Brama. "I haven't a right to ask, but I need help. *We* need help, even if Nehir won't admit it."

Brama looks down Maru. The big man is beginning to stir. "Best we talk elsewhere." She nods, but doesn't move. When Brama touches her shoulder, she nods a second time, and the two of them leave together.

IN THE SOUTHWESTERN QUARTER OF SHARAKHAI, NOT so far from the banks of the Haddah, lies the Temple of Nalamae. Save for a few special nights of the year, the broken temple lies empty. Disused. Forgotten and mostly shunned by the citizens of Sharakhai. And yet no one would dare tear it down, not even the Kings. One might ignore the gods of the desert without fear of retribution, but attempting to erase their memory entirely would be like waving a ribbon before a black laugher and daring it to charge.

The temple is where Brama decides to take Jax. It's also the very place *I* was taken, captured, and caught within the falcon's egg sapphire Brama now wears around his neck. Perhaps Brama wishes to taunt me by coming here. If that's the case, he has succeeded, for this is also the place where my most loyal servant, Kadir, died, and I feel a growing sadness and anger. The lives of mortals may be fleeting, but Kadir's blazed higher and brighter than the dim candles of most souls in Sharakhai.

Brama motions Jax to walk ahead of him into the temple. He slows, watching the way behind, wary of Kymbril's gang, wary of the assassin. No one is following, however, and the two of them head into the nave, where the temple's grand, broken dome arcs high above them. Rubble and stone and dust lie all about. The mosaics here depict life in the earliest days of Sharakhai: the river, the mount where the Kings' palaces were built, the small settlement that grew into the sprawling metropolis that eventually swallowed the open land around this temple.

The colors around Jax are bright, especially as she walks in shadow. They're more vivid than they've ever been. Surely she will be the one to release me from my prison. Or deliver me to the one who will. She's restless. I can feel it inside her: the worry over her pursuers, the desire to return to her homeland, the sad and growing realization that she no longer can.

She reaches the center of the open space and stares up at the jagged gap where the dome has been sundered, a remnant of Goezhen's presence here nearly two centuries ago. "My mother and father were murdered nearly one year ago in a temple not so different from this one." Her voice is weak, subdued. "It honored the gods of the mountains, among them Nehiran and Urajaxan, after whom Nehir and I were named. It did little to save my parents, but Nehir still thought it a fortuitous sign that the two of us were able to escape. I believed him then—that our patron gods were watching over us— but I can see now it was only my fear speaking to me, words of hope whispered to a petrified girl." She laughs a bitter laugh and stoops to pick up a stone. She turns it absently in her hand, continues to walk, taking in the grandness of this ruined place. "How foolish we were. The gods care nothing for our struggles. We soon found out from those still loyal to our family that all had been arranged beforehand. After my parents were murdered, our land was delivered to my father's rival in exchange for a ruby mine our own lord had had his eye on for decades. We hoped to rally support to restore the power of our house, but when our few allies were also killed, we knew the time was upon us to flee." She spins, flinging her arms wide like a mummer performing a play; the lights surrounding her dance along with her. "We came here to Sharakhai, but even this city wasn't far enough. The lords who conspired to kill my parents will never allow Nehir and me to live. We are the final two who have a rightful claim to our barony. They cannot take the chance that we'll reach our king and present our case. That's why the assassins follow us, even here. That's why they won't stop until we're dead."

Brama sits on a large piece of rubble. He speaks, keeping an eye on the temple's entrances. "Your troubles… Is that why Nehir took to smoking lotus?"

Without pulling her gaze from the mosaics, she nods. "That's when he started selling as well. My father knew several smugglers of the black, and allowed them to pass through our lands—with a tax, of course. Nehir was being groomed to take on more responsibility from my father, and had learned their names. He made contact with them immediately after reaching Sharakhai, thinking he'd rebuild our wealth—some small amount of it, in any case, enough to return to Malasan to hire swords and spears to aid his cause. One hundred good soldiers, he told me. One hundred is all we need. If we get that many, a thousand more will rally to our side."

"And would they?"

Jax laughs. "No. Our people did not hate our father, but neither did they love him. And with both dukes standing united, our cause is lost. Had we ten thousand, we would still fall beneath their combined might."

"So what will you do? Kymbril won't let this stand. He wants Nehir's head, too." He leaves unsaid that the drug lord likely wants Jax dead as well; he can see in her eyes she already knows.

"I'll book passage on a caravan ship."

"To where?"

She shrugs. "Kundhun. From there we'll continue on, far enough that they'll stop chasing us."

"That may work," Brama says into the cool breeze, "but I think it likely you'll need to leave your brother behind."

"I know." She scrapes the dirt from under her fingernails. "He won't want to go, but I have to convince him. He doesn't know this city, and he has yet to accept the fact that we'll never return home to Malasan."

Disappointment emanates from Brama like heat from a hearth. He's only just met Jax, but there's something about her that entrances him. His old self might already have started to woo her, to get her by his side, to cajole her into bed—his old self would have tried harder precisely *because* she would soon be leaving the city—but *this* Brama, the changed Brama, simply wants a friend. I can feel the desire in him mixing imperfectly with the acceptance that her departure is necessary.

"Finding passage on a caravan won't be difficult," he says, "nor would it be expensive if you're willing to work the ship. But buying their silence. *That* will be expensive. Now that we've beaten Maru senseless, Kymbril isn't going to let this go, and I doubt your Dukes will either."

She fixes her gaze on Brama at last. "That's why I need you. I don't know which caravan masters to trust."

"Do you have money?"

"Yes."

"How much?"

"Enough."

Brama shakes his head. "I have to know what I'm dealing with. The more you can spend, the safer a caravan master I can find for you. Skimping here might cost you your life."

I would laugh if I had form. She's staring into Brama's eyes, trying to weigh just how far she can trust him, but she's in too deep to be questioning such things. Still, Brama remains silent, waiting patiently as she takes in the scars on his face, on his hands. "Who did this to you?"

"A vile creature."

"Did you kill it?"

"No, but there are days when I wish I had."

The power within her has been muted until this moment. Now it ignites, and I can see some of the upbringing of a Malasani noble. "There are days when I tell myself I should return to Malasan and avenge the death of my parents. But then I remember how narrowly we escaped, how close we've come to death since then." She reaches down and pulls up one trouser leg. She rolls down her woolen sock all the way to the ankle, exposing three bracelets. Immediately Brama's old instincts for assessing the value of goods return to him. Two of the bracelets are gold. They're beautifully made though simple in design. Each would fetch a handsome price, but nothing like what she'd need to buy discrete, long-distance passage for two aboard a caravan ship. The third, however, is made of white gold, and is strung with small rubies and diamonds. "This is the last of what I smuggled away from Malasan, and the last of what I've managed to keep hidden from Nehir." Of the three, she unclasps the one with the rubies and diamonds and hands it to Brama. "Will it be enough?"

"More than enough. It will ensure you get help to go wherever you wish and help when you arrive as well. But first we need to convince Nehir."

The sounds of the city are distant and muted, but now Brama hears the sound of scraping, the subtle shift of leather on sand-dusted stone. Brama knows immediately it comes from somewhere in the temple. He turns toward it, waits, holding up a hand up to Jax for silence. He listens for the span of two breaths, then rushes silently toward her. Together they move toward the rear of the temple.

Brama whispers to her, "Where is your brother now?"

She hesitates, her eyes fearful as she glances over her shoulder for their pursuer. "In a room above the Dancing Mule."

Brama nods. "I'll find you there." Then he points her toward the opposite side of the stone-walled courtyard. Beyond lay the Haddah, and a dozen paths of escape for Jax if she's fast enough. Brama waits for her to leave and slips behind a tall marble statue of a woman cradling a lamb. From behind it he watches the shadowed doorways of the temple. I wish to reach out, to find the man who's following him wherever he may hide, but Brama denies me.

Across the courtyard, a stone balustrade divides a patio from the sandy yard beyond. At the yard's far end stands a grove of decorative trees, all nearly barren of leaves. It is there that Brama sees shadows shifting. A split second too late, he jerks back behind the statue. A dark line slices the air. A crack breaks the stillness as the leg of the statue is chipped by the streaking arrow. Brama feels a sharp pain along the outside of his knee. Sucking air through gritted teeth, he examines the wound.

But then, before I know what's happening, he's pulled Maru's knife and is sprinting toward the trees. I plead with him to take the protection I can offer, but he refuses; his decision to help Nehir is an embarrassing moment of weakness for him. He can see the assassin clearly now—his bow is drawn, the string to his ear—but Brama doesn't flinch.

He's going to die, I realize. He's moving with intent and pure abandon and little else. He's touching that place where he hid while I tortured him. It is a place of fear and rage and dwindling hope. I never thought to find a place of commonality with a mortal, but I too was tortured. I too found a place like this. It makes me feel no sympathy for Brama—what is he but a tool I will use to win back my freedom?—but there, in that hidden place so tightly tied to us both, I realize I can feel him more strongly than at any time except when he used me to lift Nehir's addiction.

I allow some of myself to filter through Brama, adding my rage to his. As the arrow is released, our combined power pours forth. The arrow flies, turns black as it nears us. The arrow's point digs into Brama's leather vest, bites his scar-riddled skin, but goes no further as the shaft of the arrow sprays outward from the point of impact in a brilliant fan of smoke and glowing red embers.

The assassin's eyes go wide. He pauses for a moment, his indecision clear, and then he drops his bow, sprints toward the temple wall behind him, leaps against it, and clings to a lattice of dried vines. Then he clambers over the top. Brama tries to follow, sprinting to the wall, but the wound along his knee flares; the puncture wound in his chest burns as he pulls himself up along the vines. By the time he drops to the city street on the other side, the assassin is gone. It is in this moment, while Brama is staring along the empty street, that I wonder if Brama saw what I saw. I pray to Goezhen he hasn't, for as the assassin leapt over the wall, a trace of light trailed in his wake, there and gone in a moment, a thing I'd not thought to see, but now that I have it's making me reconsider all the events that had led us to this point.

Across the street, on the sill of an open window, sits a massive copper kettle. Brama walks toward it, pulling the necklace over his head as he goes. Gripping the leather cord tightly in one hand, he stares into the ruddy reflection of his face that grows the nearer he comes to it. The reflection transforms, becomes the distorted face of an ehrekh.

"How did you do it?" Brama asks.

"I don't know what you mean."

"You know precisely what I mean. How did you ignite the arrow without my leave?"

"*You* willed it."

"That's a bloody lie." His hand is gripped so tightly my prison, the sapphire, shakes. "You worked through me of your own free will."

I pause, knowing that the wrong words here could make Brama do something rash. I'm consoled by the realization that he didn't notice the light trailing the assassin, or perhaps he did and thought it some vestige of the power I unleashed. "You cannot expect the two of us to remain close for as long as we have without *some* effect. What I did, I did to protect you."

"What you did, you did to protect *you*." He lifts the necklace, stares at its cloudy facets. "You cannot do it again. I forbid it."

"You are the master who holds the chains," I say to him, an ancient proverb, one that was once used bitterly by the powerless but in recent centuries has come to mean simple deference. He can sense the way I'm chafing at my imprisonment, but I continue. "He may have heard Jax. He may be on the way to the tavern now."

Brama stares uncertainly into the kettle, but when an elderly woman shuffles toward the window from inside, he slips the necklace back around his head and sprints headlong for the Haddah and the bridges that span it, his worry for Jax growing with each long stride he takes.

BRAMA REACHES THE DRUNKEN MULE AT A RUN. HE takes the stairs at the back of the old, misshapen tavern to the balcony that leads to four rooms situated above the common room. Brama doesn't know which one is Jax's, but the door to the second room is open. He paces toward it, body tensed, and finds Jax standing just inside. She's holding something in her hand. As Brama comes closer, he sees she's holding a severed finger in a blood-stained kerchief.

"Kymbril," Brama says.

Jax nods. Her hands are shaking.

Brama takes the kerchief from her and sees a small wooden chit, half hidden by Nehir's severed digit. There's a symbol on it—Kymbril's own—a coiled viper. "It's a message."

"I know what it is!" Her eyes are saucers. She's shaking so badly her lips are trembling. "I'm going to go there. I'm going to save him."

"You don't understand." He holds up the chit, then wraps the finger in the kerchief and sets it on a simple ironwork table near the door. "This is a marker for those who buy large amounts of black lotus or whitefire or what have you. They get it after bringing the money to men like Maru, at which point they take it to another location to pick up their purchase. Kymbril wants you, but he also wants Nehir's stash."

She looks ready to argue, but then her resolve hardens and she holds out her hand. "Give me the bracelet."

She means the one she gave him at the temple, the one bright with diamonds and rubies. "You can't buy him off, Jax. Not anymore. He wants both of you dead."

She flicks her fingers. "Give it to me! It's mine!"

"It won't *work*."

Her face screws up in anger, and she begins pummeling him with her balled-up fists, striking him inexpertly around the shoulders and chest. Brama doesn't try to stop her. He takes it all, her swings thudding into his chest, slapping against his face. Eventually she stops and simply holds herself. "I can't let him go."

"You don't have to," Brama says as he steps in and takes her into his arms. Surprisingly, she allows it, even softening as he continues to hold her. Brama speaks softly and strokes her hair, "Here's what we're going to do."

IN THE HEART OF THE KNOT LIES KYMBRIL'S MANOR, where he runs his operations. It stands drunkenly with its neighbors at the end of a cul-de-sac. Lying low as he is on the roof of the building next to Kymbril's, Brama can see the full length of the street. He's watching for Kymbril's spotters, those who look for danger and call it out before it lands on his very doorstep. There are two boys sitting at the mouth of an alley halfway down the street. Seeing them crouched, preoccupied with a game of sticks, Brama picks up the fragrant calfskin sack by his side and moves smooth and low to the nearby roof of Kymbril's building. With the buildings butting up against one another, it's as simple as dropping a few feet down over the lip of the building. Once there, he sets the sack down, removes his necklace, and ties a length of string to the leather cord. Moving to the very front of Kymbril's building, he feeds the string out, lowering the necklace until the sapphire is suspended in the corner of the topmost window below.

After securing the string to a nail, he lies flat and closes his eyes. Like the coming of dawn shedding light over a dangerous landscape, a vision of the room brightens in Brama's mind. The drapes Brama spotted earlier while surveilling the building mask the sapphire's presence, but the cloth's material is thin enough that he can see the room within. Kymbril is there, leaning deeply into a couch along the far wall, staring through the window where the sapphire now hangs. Brama's heart skips, but he realizes Kymbril's eyes are closed. He's asleep, his breath coming long and slow. He looks as though he fell onto the couch the night before and has yet to wake up.

On the roof, Brama opens his eyes and blinks. He stares at the blue sky, breathing deeply and yawning like a jackal to help clear the dizziness from his mind and body. The effects of the gem are disorienting, but he's handling it well enough. Before Brama left for Kymbril's manor, I offered more of my power to him—much more, in fact—but he's still wary of me, enough that this facile spell is the one small concession to Jax's desperate need he allows.

He closes his eyes again and studies the room, memorizing it. With Kymbril so vulnerable, he considers slipping in through the window and driving a knife into his chest, but it would be too risky. He doesn't know where Nehir is being kept, and he promised Jax he would do everything he could to see her brother safe, so he resolves to continue as planned.

I muse at how quickly mortals can fall for another soul; I suppose we're not so different in this respect.

Soon, Jax appears at the far end of the street. She walks with a tightness, hands bunched at her sides. Even far away it's easy to see how frightened she looks. A good amount of it is real, to be sure, but she's playing her part well. They want Kymbril to see her as a scared little doe, ready to bolt at a sharp sound or sudden movement. A boy struts out to meet her, dust kicking up behind him into the hot air. He holds his hand out and says something, not quite loud enough for Brama to hear, but Jax shakes her head, demanding she be allowed to see her brother.

The boy shouts at her, "You were to have brought it *here*," angry that she doesn't have Nehir's stash.

"Bring her," calls a voice from the base of Kymbril's manor.

Maru. Part of Brama regrets not drawing his knife across Maru's throat in the tenement, but if it wasn't Maru it would be someone else. It's a simple truth in the Shallows: finding oneself with a shortage of those willing to do dark work for a bit of coin only means you haven't looked hard enough.

As the boy leads Jax into Kymbril's manor, Brama waits, hoping he hasn't miscalculated. It wouldn't be the worst thing if Kymbril meets her below, but he's counting on Jax being brought to Kymbril's private offices, where it will be easier to make their escape.

Brama takes up the bulky sack, which smells strongly of fermented lotus, and crawls to the trap door leading down into the building. He sets the sack down, closes his eyes, and waits breathlessly as the sounds of the city play around him. The clatter of hooves in the distance, the rattle of wheels. The sound of children playing, a man coughing so heavily and wetly Brama wonders if he already stands on the threshold of the farther fields. Maru's voice calls up the stairs, and Kymbril wakes. The big man shakes his head, uses the heel of his hands to clear the sleep from his eyes, then opens the door to the room. Jax, guided by Maru, takes the last run of stairs to the topmost level and steps inside the room, where Maru pulls her to a stop.

Kymbril makes a show of looking her up and down. "Takes a lot of nerve, coming here empty-handed."

"You'll get the lotus," Jax replies nervously, "but only after I see my brother."

"You think you can come here, to *my* house, and start making demands?"

"You want our stash and you want us gone," Jax says evenly. "All I'm asking is to make sure he's unharmed."

Kymbril laughs at that. "Other than his finger, you mean."

Jax stares back defiantly. "I will see my brother. Only then will you see your reek."

"I don't *need* your reek, girl."

"We have a lot of it, Kymbril."

The statement sits between them like a jewel for the taking. Kymbril considers a moment, then nods to Maru, who leaves and heads downstairs. He returns a short while later with Nehir, a black bag over his head, in tow. Maru removes the bag to reveal a face that is bruised and bloodied. He cradles his right hand, tightly wrapped in a bloody bandage, to his chest. The resignation in Nehir's face is plain to see, as if he's known for months that it would come to this, and now that it has there's precious little to do but accept it.

Jax reaches up and brushes his hair, tenderly, slowly. She's positioned herself as Brama instructed so that neither Maru nor Kymbril can see the words written on her wrist. To his credit, Nehir's expression hardly changes. He becomes *more* calm, a tell in and of itself, but the gods of his homeland are watching over him, for neither Kymbril nor Maru seem to notice.

"Enough." Kymbril steps between the two of them and turns to face Jax. "Where's the ruddy stash?"

She puts her fingers to her lips and whistles. On cue, Brama stands and stomps on the trap door on the roof. Through the crystal eye he sees Kymbril and Maru staring up toward the ladder against the wall and the trap door it leads to.

"What's this?" Kymbril growls.

"Your stash," Jax says.

Kymbril raises a thumb at Maru, and Maru climbs the ladder to the trapdoor and pushes it open. On the roof, Brama opens his eyes, replacing the sapphire's perspective with his own, and makes his way down the ladder. He tosses the heavy sack at Kymbril's feet. Kymbril stares at it, then at him. Then he smiles wide, looking like a little boy who's just been served his favorite meal from his memma. Kneeling, Kymbril opens the sack and takes a good whiff of the pile of fermented black lotus petals. "I'll give it to you, Brama,"

Kymbril says. "You almost had me convinced you were innocent in all this." He stands and steps closer to Brama, pulls his shirt out and looks down his bare chest. "Where's that necklace of yours?"

Brama's only reply is to unclasp two of Jax's bracelets, the simpler ones, from around his wrist. He flips them in the air to Kymbril, who catches them with ease and stares, a quizzical look on his rough-and-tumble face. "What's this?"

"Enough, along with the reek, to let them leave the city unharmed. They'll be no further trouble to you, Kymbril. That I promise. If they come back, I'll take the knife to them myself."

"Ah, but we know what *your* promises mean."

"What Nehir did was more than foolish," Brama continues. "You've made that clear. But he was only trying to raise money to head home and avenge the deaths of his parents. A fool's dream. We can all see that now. Can't we, Nehir?"

Nehir stares at everyone in turn. Wearily, he nods to Kymbril.

Brama goes on, "They've both given up, Kymbril. They're leaving the city, far enough away that Sharakhai and their troubles in Malasan will be but a memory."

Kymbril shrugs. "You know how this city works, boy. Always mongrel dogs nipping at your heels. My soldiers see I let these two go, what will they think? Or worse, my enemies?"

Brama considers this. "What if you and I could come to some sort of arrangement? What if I remained in your employ and helped heal those most addicted to the reek?" Kymbril and Maru exchange a look. It's clear that Nehir confessed what Brama had done for him, but surely the two men had scoffed at the notion. Brama speaks quickly before either man can protest. "What I did with Nehir I can do again. I'll do so whenever you ask."

"Even if you could, how would that help me?"

"Because when your wealthiest patrons die, you lose a reliable source of income, but what if the lotus's call was removed from them before that happened?"

"I'd lose them."

"Some perhaps, but certainly not all. And if you sensed that they were falling too far, you could force them to pay coin for it. You'd win either way, Kymbril, and fewer would die."

Brama's words take me aback. This is either something Brama just thought of or purposely hid from me. Either way, in all our days together, I've never felt this from him—a spark amidst the terrible darkness surrounding him—and I wonder what will come of it.

Kymbril, however, merely frowns. "I'll admit I'm intrigued, boy. Yesterday it might've been enough to call things square. Yesterday, I was in a giving mood. But I made another deal this morning. Can't go back on it now."

Fresh footsteps can be heard from below. Brama tenses as a dark form ascends the stairs. Jax and Nehir look at each other anxiously. This is something neither he nor Jax nor I had considered.

The man is one they all recognize: the assassin. What has me transfixed, more than his sudden appearance, are the lights that dance around him. They're dazzling, nearly blinding. And I realize Jax has become as dull as an old copper coin. It's true, then. Jax's role has always been to lead me to the assassin.

He steps into the room and looks at Nehir and Jax. Apparently satisfied, he tosses a bag to Kymbril. It clinks as Kymbril snatches it from the air. Kymbril opens the bag and inspects the contents. "May your daughters find husbands and your sons wives," he says with a wide grin, then shoves Jax toward the door.

"No!" Nehir shouts, and leaps into Jax's path.

Brama is already on the move. He stomps hard on Maru's foot, twists and elbows him in the jaw. Maru reels, and Brama sends him flying backward, through the doorway and toward the stair rails.

Before Kymbril can react, Brama brings his heel down sharply onto the sack. The muffled sound of a bladder bursting emanates from the sack. A sizzling follows. Then green smoke rises from the bag.

Brama dives toward the corner of the room to avoid Kymbril's grasp.

"Away, Nehir!" Jax shouts as she too runs for the far corner of the room.

But it's too late. The assassin stabs Nehir in the belly with a sharp thrust of his knife. Nehir stumbles, tries to crawl away.

When a high-pitched whistling sound comes from the bag, Brama clamps his eyes shut, and the center of the room transforms into a burst of white light. On and on it goes, the shrieking sound, the bright light so strong it's all Brama can do to keep it out. The skin along his left side burns hot, and he worries that the concoction he'd bought from the alchemyst with Jax's third bracelet was too much, that they'd all go up in flames, but he no sooner has this thought than the light and sound and heat all subside. Soon the only sounds are the moaning of men and a sizzling like meat over an open fire. Brama realizes he's on the floor, fingers grasping for purchase. He turns himself over, sees Jax standing in the corner, eyes dazed and blinking, yawning as she shakes her head.

Kymbril is not far from her, unconscious. The front of his clothes are charred; the legs of his trousers still smoke.

Near the open door, where the sack of black lotus once was, a hole is burned clear through the flooring and the timbers to the room below. Blue-green fire licks around the hole and up the door frame, where the flames transition to something more mundane: an orange the color of turning leaves. Nehir lies in the hall, grasping his gut, pulling at the banister in a vain attempt at regaining his feet. Past him runs Maru, back into the room with his knife drawn.

Brama stands to meet him. He takes one step forward, pretending to charge, but when Maru lowers his shoulder, preparing for it, Brama drops onto his back, lifts his legs, and catches Maru's gut with both feet. Maru swings his knife wildly at Brama, slicing his arm, but Brama uses Maru's momentum against him. With an almighty thrust of his legs, he launches Maru into the air and through the window behind him. As Maru grasps for the window frame, his knife tumbles into the corner. A moment later Maru lands on the ground outside with a thud and a groan.

Brama rolls over one shoulder and takes up Maru's knife as Kymbril, mouth gaping, makes it to one knee.

The assassin, meanwhile, stands in the doorway, his left arm burned and blistered. The lights swirl around him, and I am transfixed. I can do little, but I reach out to him. With all my will I beckon him, I force him to notice the glint in window. I whisper but one small memory: an arrow that bursts into flame as it strikes his enemy's chest.

As Brama moves to engage Kymbril, the assassin moves to the window. He reaches out and grasps the necklace. With a downward tug, he snaps the string holding it in place. He clutches the sapphire in his warm hand. I can already feel his eagerness, his ambition. By Goezhen's sweet kiss, what we might do together, he and I. For a time, he will be the one in control, I have no doubt, but with someone like him holding the necklace, it won't be long before I am the master of my fate once more. Perhaps then we'll return to Malasan. Perhaps I'll allow him to accept commissions from his lords. I could do with a bit of murder to quench the fire that's been building within me. Or perhaps I'll move on, toss the assassin aside and take the form of one of his lords. It's been too long since I've been to Malasan in any case. The last time I was there it wasn't even *called* Malasan.

Brama and Jax are wrestling with Kymbril. Kymbril tries gouging Brama's eyes, but Jax raises a knife high overhead and plunges it into Kymbril's neck. Blood sprays over her, over Brama. Kymbril thrashes as the two of them stand and back away. Then the big man with the mismatched eyes goes still, his hands grasping empty air. Finally his body goes still, and Brama and Jax turn to the assassin. Nehir is there as well, on his feet, hands pressed against his stomach, his face white as salt. Together, the three of them hem the assassin in.

Brama eyes the sapphire in the assassin's hand, but he knows something has changed. He can feel it. A distancing from me, which, even though he'd come to resent it, leaves an empty space inside him.

"You don't have to do this," Brama says.

The words are for me, not the assassin, but the assassin still responds. "All of this is necessary." He grips the sapphire tight. Wills me to burn them all as I burned the arrow.

But there's something about Brama that gives me pause. I haven't seen him through another's eyes in years, and when last I had he was dull, almost lifeless. Back then, I hardly spent a moment on him, blinded as I was by my obsession with the White Wolf.

But now…

There are lights, but they are dark and difficult to see. They remind me of my lord Goezhen. Will Brama be touched by the God of Demons? Will he one day stand before the lord who made me? It is something I've given up on ever happening again, thinking my god abandoned me. But if it might be so, what a fool I'd be to pass it up. And yet it isn't up to me. Not me alone, in any case.

Nearby, the green, alchemycal fire is dead, and a mundane fire of flickering orange burns in its place. The smoke is growing, but no one pays attention to it. The assassin has opened his mind to me, enough that I can take his body from him for a time. "If I remain," I say with the assassin's voice, "will you allow me to help you?"

"What's happening?" Nehir asks, leaning against the wall. As he slides to the floor, his confused gaze flits between Brama and the assassin. Jax rushes to his side, every bit as confused as her brother, but Brama understands all too well who voiced that question.

"I will not kill for you," he says.

"You hold the reins, Brama. I only wish to help."

Brama stares, clenching his teeth.

"Brama—" Jax begins, but when Brama holds his hand up, she goes silent. Brama looks the assassin in the eye, and I know his answer before he gives it.

"Very well," he says.

And I nod back to him.

With a voice given to me by the God of Chaos himself, I whisper to the assassin's mind. I tell him a story, of how he came to Sharakhai, how he found Jax and Nehir, how he made a deal with a local drug lord to secure them. I tell him how he slit both their throats, completing his lords' mission here in the desert. I breathe into him the satisfaction the deed gave him, and he swells from it.

As I knew it would, the urge to return to Malasan after long months spent tracking his quarry here to the slums of Sharakhai is born inside him. Slipping his knife into its sheath, he drops the crystal and walks through the smoke, beyond the flames, and down the stairs.

When he is gone, Brama walks to the where the necklace fell. He picks it up and slips it around his neck.

ONE WEEK LATER, JAX STANDS AT THE DOOR TO THE room that was once Kymbril's bedroom. "There's a man downstairs asking to see the Tattered Prince. He's the cousin of the girl you put right yesterday."

"How bad is he?"

"Bad," Jax replies.

Brama stands from the chair he'd been sitting in and begins to stretch. "Tell him I'll speak with him."

Jax stares. "You can't mean to heal him *now*."

"I do, if he can convince me of his earnestness."

He heads for the pair of beds that sit along the far side of the room. Brama will lie in one, the lotus addict the other, and then he and I will work together to lift the addiction and place it on Brama so that the man might be freed.

"But you've only just recovered."

"Maybe, but I *am* recovered. Send him up."

"Gods," Jax says under her breath. She stares at Brama as if he were some unanswerable riddle. "You'll kill yourself if you keep going."

"Perhaps. But I'm giving people new chances at life."

He's used that term once or twice before, and it has struck Jax hard each time. Nehir died the night of the fight with Kymbril from the wound to his gut. They buried him in the sand the following morning. When it was done, Brama asked Jax what she planned to do.

"I don't know," she said, staring out at the eastern horizon, toward Malasan. "Part of me wishes to return to my home. Part of me wishes to leave and go to Kundhun as I'd planned." She turned to Brama then. "And part of me would stay."

It was an offer, a plea, as clear as she could make it just then.

Brama smiled, a bit of the scoundrel returning to him. "Stay for a day. Stay for a week. I'll show you parts of the city you'd never find on your own."

As she stared into his eyes, a genuine smile crossed her lips. "I'd like that."

But she hadn't counted on Brama following through on his offer to Kymbril. The very next day, he healed two of the worst addicts who'd wound up in the lowest floor of Kymbril's manor, freeing them from the prison the lotus had built around them.

In the manor, Jax strides to Brama's side and takes his hand. "Promise me you'll be careful?" She leans in and kisses him, pulling away as quickly as she'd come. "We have sights to see, you and I."

I feel him brighten from within, and a smile most genuine spreads across his face. "I will be."

The look they share is precious, one of the most beautiful things I've seen in Sharakhai, a tattered prince and a young, foreign noble. And then Jax leaves the room to lead the suffering man up.

When she's gone, Brama moves to a beaten brass mirror hung against the wall. "Are you ready?"

"Of course, my master."

"I asked you not to call me that."

In the mirror, my visage smiles. "You don't have to suffer like this, you know. There are a thousand things and a thousand more we could do together. You and I *and* the girl."

"To live is to suffer," Brama replies. "I merely wish to do something virtuous with my life for once."

I consider this, wondering where the dark lights I'd seen will take him. Where they will take me.

"Very well," I say. "I'm ready."

A STORM UNBOUND

E.V. MORRIGAN

— Moonborne —

SMOKE BILLOWED ABOVE AVENTAIL QUARTER, SHADOWY whorls staining the morning sky black. Shae froze, eyes tracing the smoke, knowing full well its source before her gaze even settled.

They've found me.

Heart thrumming in her throat, she darted along the cobbles, racing for the home she'd made in the intervening years between her old life and new. A small crowd gathered in the street before the steps to her building, eyes wide and rumors flowing. She pushed her way through the finger-pointing throng and took the stairs three at a time. The symphony of crackling flames urged her on, each breath like inhaling shards of glass. Shae pulled her tunic over her mouth and crashed through the door, which already hung crooked on broken hinges. Wafts of smoke greeted her, and she bit back a cough. The heat struck her a palpable blow, stealing the moisture from her eyes. She stumbled to a halt just inside. There, on the floor not two paces from the doorway, lay Vitra, arms extended, fingers twitching against the wood. A discarded dagger lay just out of reach. Flames danced on the far side of the room, creeping ever closer, consuming everything in their wake.

"No!" Shae knelt beside the slip of a woman and rolled her over, drawing her into her arms. "Vitra?" She brushed strands of raven hair from her ashen face, swallowing hard at what she saw beneath.

Brown eyes, surrounded by halos of red, fluttered and struggled to focus. A darkness welled unchecked in their depths. "They…they took…her." The words ignited and faded in a huff, dying embers without fuel. "I…I couldn't…stop…" Shae's eyes trailed her limp body and spied the ooze of ruby fluid that spread about a bubbling gash at Vitra's ribs. The unmistakable tang of silvertail venom clung to the wound, the flesh tainted with emerald striations. A chill crept spider-like down Shae's spine, her stomach roiling. "It was…Ero… ghast," Vitra finished with a gasp.

Shae didn't need to hear the name to know who was responsible.

"Shhh." Shae pulled her in closer, clutching Vitra to her breasts. Bloody spittle spattered her tunic with every weakening breath. "Go with Dru, my love. It's okay. I'll find Aruur and bring her home." Heedless to the approaching blaze, Shae clutched to Vitra as she went limp in her arms, her chest falling still.

Shae stayed that way until a spark struck her cheek, a fiery reminder of what must be done. She eased Vitra from her lap, cradling her head until it lay still upon the floor. Empty eyes watched Shae as she stood, taking in the ruin of their home. Aruur had been taken so it served no purpose seeking her out in the conflagration.

Still, there were things Shae could not let the flames devour. She would need them soon enough.

With a shallow breath through the meager protection of her shirt, Shae bolted deeper into the apartment. She trailed the edge of the flames until she reached the hearth, ignoring the irony of the cool chimney's stones, the fire having yet to besiege it. Shae had no doubt it would soon, so she drove her elbow into the hearth's brick facing, knocking one inside the dark shaft with a loud *clunk*. From there, she clasped at another and pulled it loose, and then another, and another, until she could lean inside and reach the bundle wedged high in the shaft. She clasped the cloth-wrapped package and yanked it free of the chimney, peeling aside the covering as soon as it emerged. Her efforts revealed twin swords: Bol and Patnja, passed down from her mother, and her mother in turn. The worn, unadorned scabbards that cradled them were comfortable in her hands but the heft of the blades was bittersweet. A plaintive hum echoed in her ears as she ran her fingers across the pommels. She ground her teeth at the sound. It was a dirge, a sign of things to come.

Though she had given the swords up, exiling them to the darkness for years in favor of Vitra's soft touch, there was no recrimination in the blades' songs, only a desire that washed over Shae like a breath of fetid air. They longed to be used, to be bloodied once more.

Shae cast one last glance across the apartment as the flames licked at Vitra's body, slowly consuming her, and surrendered to the psalm that set her veins alight. She slung the blades from her belt, the action all too familiar, and kicked the shutters free from the nearest window. The fire snarling at her back, she leapt free of the apartment and left it to burn.

THE SEVERED HAND SPUN IN THE AIR FOR WHAT SEEMED an eternity.

The man it belonged to—until just a moment before—had yet to even scream. His gaze remained focused on the whirling piece of his body as it pirouetted before him, the stump spewing blood. Shae ended him with a thrust, driving Patnja under his sternum until the sheen of its crystalline shard disappeared inside the well of his chest.

She circled her head with Bol, blade down, to parry a blow aimed at her back, the embedded moonshard guiding her hand. Steel *clanged* as she freed the first of her swords and spun about, flicking blood into the eyes of her assailant.

"You sharding bit—" A crevice opened at the man's throat, leaving his unfinished curse to spew down the front of his tunic. Shae kicked him aside and leveled her blade at the last of Eroghast's men she'd ambushed in the narrow alley outside the Al Zahir Tavern.

The place was a magnet to the reivers, an oasis for the desert Kazuks fearful of the wide ocean that lay to the west. The wafting scent of Quwarmah Al Dajaj that enraptured the air as far as the next block over was sure to draw them in, if nothing else would. She only had to wait for those bearing Eroghast's sigil, the black vulture clutching a snake, to arrive.

They'd obliged her at dusk.

"Tell me where to find your master."

His steel wavered in a trembling hand but Eroghast's lackey shook his head, the barest flicker of a snarl curling his mustached lip. "There's no shame in dying to you, Oluja. In fact, better to you than him, I think."

Shae growled and darted forward, feinting high and driving a fist into the man's liver. He gasped and crumpled to his knees.

Shae batted his sword away and straddled him, aiming the point of Patnja at his eye. She pinned one of his hands flat on the ground with her knee as he tried to catch his breath.

"Who said I was going to kill you?"

She reached down with Bol and chopped off the man's thumb.

Shae waited until his shrieks subsided. "Now tell me where to find Eroghast."

His loyalty lasted only two fingers longer.

NIGHT SETTLED OVER NAPIER YET THE DARKNESS WAS never given full rein. Sai hung in the heavens above, casting her turquoise pall over Whitegate Market, the gleaming orb standing witness. The moon's light aided by the liberal smatterings of lanterns that lined the cobbled roadways, Whitegate held the gloom at bay.

Shae resisted the urge to spit as even the name of the well-to-do quarter filled her mouth with the sour sting of bile. Here, the rule of law only recognized coin. Pay enough and you could do nearly anything. Proof of such was evident in the raucous crowd that littered the streets, hooting and howling, pampered royals sampling all the deviance the market had to offer. Street hawkers strutted their wares along Market Way, their voices raised in competitive ardor. Oiled breasts and thighs glistened in the lantern light on full display, distracting the eye from stiff leather collars clasped about porcelain throats and the glazed expressions of saari-smokers too sharded to ever fully recover.

Though Shae had once been a part of this world, her own decadence a thing of legend, she found herself out of place. Hunched in a sliver of shadow in a narrow alley, she cursed her foolishness at letting Eroghast live when she left his service. Vitra had paid the price for Shae's stupidity, her arrogance, and now Aruur was in danger. And so Shae stood, waiting, scanning the street in search of the man who would lead her to the thief lord and her precious girl.

Time passed slowly until, at last, Shae spied the peacock Eroghast's lackey had spoken of: Belan Razul. There was no missing him in the crowd. His purple headdress stood out above the gathered revelers, garish yellow robes marking him as a keeper. Twin bands of crimson offered his rank among his order, a maharat in service to the sky god Galaksus, or so his garb would have one believe. The gold rings at his fingers and his wandering eyes, which greedily took in the flesh on exhibit, betrayed the illusion. Belan strolled through the crowd, at home in the carnival debauchery where even the most inebriated of the merrymakers made way for him.

Shae lowered her chin and strode after him, pulling her cloak tight to keep her blades from sight. Unlike the priest, she was forced to slither through the throng. Dressed so plainly, her wild hair in her face to distort her features, she had already begun to draw curious stares, so she was grateful when Belan turned off the crowded thoroughfare, unwittingly guiding her down a familiar dead-end street.

"Shards," she cursed under her breath, melting into the shadow of a shop's awning as the maharat continued unaware.

There, at the end of the cobbled street, stood Napier's resident Butkada Saimoon; a moon temple dedicated to the deity of judgment and protection, Dru. Shae snarled. *Leave it to Eroghast to make his home in a church.*

Though she, unlike Vitra, had no love for the gods, it was bad omen to spill blood in their halls of worship. She could only imagine that was why Eroghast had chosen the locale to do his business. Few would dare—at least publicly—to defame the church within its sacrosanct halls.

Razul clambered up the steps and peeled one of the great doors of the temple open, disappearing into the flickering candlelight inside. The door closed with a heavy *thump*, the sound reverberating down the barren street. Still, Shae held her ground and watched. This late, it was unlikely there were parishioners inside, but she wanted no witnesses to her return, no rumors to contend with.

Time ticked by slowly as she waited, finally giving in to the need for action that gnawed at her. She loosened her cloak and let it fall away. If there were innocents within, their fate would be in the hands of their gods. *Oluja has come.*

Shae mounted the steps and flung the door open, pausing only an instant before plunging into the gloomy interior of the temple. Blood was her goal, not stealth. Her blades leapt from their scabbards, her knuckles white about their pommels as she marched inside. The foyer opened before her into a wide hall, wooden pews lining the crimson carpet that snaked its way to the dais near the far end of the Butkada. The steps gleamed ivory in the flickering candlelight, and Shae froze at seeing her quarry lounging casually upon them, Belan Razul stood at attention beside him.

"I told you she would come," Eroghast said to the flamboyant keeper, his laughter echoing through the quiet church as he clambered to his feet. Dressed in a simple black tunic without adornment, and loose fitting pants tucked into calf-high leather boots, he looked nothing like the infamous lord Shae knew him to be. "She simply needed proper encouragement. Isn't that right, my dear?"

"Encouragement?" Shae's cheeks erupted with warmth. "You killed my lover!" Her raw screech reverberated through the temple. Belan eased a step higher, his smile withering.

"And I'll do the same to Aruur should you raise your voice to me again, Oluja, my little storm." He met her gaze with steely eyes. "Care to lose both of your loves tonight? Or do you doubt my commitment?"

Shae bit her lip, inching forward in defiance of reason. "At least *you* would be dead, too."

Eroghast shrugged, his slim shoulders relaxed. "Indeed, but then who would issue the counter-order to keep poor Aruur from being diced into tiny pieces, all while being kept alive to feel every rusty sawblade amputation? Hmmmm?"

Her feet froze in place of their own accord. She tasted copper, her lip bitten nearly clean through. "I'm going to kill you, Eroghast."

"Of that, my dear, I have no doubt. But it won't be tonight, nor anytime soon for that matter." With no apparent concern for the naked steel in her hands, the thief lord strolled across the carpet and came to stand before her, so close she could smell the tang of the oil that held his long black hair in place. He reached out and ran a finger along her oozing lip, trailing blood across the tip. "I warned you what would happen should you ever leave me, did I not?" He sucked the blood from his finger, his grin widening.

Shae snarled and took a short step back. Only a child when Eroghast took her in, rescuing her from the streets of Portmar where, despite the inheritance of her mother's crystalline swords, she would have grown to be nothing more than an urchin, a whore, or a corpse, she could find little to be grateful for right that moment.

"You killed Vitra," she repeated, hating the weakness that crept into her voice.

"That, my dear, was truly an accident," he said, the rigidness of his features softening to offer up the barest flicker of regret. "She was feisty, that one, and my man was overzealous. I meant to capture both your woman and Aruur without harm." He gestured to the keeper. "He has been seen to, has he not, Keeper?"

The priest nodded.

"The maharat can show you to his…*remains*, should you so wish. The fool has been dealt with accordingly." Eroghast moved in close, throwing a bony arm over Shae's shoulder, pulling her to his side. His breath smelled of peppermint and absinthe. "You, however, are not entirely blameless here. It was you who chose to flee my service despite your blood oath."

"I was but a child when I agreed to that."

"Be that as it may, it does not absolve you of your duty. Each day that you hid from me bears a cost, my dear. One you must pay or the penalty falls on Aruur. You of all my children must understand this, Oluja. You are mine until Araqh carts your soul across the Whorl or I absolve you of your service."

"Do so now, I beg of you." In his embrace, Shae felt just as she did the day he introduced himself in that rainy Portmar alleyway: cold and hollow and fearful of what was to come. "Return Aruur to me and let us leave. *Please.*"

"I've invested too much time in you to let you go so easily, child." He released her, moving to stand before her once more, pale, liver-spotted hands bookending her shoulders. He shook his head. "No, I will not let you go. I did not cross the desert to this godsforsaken hole for nothing, but I will spare Aruur the consequences of your rebellion should you deign to do a task for me."

Shae sighed, her decision already made. *Aruur will not suffer for my stubbornness.* "What is it you would have me do?"

His leathern face brightened with his grin. "I would have you bring Valare Sudar's head to me and I will, in turn, absolve Aruur of your debt to me."

"You ask so little," Shae told him, drawing in a deep breath, letting it go stale in her lungs.

"Your sarcasm aside, this is what I require."

She nodded. "Then his head you shall have." Shae let her breath ease out, the bitterness of her decision playing across her tongue. "But I warn you, no harm will come to Aruur or I will bring your world crumbling down around you no matter the consequences."

Eroghast stepped back and bowed low, muffled *cracks* sounding at his back. "I give you my word, Oluja. Now cease your threats and abide by your own word. You have two cycles to deliver Sudar to me, no more."

Shae spun on her heels in silence and left the church, letting the door slam shut behind her as she stormed into the cool night air once more. With but two cycles to slay Napier's renowned warlord mayor, she had no time for words.

The clock of Aruur's life ticked in her ears.

THOUGHTS OF ARUUR CROWDING HER HEAD LIKE tenement rats, Shae sped her way across town to where the mayor made his residence. Born of dirt and built powerful upon his wits and prowess, Sudar took no steps to obscure his home. Quite the opposite, in fact. Once a lowly reiver, Sudar came to rule over the Dûpişk Clan, one of the largest and most feared tribes to roam the Oldenspear Prefecture. Ever since he'd come to Napier and claimed the seat of mayor, his presence had been a shining beacon as to his power of will.

Sudar reveled in his mastery over the world. Part house, part museum, an entire wing of his expansive mansion was dedicated to his success. The heads of dozens of his enemies were mounted upon the walls, their staring, glassy eyes a reminder as to the fate that awaited those who might challenge him. Around those stood displays of feral beasts, some as fearsome as the *diranê çêkiri*, the fabled three-fanged tiger, and the poisonous *dûpişk*, for which his clan was named, or the *vatra pauk*, spinning webs of acidic fury inside their stone enclosure. The most dangerous of the beasts were dead, of course, such as the great horned bull, but many of the cases squirmed with unnatural life, memories of the constant skittering behind the thin barriers setting Shae's skin to crawling. Though she'd never imagined she would go there to kill Sudar, she had visited the manse several times, hoping to show Vitra a small part of her past, to give her lover a taste of the desert no sane mind wanted to see outside of a cage.

Shae exhaled in slow huffs, pushing aside thoughts of Vitra and the maddening images that came in their wake. They would do nothing but slow Shae down, distract her from what needed to be done. Vitra was dead and nothing could be done for her. Shae would kill Sudar for Aruur, then she would concern herself with thoughts of revenge upon Eroghast. Until then, she had a job to do.

She stood outside the low walls that surrounded Sudar's home and watched as well-armed men patrolled the yard. Though the warlord mayor might not fear attack, he wasn't so foolish as to invite assassins into his home. *Still,* Shae grinned at her thought, *he hadn't done nearly enough to keep this particular assassin out.*

She waited until the nearest of the guards turned his back and strode off about his rounds, the grip of his lantern *creaking* in his hand, before scaling the wall, her gloves and padded boots silencing her movements. The plush grass on the other side muffled the sound of her landing, and she darted low toward the manse. Once in the shadows of the building, she dug fingers into the places between the stones that made up the wall and clambered to the second floor where Sudar's quarters resided, the lower levels the museum. A small balcony splayed out before her, and she scrambled over the retaining wall and surveyed her surroundings.

She'd seen the mayor address the throngs of citizens from this exact balcony several times and spied the comfortable furnishings that lay beyond the wide double doors at his back. Now, in the pitch of night, those doors were closed, but Shae had seen enough to know they would be her best choice of ingress. She grasped the latch, expecting to have to pry the doors apart, only to find that Sudar, in his confidence, had left them unbarred. Shae swallowed a chuckle and let herself inside. Thick, fur rugs silenced her footfalls as she slipped into the dark room, her eyes adjusting the to the gloom.

Shae drifted through the living quarters, weaving her way around the furnishings toward the archway at the far end of the room. Bol and Patnja hummed in her ears in anticipation, their sheaths almost vibrating in an effort to contain them.

Your time will come, she told them and eased into the hallway beyond the archway. Lanterns lined the corridor walls, yet none were lighted. The warlord seemed to prefer the dark. At the far end of the hall, she spied a wide stairwell, spiraling down to the museum below, and knew she was close. The tremble of her blades grew as she came upon what she believed were the sleeping quarters of the mayor. Their excitement was contagious, and Shae found herself clasping their pommels in anticipation. Much as she detested the reason she was there, there was no denying the primal urges inside her, the need to stalk, to hunt. She was exactly what Eroghast had made her: a killer.

She sighed at that thought as she slipped through the entryway to Sudar's bedroom, freeing her swords from their sheaths. Eroghast had been right: She would never know peace for her very essence screamed for war, her blood shrieking in her veins as she crept closer to the sleeping form beneath the furs. She raised Patnja and plunged it toward the wild mass of hair splayed across the pillow.

The furs erupted and steel clashed against steel, her blow deflected.

Shae leapt back, eyes wide.

From the bed, Sudar emerged, holding a sword, its point aimed her way. "Did you truly think it would be so easy to slay me?" he asked, letting out a phlegmy chuckle.

"I had hoped." Shae met the warlord's gaze and wondered how he had known she was there.

He drew a step closer, taking her measure as she did his.

He wore the loose pants popular with the desert reivers, their overlapping seams keeping the sand at bay while allowing ease of movement. Beyond that, he wore nothing more than an amused grin. His long hair cascaded down bare, tanned shoulders, muscles coiled and ready to spring. If his stance was any indication, he was every bit the warrior he claimed.

"Who is it that wants me dead this time?" His grin widened. "I would know whose head I need to mount upon my trophy wall once I've killed you."

Shae shook her head, declining to answer. She raised her blades and started forward.

Sudar's eyes narrowed, his gaze locked upon her swords. "Your blades are sharded?"

Again, Shae said nothing, lunging forward and slashing high with Bol and thrusting low with Patnja. Sudar flowed like water, sidestepping the first blow and parrying the second, spinning around so he stood behind her. Shae spun as well, and Sudar drew back a step, chuckling once more. His smugness filled her cheeks with fire. She advanced again.

"You'll have to do better than that, assassin," he said. "You're not the only one in possession of a moonshard." He tapped his bare chest, just below his heart.

Shae froze.

"Ah, you hadn't known that, I see." He shook his head. "Your employer's obviously a fool or he sent you to die. I wonder which it is. Do you?"

Either is likely, Shae thought, but Sudar's revelation changed nothing. Aruur's life depended on her success. Sudar had to die.

She darted forward, feinting at his chest in hopes to draw him out. But it was as if she battled in mud. The warlord swayed and met her true strike, deflecting it from his groin, then he knocked aside Patnja as she followed up. She growled and launched another attack but Sudar was faster. Her blade cleaved air but his bit flesh.

Shae hissed and leapt back, fighting the urge examine the wound at her hip. She kept her eyes locked on Sudar as he held his blade up for her inspection, the steel colored red with her blood.

"First blood to me," he said. "How fortuitous."

Shae snarled and went after him again, blades whirling before her. Sudar parried and retreated, driven back by the onslaught. Fast as he might be, the warlord only had one blade to defend against two. She forced him out into the hall. He bounced off the wall and shifted, backing toward the stairwell. Sudar only laughed as she grazed his forearm. He lashed out in return, catching Shae across her chest. She growled at feeling his steel etch a searing line across her skin. The wound, shallow as it was, drew her up short, and Sudar took advantage, barreling down the steps to put distance between them.

"Come and join me," he called out from below, his voice echoing up the stairwell. "Soon you'll be just another attraction for the peasants to ogle, one more story for me to tell."

Shae started down the stairs at a creep. She would not let the warlord goad her. Crouched low, she took each step slowly, deliberately, her eyes surveying the path ahead. She reached the bottom without incident and stepped into the wide hall of the museum where an even deeper darkness greeted her. The chitter of insects sounded all around her and, though she'd visited the museum numerous times, she struggled to find her bearings in the absolute blackness that blanketed it now. She saw only shadows.

Patnja tugged at her wrist and she surrendered to the feeling, raising her sword just in time to parry a blow aimed for her head. The warlord's toothy grin emerged from the darkness for just an instant. She lashed out with Bol and forced his retreat. His laughter rang out a moment later, and Shae heard a loud *clunk* and moved toward the sound. She spied Sudar's shadowy figure dart away and she gave chase. A sharp pain at her ankle brought her to a sudden halt. A second stinging pain savaged her heel. Shae raised her foot and stomped down and something *crunched* beneath her boot. Before she could see what had bitten her, she felt the brush of insectile legs climbing her calf. She swatted the thing aside with Bol and leapt backwards. Only then did she realize Sudar had broken open one of the cages. The floor swarmed with *dûpişk*—scorpions—a sea of snapping pincers and poised stingers. Already she could feel the creatures' poison igniting the blood in her veins. Warmth washed over her.

Shae swayed and stumbled into the case nearest her, her elbow shattering the glass that protected the three-fanged tiger. Shards rained down around her and she groaned, muffling her voice against the back of her hand. She reached into the cage for support, her knuckles grazing the stitching at the tiger's belly, which held the stuffed creature's innards in place.

"Unpleasant, isn't it?" Sudar asked from somewhere in the darkness. "My brethren can be quite cruel."

Shae shrugged off the shards of glass that clung to her shoulders, letting them crash to the floor below. A pained grunt slipped loose from her lips as another of the *dûpişk* stung her foot. She crushed it under her heel and kicked it away.

"That was most unkind of you." The warlord's dark form oozed into view, just a few short paces from her. His blade led the way. "It's one thing to try and kill me, but it's something else entirely to come into my home and harm my brothers and damage my trophies." He shook his head. "Now tell me who sent you so I can punish them once I'm done with you."

Shae slumped against the cage, doing her best to put distance between her and the warlord. The tiger toppled from its perch and fell over her left shoulder, pinning her in place. Its permanent snarl glared at Sudar as he approached.

She shook her head. "You'll get nothing from me." She held Patnja toward him in a trembling hand.

Sudar shrugged, inching closer. "Oh, you'll tell me, assassin, fear not. It's only a matter of time." He lashed out and knocked Patnja aside, the sword clattering away into the darkness. He laughed and leaned in so they were face to face. "Save yourself some agony and tell me who your master is. Speak now and I will offer mercy."

Shae sighed and nodded. "My master is…"

Bol burst from the tiger's mouth and speared the warlord through the eye.

"Death," she finished.

Sudar stiffened, his grin withering at his lips. Shae yanked her blade free and the warlord slumped to the floor. She pulled her arm free of the tiger's stuffed guts and pushed the trophy aside, rising to her feet over Sudar's corpse.

"You are not the only child of the desert," she told it, reaching down and picking up one of the *dûpiṣk*. It lashed out and stung her palm and Shae just laughed, its venom bubbling in the wound. She crushed the creature in her fist and tossed the gooey mess aside. "No one survives the Slough Marches without becoming immune to *dûpiṣk* poison."

She stared at the creatures as they clambered over Sudar's body, reminded of the moonshard buried in his chest, such being the custom of the shard-bearers. Shae knelt, brushing the *dûpiṣk* aside to bare his torso and neck. She took her blade to his throat, cleaving through the spine to free his head. Then she went after the shard. If Aruur's freedom could be bought with Sudar's head, she wondered what could be had in exchange for the moonshard. A smile formed as an idea came to mind.

Shae rose, the warlord's blood dripping from her hands, her prizes clasped tight as she made her way toward the stairs. The skitters of Sudar's exhibits sounded in the background, loud in the stillness of the museum, their whispers seeing her off.

BELAN USHERED HER INSIDE THE BUTKADA SAIMOON, stepping to the side to avoid her as she strode toward the dais without a word to the maharat.

Eroghast stood atop the stairs, watching her approach. His gaze drifted to the heavy bag she carried. "Is that him?" he asked, rubbing his hands together.

"It is," Shae answered, coming to a stop at the base of the stairs. She remained there, not bothering to offer the head to Eroghast.

"Come now, little storm, must you be so difficult?"

"Show me Aruur first. Show me she's okay."

"Such dramatics, child." Eroghast sighed and waved to the maharat, who had resumed his place at Eroghast's side.

The priest went over to a door set in the wall behind the altar and opened it a crack. Shae caught a flicker of Aruur before she was pulled back out of sight.

"There, you've seen her. Now give me Valare Sudar's head or I'll have my men take her away."

Shae nodded and tossed the sack to Eroghast. He caught it

with a grunt, a grin breaking out across his lips. He fumbled with the tie and managed to get the bag open, peeling back the edges so he could see inside. A low, rumbling laugh spilled loose at seeing what was inside. He reached in and grabbed the head by its hair, pulling it free of the sack so he could examine it. His brows rose at seeing the moonshard that filled its ruined eye.

"What is this?"

"My freedom," Shae told him. "The head for Aruur and the shard for me. Even trade for our release."

Eroghast chuckled and pulled the shard out, crystalline reflections dancing across his face in the candlelight. He stared at it for a few moments before pulling his gaze away and returning his attention to Shae.

"You know I can't let you go, child. I applaud your efforts, but you are mine until Araqh parts us. You must understand my position."

She exhaled slowly. "I do," she said, "as you must understand mine."

Eroghast's eyes narrowed as something moved within Sudar's gaping socket. The old man shrieked and went to release the head just as something dark darted across his hand, trailing a string of red in its wake. Skin sizzled at its touch and Eroghast shrieked, unable to release his gory prize, his fingers entangled in the warlord's hair.

From the wreckage of Sudar's eye, dozens of *vatra pauk* spilled forth, spewing their acidic strands as they clambered over Eroghast. The temple filled with the stench of charred flesh and the thief lord crumpled into a heap, screeching as the fire spiders spun their web, strands crisscrossing his shuddering body.

The maharat fled without a backward glance, leaving the door behind the altar open.

"Aruur, to me!" Shae shouted.

She heard the clatter of chains, followed by low, guttural screams. There was a heavy *thump* somewhere beyond the door, and then Aruur burst through, charging across the altar. Warmth flooded her veins as she saw, and Shae stepped forward as Aruur took the stairs at a run. Unable to stop her momentum, Aruur skidded and flew over the stairs, right into Shae's waiting arms.

"That's my girl," Shae whispered as she buried her face in Aruur's neck as she hugged her tight to her breasts.

Eroghast's screams fading into wet gurgles, Shae knew they had to flee. She set the dog on the floor and slapped Aruur lightly on the ass.

"Come on, girl. Let's go."

Aruur padded across the carpet on all fours, letting loose a parting howl as the pair fled the temple.

"Arrrrruuuuuuuuuurrrrrrrr!"

THE GAME

MATTHEW WARD

— World of Aradane —

EVERYTHING'S A GAME. LIFE. DEATH. WAR. LOVE.
Ambition. Oh, especially ambition. It is the master that rules us
all. It drives every desire—for what is desire but the longing for
something we do not have? The clever, it ushers to new peaks,
to prosperity and satisfaction without end. The foolish? Well,
better an ambitious fool than a lazy one. After all, the ambitious
ones never last. But the game is never a foregone conclusion.
Cleverness and foolishness are not absolutes. Recognising which
guides you at any given moment, whether your choices lead
to victory or defeat? That's the tricky part. Which guides me?
Time will tell.

There's a stone wall at my back. My hands are hitched high above my head. By rope, rather than chain. My blindfold's imperfect, less so the darkness in this dank place. Clammy air tells me I'm underground, the tang of a sunken shoreline suggests the sea is nearby. Interesting, but hardly conclusive. The Tressian promontory is a warren of sewers, caves, smuggler's tunnels—and a goodly number of crypts besides. I could be in any of them.

A gruff voice sounds. "Who's there? Answer me!"

Privileged tone, accustomed to instant obedience, if not respect. I've only met its owner a handful of times, but once would be enough. It's always enough if you know how the game is played. After all, if you're not familiar with the pieces, how can you expect to win?

"Answer me, damn your eyes!"

"Calm yourself, captain," I sigh. "I'm in no position to harm you. It appears we share a predicament."

"Solomon? I might have bloody well known."

There aren't many in the city who'd address me so disrespectfully. Most are…wary…of earning my disfavour. Not so ex-General Quintus, late of the republic's army. Probably, he feels he has nothing to lose, not after that disaster on the border—the one most are too polite to mention in Quintus's presence. For all their high-minded talk, my fellow councillors turn on their darlings like a pack of starving hounds, when the hunger is there. Especially when their own reputations are at stake. It's useful, most of the time. If only they hadn't followed the demotion by instating Quintus as captain of the city guard. I'd hoped for someone more tractable. More…flexible. Then again, a man can do worse than be judged by the quality of his enemies. And much as it pains us both, we share a passion.

"I assure you, captain, I'm as much in the dark as you are."

"Very bloody funny, *my lord*." As ever, Quintus laces the honorific with disdain.

The still air carries a chorus of small, whispering creaks. It's easy to picture Quintus's heavyset bulk straining against his bonds, his impassive grey eyes growing gradually less so as it becomes clear the knots won't budge.

Though I'm at pains not to show it, Quintus's presence worries me. It's unexpected, and the unexpected is usually the undesired. It means pieces are moving in ways I haven't foreseen. It might be nothing. Just a stray gambit from an unready opponent. Or it could be that I've been outplayed, that my ambition has exceeded my ability at last. The future promises to be very interesting, and possibly very brief.

"I didn't expect to find you here, captain."

A growl. "So you know where we are?"

I waste a thin smile he can't possibly see. "I wouldn't trouble you with a guess."

"But you know who holds us?"

I laugh under my breath. "That would depend entirely on who's in charge, wouldn't you say?"

Quintus snorts like a restless bull. He and I are clearly of similar mind. We're neither of us happy—only a fool would gladly embrace our particular predicament—but fear is as alien to the good captain as it is to me. It's a waste of energy, and clouds the mind besides. It's a shame he and I are destined to work at cross-purposes. Not opposing, not as such. Ultimately, we want the same thing. Alas, he hasn't the stomach for the journey I have planned. Today, though? Today we're allies of circumstance.

Unless I have to kill him. That's always a possibility.

"My money's on Selloni," says Quintus at last. "Caught a couple of his brigantines at harbour last week. Impounded near three thousand tonnes, all of it still bearing the brands and spilt blood of the Solokan Estates. They're getting sloppy. Relying too much on Lord Avanov looking the other way."

Poor Avanov. By now, he's finally realised Quintus isn't as malleable as his predecessor. And Quintus could be right. It could be Selloni. He's never lacked for pride. Though he struts and preens as a princeps of corsairs, the truth is, Giack Selloni's nothing but a thug with a taste for velvet and lace.

"Still, *my lord*," Quintus clearly isn't done. "I'm surprised you'd let any of your lackeys get out of hand. Unhappiness in the ranks, is it?"

"A certain dissatisfaction has been brewing, I must confess. Change is always a catalyst."

He laughs, the notes dry as dust. "Under other circumstances, I reckon I'd be glad to see this. The great and untouchable Lord Solomon, strung up by his criminal brethren."

He sounds bitter, and I suppose I can't blame him. I've not exactly been subtle. I've never seen the point. Why waste effort on legerdemain and obfuscation when fear and greed are so much more efficient? Half my fellow councillors know the steps I've taken to control Tressia's disordered underworld, but there's not a man or woman amongst them brave enough to actually come out and say as much. A promise here and there, and most are happy enough to look the other way. And for those who aren't? Well, there are promises, and there are *promises*. Without their support, there's little Quintus can do.

You want my advice? Throw off the shackles of mortality as soon as you're able. Become a *legend*. Let the tales of your deeds run before you like howling wolves, sapping resolve before intent crystallises into action. Naturally, some will perceive you as a challenge, a rung on the ladder to their own ascension. Like I said, ambition is one of the few constants in life. The trick is to stay one move ahead, to let your challenger's death and disgrace be the kindling that causes your fire to blaze all the brighter. The question is, am I still one move ahead? Is the game still following the rules I've set?

The evidence suggests otherwise.

The scrape and thud of approaching feet drags me from my thoughts. "It seems, captain, that your curiosity is about to be sated."

"Oh, be still my aching heart."

Quintus's words are weary, but his tone betrays a hidden vigour. The good captain's tightly wound. Expecting some opportunity, perhaps? More likely hoping to create one. A dangerous man, is our Quintus. Maybe more dangerous to himself than to me. Something to consider.

The footsteps approach. The warm glow of a guttering torch dances through the blindfold's weaves. Strong hands close around my arms, their grip more forceful than necessary. My bound wrists are loosed from the wall, and they lead me away. I don't resist. What's the point? I've never sought physical confrontation. It's so…unpredictable.

Somewhere behind me, Quintus proves less tractable. There's a choked gasp and a scuff of boots as one of our captors goes sprawling. Then a dull thud and a heavier grunt from Quintus as retribution follows defiance. Like I said, unpredictable.

For a time, the steady footsteps are the only sounds—those, and the scrape and splash of Quintus's heels as he's dragged along behind. Apparently, my captors aren't inclined to conversation. I smother the temptation to second-guess the decisions that led me here. The board is set, and the pieces begin their slow, intricate dance. That's where my attention must lie.

There's a creak of aged timber. New sounds wash over me. The burble of a crowd, their echoing voices thick with anticipation. Beneath it, the crackle of flames. The temperature leaps as I cross the threshold, the rush of air carrying with it the stench of sweat and stale beer.

My guide hauls me roughly to a halt and spins me around. A swell of laughter rises. The crowd's amused. I can't say the same for myself. Like I said before, I don't get afraid. But on occasion, it's an effort of will more than nature. Right now, my willpower's dangerously close to its limits.

I suppress a flinch as cold steel slides along my temple, cutting free the blindfold. Light blazes all around me. I blink away the splotchy blue afterimages. A cheer goes up from the crowd. Nothing pleases a mob like discomfort, however trivial.

At least a hundred men and woman crowd the cavern, their raiment a jumble of leathers, furs and wool-cloth. Not for this gathering the following of fashion so beloved of the nobility. Practical garb for practical folk. Nondescript enough to not draw a constable's eye. Dark enough to render every shadow a welcome refuge. Naturally, they're all armed.

Most of the onlookers are gathered around the leaping bonfire set before the ramshackle wooden stage upon which I now stand. Smaller groups watch eagerly from lantern-cast shadows against the granite walls. A few paces beyond the bonfire, water laps against a shallow shore, glimmers of light dancing across the ripples like the restless faelings of romantic myth.

A caravel's prow looms out of the shadows, its timbers as sagging and rotten as a spinster's dreams. Only the figurehead retains any semblance of former glory. Her patrician brow lends the impression of a judge presiding over court, and a steady stare warns of an ill-fate for those who defy her will. But algae discolours her alabaster beauty, and the gilded lustre of her hair has long since faded. The irony provokes a wry smile. A forgotten figurehead for a forgotten goddess. It's been long indeed since anyone in Tressia bent a knee to radiant Lumestra, patron of wisdom and judgement. It'll be longer still if I have my way. Gods only bring ruin.

My amusement does not go unnoticed.

"I'm glad you approve, Lord Solomon."

The speaker spreads his arms wide as he strides across the stage's uneven boards a half-dozen paces in front of me. Unlike his audience, he apes the garb of his betters. The tails of an emerald jacket brush his heels, and his greying hair rests upon the collar of a silk shirt. Giack Selloni, ever the showman, ever with so little to be showy about. You can dress a wild beast in waistcoat and cuffs, you can deck it with gold and jewels—you can even teach it to turn the odd witty phrase—but a beast it remains. I should know. The self-styled corsair princeps is a creature of my own making. I oversaw the capture and execution of Selloni's predecessor, and the three who preceded *her*. All died twitching on a scaffold, empty eyes staring across the seas over which they'd sought dominion. Nothing personal. The corsairs of the Outer Isles have been a power in this part of the world for centuries. I sought a leader with whom I could do business.

The search continues.

I glance at Quintus, standing a pace or so to my left. He's in no state to crow about predicting Selloni's involvement. His blindfold's gone, but he's upright only by dint of the two minders gripping his shoulders. Well, he brought it on himself. One of the minders has a fearful bruise forming on his brow. Even blindfolded, Quintus knows how to leave his mark.

Selloni steps closer, moustache twitching as he sneers. "Nothing to say? I think I'm disappointed. I'd expected a threat by now, or perhaps a heartfelt plea." He brings his hands together, palm to palm. "You *do* know you're going to die, don't you?"

Laughter rumbles across the cavern, thunder heralding the storm yet to come. This is why Selloni will never hold the authority he longs for. Tell a man death is inevitable, and you give him power.

He no longer has any reason to cooperate, and nothing to lose. He'll drag the game out as long as he is able. Hold out the possibility of hope, and your prey trip on their own feet as they scurry to claim it.

I let my gaze drift across the group standing behind Quintus and I at the rear of the stage in front of a mildewed scarlet curtain. Selloni's peers, each a ganglord with a stake in the city's criminal pursuits. Turning my back on Selloni, I give them the benefit of my full attention. It's always interesting to see who's watching, who isn't, and who isn't here at all. "You really shouldn't let your jester prattle on. He's embarrassing you."

Lithel Andri, current mistress of the Crowmarket, shifts uncomfortably beneath her feathered veil. The alleys and wharves are her territory, and they're a long way off. Too many present will remember what the Crowmarket used to be—a brotherhood of "noble" thieves, labouring to feed the starving and blunt the excesses of the rich and the criminal alike. An ocean couldn't wash away all that bad blood.

Of course, the Crowmarket of legend is long since gone. I've spent years pruning its ranks, winnowing out the genuinely high-minded rogues, opening up positions in the Parliament of Crows for those I can deal with. Behind every righteous soul, there's always two or three realists eager to take their place. Now the Crowmarket is little more than an assemblage of beggars, footpads and housebreakers. The cadaverous Andri is the last of the old Parliament, but even she doesn't lack for secrets. She's taken plenty of lives with that stiletto of hers, and ruined many more. The hulking lad acting as her bodyguard is the son of her predecessor, dead in the squalor of Blackwater Jail ten years back. She's never told young Balgan what she knows of the mother who betrayed him, and who delivered his father into the hands of the city guard. It's hard to say what Balgan knows of this. There's no reaction to my enquiring glance, but that's to be expected.

He's mute, and dull-witted besides. Not that the dull-witted are in short supply hereabouts. But even a simpleton can be a powerful piece upon the board, if properly directed.

To Andri's left, Natilya Eshlan favours me with her gorgon stare. Of all those present, she's the closest I have to a rival—certainly since the passing of the late, unlamented Lord Lavirn. She specialises in fanning the fires of hedonism into vice, and profiting thereafter by keeping the flames stoked. She knows all the bloodlines carefully concealed from family trees, knows by sight the owner of every wandering hand and jealous eye. Even I don't know how long she's plied her trade. I've heard it rumoured that she's an eternal, as ageless and bloodless as the granite walls. Possibly she is. Certainly she cannot be so young as her girlish figure implies. Her eyes are too old for that.

Natilya has longed to get her claws into me for many years now, to learn my secret yearnings and turn them to her own ends. But there is nothing secret about my desires. I love only the Tressian Republic, freed from the tyranny of gods and magic through labours without end. Every bead of sweat I shed—every drop of blood I spill—is in her service, and no other's.

Only the third and final worthy seems truly at home in the cavern. Niarr af Redegar casts a vast shadow. He's a creature of the frontier, rather than Tressia's civilised streets, and he wears his wolf pelts as trophies as much as raiment. Like the broad-bladed axe at his side, they're warnings. I have it on good authority that he could fill entire wardrobes with the flayed skin of his rivals. Perhaps he has. A Thrakkian's honour is every bit as tangled as his plaited beard and, like most such pretensions, a deception practiced upon oneself. Niarr would have us believe he's a noble outlaw, fighting the underdog fight. In truth, he's a smuggler, a braggart and an opportunist.

Still, four out of Tressia's five underworld chiefs, and all here because of me. It's gratifying. I wonder where the fifth is?

"You'll not turn your back on me!" Selloni grips my shoulders and spins me around. "You're nothing, Solomon, not any longer! This is my hour!"

He drags me to the front of the stage, giving me what he fancies is the full weight of a withering stare. Anticipation ripples through the crowd. They surge forward, desperate not to miss a moment.

I don't flinch. I don't attempt to pull away. Why should I? I'm a dead man, remember? What's he going to do? Kill me twice? I'm in no hurry for him to follow through, but I may as well take what pleasures I can in the meantime.

"*Your* hour? Oh, I see. This is all your idea? Don't tell me they're so desperate as to let you take my place?"

All of a sudden, I'm falling back across the stage, propelled by Selloni's angry shove. With my hands still tied, I've no means of fighting for balance. I lose my footing and fall. The impact shivers my elbow, and drives the breath from my body. Selloni leans over me, eyes shining.

"Why not?" he hisses. "In five years, you've shown us how much stronger we are together than apart. But you're not one of us. We've always been your toys…" He flings a hand towards the curtain and the unconscious Quintus. "…offered up to the city guard when it suits your purposes, so you can climb the Council's ranks. No more. You hear me? No. More."

I can't argue with his logic. He's right. I've done all that and more. I've no interest in letting thieves and outlaws flourish in my city, or in the Republic at large. Selloni and his newfound allies were only ever a means to an end. Playing pieces traded for advantage. Before I took an interest, they were tearing each other apart, and the city alongside. I couldn't allow that. Not my city. So I took over. It was only ever a temporary measure. I've more important things to do than administrate a nest of vermin. Not that there's any point in saying so.

Finally, I haul myself into a sitting position. "Selloni? You're a fool."

He laughs off the insult, and slams a boot into my gut. I hear the *crack* of my head bouncing off timber before I feel it. For the second time in as many minutes, I'm fighting for breath, and this time the room's spinning like a child's top. I'm not even halfway recovered when Selloni kneels beside me, the point of his dagger pressed against my throat. There's a mad gleam in his eyes. Even if I were inclined to beg, it wouldn't do any good. I've pushed him too far for that.

Heavy footfalls thump across the stage. "No! He's mine. As agreed." Niarr's bellow rumbles like mountains grinding together.

Selloni rises to his feet in a swirl of emerald velvet, a little of the madness fading from his eyes. "Of course. As agreed." He sheathes the dagger with a flourish and withdraws to the front of the stage, but he's fooling no one. Without Niarr's intercession, things would have grown a great deal more interesting. Not that I've any reason to celebrate. I know exactly how Selloni won the Thrakkian to his cause.

Niarr's meaty hand clamps around my throat and hauls me aloft. He's a good head taller than I. My feet don't even reach the floor. The stench of his furs is overwhelming. Or perhaps it's not the furs. Some Thrakkians have a profound aversion to bathing—some superstition about a long-vanished nymph goddess, if memory serves. I imagine every time Niarr passes a river, the fish downstream sigh with relief.

"For three years now, I've sworn your death. For Ana."

It's not something I'm proud of. Niarr resisted my approaches for the longest time, even when I threatened to have his beloved daughter killed inch by inch. When he refused? Well, I didn't have a choice, did I? Like I said, I'm not proud of it, but necessity must win out. Once set, the rules of the game must be observed.

Do I feel remorse for the death of Ana afa Niarr? Of course not. That particular apple was as rotten as the tree from which it fell. Not that it matters. Ana could have been the most virtuous of souls and it would have changed nothing. She mattered only as a gaming piece, in life and in death. Still does, as she's now the token with which Selloni bought Niarr's loyalty. It's something of a surprise. After all, Niarr has another daughter upon whom he dotes just as much. He must be *very* certain of today's outcome.

Niarr's grip tightens. I can't tell whether he intends to choke me, snap my neck, or both at once. The crowd cheers. They don't care. They want blood.

"That's the trouble with the theatre," rumbles Quintus, blinking away his unwanted nap. "I always fall asleep before the finale." He clears his throat. "You do know you're all under arrest?" Even pinned by his minders, he manages a solemn dignity that Selloni and his peers will never master. He's barely forty, but the manner of a disappointed patriarch suits him better than a man of twice his years.

Selloni roars with laughter, and the crowd join in. "I doubt that, captain." Selloni waves a graceful hand towards the curtain. "Mistress Andri claims your hide. The Parliament of Crows are inundated with petitions. The people want justice for sons and daughters led to their deaths under your command. Your head will go to the Roost, and your bones scattered across the city for the rats to gnaw upon."

"Aye, we'll see about that." Quintus's tone remains defiant, but his posture wilts, just a little. It's not fear. I can practically see the ghosts of the dead swirling about him. A guilty conscience is the mark of a good man. It's also the prerogative of a fool, if the distinction can be made. He did what had to be done. That should be an end of it. The living are burden enough; let the dead remember themselves.

Yet there's something in Quintus's eyes. Not fear. Not remorse. Not even defiance. Expectation. Even dangling from Niarr's grip, it takes me aback. Does he know? It doesn't seem possible, but I'm already suspecting that Quintus is not someone to underestimate. I catch his gaze, and the lack of acknowledgement is all the acknowledgement I need. Well, well.

The chant begins as a murmur, soon swelling to a hollow roar. *Kill them! Kill them! Kill them!* The cry echoes around the cavern, as rhythmic as a heartbeat. Selloni, once again revelling in the role of showman, offers a deep bow to the braying masses. It's a safe audience for him, eager to cheer him on. Most are his crewers, or at least his dockside fences and informants. This cavern is one of his favourite nests.

Of course I know where I am. I've always known.

I twist just enough in Niarr's grasp to stare at the new owner of Quintus's hide. Lithel Andri's eyes are fixed on a knothole in the planking. She has no stomach for this. The way this gathering's going, that'll get her killed sooner rather than later. There's no honour amongst thieves, whatever people say. There's only fear, and the will to do what must be done. I'm Niarr's price. Quintus is Andri's. And what of Natilya Eshlan and her ageless stare? The answer comes easily enough. Though I doubt Selloni knows it, she'll be the true power, whispering, manipulating. Selloni seeks a throne, but all he's really done is taken his leash from one master and given it to another.

Ambitious fools never last.

Four ganglords, seeking profit by my death. But where is the fifth? The answer comes just as Niarr renews his assault on my abused neck.

A hooded figure emerges from the crowd without fanfare, but the chanting dies with its approach. Crimson robes gleam like blood in the firelight. The newcomer is alone, but from the stumbled steps and widening eyes amongst the audience, you'd think there were dozens. Niarr shoves me back across the stage, into the waiting arms of the minder who led me from the cells, and places a hand to his axe. Natilya goes pale as the corpse she may or may not be. Lithel Andri takes a half-step back, then recovers herself, doubtless hoping no one notices. Quintus watches impassively, even as one of his minders makes the sign of the rose to ward off evil. And Selloni, predictably, decides to brazen things out.

"You're not welcome here."

The figure bows low before the stage, black-gloved hands spread wide. "I come as an emissary."

It's a pleasant voice, as far as these things go. It possesses a strange timbre, almost metallic, not readily identifiable as male or female. The shapelessness of the robes adds to the ambiguity. They hang unevenly, and puddle on the ground like wax from a candle lit too long.

"I've no words for your mistress." Selloni's tone grows firmer, more confident.

The emissary straightens and climbs the creaking wooden stairs. No one bars its way. Doubtless they're recalling the rumours they've heard of Tressia's fifth and newest criminal power. She's called many things. The Red Lady. Mistress Arlia. In the wall-ward slums, they name her Baszoria, after the fabled witch who bathed in fresh blood under each new moon. None of these are her real name, of course. They're just words to lend a little shape, to clothe the unknown. An identity for the fear she works so hard to propagate. Magic may have passed into legend hereabouts, but the dread of it remains. She understands this.

They say she has no servants, only slaves, their souls ripped from their hearts and set in glittering gemstones for her pleasure. They say she is older than this city, older than the Republic, older than the very hills themselves. They say she commands magics not seen in Tressia since the time of Sidara. *They* have much to say, and a great deal of it is wrong. I know the truth. Or at least a portion. It's the only real leverage I have. One last throw of the dice.

The emissary halts a pace from Selloni. "My Mistress asks very little. Just a seat at the table. As an equal. All will profit handsomely." There's a curiously soothing note to the voice. It longs for agreement. It entices acceptance.

Selloni's cheek twitches. Not much, but enough, if you're looking for it. He knows something's off-key. I'm impressed, after a fashion. I wouldn't have credited him with the intelligence. "Your mistress has no place here. I'm not impressed—*we* are not impressed—by the theatrics of a Thrakkian bog-witch."

"I concur." Lithel Andri steps forward, her thin face hardening into resolve for the first time since my arrival. "The Crowmarket will never embrace Mistress Arlia. If she comes as a friend, she should have presented herself as such from the first, not contested our territories."

"Agreed." Natilya makes her pronouncement with all the finality of an empress disposing execution—a tone I've been unlucky enough to hear first-hand in a different game altogether.

Niarr holds his tongue. I doubt he cares either way, so long as coin flows into his pockets.

Selloni cracks a smile. I'll never know if he'd have had the courage to follow through on the decision alone, but with his newfound colleagues at his back? Well, now he *can't* back down. "You have our decision."

A murmur ripples through the crowd. Quintus's expression may as well have been carved from granite. Were I a betting man, I'd wager he wasn't expecting this, but you"d never know it from his face.

The emissary cocks its head. "But you've not yet heard her terms."

Before Selloni can interrupt, the soothing voice recounts a list of concessions and trades that Mistress Arlia is prepared to make. It's a generous offer, from what I hear of it, but I'm not really listening.

My attention's given over to the woman standing at the side of the stage, her arms folded across her chest and her back propped against the rough stone of the cavern wall. She meets my gaze and holds it for a moment, her perfect lips hitching into a lopsided smile. Like Natilya, she looks young. Like Natilya, her appearance is a lie. No one else spares her a glance. It's as if she and I exist in a world apart. Only when the colour fades from my surroundings, do I realise that's precisely true.

The woman pushes away from the wall and advances in a swirl of crimson skirts and black hair. Rubies glint at her pale throat and silk-sleeved wrists. Her footsteps are the only true sound. Everything else is muffled, as distant and weary as my surroundings. Everything but the soft chuckle of her laughter.

Enough with the sideshow, with the distractions. This is where the real game begins.

She halts in front of Niarr, green eyes glinting at me. "I received your invitation."

I nod towards Selloni, now gesticulating wildly in reply to the emissary's terms. If nothing else, I'm grateful to be spared another round of verbal posturing. "He'll never agree."

"I know. But you'll forgive me my foibles?" Her smile broadens, then vanishes as she crosses the remaining distance between us. "What do you offer?"

"A truce. A year to consolidate your new territory, unhindered by me…or by the Council."

A slender eyebrow arches. She curls her lip in disgust. "Have I come all this way for that?"

"No. You came because I guaranteed all your rivals would be in one place. Because I guaranteed you an audience. And, I think, because you were bored."

She shrugs. "Perhaps that's true. But I didn't ask you for anything. You have no hold over me unless I allow it. You're my rival as much as they. Why should I spare you?"

The threat hangs on the air. I don't doubt she means it. This is the moment where the course of the game turns. Defeat or victory rests on my next words. I start with a name. "Fitzwalter."

She stiffens. Just a little, but enough. "And what do you think that buys you?"

She could kill me at any moment. That she hasn't yet means I'm still in the game. "By itself, nothing. It's a warning. I know who you are, even if these fools do not."

Her beauty turns cold. I have her full attention now. In truth, I don't know the importance of the name—not in any great detail, anyway. It's not a Tressian name, and if my sources speak truly it hails from very far afield indeed. Much like Arlia herself. Beyond that, my information is sketchy at best. Fitzwalter could be male or female, living or dead, a beloved ally or a hated enemy. That's not the point. What matters is that it means something to *her*. Knowledge is rarely as complete as we might wish. Facts float upon a sea of conjecture and guesswork. The trick in these circumstances is to present what you know in such a way that your opponent believes the knowledge left unsaid is the most powerful of all.

She shakes her head in dismissal, but the accompanying laughter is hollow. "You know nothing of me."

Just like that, the balance of power between us shifts. If she truly believed that, I'd already be dead. She can't kill me until she's certain.

"Then let me prove you wrong."

The words come with a confidence I don't yet feel. But I'm an old hand. Old enough to know that appearance is everything. I may deride Selloni for his theatrics, but I'm as guilty of them as any. A firm jaw, a level stare and you can fool them all. Because deep down, people *want* to believe. They want their secrets laid bare. It validates them, gives meaning to who they are and what they've done. I couldn't do my work otherwise.

"Selloni thinks you're a Thrakkian, but the realm you hail from is more distant by far. You're certainly not here by choice. And impressive as this little display is, I know you're but a shadow of who you once were."

It's guesswork, all guesswork, no more validated than the wharfside diviners promising to reveal the future through a deck of scuffed pentassa cards. But like I said, people want to believe. Even people who aren't really people at all.

She steps closer, eyes blazing. "I think I'll kill you now."

But she makes no move to follow through. This time, the threat's empty. I may not know much about Mistress Arlia, but she knows me. Or at least she knows my legend. Ask anyone in the Republic, or a hundred leagues beyond in any direction. They'll all tell you the same stories. Solomon *knows*. Solomon *always* knows. Oh, she's too canny to take every tale at face value. Given time and experience, she might even come to split truth from fable. But not yet. Not before this particular game has ended. For all the uproar she's caused these last few years, the Red Lady is a stranger here, while I've worked hard to become a constant in an inconstant land.

I savour the moment. In many ways, I wish she hadn't moved us into this grey world, beyond the sight of Selloni, Quintus and the others. I shouldn't crave an audience, but I do. How else do legends grow? I swallow the impulse. It's unworthy of me. What I do, it's not about personal ambition.

"I know about the temple buried beneath the Hayadra Grove. I know what you've hidden there. I know it's what gives you the power to perform these little…tricks of yours." With that my gambit's revealed. She has to know what's coming now, but that doesn't diminish the pleasure. "If I don't walk out of here, my operatives will act. She'll be gone. You'll be gone. Or we can have that truce."

She goes rigid as a board, fists clenched so tightly that red rivulets appear where lacquered fingernails gouge her palms. I'm not guessing. Not this time. Always save the best for last—it lends verisimilitude to the half-truths that come before. If I'm honest, I'm not certain my operatives can do as I say. There's still so much I don't know about her reach. As for the rest? I no longer have to join the dots—Mistress Arlia's doing that for me. Behind her eyes, she's weaving together the pieces in a way I never could. I don't have to convince her. I never did. I just needed her to convince *herself*.

"A seven year truce."

She spits the words. It's the sound of concession, of pieces toppled to the board. I restrain a smile. Whatever tale I tell of this moment in years to come, this was no foregone conclusion. It's important to remember that. An acquaintance of mine had a saying: *Arrogance is more dangerous than a sword.* Words to live by.

"Five."

She nods, swallowing her displeasure. "We have a bargain."

A bargain. I've heard no sweeter words all day. If Arlia's what

I think she is, then she's incapable of breaking our accord. Gods can't go back on their words, nor can their shadows. Nor can I, for what it's worth. Another part of my legend—the carrot to the stick.

She turns away, looks over her shoulder, as if the next words don't matter. "And these others?"

"Enjoy yourself."

She smiles, confirming my words as sentence of death, and drifts away into the crowd.

Colour bleeds back into the world. The sound of the crowd rushes into my ears, like I've broken a river's surface after too long underwater. They're chanting again, the words lost in a dizzying swell of emotion, but it's different now. They're no longer forming words. It's a primal sound, all pulsing rhythm and hate. Those eyes I can see are wild as beasts. I've seen that look before. Demons have that fury, at their core, but mortals sometimes harness it without thought. After a siege, when slaughter beneath the walls is repaid by a massacre within. When a parent returns to a house naught but ashes, the charred remains of their children yet inside. It's a hatred that goes beyond reason, beyond words.

Then I see Arlia. She's sitting astride the caravel's bowsprit, her crimson skirts draped across Lumestra's just visage. The metaphor doesn't escape me. Reason drowned in red. That's when I know it's Arlia's doing. She's wide-eyed with anticipation. With hunger. More than ever I'm glad I struck that bargain.

Selloni knows something's wrong. Like the rest of us on the stage, the madness hasn't touched him. But where Selloni's peers—even Niarr—stare aghast at the baying mob, he's still speaking with the emissary. The roar of the crowd swallows his words long before they reach me, and his eyes flick nervously across the chanting throng. He knows this sight better than I. He's brought madness and slaughter to many a harbourside.

A clever man would flee at this moment, but as I've said before, Selloni's a fool. He doesn't understand what's happening. He doesn't know the game he and I played was but a prelude to the main event. All he knows is that the crowd wants blood.

"Don't do it, Selloni." Again, Quintus reads the situation more clearly than I'd expect. Perhaps it's the worried gleam in Selloni's eye. More likely it's the mood of the crowd—the expectation in the air. Madness is so often self-sustaining. I'm sure Quintus saw enough of that on the border. I wonder how he feels about it loose in the city.

Selloni crooks a warning finger, a snarl upon his lips. "Your turn comes soon enough, captain."

Steel glints in the firelight. The dagger that so lately graced my throat slides into the emissary's chest.

The emissary goes limp in Selloni's arms, but there's no blood to mark the strike. There's no body, just shapeless, empty cloth. Selloni's triumphant cry dies on his tongue. The roar of the crowd redoubles. Selloni spins on his heel, scattering the robes to the ground. He sweeps his hand towards Quintus and me. "Kill them both. Now!"

He's an age too late. The rabble surges up the stage's timbers, trampling one another in their desperation to reach the crest. They reach Selloni before he has time to turn. No weapon is drawn—they're too lost to Arlia's madness. Hands tear at his limbs, bearing him backwards. A heartbeat more, and he's lost amongst them. His screams gurgle away almost as soon as they begin, drowned out by wet, meaty thuds.

The pressure on my arms vanishes. My escort knows the score, certainly better than his late, unlamented master. Stumbling footsteps rush away behind me. I don't even watch him go. He doesn't matter now.

Niarr rushes forward, weapon drawn, to defend an ally already dead. The Thrakkian was never quick on the uptake. Or maybe it's his complicated honour at work again. His axe bites deep. The leading edge of the feral tide crumples in a bloody spray. But those following behind are beyond fear. Two bodies fall beneath the bite of Niarr's blurring axe. Then he too is dragged into the vengeful mass.

"What have you done, Solomon?" Lithel Andri spins me around with strength I hadn't expected. The feathered veil can't hide her desperate eyes any more than it can block her spittle. She glances to where Arlia sits serene upon her perch. Apparently I'm not the only one who can see the Red Lady now. "What have you done, Solomon?"

I'm not surprised Andri put everything together. Most of what I know concerning Mistress Arlia came from the Crowmarket. It's just possible there's a deeper connection I haven't made. Not that Andri seeks to share that knowledge. I barely see the stiletto move. It's a glint in the firelight, nothing more.

The greasy *crack* is barely audible above the howling of the mob. Andri drops, her neck lolling at a decidedly awkward angle. Balgan snatches the stiletto from her falling hand, severs my bonds and stares mutely at me for approval. I think he's worried he overstepped our agreement.

I pat the hulking youth on the shoulder. "No, that was exactly right."

The truth about his father's death was all it took. Balgan doesn't need to know that he's just killed his mother. It's a poor parent who disowns a child out of loathing for their imperfections. Or perhaps it was the other half of the parentage that severed the maternal bond. Not that it matters now. I'm actually rather pleased about the symbolic justice. Perhaps Lumestra and I have something in common, after all.

If Niarr's defiant roars are anything to go by, he dies harder than Selloni, but he dies all the same. The mob cheers. Hungry eyes glance in my direction.

Arlia has abandoned her perch to walk in the mob's wake. She doesn't meet my gaze. She's lost in ecstasy. She may have stoked these fires, but now she's feeding on them. I had no idea she had such power. She's anarchy in a silk dress. She's everything I despise. It's no consolation that her star was in ascendance long before today. A year, at most, and she'd have subsumed her rivals without my aid. All I've done is provoke events in exchange for personal advantage and a period of stability for my beloved city. It's not going to be enough. Five years isn't going to be enough. I'm going to need help. Someone who understands what's at stake.

It won't be Natilya. She's disappeared as surely as if she was never here. The self-preservation instincts of the ageless on display once again.

That leaves Quintus. Quintus, who's watching me the way a hawk watches a rabbit—when he's not watching the mob, anyway, or flicking his gaze longingly to an exit he knows he'll never reach. There's a sword in his hand and a crumpled minder at his feet. The other minder is still at his side, trying and failing to replicate the captain's imperturbable expression in the face of imminent death. It doesn't exactly tax me to put the pieces together—his man on the inside, just as Balgan was mine.

I was correct before, when I said Quintus and I were equally in the dark—which is to say nowhere near as much as Selloni and his peers believed. Despite appearances, neither of us came to this place unwillingly. Both playing the same game, if for different reasons.

I sought to stabilise the city's underworld. Even with my guidance, it's been too fractured of late, too unpredictable. Uniting it under a guiding hand, one I could predict, that was the goal.

Quintus wanted the same, in his way. Selloni, Niarr, Andri and Natilya all in the same place, ripe for the taking? A lawman's dream. Net the big fish, leaving the others easy pickings. It wouldn't have worked, of course. Remove the big fish, and the lesser will fight like demons for the scraps. But the goal? I can't fault that.

"I've a hundred constables within a bell's toll of this place, *my lord*," Quintus growls, "but I reckon we'll be dead long before they get here, don't you?"

The mob gives no warning. The howls come in the same moment as the screams. But this time, their fury is directed inward, upon one another. If anything, it's worse than before. It's something about the scale of the frenzy—a hundred desperate souls rending and tearing in ensorcelled madness. It's the welter of wet, ripping sounds and the stench of spilt blood. I've seen worse, but never so close. My stomach churns at the coppery tang. There's no art to this, no necessity. This is slaughter for its own sake. But even now I barely consider the consequences for myself. This is what Arlia will make of my city, if she's given the chance.

It's too much for Quintus's inside man. He doubles over, something wet and unspeakable slithering from his throat. For his part, the captain looks on unflinchingly, as does Balgan—though I suspect for different reasons.

The thrashing slows. Half the mob are lifeless upon the bloody stage. Others are twitching fitfully as the life leaves them. I have eyes only for Arlia. She's still atop her perch, lost in rapture at the slaughter she has wrought.

Arlia only opens her eyes when the last body hits the bloody stage. She glides serenely through the fresh carnage, not sparing a glance for the ruin at her feet. The trailing ends of her skirts ripple as they touch the gore. I occurs to me they may not be cloth at all.

She flashes a mocking smile. "Our truce begins now."

She doesn't have to say anything else. She's made her point. She sweeps the mildewed curtains aside and is gone. Not a one of us moves to stop her. Even Balgan knows better.

"Oh, I'm locking you up for this, *my lord.*" Quintus bears down on me with the inevitability of an avalanche. "They'll hang you from the nearest bloody tree." There's an unfamiliar tremor to Quintus's voice. Then again, one does not look upon five-score mangled bodies without being moved by the sight.

I contrive to look appalled. "For what, exactly?"

Nothing's changed between us. Quintus has no proof. He doesn't even know why I was really here. Much as it twists him up inside, for all he knows I'm just another victim. Not that it'll stop him wanting someone to blame.

He rounds on me, storm clouds gathering behind his grey eyes. "I heard every word. Fitzwalter, the Hayadra Grove, all of it."

So the Red Lady brought Quintus into the grey world with me? In hindsight, it's obvious. Quintus and I are both agents of the Council. The terms of the truce left her unable to harm us, so she instead sets us at each other's throats. Clever. Ambitious. But she's underestimated us, just as I underestimated her.

I advance to within a pace of Quintus and press my wrists together, inviting shackles. "Then arrest me. Parade me through the streets. Throw me in the Pit. Hang me from the tallest tree in the city. Arlia won't give you trouble for some time yet. She'll have her hands full once word of this massacre spreads. Every racketeer and coshman of standing will be out to stake his claim now Arlia's removed their masters and mistresses. But in five years, she'll be ready. I hope you're ready too."

A vein throbs in Quintus's cheek. I know what he's thinking. Even if he can make the charges against me stick, which is unlikely, not one of my fellow councillors will believe the rest of it. They've spent decades systematically purging magic from the Republic. They have no defence against someone like Arlia, which means they won't want to believe. Which means they won't act. Not until it's too late. Democracy is merely another word for inaction.

Though Quintus is loathe to admit it, he needs me. Just as I need him. Because the truth is, we have something in common. That something is our ambition, and what it serves. We act not out of desire for personal gain or status, but so our city, our republic, can survive, and maybe even prosper. I may deride Quintus's methods. He may abhor mine. But today, and for the next five years, that which unites us is greater than that which divides us.

I only hope Quintus admits as much *before* he strikes my head from my shoulders. Otherwise "awkward" won't cover it.

Quintus turns away. The sword slips from his grasp and clatters to the stage. When he speaks, it's like he's dragging the words from the very bottoms of his boots. "Get out of my sight, *my lord.*"

Motioning for Balgan to follow, I comply. Another game lies ahead. A game five years in the making. It's time for the first move.

BLOOD PENNY

DEBORAH A. WOLF

— The Dragon's Legacy —

1: Dark Wishes of the Heart

KANATI WAS TELLING MOON-TALES TO THE CHILDREN.

He sat as he often did, cross-legged beneath the branches of the cherry tree in front of his family's teahouse. He wore a boy's robe of common silk, sashed with gold to mark him as the favored son of his House, yellow brocade upon his sleeves and hem marking him as one of the Emperor's own. As if his twilight skin and moonsilver hair and eyes left any room to wonder about his parentage. His hands were busy, always busy, even as he ensorcelled the children with his stories; just now he was plucking blossoms out of a shallow wooden bowl and stringing them together.

Awitsu stepped deeper into the shadows, gathering them about her even as she gathered the scratchy, filthy edges of her hempen robes. She was daeborn as well, but there would be no fine brocade or golden silk for her. Awitsu was beloved of nobody.

The children sat on the low stone walls, they floated flower-petal boats in the mossy fountain, they lay scattered about the small garden like so many blossoms shaken loose by the wind. Pretty and pink and sweet-smelling, she thought, easily crushed, easily bruised. Sweet to look at, but never to touch. They stared wide-eyed at the storyteller, and more than one of the girls had tucked pink flowers into her hair.

> "Akari faced the Huntress then, and terrible his flame
> But, lo! She drew her sunblade forth, and he beheld in shame
> Upon her blade in darkness Zula Din had forged his name..."

Kanati wove his spell with all the skill of a trueborn storyteller; his voice was low and soothing, smooth as water over dark stones. That voice had eased her hurts and worries for as long as she could remember, and Awitsu scowled to think his magic might be stolen by the village girls with their cinnamon skin and pretty round ears. She gathered the darkness into her heart, used it to deepen the shadows that concealed her, even as Sajani Earth Dragon had hidden from the wicked Huntress.

> "The moons hung low and pale with woe, the stars fled from the sky
> The Song began to shatter when it heard Sajani cry
> And then the King began to sing the Dragon's lullaby.

And this is why the Huntress, though she stole Akari's will
Though she and her Hound searched the world around, she
never made that kill.
The Four Winds wept as the Dragon slept. O, Listen! They
mourn her still."

Kanati smiled at the children as he strung the last flower and
tied off the silken cord. "And this is how Zula Din enslaved Akari
Sun Dragon by using his true name, but failed to kill Sajani. For
Sajani Earth Dragon sleeps still, and the Dragon King built his
great fortress Atukos upon her back, and so it shall be until the
end of time." And he sat back against the tree, still smiling, and
cut his eyes towards Awitsu-in-Shadows.

She could hide from anyone in the world, but never from Kanati.

"Is the dragon real, Kanati?"

"Of course she is real."

"Can I see her?"

"No, Nanli, Sajani sleeps beneath Atualon, and that is as far
from Peichan as the Sun Dragon flies. But sometimes you can hear
her in your dreams."

"In my dreams?" The little girl squeaked in excitement.

"Yes, you can hear her in your dreams, and she can hear yours.
The stories say that some day, the Dragon will wake, and she will
make all our dreams come true."

One of the older girls, Daiwei with flowers in her curly dark
hair, covered her mouth with her hand and giggled.

"All our dreams, Kanati?"

He blushed.

Awitsu let the shadows fall from her and stepped into the
sunlight. Let them see her, all of her, from the velvet-soft tips of
her antlers to the pale filth of her little bare feet. Daiwei drew back,

pretty little mouth pulled back in a grimace, but Awitsu did not wait for the poison to fall from those painted lips. She lowered her head, shook her antlers at them, and whispered, "Even my dreams, Kanati? Even mine?"

"Even yours, Awitsu," he sighed.

She crossed her arms over her chest, still bony and flat as a boy's, and stared at the other children with hard eyes until they all got up and left. Daiwei and her friends rose last, and as they went they tossed glances like daggers back at her, and their hands fluttered like butterflies before their mouths as they giggled. Awitsu did not much care.

Let them laugh, let them mock. Awitsu did not need to wake a dragon—she had found a way to make her own dreams come true. And when they did…

"Why are you looking like that?" Kanati put his bowl aside and stood, stretching like a cat. His shadow fell across her face and Awitsu shivered with delight. He was almost a man grown, and so beautiful that now everyone could see it, not just her. She tried not to think about what that meant, that next Feast of Daeyyen would be his sixteenth year, and after that she would truly be alone.

Unless this worked.

It had to work.

"Looking like what?" She did not move as he came to her, and looped the flowers about her neck, and kissed her cheek. She had known they were for her, but her heart leapt anyway.

"Like you have a secret. A wicked secret."

"Probably because I have a secret." She let a smile, a real smile, steal across her face. Her cheek was still warm where he had kissed her. "A wicked, wicked secret. Come see." She took his hand and turned towards the path that would lead them out of the village and up the mountain beside Cold Spirit Stream, and beyond that…

"Are we going to get in trouble again?"

"No." She spared a glance over her shoulder. "Not unless you let us get caught."

He sighed again, but let himself be led. So it had always been between them, and so it would always be.

If this worked.

It had to work.

AKARI SUN DRAGON HAD BEGUN HIS PLUNGE TOWARDS the ocean by the time they got there, and Awitsu's feet were cold and slimy with muck. Her ankle throbbed from a slip in the river, and she had skinned the palms of both hands, but it was worth it, it was worth every bit of it to see the look on his face as she pulled aside the heavy curtain of vines.

"Awitsu," he breathed. "Awitsu. How did you find this?"

She grinned and held back the vines, slipping through in his wake and letting them fall as they would. "You told me where to look."

"What? I never…"

"You did," she insisted. "Do you remember the story you were telling last two-moon, about the witch and the stars and the blood of the innocent? I fell asleep by the river thinking about that, and when I woke up the stars were out, and I thought, oh! The witch is Hag Nagui, see, and her wand points towards the Bleeding Sisters, and the drops of blood lead straight to the Hangman's Bucket! See, see? It was all right there, in your stories!" She bounced on the balls of her feet and clapped her hands, willing him to share in her delight.

"Clever girl." He smiled and tugged at a tine on one of her antlers. He was the only soul in all the world she would allow to do such a thing. "I wonder what this place is…look at the roots, how they have grown over the buildings." He took a few slow steps down the crumbling stone stairs towards the floor of the narrow valley. "It looks like nobody has been here for a hundred years or more."

"Longer than that," she told him. "You will see. Come on! Before it gets dark." And she hurried down the path before him.

The path was narrow and steep and the footing treacherous, but Awitsu was nimble as a deer, and Kanati more graceful still. They were swift and silent and quick as ghosts upon the wind, scarcely disturbing the dead litter of last year's leaves and the thin yellow blossoms of baobing. Kanati exclaimed as they came upon the round stone buildings with their narrow windows and caved-in roofs, and exclaimed again as they clambered over tree roots as big around as they were tall and intent on reclaiming this place for Sajani Earth Dragon. These things were interesting, but rocks and roots were not the reason she had brought him here so late, late enough that she would be back home too late for dinner but just in time for a beating. Rocks and roots would have waited for another day. But this…

"Awitsu!" He stopped short, and his breath made her name into a prayer. *Aaaah-wiiiiiit-suuuuu.* "Awitsu, what is that?"

They had come upon a circular clearing where nothing grew. The low stone houses stopped abruptly and seemed to take a step back. The space was wide, and quiet, and utterly devoid of life. The wind, like the stone houses, seemed to shun this place, and the birds fell silent as they drew close. Awitsu tugged at her friend's sleeve, urging him closer.

"Come," she said.

Come, come, echoed the voice of the Well. It crouched in the middle of the clearing like a spider in her web. And it called to her.

Come.

Awitsu followed the prints her own feet had left in the ash and grit earlier that day. The air had an acrid smell and felt heavy in her lungs, but her heart was light as a feather as she heard Kanati behind her. She had been searching for so long, and she was so close

So close, whispered the Well, *so close*

To having all her dreams come true.

Her hands rested like pale birds on the edge of the Well; the stone was cool to the touch, rough and gritty. A breath sighed up to her from the bowels of the earth, an old smell and deep, the smell of things best left hidden.

His hand covered hers like a shadow across the face of the moon. "You know what this is."

"I know."

"The Witching Well."

"Toss in a blood penny," she whispered, "and the darkest wish of your heart will come true."

His stories had told of this well, this place. Dark stories, blood stories, not moon-tales for pretty little girls with eyes full of mist and flowers in their hair.

"What happened to them?" She pointed with her antlers towards the little houses. In the dying light they looked like a ring of staring skulls. She asked, but she did not really care. They were just people, after all.

"The stories do not say," he answered. "No story I have heard. They speak of the Well, and the penny, and the wish. But never of what became of the village." His eyes caught the new-moonslight as Didi peeked over the mountaintops, and his hair curled about his shoulders like fog as he gazed upon the dead village. "Something bad, I think."

"I think so, too." She did not smile, because that would upset him.

"We need to start back. My parents will worry."

Her father would not worry. He would beat her, but he would

have done that anyhow. But all she said was, "The darkest wish of your heart."

"You would have to have a blood penny to make it work. Where are you going to get a blood penny? My father's father fished the cold waters his whole life, they split open the skull of every sea-thing child they ever caught, and in all his years he only saw one." Kanati's eyes were moonsilver, catching the starslight and burning with pity. "The man who found it bought his freedom and was never seen again."

"Coin enough to set you free."

"Even so." He patted her hand. "Come on. I'll lead—my night vision is better than yours."

And still, she thought, *you can be so blind*. "I have one," she whispered. She had never dared say the words, never dared think them, until this moment. Her heart beat so loud it seemed she could hear an echo deep, deep in the Well.

He stopped and turned, his mouth such a perfect 'o' of surprise that she almost laughed. Almost. She did not want to hear the Well laughing back at her.

"What did you say?"

"I have a blood penny."

Blood penny.

Blood penny.

"Awitsu…"

"Do you remember three years ago," she told him, stumbling over the words in her haste to pass them by, "when the shongwei pup washed up on the shore near Houlen?"

"I remember," he said. "Its head was smashed, and the fishermen who found it thought there might be a blood penny. But there was none."

"There was." She refused to look away from his face. "I found it first. It is mine."

Mine.

Mine.

"And you kept it all this time?"

"It is in a safe place." Buried beneath the Blood of the Child on her mother's grave; nobody would look there.

"Awistu, you silly girl, that is your freedom, right there!"

She shook her head. *Blind.* "Coin enough to set one free," she whispered, "but never you. Never me. We are daeborn, Kanati. The Emperor will never let us go. And besides," she shrugged, "my father would have just taken it from me and claimed it for his own."

Kanati stepped close and took both her hands in his. "What will you do, then?"

Delpha had risen behind her little sister, and both moons peeked over his shoulder to hear her answer.

"I will wake the blood penny with the blood of the innocent, just as the stories say," she replied, "and then I will make my wish." *Make them pay.*

Make them pay, agreed the Witching Well.

"Will you stop me?"

Kanati stared at her for a long moment. He was so beautiful. He reached out and traced the livid bruise beneath her eye, the one she had gotten last night. Witch child, her father had called her. Daespawn. *Not my father,* she reminded herself again. *Only my mother's husband. My father rides with the Wild Hunt.*

But it still hurt.

"No, little flower," he said, and leaned to kiss the tip of her nose. "I will help you."

2: Blood of the Cock

"I DO NOT SEE HOW THIS WILL HELP." AWITSU KEPT HER voice soft, though nobody but the daeborn children would ever dare take this path at night.

"We must bathe the blood penny in the blood of the innocent, by the light of the full moons," Kanati explained. "That is the only way to wake it."

"Yes, but it is a stolen chicken. How is that innocent?"

"The chicken is innocent. Your father is the one who stole it. Are you sure he will not beat you for this?"

Awitsu hugged the burlap sack close to her chest, muffling the struggles of the scrawny black cock. "He was drunk when he stole it, and that old woman never comes into the village. Nobody will ever know." It was only a little lie, but he glanced back at her and scowled.

"One day, somebody will beat him."

Or make a wish, she thought.

They climbed the steep path by moonslight as they had so many times before. The ginger was blossoming, and the pale night jasmine. Somewhere in the distance a wyvern was singing, sleepy low notes that rumbled through the air like thunder as it bedded down for the night.

"Tree wyvern," guessed Kanati. "Have you ever seen one?"

"No."

"Neither have I. I would like to."

"So would I." The cock had gone limp; Awitsu lessened her grip, lest she kill it before time. "But only if it had a full belly."

They emerged from the forest at last, leaving the trees and the scent of flowers for the bare, scorched top of Bone Mountain. It was bathed in moonslight, ringed with jagged boulders and crowned with a circlet of bamboo platforms, freshly built and awaiting the dead. No scent of night jasmine lingered here; this was the place for sky burials, it stank of death and char and wyvern-musk.

Awitsu dropped the sack, and the bird inside flopped around a bit, squawking softly. It was not dead yet; that was good. "What do we do now? Did you bring a knife?" Her father kept his knives in a locked box, after what happened last time.

"I have this." He held up a boy's machete. "Awitsu, you do not need to do this. Listen to the stories…blood magic never ends well."

"Listen to the stories, yourself." She scowled. "What will they do, beat me? Send me away? Sell me to the comfort houses? The life of a daeborn never ends well, Kanati. I have nothing to lose."

"Well, I do."

Awitsu looked at him, one with the night, fine and shining as the stars, and shook her head. "No more than I. In ten moons, it will be the Feast of Daeyyen again, and you will be gone forever. It is written."

His face went hard at that, but he handed her the machete without another word. It *was* written.

Awitsu chose a low, flat stone. It was deeply scored, scarred by wind and time and the claws of battling wyverns, and Awitsu had slept upon it on more than one occasion. Wyverns and dead things were better company than her father was, when he was drunk. And he was drunk more often these days than he was sober.

Not my real father, she reminded herself. *My father is a pirate king; he sails upon the moons' dark seas, and wears a crown of stars.*

She hauled the struggling cock out of the bag feet-first. He was a pretty bird, dark and shiny as a beetle's shell, of the breed known as Silent Night because of the color, and because these cocks did not crow. They were witch-birds, bad luck to see, worse luck to touch. Her father had stolen this one from the herbwoman who lived in the deep woods, and Awitsu hoped his luck would be the worst of all. She flipped the cock onto his back on the rock—gently, there was no need to make the bird suffer—and held him down with one hand as she raised the machete high overhead with the other.

"Awitsu, let it go." Kanati's voice was as soft and low as the wyvern's song. She looked up at the sorrow in his words. "Please, let it go."

Too late. She brought the sharp blade down with such force that it shattered upon the rock; a shard hissed through the air and scored her cheek, just under the eye. Blood trickled down her face like tears, and she dropped the broken hilt even as she loosed her grasp on the rooster. Too late.

"I am sorry," she told him, and she was. "I broke your machete."

Kanati stepped close and wiped the blood from her cheek with his sleeve. "Ah, Awitsu," he mourned. And then, "Awitsu!" He grabbed the front of her rough tunic and hauled her away from the rocks. His eyes were as big as the moons, his face a mask of horror.

Awitsu looked to the rock where the dead cock lay. But the rock was bare, and the cock was not dead.

"Ohhhh," she breathed, and covered her mouth with both hands, smearing her cheeks with cocksblood. "Oh, Kanati!"

The rooster stood in place for a long moment, long enough for her to see that half its head was missing, and the other half lay, horribly, upon the rock. It fluffed its feathers and twitched, and twitched again, and then it took off running down the path and into the woods. Awitsu stood, shaking, just as the bird had, and then she too was running, running into the dark, running away. She heard Kanati calling her name, and off in the woods somewhere a jaguar screamed, but she paid them no mind. If she was lucky the cat would find her and have her for its dinner, or she would trip in the dark, fall down the mountain and break her neck.

Never in her life, not from the moment her mother had set eyes on her moons-king father, had Awitsu ever been lucky. She ran into the dark, deep into the woods. Branches and blackthorn tore at her face as guilt tore at her heart, she ran until her legs faltered and the breath sobbed in her chest, and when she could run no more Awitsu fell to the ground and curled herself into a little ball. Though the night was chill she did not bother to seek shelter or even cover herself with a blanket of leaves. Let the night do with her as it would, she was tired of running. She took the blood penny from her pocket and clutched it to her chest, and fell asleep wishing that she might never wake up.

She would not be so lucky.

AWITSU WOKE WITH THE BREAKING DAWN, BONE-SORE and heart-sore, and her mouth tasted as if she had been licking the top of Bone Mountain. The blood penny had fallen from her grasp as she slept. It was smeared with the cock's blood, and she supposed it had bathed in the light of the moons, but it was as dead as it had been when she pried it loose from the skull of the sea-thing child. She wiped it on her tunic and put it back in her pocket with a sigh, and then shook the leaves from her antlers and headed home. There would almost certainly be a beating for her this morning, but there might be breakfast as well, and she was hungry.

As it turned out, neither a beating nor breakfast waited for slaggard little girls who slept who-knows-where until the sun was well awake, and skipped home demanding breakfast and a bath and silken gowns. Her father had forgotten the rooster, sure enough, and that was a good thing; he had some coin from a night spent gambling at the Emperor's comfort houses, and that was another good thing, as it put him in a fine mood. Awitsu hid the blood penny, bathed as best she could in a bucket of cold water behind the shed, and changed into her better rags before setting off for the market with enough coin for a sack of potatoes, a sack of onions, and a measure of flour. "And mind you do not waste it, girl," the man she called father had warned her. "If you cheat me, daeborn or no I will kill you myself." She had nodded, and taken the coin, and in truth nearly skipped into town, almost happy. It was too bad about the rooster—she could have made them a stew.

Foolish girl, she would chide herself later, *to think your luck had changed.*

She could hear the commotion before she stepped into the market square. Had she been a little older, a little wiser—or even a little quicker—she might have turned and run away, and avoided trouble altogether. As it was, she stepped full into the light of the sun just as a headless rooster ran around the corner of the tanner's cottage. The butcher ran after it with two of his boys, and a woodcutter behind them. Children and women fled screaming at the sight. It was so like one of Kanati's moon-tales that Awitsu could not help herself; laughter burst from her like a spring flood, loud and clear, rising above the cries of panic. She could not have proclaimed her guilt any more clearly than if the rooster ran to her and dropped dead at her feet.

The rooster ran to her and dropped dead, plop, at her feet.

The whole town went as quiet and still as the top of Bone Mountain on a moonlit night.

Awitsu could not move—it felt as if she were grasped in a wyvern's claws and it was squeezing the breath from her. *No,* she wanted to say, *no.* But the words did not come. She looked up into the shocked faces of the townspeople; in that sea of fear, only one looked at her with anything besides hatred, and that was her friend Kanati.

Awitsu, he mouthed. *Run.*

But it was too late.

THE JAILHOUSE WOULD NOT HAVE BEEN SO BAD—THEY gave her a clean robe to wear, closer to new than anything she owned, and clean straw to lie on, and fed her twice in one day—if only the old jailman would stop talking about executions he had seen or heard about, or carried out. Hangings and drownings, stonings and burnings, and then of course one could be impaled on a sharp stake. Awitsu thought that sounded the worst. After two days of the crazy old man's reminiscences, it was nearly a relief when they finally came for her. She did throw up, but only a little.

They bound her arms behind her back, and led her through the streets to the town square. Everybody she knew was there, and some folk from other towns as well. Even the old herbwoman was there; Awitsu could see her dead-bird hat and the raggedy plum-colored robes, garish in the morning light, and her heart sank even further.

When her legs failed, the two men who had come for her took her by the arms, not ungently, and carried her the rest of the way. Awitsu's head spun so that for a moment she saw a well, a dark well crouching in the center of the clearing like a spider in her web.

The men let her arms go, and she fell to the ground as the rooster had fallen, plop, in the dirt.

"We are here."

Awitsu looked up and saw the town's elders, two old men and an ancient woman who used to dive for pearls. One of the old men had been the village mayor for years, and the other she recognized for a kindly soul who had slipped salt candies to her, not so long ago. His face was still kind, but his mouth was drawn down, and his eyes were heavy with sorrow.

"We are here," the crone continued, "to decide this matter before us. The child Awitsu had been charged with witchcraft, sorceries, and blood magics."

"She is no child," cried a woman in the crowd. "She is daespawn!"

Daespawn.

Daespawn.

Awitsu shook her head to rid it of the echoes; surely the Witching Well was too far away to speak to her. Perhaps the food she had been given was drugged.

"The child is daeborn," agreed the candy-man, "but she is a harmless little thing. Can any here claim to have been harmed by her?"

"She killed her own mother," insisted another woman. Awitsu knew this one; her daughter was a pretty little thing, and wore flowers in her hair. "Her own mother!"

"The woman Aelani died saving her child from drowning, but she chose to do so. The child cannot be held responsible," answered the old woman. "It is written."

"It is written," agreed the old men.

"And besides," the third elder spoke reluctantly, "The daeborn are the Emperor's Own. She cannot be killed but for good reason."

Drown her. Stone her. Burn her at the stake, thought Awitsu. She wanted to throw up again. The old herbwoman was staring at her… and smiling.

The candy-man looked about him, and then directly into her eyes. "Child Awitsu," he asked in a sad and formal voice, "an ensorcelled beast was seen in the village, and that beast ran to you and died at your feet, proclaiming you guilty of witchcraft. I saw this with my own two eyes, or I would not have believed it. What do you have to say on this matter? Are you guilty of witchcraft?"

"Do not lie," warned the old woman.

"It is a very great crime to lie to your elders," agreed the third old man.

Awitsu bit her lip and stared at her feet, still clean from her bath. She had thought about this answer and little else for the past two days.

"I am guilty," she whispered.

The crowd gasped.

"Awitsu?" The old woman asked, and her scratchy old voice was harsh as a crow's. "Do you admit to witchcraft and sorceries?"

"Oh, no." Awitsu shook her head, mindful of her antlers, and looked up to the elders with eyes as wide and innocent as she could make them. "I am guilty of stealing a chicken. I found him in the woods, and I did not know who he belonged to." She let her voice fall to a whisper. "And I was hungry."

Hungry.

Hungry.

"You admit to stealing a chicken." The candy-man puckered his lips.

"I thought that I might bring him home to my father, and I could make him a soup." She sought the crowd for her father's face, and found him between the butcher and one of his boys. Oh, he looked so angry. Awitsu took a deep breath and continued, "But I have never killed a chicken before, and I was afraid I might cut myself with the sharp knife, so I closed my eyes, and…" She made a chopping motion with her hand and looked down at the ground, wishing she could let a few tears fall for effect. "I did it wrong, and when the cock ran off I was too scared to tell anybody."

The candy-man was making soft strangled noises behind his hand, and the old woman laughed out loud.

The last elder cleared his throat. "So you…" he cleared his throat again. "So you tried to kill this rooster and make it into a soup."

"Yes," she agreed, and scuffed one foot on the ground. "For my father."

"I do not need you to bring home food," spat her father. Oh, he was soooo angry. Awitsu flinched for real then; maybe being drowned would not be so bad.

All three of the elders and no few of the villagers looked away, uncomfortable. The elder lady rapped the ground with her cane and got everybody's attention.

"Does any person here claim to own this rooster?" she asked.

The herbwoman stared at Awitsu and shook her head, but said nothing.

"Anyone?" Asked the old mayor.

"Perhaps it was a stray from another village." This last came from Kanati's father. Awitsu thought of the lemon rolls she had stolen from the teahouse some moons back, and was shamed.

"Well," said the old mayor, "I see no sorcery here, just a young girl who is not very good at killing chickens." The old lady cackled out loud at this, and Awitsu let her breath out in a long sigh.

"I agree," said the old woman.

"And I," concurred the candy-man. "And as no one admits to owning the black cock, I think we can say no fowl, no harm." He looked straight at the man Awitsu called father as he said this.

No doubt he thought it would help.

3: Blood of the Child

THE RAGGEDY WHITE KITTEN HAD SHOWN UP ONE DAY as Awitsu was gathering wood. Small cats were rare enough that even this wretched orphan would have brought good coin, and he might have been a pretty thing after a bath and some dinner. But

Awitsu had other plans.

It had taken her a full two-moon and a stolen bottle of rice wine to escape her father's notice; she slipped from the house to the liquid burbling sound of his snoring, gathered up the mewling cat from the smoke-shed, and flitted like a wraith through the woods to her mother's grave. Kanati was waiting for her, but he frowned when he saw the kitten.

"Awitsu, what are you doing with that?"

She clutched the scrawny thing to her chest. He was so soft, hot as a bag of embers, and his heart beat quick as a bird's. He must have read the answer in her eyes, because Kanati shook his head and held his hands out.

"Awitsu, no. No, you cannot do this thing, it will stain your soul. Give him to me, I will sell him for you and you can keep the coin. And I brought you a gift…see? I made them. For you."

She beheld in his outstretched hands a pair of shoes, woven from the pale red bark of the grouseblood willow.

"Grouseblood." She stroked the kitten, and he began to purr. "Like in the story."

"You remember." He smiled, but his eyes were sad.

It was the first story he had ever told her, back when they were very young and he had found her hiding, here, and crying because the other children had mocked her bone-white skin. The story of Willow Grouse Girl, so pale and beautiful. Kanati placed the shoes upon the ground and backed away; Awitsu slipped her feet into them, feeling as if she had stepped into a dream. They fit. Of course they fit.

They were so pretty. "I have never had shoes before."

"I know."

She took a deep breath, and then looked her friend in his moonsilver eyes and said, deliberately, "Thank you, Kanati."

He gasped. One did not thank the daeborn; such a thing was fell luck, the worst luck, until the debt was settled.

And then he smiled. "The kitten."

"What!"

"That is my price. The life of this kitten for your debt."

Awitsu scowled and sank to the ground. The kitten was still purring; he had closed his mismatched eyes and began to knead the front of her rough hemp robe as if she was his mother. "You tricked me."

"You tricked yourself." He sat beside her, and took a small bundle out of his pocket. He handed it to her, and Awitsu's stomach growled at the smell of redspice bread. "You did not want to hurt him."

Kanati would not take a share if she offered. "No," she admitted around a mouthful of sweet bread. "But how else am I to wake the blood penny?"

"You are still determined to make that wish?"

She shrugged, and tried hard not to wince. It had been a full two-moon since her trial, and still she ached from the beating that had earned her. She had thought that surely this time she would die.

He must have seen—his face took on the still look of deep water, dark and cold with secrets lurking just below the surface. His eyes shone like silver pennies in the moonslight, and he bared his sharp teeth.

"Awitsu? Are you hurt?"

She started to shrug again, thought better of it, and took a careful mouthful of bread instead. Her teeth still hurt, too.

"I will do this thing, if it is your wish."

Awitsu looked down at the kitten, sleeping now with his tiny claws caught in the rough fabric of her robe. "No, let him live. He deserves a chance."

"So do you. You are innocent…*hey*!" Kanati almost shouted, and the little cat came awake with a hiss. "Blood of the innocent, Awitsu! We just need to prick your finger…"

"No, Kanati. You are a storyteller; you know that is not how these things work. There is always a sacrifice." She had already tried her own blood, besides. Just in case.

"A sacrifice…or a riddle." His eyes lit, and he reached out to the glossy-leaved bush that covered her mother's grave like a blanket. Even so early in the year, its branches were heavy with…

Blood of the Child.

"Blood of the Child!" He exclaimed, leaping to his feet. "Blood of the innocent! Awitsu, hand me the blood penny." And he reached for one of the fat red berries.

Awitsu knew better—she had spent more time in the woods than he had. And besides, he had never been hungry. He did not know which berries one could eat, and which berries would kill. She watched in horror as he reached for a cluster of fat berries. One of the berries in his hand burst, as if it had been waiting for his touch, and the juice sprayed across Kanati's hand, his fine clothes, his face. He jerked back as the wicked thorns grabbed at his flesh and, without thinking, brought his injured fingers to his mouth.

"Kanati, *no*!"

But it was too late. He turned to look at Awitsu, and opened his mouth…

…and slumped to the ground, senseless.

"Kanati!" She screamed, and his name tore from her heart like a piece of soul. Awitsu dropped the kitten and scrambled to her friend's side. His face was a terrible color, like a two-day bruise, and the eyes were rolled back in his head so that only the whites showed. He did not move, or speak, or seem to breathe, though she shook him so that his head lolled from side to side. "Kanati, no! No!"

No

No

Noooooo

And then…

"What is this fuss all about, child? If you keep screaming like this, you will bring the whole village down here. And neither of us wants that to happen, do we?"

Awitsu looked up, panting, hands still fisted in Kanati's robe. It was the herbwoman, in her painted purple robes, and a wreath of green leaves rested upon her wild mop of gray hair like a wild-thing crown. Another time, Awitsu might have been afraid, might have run.

"Help me," she sobbed instead. "Help me!"

"Help you with what? Oh, the boy." The herbwoman shook her head, smiling a strange smile. "Got into the baby's blood, did he? You should know better, child." She clucked her tongue against her teeth and knelt beside them, picked up Kanati's hand and let it fall again, looked into his mouth, thumbed back his eyelids.

It was more than Awitsu could bear. "Is he dead?"

"Only mostly dead." The herbwoman let his head loll back against the cold ground.

"Will he die?" Oh, it was all her fault; it was always her fault.

"Not likely. He will be mostly dead for a while, like a bear sleeping through winter. But he needs to be given an antidote before he wakes—Blood of the Child does strange things to people. I have known men to fall into walking nightmares that lasted a lifetime. I have known men to go mad from it. And I know of one woman who woke from this sleep with the ability to see sounds as color." She smiled that odd smile again. "But I have no idea what might happen to a daeborn under its spell. Nothing good, I wager."

Awitsu's breath stilled in her chest; she had heard enough stories to know how this one would go. "Do you have the antidote, then?"

"Of course I do, child." The woman reached into the top of her robe and pulled out a stoppered vial.

"What do you want for it?" Awitsu bit her lip and tried to look small and pathetic. "I am very poor."

"Oh, sweet little child, you know those doe eyes will not work on me." The herbwoman laughed, and her body shook like a sack full of potatoes. "There is always a price that can be paid, you know. The fleece of a golden ram. An apple from the tree of life." She leaned close, and her breath smelled strongly of cardamon. "The heart of a daeborn child, perhaps."

If she had tears, Awitsu would have wept. "Yes," she whispered. "Take me, instead. Only let him live." She was doomed anyway.

"Oh, *pshaw*, I was only joking. What kind of a life have you had, to be so serious at your age? What are you, eleven?"

Awitsu realized that she was gaping like a simpleton. "Thirteen."

"Ahhhhhh." It was not a word, so much as a sigh. "Thirteen. Not long before your own Feast of Daeyyen, then, is it? And this one…he is fifteen, yes?"

"Yes."

"So, next year, then."

Reluctantly: "Yes."

"You know, I had a daughter once. She was more beautiful than a moons-lit night. I loved her more than there are stars in the sky."

"You had a daughter?"

"Do not look so surprised. And close your mouth. I was a great beauty, in my youth." She held the vial up to the sky and twirled it around in her fingers. Liquid swirled inside, dark as a whispered secret. "My Ahnpei was daeborn, just as you are. I kept her hidden, kept her secret, so that nobody would know. But in her sixteenth year, they came and took her away from me." A single fat tear rolled down the herbwoman's withered cheek.

For the first time in her life, Awitsu was stunned to silence.

"I cannot just give you the potion, you know. It does not work like that. But for you, I think the price will not be so great. I will sell you the antidote, for, shall we say…" she looked deep into Awitsu's eyes, and their hearts were kindred. "A white kitten? I am lonely, and could use the company."

As she pressed the vial into Awitsu's palm, the herbwoman leaned in close and whispered: "Now, what would a young girl be doing, messing about with a cock's blood, a tiny kitten, and a handful of Blood of the Child? It is almost as if you are trying to work some dark magic. That is forbidden, you know. Daeborn or not, you would be killed for such a thing."

Awitsu tried to pull away, but the old woman held her fast. "Let me go!"

"Not so fast, child. I still need to tell you three things, you know how this goes. First, your friend is going to be very sick when he wakes up. He will need to eat something, though he will not want to. Second, the two of you need to keep away from these berries. I have no more of the antidote, and if he were to get a second dose, I really do not know what might happen to him. And third…"

"Third?" The old woman's fingernails were digging into Awitsu's hands, and it hurt.

"Third, if you wish to wake a blood penny, you are going about it all wrong. It is not simply the Blood of the Innocent, you know." She let go of Awitsu, and sang:

"Heart of Illindra, Soul of Eth,
Blood of the innocent condemned to death.
Under the moons, combine the three,
Coin enough to set you free."

"Blood penny?" Awitsu gave the herbwoman her most innocent look. The old woman snorted and scooped the kitten up in one hand, and struggled to her feet.

"Suit yourself."

"What does that mean…'blood of the innocent, condemned to death?'"

The herbwoman shook her head and turned to leave. "Did you learn nothing when they locked you up? Our jailhouse if full of them, child. Take your pick."

And then she was gone, leaving Awitsu alone with a mostly dead friend, her mother's grave, and the light of the cold, cold moons.

4: Blood of the Condemned

KANATI ARGUED THAT THEY SHOULD WAIT FOR THE next two-moon; but for the warning in her heart, Awitsu might have agreed. The night was old, and if she did not get home soon her father would wake and find her gone. As the sky greyed around the edges, she thought that they may already be too late.

At that thought—*we may be too late*—Awitsu firmed her mouth and resolved that they would finish their quest this very night.

"Who knows whether we will have another chance, next two-moon?" she asked. *Who knows whether I will still be alive, next two-moon?* was what she meant. Kanati, as he always had, read the thoughts between her words, as a seer may find answers in darkness between the stars. He followed as she led.

The old guard was asleep with his feet propped up before him and an empty cup at his elbow. Awitsu closed her eyes in a brief moment of gratitude for men and their weaknesses as they slipped by him and through one of the heavy wooden doors. This was not the room in which she had been kept, but a gloomy, stinking pit filled with chained men and emptied of all hope. Awitsu let Kanati go before her—his moonsilver eyes were better than hers for cutting through the darkness. And besides, if she had admitted it to herself, she was afraid.

Kanati picked his way across the bodies and outstretched limbs of the breathing dead. The moonslight bled in through the windows just enough that Awitsu could see him stoop beside a bundle of filth and rags. He crouched unmoving for a long, silent moment and they listened to the gurgling, rasping breaths and the occasional low moan. Awitsu held one hand over her face and ghosted across the room to stand by him as he fumbled for his knife. Though her bones shuddered and threatened to turn to water, she would not have him do this thing alone. She knew the man who lay huddled at her feet: he was a poor man and a failed thief, and the only reason he was still alive was that his family had not yet paid the blood-money for an execution and burial. She supposed that he might be innocent of theft, but he was certainly guilty of having poor luck.

He is dead, anyway, she thought, angry with the man for no reason she could explain. *He deserves this fate, not I.*

The walls whispered in the night, mocking her with the voice of the Witching Well:

Not I

Not I

Not I.

The puddle of filth and misery stirred, and his eyes went wide in the moonlight.

"Murderers!" His voice was as thin as his arms that flailed against the chains, but carried surprisingly well. "Murderers!"

Up went the cry. "Murder!"

Murder, laughed the Well.

Murder.

Awitsu turned to flee, but she ran straight into the jail-man just as the headless rooster had run to her in the marketplace, and his fist connected with her jaw,

And down she went,

And down she went,

And down into the dark she went.

AAAAAHHHH-WIIIIIIT-SUUUU, MOANED THE WIND AS IT ruffled her hair. *Aaaahhh-wiiit-suuu,* wept the stars as they danced about the sky.

"Awitsu," whispered Kanati, his voice low and urgent. "Awitsu, wake up!"

She woke. And then she wished she had not, for the side of her head throbbed and burned. It was a song she was altogether too familiar with, the *thrum-thrum-rumble* of her own blood in her own ears, and she was suddenly done with it. She was finished with men who hit her and left her to weep in the dirt at their feet, as she was finished with pretty little girls who wore flowers in their hair and laughed at her behind their hands.

"Kanati," she rasped, and spat blood from her mouth as she sat. The room spun and the Well laughed at her pain. Awitsu held her head and waited for it to stop. "Where are we?"

They were in a deep, dark, breathless place. She could feel the walls pressing in upon her, and a great weight pressing down from above. Had they been buried alive, then? That is one way her father had told her the daeborn should be killed. *Drown them, burn them, bury them alive,* he would sing. And then he would laugh. But he was not her father—*her* father was a powerful sorcerer, he would blast the walls of this prison apart and set her free.

"I am not sure. A dungeon, I think. There is nothing besides us down here, not even rats." Kanati hated rats. Awitsu rather liked them, stuffed with wild onions and rubbed with salt.

"I wish I had a rat," she said. Her head hurt.

"Awitsu, *hssst*! Stay awake, now. We are in trouble, and I do not think my father can help us this time."

"I am always in trouble."

"No, I mean real trouble. I heard them talking as they brought us down here. They mean to sell us both to the Emperor's comfort houses, and be finished with us for good."

"But they cannot—we are daeborn."

"They can," he answered, and his voice was strangely thick. "Our families will have to pay a blood fine, but they can do it. And they will."

He was *crying*.

Awitsu had never felt so low in her life. This was Kanati, her Kanati, and she had brought him nothing but grief and pain. She crawled to him and put an arm around his shoulders, and when she felt them shake her heart screamed into the dark.

"I will tell them," she whispered. "It was all me, all my fault. I will tell them." And then she would die, and he would be free.

"Do not be stupid," he answered, and hugged her back. "We are daeborn. They would have killed us both, in time. This just gives them an excuse."

"I do not want to die, Kanati. I do not want to go to the comfort houses."

"Do you know what I want?"

"To get out of here?"

He laughed and squeezed her. "That, yes. And I want you to make that wish."

"Oh, well, in that case, all we need to do is fly through these walls and wake the blood penny." She giggled, and felt the walls draw away from the sound.

"I think I know a way we can get out of here."

"What! How?"

"Well, it is stupid. Almost as stupid as us getting in here in the first place."

"I am good at being stupid. Tell me, how?"

"I still have some of those berries," he told her. "Blood of the Child. A whole pocket full of them. We could eat them, and then they will think we are dead, and leave us on Bone Mountain."

"Kanati." Her voice was a dark prayer. "There is no more antidote."

"No, there is not."

"The wyverns might eat us before we wake."

"They might."

"And the herbwoman said she does not know what might happen if a daeborn eats them." *Nothing good,* she had said.

"I told you it was stupid."

"You were right, it is stupid." She threw both arms about his waist and laid her head on his shoulder. "I love you, Kanati."

"I love you too." She could feel him shifting as he dug into his pocket. His hand was warm, the berries cold as he pressed them into her palm. "Are you ready?"

"What do they taste like?" She brought her cupped hand to her face. They smelled like fresh-turned earth. Like an open grave, like a field fresh-planted.

"Sour. And then sweet. Like you." He kissed the top of her head. "Are you ready?" His free hand sought hers, and squeezed.

She did not answer, but brought her hand to her mouth and let the berries spill onto her tongue. They were bitter, dark and bitter, and then…

Sweet.

5: Blood of the Beloved

THE WYVERN HAD BEEN TASTING THE AIR OVER THIS *latest offering, and trying to decide whether that odd tainted smell was poison or just another way for the silly humans to try and mask their scents. When the meat sat up and shrieked at her she was startled backwards and lost her grip on the perch entirely; had she not been so young and agile, she might have fallen full upon the ground. As it was, she trumpeted her displeasure as she swept over the bare earth and then up, up, filling her wings with wind and her lungs with the scent of the open sky. She called again, and this time her cry was answered by a series of bone-rattling notes far to the east. It was a male; a fine, strong male, by the sound of his song. She abruptly forgot all about the little doings of lesser creatures and turned her back on the dying sun.*

The path split before Awitsu; one way led down and to the left, a dark trail charred and choked with blackthorn. The other rose up and to the right, a wide and shining path, gently sloped and neatly paved. *I know this story*, she thought, *I know the way*. She turned towards the hard road and a hot wind rose to greet her, stinking of brimstone and carrion and long, sad songs.

And then she thought, *No. I am tired of this path. It is time for me to choose another.* So she opened her eyes and looked Death full in the face, and screamed. Death in the form of a young wyvern screamed back at her and fell, startled by the sound of her voice. Awitsu lost sight of the creature for a moment and thought perhaps it had plunged to its death, but before she could draw another breath the wyvern rose before her, a vision of bronze-and-green scales and spikes and cold yellow eyes. It blotted out the fading sun, bellowed, and prepared to strike…and then, for no reason she could see, flicked its tail and shot away over the mountains.

She did not know whether to laugh, or cry, or wet herself. If she did not get down off the platform, she might do all three.

"Awitsu?"

She peered over the edge of the bamboo platform. "Kanati!"

"Are you okay? Can you get down, or do you need my help?"

"I am okay, I think." Not really, but she had been worse. "I have to pee."

"I do too, after that." His face was pale in the fading light, but Kanati's eyes shone like the moons. "That was incredible."

She might have chosen a different word, but Awitsu supposed he was right. She half-climbed, half-fell to the ground, and barely made it to the bushes in time. She felt sick to her stomach, and dizzy, and…faint. Thin. Like wine that had been cut with water until there was hardly any color left to it at all. And of course she had chosen to squat behind an itchvein bush; she could hardly wipe with *those* leaves.

"Here you go." A handful of leaves—safe leaves—thrust around the bushes.

"Kanati, would you…oh. Thank you."

Her guts felt better after that, but her head still felt sick and strange. And her antlers itched.

We could probably get a drink at the river without anyone seeing us. I am thirsty, too.

"I am thirsty. Do you think we could…" She broke off and stared at Kanati. "Wait…how did you know what I was going to say?"

He stared back. *I never said that out loud.*

She shut her mouth with a snap, and tried: *Is this because we ate the berries?*

I guess so. Either that, or we are dead.

I think the wyvern would have eaten me, if we were dead.

The wyvern might still eat you if she comes back. Best we leave before she remembers her dinner.

Best we leave before the villagers come for us.

They will not come. Why do you think they left us here? They think we are dead already.

Awitsu tested the thought as one might prod a sore tooth: left for dead. She supposed she felt bad for Kanati's family, but they would have lost him anyway, at the next Feast of Daeyyen. As for her father, she hoped he spent the rest of his life paying the Emperor for her early death.

…yes. I do.

Do you know what I wish? She laughed even as he answered the thought. This was going to take a bit of getting used to, but she liked it.

There was no further need of words. She took Kanati by the hand and led him to the river. When they had drunk their fill, and as the moons rose in full and somber witness, they took the path to the Witching Well one last time.

IT WAS A BEAUTIFUL NIGHT, STILL AND FRAGRANT, AND the skies were so clear she could see every star in Illindra's Web. The ground at her feet, the stars in the sky, and the moons at her back all seemed to know of her purpose. Know, and approve. Awitsu could feel the Witching Well at the end of her path, and Kanati at her side, and for the first time since her mother died she did not feel alone or even afraid.

The stone houses of the village drew back from them, mournful and afraid, but did not seek to deny them passage. *Nothing would,* she thought.

Nothing could, agreed Kanati.

We are daeborn, they thought together. And it was good.

The Well sang to them in her sweet low voice, the song of the crone, of vengeance.

Vengeance, best served hot, Awitsu thought with a smile.

Vengeance, best served cold. He squeezed her hand, and let it go so that she could fetch the blood penny from her pocket.

"Serve it up with meat and wine," they sang aloud, and then Kanati held a finger to her lips, and his eyes burned with a cold blue fire.

"Ten years old." He cupped her hand in both of his; they held the blood penny together. It was smeared with her blood, and now with his as he drew his palm across it. They had beaten him, too, she realized. Beaten them both and left them for dead. "Ten years since she died, and you have been alone ever since."

Dead, crooned the Well,

Dead

Left her for dead.

"He put her in the water and left her for dead," she cried. "And I could not save her. I was just a little girl."

"I remember." Kanati put his arms about her and held her tight. "I remember. Make your wish, Awitsu, it is your right. The darkest wish of your heart."

She pulled back from him, and held the blood penny high. Bathed in moonslight it glittered, it sparked, and then burst into light like blood made fire. The Witching Well burst into song, a fell song, a dirge, a canticle of bone and ash.

Vengeance is mine, she insisted.

Mine, cried the Well,

Mine.

Vengeance is yours, Kanati sang in her head, *as I am yours.*

And then he smiled at her, a smile as bitter and sweet and full of promise as the night, as bright as the stars that lit it. Bitter as Blood of the Child, sweet as innocence found after all else has been lost.

You see me, she thought, stunned. *You* see *me*.

Silly girl, he replied, *I have always seen you.*

You are beautiful.

You are beloved.

You are my Awitsu.

The starlight, the moonslight shimmered across the blood penny.

Come back to us, they called her. *Come back.*

Come to me, cried the Well. *Vengeance is ours. Come, come to me. Bring to me the blood penny, sing to me the darkest whispers of your heart, make a wish. Make a wish. Awitsu is beloved of nobody.*

Awitsu closed her eyes and let her face be bathed in light.

I am beautiful, she thought.

I am beloved.

I am his Awitsu.

"Heart of Illindra," she whispered. "Soul of Eth. I choose life over death." She curled her fingers over the blood penny.

It *burned*.

The Well screamed, a horrible sound full of blood and wrath and old bones, and then it fell silent.

Awitsu opened her eyes, and smiled, and handed the blood penny to Kanati. "I do not want this any more," she told him. "You can have it."

"Are you sure?"

Beautiful. Beloved. "Yes. I am sure. I have…changed my mind about making the wish."

He took the blood penny, dead as it ever had been, and slipped it into his pocket. "What do you want to do, then? Where do you want to go? We can hardly return to the village."

"I do not want to go back. I want to go to Atualon."

"Atualon?" He laughed.

"Yes," she told him. A slow smile spread across her face, warm and strange and wonderful. "I want to go to Atualon, and find the sleeping dragon."

And they did.

But that is a moon-tale for another time.

BETTER THAN BREATH

BRIAN STAVELEY
— *Chronicle of the Unhewn Throne* —

THE SMALL BARN STINKS, PARTLY BECAUSE ARON spilled manure all over the floor a few days ago—he's too young, really, to use the wheelbarrow; his little hands barely fit around the handles—and partly because the sick son of a bitch I've got hanging from the rafters has shit himself several times.

Outside it's a pleasant evening. There's a salt breeze blowing in off the sea. The sun's painting the clouds a resplendent red. The kids are playing up on the hill beneath the old oak, some game that has Caldi laughing so hard she sounds like she's crying while Aron keeps tooting on a stick he says is a horn, rallying the other three to do battle against some invisible foe. I'd rather be up at the house sitting on the wide front porch that my grandfather built. I'd rather be watching the children and the sunset, sipping a glass of wine, basking in what has to be one of the last warm days before winter.

And instead, I'm in here, in a barn that reeks of manure and piss and human shit.

It's not that I don't care to clean it up, or that I'm squeamish. I'm a mother. I have four kids. I've scrubbed enough soiled pants and dirty butts. Normally, I wouldn't bat an eye at one more steaming pile.

This is different, though. The man roped to the rafters must weigh half again as much as I do, and he's strong—wide shoulders, big hands. He didn't go down right away, even after I smashed him over the back of the head. It makes me tremble all over imagining what would have happened if I hadn't been in the root cellar when he snuck into the house, if he'd seen me before I saw him, if he hadn't been distracted by the children.

What if he'd come in the night, after I was asleep, when I couldn't defend myself? What if he'd come when I couldn't defend my children? My breakfast rises at the thought of it.

I need to be careful, even now, even with him tied up. I need to be more careful than I've ever been in my life, which is saying something. I can't get close to him. He could still lash out with his leg, maybe knock me unconscious. I could clean up his shit the other way, my secret way, but then he'd see it, and he'd know what I am.

I haven't decided what to do with him yet; maybe there's a way to leave him alive. Even after what he tried to do, after the way he almost destroyed my family, I don't want to kill him. I've never killed a person in my life, and I don't want to start now. I didn't even want to hurt him. All I want—all I've *ever* wanted—is to be left alone, for my family to be left alone.

The man groans. A moment later, a trickle of blood runs down the side of his leg, sluicing through the grime. Earlier, after I had knocked him unconscious, I stripped off his clothes. I couldn't take the chance that he had a knife hidden on him somewhere, but it was more than that. He'd come into my home, into my *home*, made me feel naked and vulnerable. I wanted him to feel some of that vulnerability. I wanted him to know what it's like to be naked and powerless. I'm not proud of the impulse—I wish I were stronger—but here we are.

He doesn't look like a criminal. He might even be handsome, if he weren't filthy and bruised. Broad shoulders, calloused hands, weather-beaten skin—probably a fisherman from one of the little villages down at the coast. The fact that he came all the way up here, all the way into the foothills, chills my soul. If he could make the trip, others could, too. They *would*, if they knew what I was. There would be no way to stop them. And if they took me, if they killed me, how would I protect the kids?

I realize, now that I'm thinking of the kids again, that I can't hear them playing. The laughter from up on the hill has gone silent. A sliver of ice slides along my spine. I check the gag on my prisoner once more, getting just close enough in the dim light to see that it's still in place, then I turn to the door of the barn.

I lift the latch, fingers trembling, open the door. Even the washed-out light of the sunset is enough to make me squint.

"Aron!" I shout. "Caldi! Juni!"

I can't see them. All is quiet up on the hill. There are no children on the porch. None under the tree. Panic closes its fist around my heart.

"*Aron!*" I scream again.

His voice, when he replies, is right at my knee. "I'm here!"

I look down to find him beaming up at me, small face glowing with delight. "Got you!" he announces.

Relief washes over me, so hot it hurts. I drop to my knees, wrap his spindly four-year-old body in my arms, and press his face into my own. He smells a little like a puppy, a little like a little boy—hair wet from splashing around in the creek, dirt caked on the back of his neck. He smells like my son.

I pull away, kiss him, but then another fear takes me, this one a rusty, gnawing dread—the barn door isn't quite shut, and a dozen paces behind me the intruder is hanging naked from the rafters, bleeding onto the dirt floor.

"Mama!" says Caldi, clambering out from behind the water barrel. She is beaming. "Mama!"

She toddles toward the open door while I grope behind myself, trying to drag it shut with one hand while holding off the two children with the other.

"No!"

The word is half a scream as it tumbles out of my mouth. I seize Aron by the arm, more roughly than I mean to. His forehead crinkles, then his mouth falls open in a sob.

I never grab him like this. I never yell at him. I don't yell at any of them. Of all the places in the world, this old house on the ridge is supposed to be safe. I am supposed to *make* it safe. I shouldn't be twisting his wrist and shouting, but I can't let him get past me.

Finally, I fumble the door shut.

Aron is sobbing. Caldi's mouth is wrenched into a baffled pout. I might be imagining it, but I think I can hear the man hanging from the rafters thrashing, tearing the ligaments in his shoulders as he tries to rip himself free.

"I'm sorry, Aron," I say, wrapping an arm around his shoulders. "I'm sorry. You *startled* me."

He stops crying halfway to the house. By the time we reach

the porch, he's grinning like normal, like my son, asking me what we're going to have for dinner.

"The other kids went back down to the brook to try to catch a trout," he proclaims. "Can we have spices on it? The good spices?"

"Of course we can," I say, kneeling once more to wrap him in my arms. Caldi comes up beside us and nuzzles her way into the hug.

"Fam-i-lee," she says, pronouncing each one of the syllables.

I feel their love blossom like sunlight inside my chest. In that moment, I'm not afraid at all. The intruder doesn't matter. I feel invincible, like I can do anything.

I WAIT UNTIL WELL AFTER MIDNIGHT, THEN CHECK ON the children. Aron is sprawled half off his cot, mouth agape, snoring quietly. Caldi is curled in one corner of her crib, Juni in the other. Even Willim, who is almost six, sleeps like a baby, his blanket clutched tight in his hands. I watch them for a while, partly to be sure they're asleep, partly because there's nothing more beautiful than a sleeping child.

On the other hand, I feel vulnerable when they sleep, powerless without their little eyes on me. I feel lost. It's in the middle of the night that I'm most aware it could all be taken away, that this family I've built could be shattered like a dropped crock.

"I'll keep you safe," I murmur as I swing the door shut behind me. "Mama will always keep you safe."

The night is cold as I step out onto the porch. The stars are sharp. A shiver slices through me, flaying me to the bone. I glance down at the knife in my hand. It's not a weapon. Why would I own a weapon? My mind is my weapon; my children my strength. The knife is just a normal knife, the same one I use to clean the chickens every fall. It seems like a ludicrous thing to use to kill a man, but flesh is flesh. I keep the knife keen. The prisoner's skin will open beneath the steel.

I've decided to kill him, I realize. There's no other way.

He's awake. I can see his glassy eyes as I light the lamp hanging from the rusted nail just inside the barn door. A part of me has to admire his strength. Two days hanging from the ropes, two days without food or water while I've been trying to decide what to do with him, and his eyes—a blue so pale they're almost gray—still manage to focus, first on the light of the lantern, then on my own gaze.

"Aron," he manages. The gag has come untied. No, he has chewed through it. His voice is a hideous, wasted thing, raw with lack of water, barely more than a whisper—but the name is a knife in my side all the same.

"Don't talk about my son," I snarl. I've crossed half the distance to him before I realize it. I stop myself, then take two deliberate steps back. I have to be careful while the children are asleep. I'm not as strong as I would be during the day.

The prisoner twists against the ropes. "…hurt him…" he groans.

"You will *never* hurt him," I say. My breath feels like briars in my lungs. The night, which seemed so cold as I walked between the house and the barn, is suddenly hot as a midsummer day. I'm sweating—my brow, my palms. My legs feel weak, as though yesterday or the day before I'd run all the way up and down Burnt Mountain.

"You will never hurt any of them," I say, more quietly this time.

I'm weaker at night, when the minds of my little ones are all tangled up in their dreams. I can't light him ablaze with a glance, or shatter his skull with a thought, but most people live their whole lives without that kind of power. Most people come out of the womb normal, untwisted. This fisherman, for instance—all his twenty-five or thirty years he's had to make do with the strength of his hands, the quickness of his wits, whatever stubbornness he's got. No secret well of power for him, no leaching strength from a child's love.

I study him, dangling from his bound wrists like a slaughtered pig. I've grown so used to my power that I rely on it, but that's foolish, dangerous. There are other ways. I set the knife aside, and then, almost without looking, I reach up to where a long-handled shovel hangs from a peg just inside the door.

The fisherman tracks me with his eyes, then starts to thrash all over again, weakly now. I shake my head. The shovel—a shovel I've used a thousand times—feels heavy as lead in my hands, almost too heavy to lift.

"I don't want to do it this way," I say, stepping closer to him, but not too close. "I wanted to do it fast, painless, like slaughtering a hog." I bite my lip. "But it's too risky. You're too dangerous."

His eyes bulge. "*I'm* too dangerous?"

"You tracked me here, to my home…"

He bares his bloody teeth. "You're a *leach*. An abomination…"

I hit him with the shovel then. The motion feels wrong, awkward, as though the tool itself resists being used to this end. The blow lands flat against his hip, and he hacks out a groan.

"All I wanted was to be left alone." My voice sounds like pleading in my ears. I'm beating a man to death with a shovel, but I want him to see, to understand. "I don't bother anyone," I continue. "I don't hurt anyone."

Absurd to say, watching him writhing there in front of me, but I didn't want to do this. I wanted to spend the last days of autumn baking pies for the children, watching from the front porch while they played in the leaves. I wanted to spend the chilly evenings by the fire reading to them, the old, wonderful tales about the taming of the Kettral or Yureen Fan's voyage across the roof of the world. I wanted to fall asleep knowing they were safe in their room down the hall, dreaming their beautiful dreams.

And then *he* came.

I stare him in the face, hefting the shovel for another blow as he forms words with his cracked, bleeding lips.

"You stole my son."

I shake my head. My whole body shakes. It feels as though he has reached in and wrapped a hand around my shuddering heart.

"No," I whisper.

"Aron," he groans. "My boy. You came into my house and you *stole* him."

Icy waves of nausea wash over me. My legs falter like a newborn calf's. I can feel Aron in my arms, feel the memory of it, his tiny body warm beneath my cloak, tucked against my chest as I flee into the night. Years ago now. Years ago, but not forgotten.

"I love him." I don't realize for a moment that the words are mine. "I love them all."

"You *stole* them all. And now we're coming to get them back."

My head rings like a gong. *We?* He's alone. He's been here for days. There was no one else with him.

He reads my terror and smiles.

"That's right. I told the others I was coming here, the other parents. I didn't think it was you—I've been looking for so long, in so many places. I didn't think it was you, didn't think I'd find him, but I told the others... If I wasn't back by the full moon... something happened."

I glance out window. The moon glares, full and unflinching.

My prisoner spits onto the floor again and smiles. "They're coming."

My heart is a wild thing inside my chest, trapped, panicked. I can't breathe. Then, when I drag in a huge breath, I can't find a way to exhale. My body is a skin stretched to breaking.

I drop the shovel. There's no time to kill the man now, and no point. *They're coming.* I need to get the children, get them out and away. I have no idea where we'll go. There's no time for ideas. We just need to be *gone*.

I'm halfway up the hill to the house, stumbling through the rough stubble of the field, when I see the lanterns, hear the voices. I can't make out the numbers, even in the full moonlight, but there must be a dozen. More than a dozen.

"Willim!" I scream. "Aron!"

I need the children, need to get them out, but more than that, I need their strength if we're going to survive this.

"Willim, *help!*"

The men and women on the road respond to the cries more quickly than my children, surging up the path in a wave of shadow and lamplight. Swords flash with reflected fire. Shadows twitch over the ground as they approach.

I have nothing in my hands, no weapon, not even the small knife I left back in the barn.

The crowd surges up the hill toward the house, ignoring the barn, ignoring everything but me. They can see me now, that's clear. They are fury made flesh. Their voices deafen.

I reach the porch, stumble, drag myself up, start hauling the rocking chair toward the door—a futile, stupid effort to block it, to keep my children safe—when Willim bursts out. His eyes are wide and frightened in the moonlight, but I can feel his love, feel it pouring over me, through me, lifting me up, making me strong.

"Mama?" he manages, staring down the hill toward the mob. He hasn't called me *mama* in years. It's been *mother* or *mom*. He doesn't like to sound like the babies. "Mama, what's going on?"

Before I can answer, Aron tumbles out, then Caldi and Juni half a step behind him. My blood is on fire with their love, their trust. Moments earlier, fleeing up the hill, I felt like a lame rabbit harried by the hounds. Now I am a pillar of rage, a shield for the unprotected, a scythe for the savages who have come to shatter my life and the small lives behind me.

I spread my arms. "Behind me, children. It's alright. Just stay behind me."

The mob has slowed a dozen paces from the porch, faces twisted with hope, anger, terror. They're right to be terrified. I could tear them apart from here, tear them apart without moving. That is the strength my children give me. That is what it is to be a leach.

I study them, trying to decide how best to end this threat, how to slaughter them most quickly, when I feel a small hand, still warm with the heat of the covers, slip inside my own.

I glance down. *Aron.*

"Who are they?" he whispers.

"They're…"

I hesitate. I want to tell him they're thieves. I want to tell him that they're monsters, destroyers of peace. I want to tell him the truth—they've come to rip apart our family, to tear down our home, to annihilate the love that binds us together. *They're nothing to us,* I want to say. *Nothing to fear. Nothing at all.*

For some reason, I can't say the words.

"Give us back our children!" a woman shrieks. "We'll leave you alone, just give us back the children!"

"Juni!" A man's voice, choked. "Sweet Intarra's light, it's *Juni!*"

I raise a hand to destroy them. It trembles in the moonlight. I could light them all ablaze, but what kind of mother sets fire to thieves in front of her own children? I could crack their ribs inside their chests, but what mother lets a baby see that? I can feel the love of my children, more vital than my own blood, coursing inside me. I can feel it, but I can't use it. I won't.

Emboldened, a few of the parents edge closer.

"She can't reach her well," someone shouts.

"She's got no power!"

They're wrong. Entirely wrong…and yet not wrong at all.

I turn away from them, away from those awful faces. I kneel down to gather my children in my arms. They're trembling. Caldi sobs. Tears burn down my own face.

"What's happening, Mama?" Aron whispers. "Who are they?"

"Good people," I reply. The words taste like rust. "They're going to take care of you now."

Caldi screams and Juni joins her. "I don't *want* them to take care of me!" Over and over and over.

"It's alright," I tell them, hugging them close even as the hands close over me, on my shoulders and arms, pulling me away, tightening around my neck, dragging me off. "It's alright." I try to turn to face my assailants. "Be gentle…"

There's so much I want to tell them, how Aron wakes in the night sometimes crying, how he'll go back to bed if you fix him a cup of warm milk. I want to tell them that Caldi gets sick if she eats too many bruiseberries. That I promised Juni a tiny harp on the solstice. I want to tell them that Willim's favorite stories are the ones with Kettral, that Caldi doesn't like blue, that Juni wears her socks pulled all the way up. There's so much, *so* much, but I can't. The hands are too tight around my throat. I could burn them to ash, but not in front of the children.

I close my eyes and feel it flow through me, their love, all that love, better than breath, than light, than life, bright as the autumn sky.

A FOUNDATION OF BONES

MAZARKIS WILLIAMS

— Tower and Knife —

ADAM GRIPPED THE ROCK ABOVE HIM, FEET SCRAMBLING for purchase below. He had been to Mogyrk's View five times and still had trouble with this last yard, especially now. Arms shaking with effort, he got his elbows over the lip. Silently he thanked Mogyrk that at this height nobody could see his awkward wriggling. Though he was just a young priest only four years out of training, the congregants already saw him a certain way: confident, powerful, strong. And he had been strong, he told himself: he had not chosen the easy path but the right one. He pulled one knee over, held fast, and heaved himself up onto the flat surface. For a moment he sprawled, breath knocked out, heart pumping, eyes squeezed shut against the world. Then he drew himself up, took a deep breath, and looked. Nothing had changed. The world spread out all around him as it always had. To the northeast, a chain of blue mountains led to Yrkmir, the heart of his church. To the southwest and far below him lay his home, Mondrath, huddled against the mountain, its brightly painted houses lining each side of the river that fed the valley beyond. Then there was everything in between and all that was afar. Cerana, the ancient enemy, to the south; the Felting people to the west; and past them, the great markets of Kesh.

Closer in, halfway down the slope, Adam could see blue fabric hitched up against a pine. The wind lifted it from time to time with a swaying of needled branches. Every few seconds he saw a hint of sandy hair or a light-coloured thing that could be a twisted limb. Then the wind would die down, and only the blue—Mogyrk-blue, sign-blue, pattern-blue—remained.

Adam had come to the god's view before to look out along the path of his life, and he imagined Mogyrk had done the same when He lived. Adam had always believed that in the coming years he would be called closer and closer to the seat of the Sacred Church until finally he would stand in its sanctum, wearing one of its highest robes of office. But now he was no longer certain. Had Mogyrk known His future, known He would die for the power he had granted his priests? Had He ever had doubts?

He wiped a tear from his eye. He had finally made his decision but there had been a price to pay. He told himself it did not matter. The boy was safe.

ADAM REMEMBERED THAT DAY IN THE SANCTUARY WHEN he saw who Didryk truly was. The boy had been there with perhaps five other students—he did not remember the names of the others.

They were not important. Stuart March had been there, too, as the official teacher of the youngest pledges. It had been raining outside, and the light was grey and dull.

Didryk sat down apart from the other children. "I'm going to draw a picture," he said. Stuart frowned but said nothing; the boy was the Duke's nephew, would perhaps become their ruler someday. He was treated differently to the others, even then, before they knew what he could do. He sat down and began drawing on the floor with a piece of chalk, creating half-moons, circles and squares, connecting them with lines so precise Adam could not help but imagine a divine hand behind it. When the boy had nearly completed a rough circle, Adam grew concerned. Discovery of a talented child led to a sequence of events that Adam would rather avoid. He settled into a crouch beside Didryk, blocking Stuart's view. As Austere in Charge and friend to the duke's family, Adam had more authority over the boy than anyone. "Didryk," he said.

Didryk looked up with his deep blue eyes and smiled. Adam smiled too. There was something about the boy that was both joyful and infectious. Not only was he spoiled by his nobility, but also by the way people reacted to him.

Adam made his voice serious. "What kind of picture are you making?"

"Kavic hurt his thumb."

"That does not answer my question, Didryk."

Didryk sighed the way a parent sighs when asked to explain something simple. "If Kavic goes in my circle, then his thumb will be healed. See? I found this sign of Mogyrk in a book...and this sign..." He pointed as he spoke. "Those are secret Names for healing."

"But you know, child," Adam said, "pattern-making is difficult, let alone healing. You risk doing more harm than good until you have had a great deal of practice. You are only seven and—"

Didryk shook his head. "My circle is perfect," he said.

With shock, Adam had to admit that it did look nearly perfect. That was why he took the corner of his robe and wiped away the chalk marks before they were lit by Mogyrk's power. Even acolytes, grown men with years of training, could not always light their circles. "Rejoin the others," he instructed, keeping his voice even though his heart was beating fast, "and I will speak with you later."

Didryk clamped his mouth shut against some protest and nodded. Tears threatened in his eyes. But it was not the time for Adam to baby him. Already too much rested on the boy.

THAT EVENING ADAM CLIMBED UP THE MOUNTAIN, passing bluebell and poppy and pine until at last he sat upon the high view. He had learned, as all austeres had learned, that one day a child would be born to Yrkmir who would be gifted with Mogyrk's Signs. This child would become a healer, and this healer would free the god from death and bring about the new world. Therefore when gifted children were encountered, they were sent directly to the seat of the Sacred Church. But there was one problem. This child had not been born to Yrkmir. He had been born to Fryth, a colony—a reluctant colony—of that great empire.

Still catching his breath Adam looked down upon Mondrath. From here he could see the manse, its flags gleaming in the moonlight. The Duke of Fryth, the Iron Duke as he was called, was one of the only leaders to have ever mounted a successful resistance against the Church of Mogyrk, and he remained an ardent pagan. Peace had been achieved only by sacrificing his nephew to a life in the priesthood. That nephew was Didryk.

Adam's loyalties were split. He was Fryth born and bred. Didryk might become his duke one day, and if he were as powerful as he seemed, he could also become First Austere. Adam caught his breath just thinking of all the power that would belong to Fryth if that occurred. But it could not, if the boy were sent to Yrkmir.

And as an austere, Adam could not turn from Yrkmir.

He fell to his knees and begged for Mogyrk's help. If he told the church about the boy, they would take him, and that had an unexpected sting to it. He had grown accustomed to Didryk, to his sunny nature, to his happy self-assurance. He could only imagine what would happen to him inside the halls of power in Yrkmir.

Mogyrk gave no sign. Adam needed time to think. To do that he needed to keep Didryk's abilities secret. He climbed down in the growing dark, having decided to betray everyone. Everyone, except the boy.

STUART CONFRONTED HIM LESS THAN TWO WEEKS later. He was a square-shouldered young man whose grey eyes reminded Adam of the duke's. "Why do you have the young king in private lessons?" he asked. Stuart liked to call Didryk 'the young king,' but whether it was an insult or prescience, Adam could not discern.

"He has sympathy for the other boys. He picks up things so much more quickly than they do." When telling a lie, always veer close to the truth.

But Stuart was smarter than Adam thought. His eyes narrowed. "How quickly?"

"Quick enough. He'll make a good acolyte." Adam made the comparison in his voice. *Better than you.* He brushed imaginary dust from his robe, yellow to Stuart's blue. "Is there anything else?"

"It's just—austere—I don't mean to—" Stuart gave an exasperated sigh. He was Yrkmir born: it must irk him, Adam realized, to stand below a Fryth in rank.

"Then don't." Adam stepped closer. "I know we are often informal out here in the colony, so far from the centre of the church.

But the fact remains I am an austere and you are an acolyte."

Stuart nodded acceptance at the same time he continued to object. "It is only that I was put in charge of the boys' lessons, but now one of them has been taken out of the class."

"I think you will find your job easier because of it."

Stuart was not pleased, but at last he turned and left. Adam sighed and fingered the book he was going to show Didryk, one that he himself had not mastered until he was sixteen. He turned and opened the door to the small room where the boy waited. It was not wise to leave him alone too long lest he begin to draw patterns of his own creation, and who knew what might come of that.

Didryk smiled, his whole face lighting up with pleasure to see him. Adam felt a corresponding happiness within himself, but he kept his face stern. "This is an important day, child. We are going to tackle a new book."

The boy's gaze fell to the title written on the spine. "I saw that," he said. "Acolyte Stuart showed it to me."

At once Adam went cold. "Why? When did he show it to you?"

"Today. He opened it up and asked me if I could tell him what the patterns meant." Didryk wiggled in his seat, dark hair flashing in the light from the window.

Stuart must have seen, that day in the sanctuary. Seen, and said nothing, and watched. "What did you tell him?"

"Nothing. You don't want him to know, do you?" At this Didryk stood and paced to the bookshelf. "Am I also not to tell my uncle the duke? That I can make patterns?"

"That is your decision, child. I know it is not well to keep secrets." Adam rubbed his chin. "It is only that—"

"I know," Didryk witterrupted. "If he knew I was good at patterns, he would make me hurt people with them when he goes to war. I don't want to hurt people."

"No, not that. Your uncle does not need to go to war ever again. He is under the protection of Yrkmir and the Sacred Church."

Didryk puckered his lips at that, but did not argue. Adam cleared his throat. "The Light of Mogyrk…" he pointed at the book. "We austeres have the power to bring it to the whole world. Politics and wars should not concern us except as a tool to bring people into that Light."

"That's not true," said Didryk, opening the book to a random page.

"What part is not true?"

"The Light. Mogyrk is always in darkness because He is dying."

Adam had to tread carefully here. If Didryk were but a few years older there would be serious consequences for such heresy. But he knew that the concept of a god giving his life and yet remaining present was a difficult concept for children. "Mogyrk is dead," he reminded the boy.

"No," Didryk insisted, "he's not."

PERHAPS DIDRYK IS THE DEVIL.

Adam sat at church council, austeres to either side, barely listening as they discussed donations, building projects and library duties. The child showed extraordinary talent, especially for healing, and yet he spoke heresy. More clues: he charmed everyone. He warmed every room he entered. Even Adam, who had never cared for children, looked forward to Didryk's private lessons. And yet the boy spoke falsehood with such certainty. *Mogyrk is in darkness, not light.* He could be the deceiver himself. That was the other, little-known reason why the church insisted all gifted children be sent to Yrkmir: in case one of them was fated to destroy it. His stomach twisted.

No, Didryk was not the deceiver. He was just a child. Adam had to remember that. Destroyers were killed. Children were taught, and loved.

"...duke's nephew..." Stuart's voice penetrated his thoughts, and he sat up in his chair. "Pardon?"

Austere Brandt, older but of lesser rank, explained. "March here tells us that you have taken young Didryk into private lessons."

"I have." Adam nodded, and nodded again, feeling uncharacteristically nervous. "Yes, I have. You see..."—he glanced at Stuart—"You see, I did not want to insult the acolyte, but the duke is quite particular. Very particular, in fact. And so I took it upon myself to avoid...*an incident*." Nobody spoke of the duke's pagan leanings or his hatred of Yrkmir, but today, he could hint at it. Stuart was Yrkman. Let them make what they would of that.

"An incident," Stuart echoed.

"Yes. Yes, exactly."

Brandt scratched his white-whiskered cheek. "It's peculiar, I'll say that. Stuart was given stewardship of the children."

"Speak to the duke," Adam replied. "I am sure he will support my decision." He knew this was true, but he also knew that Brandt would never approach the duke: he was not of the correct class.

Brandt waved the issue away as if it were an annoying fly. "No need for that. You are the austere in charge here."

"But I do think..." Stuart began, and then slumped back in his seat, blue robes uncharacteristically rumpled. His surrender was feigned; Adam would have to keep an eye on him.

"Well," said Adam, standing, "if there is nothing else." He left the room and made his way to the library. There he stood and stared at the books, all the books which Didryk would devour and make his own. But to do that he must survive. Didryk must not speak his heresy to the other austeres. At the very least he would be severely punished. At worst he would come under suspicion and be sent to the Numbers, priests so elevated they were titled by their proximity to the Seat: Second Austere. Third Austere. Fourth.

Adam shuddered to think what they would do to the boy. And to Adam himself—for hiding him.

He had to convince the boy that he was wrong, and quickly.

ADAM TOOK DIDRYK UP THE MOUNTAIN PATH. HE OFTEN took acolytes out in nature, though they were usually older at this stage of their learning. Seeing Signs working in the real world always boosted understanding among the less gifted. Didryk for his part did not lack understanding but rather solemnity. Seeing the real forms of the Names he had memorized might make him a more careful student.

The climb also promised privacy.

Didryk ran, laughed and found stones to throw despite the steep climb. Adam found himself laughing also. He could not remember the last time he had laughed like this, deep from the belly, with no self-consciousness. He resisted the urge to tamp down Didryk's enthusiasm, to turn this sunny mountain scene into a grey school room.

When the lessons began Didryk still laughed. He ran from tree to rock to bush, Naming each with a swirl of his finger and running to the next. His holy vocabulary surpassed that of a man three times his age. At last he tired and came to sit beside Adam on a boulder.

Adam handed him some ham and a piece of bread from his pack, and together they looked down upon Mondrath in silence.

After a time Didryk asked, "Can we come back to the mountain tomorrow?"

That would mean too many questions from the other priests. "No. Next week perhaps. But I want to speak to you of something important before we return to the church."

The boy sighed and nibbled his bread. Adam took it as

acquiescence and drew a deep breath. "Didryk, what you said before, about Mogyrk not being dead, but only dying—"

"It's true." Didryk turned to him now, eyes bluer than the sky. "I did not lie."

"I did not say you lied, child. I think you are only mistaken. The God died for us, to give us these Signs to control our world. If He were still alive, then the Signs would not work. They would still be tied to Mogyrk's soul."

Didryk frowned, working this out in his mind. "But I can feel Him."

"I have given that a lot of thought. Because you are so talented, you can remember Mogyrk better than others. You remember His pain and His sacrifice. Let it be a reminder to you in the coming years. And do not speak again of Him being alive. People will think you are taking His sacrifice lightly." He watched the boy's face, watched him make his decision, trying not to seem too anxious.

"All right," Didryk said, "I won't talk about it anymore."

Adam paused, a piece of bread halfway to his mouth. "Have you talked about it with anybody else?"

The boy's gaze shifted to a nearby tree. "Not really."

Adam rubbed some crumbs between his fingers. The boy had spoken to someone, but whom? If he pressed it, the boy would lie; he could feel it. If he did not know better he would have thought the boy was protecting someone.

Adam's heart clenched. In becoming an austere he had never thought he would feel so frightened, that he would care as much as he did at this moment. When did he become less of an austere and more of a father? His mood having changed, he swallowed the last of his food and stood. "Come. It is time to return." On the way down the mountain, as Didryk waved a large stick like a sword, fighting trees and rocks as if they were Cerani soldiers, Adam thought about how to protect him. If the other priests learned of the boy's convictions, he did not think he could fight the crushing weight of the Sacred Church.

And yet perhaps that was best for Didryk. Adam found himself reconsidering all the arguments he had entertained on that first day, and coming no closer to a decision. Instinctively he felt Fryth was safer for the boy, but perhaps his affection tilted that instinct.

Didryk tripped and skidded across the rocky ground with a little shriek. When he sat up, Adam could see that his shins were scraped and bloody. Didryk looked at his wounds for a moment, then shrugged and got to his feet.

"Let me look at those cuts," Adam offered.

"I fixed them," said the boy.

Adam leaned down and ran a finger under the boy's knee. Where he rubbed the blood away, there were no wounds—yet there had been no Signs, no drawing of circles nor incantations made. The boy had merely *looked* at himself. Adam shook his head. "I didn't see you..."

"If you know the Names, you only have to imagine them," said Didryk, picking up his stick again and waving it lazily in the air. After that he did not run, and walked beside Adam quietly.

Adam had to remind himself to put one foot in front of the other and keep his breathing steady. Didryk had healed himself merely by looking. It was unheard of. Impossible. Could he really be the child that was predicted? The one who would release Mogyrk from death? For once Adam did not wait to come to a rational decision but rather allowed the god's presence to fill him. It was true. Didryk was the child who would bring about the new world. Adam's instinct to protect him had been correct, and it was even more important now. And then he halted.

Mogyrk is alive.

Didryk took his hand and tugged. "Are you sick?"

"No, no I am not sick." Together they walked, the boy carefree, the man shaken.

As they neared the bottom of the slope, Didryk let out a whoop and ran ahead. Acolyte Stuart waited beside the church with open arms, and Adam felt all his wonder fade to suspicion. Stuart lifted the boy into the air. "How was your hike?"

Didryk pressed a finger to Stuart's mouth. "Shhhhhh."

Adam's heart filled with dismay. Now he knew to whom the boy had been speaking.

THE SANCTUARY WAS BUILT TO FACE SOUTH, TOWARDS where Mogyrk was said to have died in the deserts of Cerana. That meant the windows faced east and west, bringing sunlight in both the morning and the afternoon, beams that lit the study-tables and put a glow upon the vellum pages. Stuart's students were bent over various shapes and diagrams, faces drawn in concentration. Didryk sat alone at a table between two windows, head resting delicately on one finger, bright eyes focused somewhere in the distance. Adam wondered if Mogyrk also looked so otherworldly, even as old as he must be. The sunlight gathered around the boy like a cloak. Stuart, standing over him and speaking in a low voice, looked entirely mundane by comparison. Even where the sun lit his blue robes, it only served to bring out the same colour in the boy's eyes.

Was this how it felt, to be in the presence of greatness? Had Mogyrk had teachers and friends who looked upon him and felt this way? But Adam could not stand here in awe; he must continue to play his part. He strode from the doorway made his voice sound hearty and unconcerned. "There you are! Stuart stole you for a time. But now we must get to work."

"I apologize for detaining your student," said Stuart with a thin smile. "I am conducting the yearly aptitude test."

Adam clenched his fists. "Well, are you finished asking questions?"

"Yes." Stuart turned away and picked up a quill. "At last. I will send the report to you when it is finished, austere."

Adam's stomach turned. If Stuart knew of the boy's heresies, he might not count him among the promising students of Light who travelled to the Sacred Church each year, but rather, among the wicked ones, hustled in a side door and never seen again. But at least the report would cross his own desk first. "Come," said Adam, beckoning to Didryk, "come away."

As Didryk started towards him, Stuart said, as if he had read Adam's mind, "Very interesting. Very interesting indeed, austere."

"STUART SAYS I CAN GO TO YRKMIR."

"What?" They sat together on a bench outside the sanctuary, eating another lunch of bread and ham. It was becoming difficult for Adam to remain the stern teacher. He knew at some point in their relationship, the boy would become the teacher and he the student. And yet Didryk was still too young to negotiate the paths of the Sacred Church, to know how to avoid men like Stuart who only *seemed* kind.

"Stuart said he will take me if I wish. He will take care of me, now that my parents are gone."

Adam understood why Stuart had offered himself as the delivery man. If Didryk were discovered as a dangerous heretic it would do the acolyte's career well to have been the one who caught him. On the other hand, if his heresies were not discovered, Didryk would favour him as a father figure when he inevitably gained power. Stuart could not lose. Adam had not given him enough credit.

"Do you want to go to Yrkmir?" he asked. "Leave your family and all of your friends?"

"I would learn more," said Didryk with a little shrug.

"Perhaps. Perhaps not. It would depend on what they thought of you. Didryk, have you thought any further about the things you said about Mogyrk?"

"I don't talk about that any more," the boy assured him.

"I will not be angry, child, whatever you say."

"Nobody wants to hear what I have to say." Didryk kicked a stone away across the garden.

Adam pressed on. "I merely want to be sure you are thinking about these important things as well as the patterns you can make. Faith is not a game."

Didryk stood and faced him, blue eyes fierce. "I never said it was a game."

"You did not, but I want to be sure you are thinking about this the right way."

"The right way." Didryk mimicked him, and then, turning away, muttered something that Adam could not hear except for "...Stuart."

"Do not be rude, child. What did you say about Acolyte Stuart?"

"Nothing." Despite Adam's rebuke, the boy kept his nose in the air and his back turned. "It is just that some of the other priests are nice to me and you're not."

"It is not for me to be nice to you, child. It is for me to teach you and protect you."

"Perhaps I should go with Stuart," said Didryk. "You're not nice to him, either."

Adam stiffened but maintained a patient expression. "If you are done being angry, we have some Signs to learn today." At that the boy turned back to him, blue eyes wide and eager. He loved to learn. That was always the way to draw him. But it would not last long. Eventually Didryk would surpass his abilities and abandon him for someone he liked better—and be caught.

ADAM WAS HALFWAY UP THE MOUNTAIN WHEN HE heard running footsteps behind him. "Adam!—Adam!" Stuart's voice. He came to a halt, bringing his face into control before turning. "Ah! Stuart. I was on my way to Mogyrk's View. You are welcome to join me."

"Good. I thought it was time we discussed the young king, if it suits you, austere." Showing a little deference for once, Adam thought.

"He would not be a king, you know." Adam said, stalling for time, "The highest title he could reach would be duke, and that only if his cousin dies or steps aside."

Stuart said nothing in response to this, only smiled inwardly as if at a private joke.

"What is it you want to say, Stuart?"

"That I know what you are hiding. The boy is gifted. Extremely so. But as a Fryth you are concerned about Yrkmir."

Adam gave away nothing, but kept walking with the other man at his side.

Stuart began panting slightly as the slope grew steeper. "But Didryk. He has views. Views I think should come under the study of the Numbers."

The idea of the Numbers questioning Didryk made Adam shiver. "He is just a boy."

"A talented one. I have been watching him. He could be very important, one way or the other."

"One way or the other?" Adam quickened his pace.

"You know the clues even better than I do, austere." Again with the deference. "You know the dangers in leaving the boy unreported."

"And the dangers in reporting."

"I know that...you have known the boy...since he was born." Stuart was rapidly losing breath. For someone not accustomed to the climb he had actually done quite well. But now he was winded, slowing. "But this is about the church...not you."

It was at least a little bit about Adam, since he was likely to die beside Didryk if the boy were found to be a danger. But he put that aside. "It is about more than the church, Stuart. It is about the future. He is the child from the texts, I know it."

Stuart barked a laugh and then, seeing Adam's face, said, "You're serious."

"You think the child cannot be so low as to come from Fryth."

"I think the Numbers...know more than I on the subject," Stuart replied, "but you think...the Numbers will be mistaken about him. That they cannot see the Light as you can."

"I think the Light is difficult to see so far north."

Stuart cracked a smile at the pun as he steadied himself on a boulder. "You border on heresy. The only thing we can do...the thing we must do...is put Didryk in the hands of the Sacred Church. Otherwise why are we austeres?"

Stuart would never be convinced. He would make sure Didryk went to Yrkmir, and Adam did not know what to do about it. If only Mogyrk would send a sign. The acolyte coughed, and Adam feigned concern. "Are you all right? The next part is steeper, and we'll have to go single file."

"Perhaps next time I will go with you," Stuart said. "For now, it looks as if I have become unaccustomed to walking outside the city where the roads are flat. But please, consider what I have said. I do not want anything to happen to you."

Any doubt about whether Stuart would report him vanished. The best he could hope for was disgrace; the worst, a heretic's death by fire. And yet he found he was still more worried about

Didryk. "And the other priests? What have they said about the boy?" He did not look forward to the next council meeting and his inevitable defeat.

"I have not told them."

Of course. He would not have shared his prize. For the first time Adam was grateful for Stuart's ambition. It gave him a little more time. "I'm going up," he said, "I will see you in the sanctuary." He turned and began up the narrow path, keeping close to the cliff to avoid a sharp drop to his right. Once again he wished Mogyrk would show him what to do about the boy. Stuart's silence aside, the time was coming when he would have no choice than to adjust to what had already been decided. How had he failed Didryk so drastically? Shame curdled in him.

"Wait!—Wait!" Stuart was still behind him, one hand on the rock face, the other waving up the slope. "What is it like to stand at Mogyrk's View?"

"You can see everything." Adam's attitude changed; after all these difficult weeks he spoke to Stuart as one priest to another. "It is an inspiration."

"Have you ever had a vision there?"

"No. I pray for one but...no."

"I have rested a bit. Perhaps I will after all—" Stuart took a step forwards, but his boot slid on some loose rock and he lost his footing. As he fell he scraped his cheek on the cliff face. Blood smeared his face and then streaked the ground beneath him as he continued to slide.

Adam hurried down the narrow path. "Stuart!" The acolyte was now sideways to the drop, one leg on the path and the other hanging over thin air. He scrambled with his hands to find a hold on the jagged rock. "Stuart!" Adam knelt by the struggling acolyte.

Wait.

This is my sign from Mogyrk.

Adam stood and backed away just as Stuart reached for his hand. This was how he could protect Didryk. Without Stuart, nobody knew about the child.

"Adam! Help me! Hold onto my wrist!" Stuart flailed again, his fingers only digging into more loose rock. But somehow he held on.

Part of Adam walked away then, down the narrow path. He watched it go.

"What are you waiting for!" Stuart cried out.

Adam looked down at the acolyte. "Mogyrk lives." His message to a man about to die. His confession. His promise.

"Mogyrk—alive? Heretic!" Stuart's eyes grew wide. "The boy has deceived you! Take my hand! Take my—" Before he could finish, Adam kicked out, his boot meeting Stuart's hip with a thud. Still the man held on, so Adam stood on his hand, twisting those strong fingers, making sure they lost their grip. "Adam! Please—" Stuart's words were lost in a scream as he tumbled down the mountainside. Adam took a small step forwards and looked at what he had done. Stuart had fallen down to the treeline and come to rest against a fir. He was not moving.

Adam felt neither shame nor guilt but only the aftertaste of bitter resolve. He had chosen his path and must follow it now. He turned and began his way down to the church.

"ADAM!" DIDRYK RAN TO GREET HIM, ONE HAND holding his favourite book. "I was waiting for you. I have a question about—" His face turned pale. "Why is there blood on your robe?"

Adam looked down to where Stuart's blood made a rusty stain along the hem of his robe. "I am afraid there was an accident on the mountain." For the first time, he started shaking.

Didryk backed away. "Stuart..."

"Yes, he was coming with me to Mogyrk's View, but his boot slipped. I'm afraid he...he fell over the side." He hadn't lied, not technically, but the boy saw something in his eyes, something that made him back away. For the first time, Adam saw fear on Didryk's face.

"Didryk..." He reached out, but he was shaking even more now, so much that he worried his muscles might pull apart.

The boy ran away, darting between the church and the cookery, ducking under a ledge too low for a grown man to follow.

ADAM STOOD ON MOGYRK'S VIEW, WATCHING STUART'S blue robes stir in the wind. Didryk had not spoken to him since the day Stuart fell. When he looked at Adam, his eyes were hard and cold. The boy had changed, because of him. If someone had asked him weeks ago if he was willing to lose the boy if it meant saving him, he would have said yes. But he would not have expected this pain he was feeling.

Stuart's sacrifice had been effective. Adam had succeeded. Brandt lacked the curiosity to look at Didryk, and everyone else was under Adam's control. He had removed the child entirely from instruction and started him on militia rotation. He had hidden the books so that Didryk was unable to teach himself. That would hold him, for a time. It would hold everyone for a time. And then, when Didryk was old enough, he would take over. He would rip authority from Adam, cast him down, and fulfil his fate alone. He had given the boy the freedom, the opportunity, to do that.

He wiped away another tear. He did have doubts. Did Mogyrk have doubts, also, before he gave his Signs to man? He had given Didryk a chance, yes, but what world would there be for him? His path had been cleared with murder. What good could proceed from that?

He had given the boy a foundation of bones.

THE AGING OF A KILL

PETER ORULLIAN

— Vault of Heaven —

THE AIR CARRIED THE SWEET SCENT OF RIPE GRAPES.
The sun above hot, but not unpleasantly so. Audra Vance sat back
on her heels and looked up the long vineyard row. Harvest time.
Wine-making season. She placed a cluster of grapes into a wicker
basket, taking pleasure in such a simple routine task. Simple was
always better. Beside her, Jenn Jonsan, ten years her senior, sat
flush on the ground and mopped her sweaty face. Together they
observed a mild quiet, before Jenn broke the silence, "It wasn't
always like this. Autumn in the vineyards, I mean. I built up to
this by sending others to die."

The words sounded like confession. But not regret. Their sound
settled into the grape leaves and dry ground and made this corner

of the vineyard feel private, important. Two years. Audra had been in the employ of the Second Counsel of the Court of Judicature for two years, waiting for this admission.

The admissions always came. The only question was time. Hard work helped the words along. Perhaps they were like toxins that needed to be sweated out of the body. Or perhaps weariness lowered one's defenses.

"Me, too," Audra replied.

"Really?" said Jenn. "And who have you killed?" There was humorous sarcasm inside the question. Not mean-spirited. More amused than anything else.

Audra gave the second counselor an even look. This part always came, too. "I was trained a Dannire."

Jenn's thin smile flattened, her critical stare sharpened. She sought any crack in Audra's demeanor or conviction, to prove her a liar. But unsmiling faces and critical stares have no effect on a woman who's spent a life killing. And Audra didn't lie.

A look of approval and respect rose on Jenn's face. Not the usual bit of fear. That was the way with politicians. They didn't have a good sense of their own mortality.

"My abandoning gods," Jenn remarked with some delight. "I would never have guessed. I thought the Dannire more a Reconciliationist fable. You know, to inspire conformity to church doctrine."

Audra shook her head once. "Been a while since you've sat in a pew, I'm guessing."

"Hard benches for soft minds," Jenn quipped. "I figured the Dannire were the religionists' way of pretending they had real strength."

"Other than faith, you mean," Audra countered, a wry smile on her lips.

"My faith is in the strong law." Jenn mopped her face again, her eyes distant as one seeking to recall forgotten information. "As I recall, the Dannire worked against enemies of the faith. Killed without conscience or the consequence of sin. Took contracts without payment."

Jenn shared a look with Audra, as though seeking confirmation. Audra stared back.

"Wonderful, then," Jenn finally said. "Two women of consequence harvesting grapes in wine season. Should make for wonderful stories to pass the time."

Audra gave that another thin smile. "You believe me then?"

"Tell you what," said her employer, the woman's voice suddenly that of the counselor who examines and argues and judges. "Give me the story of someone you've killed. A Dannire story. Let's have some evidence."

Audra nodded. "I see. I'm to be cross-examined, then." She gave an easy laugh, the sound flat among the vine rows. "How about this—"

I SLIPPED ON MY DISGUISE AND FOUND MY WAY TO one side of the great platform on the day of the public court. Comes once a year. A throwback to before the Court of Judicature, when the crowd served as immediate jury and justice. Now it was almost theater. But the sentencing stuck. That was the important part.

It took place in the great square. And it was a fine day for it. Crisp feeling in the air. Autumn sun. Stones let up tendrils of steam as they warmed from the frosts of night.

On one side of the platform stood a young girl, twelve years old she was. On the other side stood a man, forty if he was a day. A second man, dressed in a jershire—the ceremonial robe of justice, long to his toes, and crimson as blood—paced casually between them.

"Who knows the challenge?" the mediator asked.

"I do," I said, and mounted the platform on the girl's side, giving her an imperceptible nod as I passed.

"Very well, I give way to you in this dispute," said the mediator, who promptly left the platform.

I stopped dead in the middle of the rough planks, and eyed the two gallows looming over the defendants. They were meant to suggest that either could be at fault. Somehow their promise, in the light of strong afternoon sun, was just twice the death.

I then looked over the crowd, which stretched out of sight. Well mannered, they were. No one shouting or laughing or holding private conversation. They waited on my adjudication of the challenge. It would not go as they expected.

I gave the man a hard stare, and turned in the direction of the girl and strolled toward her. "He is not the first man to be found in your bed, is he?" I asked in a way that made clear it wasn't a question.

There were a few gasps from the mob. Some sounded like distaste at the accusation. Some sounded like surprise that I was harping the girl and not the man.

The girl looked up at me, trust in her eyes. "I live at the foundling house," was all she said.

For most of the crowd it was explanation enough. The ugly truths of orphan life were widely known.

"But you've a taste for older men, haven't you?" I countered. "A unique desire for a girl your age."

The girl said nothing, dropping her eyes to the rough platform planks. Some would see it as shame. I knew better. She let her chin dip to complete the air of disgrace. As her hair fell forward, the peeling skin on the back of her neck came into view. Scilla sickness. It had progressed.

I left off, and paced to the man at the other end of the trial platform. "She's awfully young to bed down," I remarked. "Are we going to find more girls plagued by your oily shanks?"

The man offered a nervous smile. Shook his head violently. "I didn't know the lass's age. She came on strong, and look at her. She's fully a woman, don't you think? A bit of facepaint and she could be your sister."

I hate men who use horseshit flattery to try and ingratiate themselves to me. The insult of it burned behind my teeth. I took a long breath to moderate my response.

"You're saying she's the only one, then," I said. "And that a man your age can't possibly rape a child if she looks old enough to consent."

"She came at me," he argued. "All adult-like. And from what I know, there's no law preventing two loving people from enjoying each other's company." His nervous smile rose again on his pocked face. It stretched his skin in white bands around puckered scars.

"Loving," I muttered.

He nodded, tentative, shifting from one foot to the other.

"You're saying she's the only one, then," I repeated.

"Of course," he yelled. "What do you think I am?"

A goddamn liar. And bugger. I knew full well he visited the foundling houses on a weekly rotation. Paid hush money to some of the stewards, made hollow promises to the rest. That bit of knowledge had been easy to come by. Tailing a man who has lust on his mind is an easy thing. He's led by his loins, and leaves caution at home.

I stared back at him long enough that he'd know I knew the truth. That crack of worry on a guilty man is a sweet thing to witness. I nodded imperceptibly.

Then I stepped slowly back to the girl. "Did you come at him?"

She shook her head.

"Did you fight his advance?"

She shook her head again and repeated, "I live in the foundling house." *Foundlings have no rights*, her words seemed to say.

"And yet you've accused a ranking member of the Society for Social Reform of rape," I said with some regret. "Without evidence of attack…without even your own refusal of his proposition… Did you know that false accusation of a leader of Social Reform is a high crime?"

"I don't care for the betrayal, either," shouted the social reformer. "You've sullied my reputation." He pointed at me. "You find her guilty, you hear me?"

Some men you just can't wait to slip cold steel into.

I turned back to the girl. "Anything more to say?" I asked. Hard thing to try and balance compassion and objectivity. It's like listening to a sophist talk about love and marriage. Some things, some words, only have meaning because of the way they make you feel. Otherwise, they're horseshit.

She gave me one last look. There might have been a plea in it. It was hard to say. A long moment later she simply shook her head again. *Goddamn brave lass.*

At the rear of the platform, a barrel-chested man stood stock-still in a full hood with only eyeholes cut for seeing. I nodded to him. He came forward, lowered the noose, and helped the girl step back beneath the crossarm. He tied her hands with a gentle touch. He then pulled a hood like his own, except without holes for seeing, over the girl's head, and tightened the noose around her neck.

This wasn't a typical gallows. No trapdoor. No drop lever.

The big man then stepped back, and took hold of the rope, waiting on my signal.

"For the accusation against a member in good standing of the Society for Social Reform, we sentence…" Silent gods, her name.

What was her name?

"Sarah," the girl quietly offered, the sound of it muffled through her hood.

Goddamn brave.

"Sarah," I repeated loudly for the crowd, "to hang. By this, justice is done. Let anyone argue," I invited, as was the tradition. "But a word of caution. Once you let an urchin dictate justice, beware the streets. They'll fleece you and stick you and call it your fault." A harsh statement they'd remember her for.

A mild wind passed over the great crowd. None spoke up. They only gazed on, some eager, some curious, some with a flat look in their eyes.

I gave it another few moments, then quietly spoke a word. Not a word anyone would know. And only loud enough that Sarah could hear it. To activate the poison in her blood. Her eyes shut, and she slept. Deep and unwaking.

I nodded the signal.

Without ceremony, the barrel-chested man pulled the rope, and raised Sarah off the platform. The girl didn't kick or struggle. She swayed a bit. The crowd grew dead quiet. A heavy blanket of silence fell down around us all.

"SO YOU USED THE ANNUAL PUBLIC TRIAL TO KILL A child?" Jenn remarked. "That's your killer's story?"

Audra remained silent.

The second counselor laughed. "The insinuation of a young girl's shabby box to condemn is hardly new. I've been doing it in private chambers for years. I swear," she said, smiling, "I'm the only real protection our esteemed pedophiles have in this country."

"I know." Audra plucked a grape and placed it on her tongue.

"Still, I'm not quite sure I understand." Jenn's brow furrowed with concentration. "Was it mercy? Killing the child, I mean? You being a holy clipper back then, I would have expected you to put a knife in the shanky reformer."

Audra thought about the girl. About Sarah. "Some killing is at request. Some for personal conscience."

"That's cryptic," said Jenn.

"Do you mean like the logic of a counselor who protects pedophiles?" Audra stood, picked up her basket of grapes, and headed for her small quarters off the main lodge.

Counselors in general took their posts in order to give their self-righteousness some authority. It would be burning in Jenn that Audra hadn't let her have the conclusive word in their exchange. Small victories have their sweetness.

The following morning they met at the mash vat, a wide deep oak tub filled to the knee with grapes. Jenn sat to one side methodically washing her feet and legs. Her brow was still pinched.

Audra had barely sat when Jenn set in, "You can't have been working for the Church of Reconciliation, then. They'd never authorize the killing of a child."

Audra let the latent question lie while she washed her own feet and legs and stepped into the vat. As she began stomping grapes, she replied, "Dannire work for themselves."

"That might explain why they seem more a fable than a real institution," Jenn reasoned. "But it doesn't explain the connection to the Church."

Jenn climbed into the vat and began to mash grapes. Together they stepped high and slow, feeling the juice squish between their toes. Audra never lost her balance. Jenn held the side of the vat.

"When there's damning work to be done, the Reconciliationists call on the Dannire." She paused, gathering a second thought. "And Dannire share certain ethics and ideals with Church-folk."

"Meaning a woman like me has no ethics or ideals," Jenn challenged.

Audra let that go. She wouldn't be baited. "A kill is made for reasons. Not gain."

"Everything is gain," Jenn countered. "No one does a thing except for advantage. Coin is the most obvious, but certainly not the lowest."

The smell of grape mash rose in waves around them. It carried a tart, pleasant scent. Their feet made sucking noises as the grapes became a thick slush. Mashing was meant as a civilized bit of work. Genteel. Something that would become a story to tell at polite gatherings in the company of influentials. *Everything is gain.*

Audra felt the tug of another wry smile. "No," she agreed, "not the lowest. It reminds me of the time…"

I STRODE THE POLISHED MARBLE FLOOR OF THE ENERI Bank. My footsteps echoed out over empty chairs and desktops and up the high-vaulted ceilings. I'd come after hours. More conducive to my business. The lights still burned full, shining off brass-hooded lamps and gleaming on other instruments of measure. The whole place held a feeling of latent industry. One could almost hear the buzz of focused conversations that hummed here during the day. Just now, only one ministry banker occupied the cavernous offices. My appointment.

I settled into the chair opposite her, waiting patiently as she concluded some calculations. I'm not new to math, or even ledger-work, so I could see she was deliberately stalling, making me wait. The game of power had already begun. I was going to enjoy this. I removed one of my short knives and began to work it with an oil rag.

Eventually, the woman dabbed her pen with a cloth, set it aside, closed her book of accounts, and folded her hands atop the ledger.

The look she gave me was practiced patience. She wasn't naturally given to this part of her job—dealing with clients. She preferred accounts. I'd seen as much in her private affairs—she hired agents to manage land holdings, public businesses like meal houses and liveries. But she was mighty with her registers. Those she managed during the day. And those she managed when the bank was closed.

"You want to establish an account?" the patient-faced banker asked.

I ignored her question, and continued working the knife-steel. Not in a threatening way. More as an irrelevant task that was more important than answering her question.

"An account?" the banker repeated.

Without looking up, I replied, "I have a considerable sum of money that needs to appear legitimately earned."

"How did you earn it?" she followed.

Straight-talker. This should go well. "How is that your concern?"

"There's an art to cleansing ill-gotten money," explained the banker, tapping her ledger. "The industry you name should bear a relation to the actual source."

I knew all this. I'd read her ledgers. But I led her down the path. "I don't follow."

Her patient smile faltered at the edges. She blinked slow and drew a deep breath. "A pirate's bounty," she further explained, "might be listed as mariner shipping. In an audit by a legal agency, a rational explanation for the confusion can be offered. Accusations dismissed as one man's misunderstanding of your business practices."

"Clever," I congratulated her. "But what if we're talking about a large sum? An amount any intelligent person would know isn't standard fare for dockside trade?"

"Look around you?" she invited. "Does it look like we can't handle a large exchange?"

I didn't look around, instead tightening my focus on the banker and choosing my words carefully to coax the desired response. "I'm not here in the light of day, when you no doubt scribble in a different ledger—one for the ministry bank. I'm here now, with *private* business."

The woman shook her head, her impatience getting the better of her. "Wrong," she blurted. "You're here now because you're cagey. There *is* no other ledger for the ministry bank, and you may be glad of it. To cleanse money, you put it on the public record. You make it available to auditors. You invite them to scrutinize its source. When you do these things, most actuaries won't bother. They're trained to look for anomalies. And it's not healthy for them to find fault with large accounts, in any case. What do you suppose would happen to our solvency if foreign depositors pulled their money from our vaults because an auditor found us incompetent?"

"You take foreign deposits?" I asked, knowing full well she did. It was a point of personal pride for the woman.

Her flat pudgy face took on its first glint of delight. "Eight nations, all told," she said, leaning back and knitting her hands just beneath her impressive bosom. "My design. We're the first deposit house to establish banking across borders. Our depositors can travel without having to risk carrying large sums. They may travel as far as Reyal-Te, Ebon, hells even Nallan, and draw funds there."

I nodded as though impressed. "And shop owners from those regions may come here and do the same?"

"Exactly." The banker's smile was self-satisfied, and would be short-lived.

Because I knew all this, too. And more besides. "Remarkable as all that is," I said, "it doesn't explain the fact that you personally hold twelve discreet businesses throughout the city. That's more than a ledger salary would support. So, come now. I'm here to deposit a fair sum, taken in a less *conventional* manner. I want to know that my banker is shrewd. Not simply good with math."

Her smile fell. She sat forward, her chair creaking beneath her weight, the sound of it rising into the vaulted climbs of the bank. "You stay the hell out of my business."

I stared back with a look of apathy.

After a long moment, she gave a nod of slight concession. "Transactions of state are…*complicated*," she began, seeming both reluctant but eager to explain. "A practiced hand might find as much as eighteen percent of the deposit hard to account for. Not to mention the interest—"

"Which has a *reported* percentage and an *actual* percentage," I finished.

Her smile returned as one who believes she's found a sympathetic soul. "Exactly," she said again. "What's more, there are times, however unfortunate, when the bank must seize funds from a defaulting foreign national account."

"With you deciding what 'default' means," I added.

She didn't bother to acknowledge the obvious. "Legal recourse in such an event is costly for the depositor," she continued, "and rarely successful if attempted at all."

Then the banker laughed a bit, the sound of it like she was not used to doing so, as though her throat had forgotten how.

"Whose national funds have you seized?" I asked, laughing with her.

"So'Dell, Kuren, Ebon." She waved a hand as if the list was too long to enumerate. "Sods, all of them. If you can't take care of your money, you don't deserve to keep it."

While her laughter continued, I drew a small leather bi-fold from my cloak, untied the leather strap, and opened it. I removed the topmost document and gently placed it in front of her, orienting it to be conveniently read.

"What's this?" she asked, leaning forward.

"It's a contract for your life."

"A what?" She began to read, her face sobering by degrees each passing moment. Smile fading. Cheeks slackening. Eyes widening. Fingers trembling.

"The one you hold is unique," I explained, speaking conversationally. "The Solida cutters. Court assassins from Ebon. They begin by killing all known kin of the mark, taking pieces of the victim as evidence of the kill. These they show to the mark before slowly dissecting her. Only when she is near to death do they cut her throat as a mercy."

The banker looked up over the document at me, as one wishing to hear that what I'd said wasn't true.

In response, I placed a second contract before her. "Nallan alley backers. Killer sect known for extreme nationalism. They want you, too. Their art is making death look accidental."

After another long moment, she forced her unpracticed cackle. "A ruse. You're gilling me for a better rate. Dead gods, and I almost believed you."

In response, I placed a third contract before her. "Your lover, Katrine is it? Down to Riven Port on an inspection run. Checking your warehouses."

The woman shook her head in denial of what came next.

"So'Dell death squad has her." I reclined, looking up into the heights of the bank, so like a cathedral. A church to the faith of coin. "It's an interesting approach for a cutter guild. Effective. Emotional leverage. I wonder," I speculated casually, "if you see Katrine as another asset? Or if you'll take her place as the contract expects."

Her face slackened in surprise and horror, her mouth gaping. Then another tentative smile. "A fine game. But no. Why would I be hearing about it from you and not these assassins?" She visibly relaxed.

"Because a Dannire asked," I said.

She pointed at me. "You?"

"I'll give you a tip for free," said I, carrying on with the language of commerce. "Katrine's life isn't worth a spit. If she's not dead already, you may trust they'll never let her simply return to her philosophers. That's where she wiles away the time, no?"

The banker nodded, the realizations appearing to pile up behind her distant eyes.

I wasn't one to rush things. So, I sat, waiting. These moments were worth the savor. And they went one of two ways—there'd come defiance or contrition. I typically bet with myself which way each would turn. I was betting defiance this time.

Could have been ten full minutes. But eventually her eyes focused. Her countenance hardened. *Lovely, defiance then.*

"Guard," she intoned coolly.

Four men appeared, one from each corner of the bank. They wore the bank insignia. Had each, in fact, been in the bank's employ for no less than four months. They were being paid handsomely. By me.

"The official record will show that you broke into the bank after business hours," she stated with new confidence. She leaned back, steepling her fingers. "I'll have a bruise or two. Maybe a cut. But how grateful I'll be for our night guard, who subdued the threat. Though, they'll have killed the thief in the exchange."

I wasn't opposed to a bit of good theater. So, I clapped for her story. The sound of it like sharp reports in the largely empty bank.

"You should have been an author," I said. "Less risk to it."

The woman didn't wait. "Take her down," she commanded.

The guards stood pat. The banker showed the four an angry look. "I said Take. Her. Down!"

No movement in the wide bank.

"It'll come to you," I said, steepling my fingers in mockery. "Give it a moment."

She needed only half that, her brow tightening almost immediately. "Gods-damn clever. And who are they?"

"Allow me to introduce countrymen from Ebon, Reyal-Te, So'Dell, and Nallan." I gestured to each man in turn. "Nations who've had the bad luck of closed accounts at this bank," I caught her eye, "at your hand."

"I see. A poetic kind of justice." She swiveled to face the Nallan man square. "And what is she paying you? I'll double it."

Abandoning gods, was this woman cocksure! Wonderful!

The man said nothing. Didn't move. She tried each of them with the same result.

When she finally turned her attention back to me, I smiled sadly. "Contract cutters, unlike this fine institution, don't default on their contracts."

"The ethics of murder," said the banker. "High moral ground you stand on."

Now my patience had run out. "You've options," I explained, dropping the last of the contracts from my bi-fold on top of the others. "You may choose which of these best suits you as a means of death. Or…" I drew this out, savoring, allowing the impact of her final choice to have its own moment. "You may do it yourself. Here. Now."

"What, kill myself?" She laughed—her most genuine laugh of the evening. "You're mad."

I gathered the contracts and put them away. "I'll only ask one more time. Then, I will walk out of this place, and leave you to your chances."

She looked around at the cutters. Indifferent eyes met her on every side. Something in the silence must have gotten to her. A mortal feeling, perhaps.

"How would I do it?" she asked.

I dug one gloved hand into my inner breast pocket and flipped a coin onto the desk before her. "Salvin metal. Deadly to the touch. Just pick it up."

The coin had been fashioned into the likeness of a penny. I liked the symbolism of that—dying for one last penny.

To her credit, she didn't waver in picking up the coin. She didn't do it swiftly, or desperately, but she didn't hesitate either.

"It'll be painful," I told her. "You'll froth at the mouth. Drool. Empty your bowels. But if you keep hold of that penny, it'll do the job."

"You're an alley bitch," she said as I stood and set to leave.

"Coming from you, madam, I take that as high praise. Goodbye."

"YOU'D HAVE MADE A FINE COURT COUNSEL," JENN remarked.

"How so?" asked Audra, stepping from the vat and wiping her legs of grape juice with a towel.

"The art of leverage to force a favorable choice." Jenn spoke matter-of-factly. "Most dissents aren't argued and won in the court halls. They're negotiated with threats and promises well before they're heard by a judging authority. The court is simply the pageant to share what's been agreed to beforehand. And successful counselors know how to compel complicity."

She was more right than she knew. Save one thing. "Dannire address wrongs."

"Are you talking about morality? Really?" Jenn sounded incredulous.

"It's clear the courts don't do it," Audra observed. "And

counselors sure as every hell don't."

Jenn laughed her caustic laugh. "So Dannire deal death as punishment based on their own sense of justice. That sounds entirely different. Who do the Dannire answer to, then?"

Audra gave her a patient look. "It's not who we answer to, but who we answer for."

"The cryptic response of a killing sect." Jenn finished cleaning her legs and pulled on her sandals.

Audra did the same, and fell in beside Jenn as they walked back to their rooms. "Sometimes the Dannire are asked to step in when the wrong is far-reaching. Say, to kill a murderous general who is slaughtering populations."

"Altruism, then," Jenn quipped.

"But more often, the Dannire see to small wrongs. Quiet abuses. Indignities that ruin a single life." Audra let that sink in.

"The Court of Judicature could bring the Dannire to trial—"

"They could try," Audra said, ignoring the rest of Jenn's comment. "But the Dannire don't regard the law you so artfully… navigate."

"Abuse, you mean to say," Jenn corrected with a smile.

Audra nodded to that. "We simply don't answer to it. Any more than we answer to the accepted laws of heaven."

"You *kill* for heaven," Jenn said.

This time Audra shook her head. "More accurate to say we have the *peace* of heaven. That's a deadly tool when one's job is death."

"I could use me some of that," Jenn joked.

They each laughed at the idea that Jenn had a conscience.

"Not caring is different than having an assurance," Audra clarified.

Jenn didn't rebut that, and seemed to chew on it as they continued walking to their rooms. Maybe fifty strides from the houses, Jenn's husband, Bur, and young son, Kaleb, emerged from the door and greeted them.

The boy was eight years, and a bit on the small side for his age. He ran into his mother's arms. "Did you bring me grapes?"

"Oh, all hells, I forgot," said Jenn. "Sorry, bean."

Audra drew a small cluster from her pocket. "What you forgot, was that you asked me to carry these for you," she said. It was a lie. But for children, some lies are the right ones.

Kaleb snatched them up and popped one in his mouth. "Thank you," he said around the gob.

"Yes, thank you," Jenn repeated to Audra. It was the first genuine thing she'd said all day. At least it sounded that way. For all her sins and abuse of her position in the court of judicature, her love of her family was real enough. Audra had seen it up close over the past few years. Maybe most powerfully at her daughter's funeral. Death is a sad event. But you learn much by watching its mourners. Jenn hadn't needed her court tricks to show real emotion that day. It was refreshing to see.

"I'd have paid to see you tromping grapes," Bur, her husband, offered. "Such a menial task for a woman of the court." He was smiling, but as a man whose wife led him like a dog on a rope, the truth inside the words weren't hard to see: He liked the notion of her being made to perform the uncomely tasks.

"Not menial, Bur," she chided. "Civil. We're on the journey of the grape. Participating in a thousand-year-old process. Gods you're thick."

He gave Audra a sheepish look. "I was only having a bit of fun. I hope you enjoyed your day."

Jenn rolled her eyes, but gave Bur a conciliatory pat on the arm. She did care for him. But her respect for him came in waves. Honestly, Audra was surprised the man hadn't moved on from Jenn years ago. Did he not respect himself?

But she'd seen it before. The simple truth was that fathers bear all manner of indignity for the sake of those they love. The ugly truth was that some women knew it, and abused these men's decency. It was one of the things she hated most about her own gender.

"Maybe your husband would learn something from one of our stories," Audra suggested.

"That'd be a good trick," Jenn quipped.

Audra quickly shared the context of her and Jenn's conversations over the past few days. He didn't seem entirely surprised that his wife would have an assistant with such a history. But he sidled up protectively beside Kaleb, resting a hand on the boy's shoulder.

Audra smiled to see it. "Ladies have their flaws. Once—"

I ENTERED BY A WINDOW AND CROUCHED, LISTENING behind a low wall as the young women shared their escapades. I knew all their voices. Voices are like fingerprints. The sound of each coquette brought to mind her face, her family, her daily routine, her biases. Everything. I knew these girls. Had followed each of them for weeks. Had learned to hate them.

They sat in a circle in a lavish apartment deep inside the merchant district. Quarters here weren't just expensive; they were owned or rented only if your surname had the right pedigree. Or political station. Fixtures were polished. Wood oiled. And the air carried the scent of rare chocolates and foreign fruits that would cost a month's salary for most city-folk. Privilege is what it smelled like.

And privilege breeds boredom. Which breeds unkindness.

"Enough chitter, I hereby open this meeting of the Society of Ruin," said Ann. "We've two initiates whose admission deeds we need to hear and judge. Melisa?"

Melisa cleared her throat. New money. She wanted to belong, but she didn't have good examples of unkindness at home. "Well," she began haltingly. "There's a suitor. I've known him since I was thirteen. He's always thoughtful. Brings me dalla flowers after the rain. When they're the sweetest—"

"You're betrothed?" interrupted Ann. "Please tell me you're betrothed. And that you love him, besides."

"We were to be married," Melisa confirmed. "I thought I might love him. I know he loved me."

"How did you know?" asked another coquette, Christina. "Not kisses and promises, I hope."

Melisa paused a moment. "He didn't decide for me."

"They all do that in the beginning," said Ann, impatience edging her tone. "What did you do to him?"

Melisa was silent for longer this time. The silence said much. Regret. Shame. Second thoughts. "I told him not to call on me again. Told him I didn't love him." She stopped, seeming to gather herself. "I told my father he tried to force his loins on me. He was beaten, expelled from his counting house, disinherited."

Ann tittered at that, bringing the rest of the girls into a chorus of the same. "Lovely. That'll do for membership to our association. But you look apologetic. You'll need to harden yourself. The first time is forgivable. But no more." A shifting of her dress, as she repositioned. "Now, Loni, do tell."

The silence this time was different. Not shame-filled or regretful. This was a pregnant pause. Eagerness to tell. Loni was old money. Some of the girls thought maybe too old. She had an easy way about her. She didn't worry. "Well, Ann, I thought I should do something…profound. Something to really impress."

"Ooh, I like the sound of that." Ann clapped twice. "Let's have it."

Loni didn't hesitate. "I paid *your* suitor a visit."

The hush that followed lay heavy and violent. "Why?" Ann said softly.

"I had an idea," Loni replied with the most practiced nonchalant tone Audra had ever heard. It was hard to believe this was her inaugural ruin. "I wondered if I could do something to upset you. You, who lead this pack. And at the same time end the tiresome stories you inflict on us when we gather at your hem."

"Oh?" said Ann. Such a beautiful response. Audra knew it inside from out. Nothing these girls ever did was a surprise to Ann. Or at least that's what Ann thought. She had members of the Storalaith House tailing each of them day and night. Information gatherers. She was playing her part to Loni's revelation.

"Yes," Loni went on. "I bedded your man. And he went down rather a willing horse, I have to say. Whether because you keep your knees locked or because you don't, I can't say. But the lad fell for me. Renounced his vow to you. And I promptly put him out."

Ann let out a long exaggerated gasp. "Oh, no, you didn't do *that*? How will I ever survive it?"

A stunned silence stretched out.

Then, softly again, Ann began to speak. "The pity is that your ruin is more worthy than any of our current members. And if I had a forgiving mind, I'd take you as a sister."

"You n-n-knew?" Loni stuttered.

"My sippy bird, of course I knew." She spoke as though this was all long history. "And no real member here ever creates a tie they aren't willing to sever. That's the key to happiness. Or haven't you been listening these few weeks?"

"And you let me bed him?" Loni asked, incredulous.

"I did more than that." Ann resettled herself in her seat, as if preparing for a performance. "I marched Rane right into your father's business offices and made him fully confess it in front of your da, and all his senior staff." She laughed as if the memory amused her. "And not just the sex, mind you. But how you did it casually, knowing he and I were in love. And then put him out."

"My silent gods," fell from Loni's lips.

"Delightful," Ann squealed. "Yes, the impression we made was that you were a ceiling-looker. A real slut. And that you had no regard for friends or the sanctity of another couple's love. Now that I think about it," she said with sudden glee, "we helped them feel the Society of Ruin." She paused a long moment. "And they hate you for it."

"I'll kill you," said Loni, seething.

"There's quite a welcome party awaiting you at home," Ann remarked with glib self-satisfaction. "You should run along and see what's left of your dowry and family promise."

"I'll kill you," Loni repeated.

And that was my cue. I stood, startling the gaggle of girls. "Mind if I join?"

Ann didn't look the least put out. I had to admire her self-assuredness. She simply didn't believe someone would or could do anything to harm or upset her. That's what would make this night so sweet.

"You wish to join?" said Ann. "You've a fine form, but you're nigh onto thirty. I think you're a bit old for fetching reputations to ruin."

"Oh, I don't need to join your society. I have a sisterhood of my own." I took a seat among them, looking around. It was the first time they were seeing me, though I'd been in each of their company a good many times.

"Tell us, then," Ann prodded. "Of this sisterhood."

I turned back to the ruin leader. "We learn things," I offered. "With long patience, and much listening, and by positioning ourselves in the right places. We learn things."

"Rather obtuse," Ann observed. "Care to be a little more specific."

"Gladly," said I. "Let's take your Society of Ruin. You're whole purpose is to destroy the reputations of young women."

"Or men," Ann quickly put in.

"Yes. And this is done for sport." I smiled to myself, knowing what was to come. "The most artful of deeds makes the sinner look innocent in the affair."

"Sinner?" Ann wrinkled up her nose. "I don't use that word. It doesn't mean anything."

"Glad to hear it," I said. "Please keep that in mind."

The other girls began to squirm, stealing glances at my knives. They needn't have feared steel. In fact, they may have use of it momentarily.

I turned to Loni and began. "You. For you, I ensured Ann here knew your plans, so that she could turn it back on you the way she did. Her own informants would have missed it." I looked at Melisa. "Your former suitor was *not* disinherited. That's only what you were told to make your shame complete. No, he's next in line to his father's accounts. And has taken up with another young lady already. A Miss Ann Reyal."

Melisa turned angry eyes on Ann. "What?"

"Your detachment needs work," Ann said to Melisa with a lack of concern. She then pointed at me. "You're good. I could use someone—"

"Katie," I pushed on, staring into the bright eyes of the intelligent young musician, "You were expelled from the conservatory a few months after you started attending these little gatherings weren't you? A bright future as a cellist. Took you away from your commitment to this group, didn't it? I smiled at her sadly. "Until

Ann met privately with the Maesteri. Told him you had stolen your two performance instruments. Such was your drive to sit first chair in the orchestra. And when they searched your room, what should they find but two stolen cellos. That announcement reached every music school across the Eastlands. You were expelled. Music thieves are hanged in some provinces. Your father's money kept you out of prison. And here you're especially safe, aren't you? Not to mention that you have time to give Ann her audience."

Katie's jaw flexed as she clenched her teeth repeatedly, too angry to speak.

Mary came next. A contradiction of a girl. Devout for one part. Vindictive for another. I understood this one better than the others. "And you, Mary," I said, seeing her screw herself up to hear what I had to say. "You were your father's hope for succession as a blackcoat, weren't you? Clergy. A high seat in the Church of Reconciliation."

She shook her head at me. Not in denial, but as if she'd have me get on without the preamble.

"A little doubt can destroy so much, can't it?" I asked with heavy sarcasm, and let the question linger a good long while. "And honesty. Honesty kills, too."

"You told my mother of my struggle with faith, with the abandoning gods." There was something deeply cold in her tone.

"Not directly," I explained. "I heard some of your private prayers, where you wrestled with the big questions. Some of those you wrote down. That's the Reconciliationist way—with those who are devote, anyway—document, commit to diary. And I made sure Ann got a gander at your writings. Her information gatherers would have missed these, given your careful concealment of them in the canon library."

"You're a bitch," Mary spat.

I'd been called much worse. And I knew the blame would shift quickly to the real source.

"And you," Mary said, pointing at Ann. "I was removed from the rolls of Reconciliation. Denounced."

"Oh, shut your hypocritical lips," said Ann with a flip of her wrist. "You come here with ruin deeds to be a part of our group, but show up to the cathedral with visions of wearing the high vestments. I did you a favor. Pick a path already."

Mary got to her feet, her fingers balling into fists.

It was working. The temperature in the room was rising nicely. I made my last revelation.

"And Christina, yours is simple. Two children with a husband you do love—a family started when you were fifteen. And here you are at nineteen, learning that your affections are for women. So what to do?" I stopped, seeing her ready to speak.

"Just live through it," she said. "For my small ones."

"Then why come here?" I pressed, knowing the reason full well.

She shook her head. I spared her the revelation of her lust for a few women around the circle. But I did give her reason for new hatred. "Your secret's been shared with your husband. A good man is your Jon. But when his parents learned of it, they had papers drawn up, legally taking custody of your children."

"You told them?" Christina's face twisted with rage.

"No, Ann did. At first she was seeking leverage over you. Over all of you. But in your case, Christina," I told her, concluding my round, "she may not have anticipated the actions of your husband's parents. A miscalculation on her part."

Christina's head turned in a comically slow fashion to face Ann. I knew the look: murderous intent.

"You're all overreacting," Ann declared. "We're the Society of Ruin. I'm your leader. Of course I would need some assurance of your loyalty."

"Poor try," I said. "You love the thrill of it."

"Of what?" she asked, oblivious to the rising storm around her.

"Betrayal." I thought a moment more. "Which is more potent when it comes between two friends. Or six."

I pulled a leather roll from a clutch on my belt. Unrolled it. Six knives, each in its own sleeve. I removed them, placing one in front of each girl. Then I rolled up the leather, stood, and strode to the window. By the time I looked back, each girl had taken a knife in hand.

Desire to do death can be felt. And it grows as the action nears. This room thrummed with it. Ann had plotted. I'd made some of that easier. And I'd exposed it all.

Ann caught my eye before I ducked out the window. "You're a bitch."

I smiled. "I'm just better at ruin than you." With that, I stepped back into the night, leaving the Society to its own.

"YOU PUT AN END TO SOME PROMISING YOUNG CAREERS," Jenn said. She took her son's hand and turned to the door of the house.

Bur held Audra's gaze a long moment, then followed her in with a troubled brow. He was a man who lived too much in his head because he wasn't allowed to say the things he felt. *He'll die of mental illness*, Audra thought.

The following day the vintner took them to a bottling warehouse. A small affair. Oak paneling. Smelled of aging barrels. A good, patient smell. Jenn and Audra sat at a table with a crate of bottles between two barrels with brass spigots. The vintner showed them what to do, then left them to the work. They filled one bottle at a time with the blend that had formed over the last few weeks after the admixture of yeast.

Red wine. Dark as blood.

They worked in silence until the door squeaked open, and five men and women ducked inside. All were lean. All wore the indifferent expressions of hired cutters.

"You think I'm here to kill you, then?" Audra asked, finishing a bottle and putting the topper on.

"I just got to thinking, after your little story for Bur last night." She turned a spigot and began to fill another bottle. "You never really know someone. And your friends wind up with too much personal information about you. So, you're either still Dannire. And maybe here to kill me. Or you're a very good aide, and have been with me long enough to know of things I'd rather you didn't."

"So, killing me is safest, regardless of who I am." Audra nodded to the logic. "Practical."

"I think so, too," she replied, continuing to fill her bottle.

The cutters came in, forming a wide circle around the two women. Jenn finished filling her bottle of wine. She put the stopper in, placed it in the crate, and stood up. "I've enjoyed our association," she said rather genuinely. "But nothing so much as these last few days. I'll say I've learned something from your killer ways. Thank you for that."

"My pleasure," Audra said. "Will you be staying to watch?"

"Wouldn't miss it," she replied with a smile.

As Jenn backed up to the wall, the men tightened their circle. Much as Audra had done with the Society of Ruin, she pulled her leather roll from the clutch on her belt. She laid it out on the table, and drew the knives.

"Gentlemen and ladies," Audra announced with good humor, "this is a dance we all know, and which we get to do together. Best of luck."

A broad-shouldered fellow, came in fast from her left. He feigned a sword stroke with his left hand, and came up underhand with a knife throw out of his right. Old move. Audra waited until the last moment, side-stepped, and flicked a knife of her own. A good throw is in the wrist. This one buried steel deep in the man's throat. He dropped to the floor clutching at the hilt sticking from his neck. A gurgling sound rose as he gasped a few breaths.

A woman, wiry type, didn't wait on the first cutter to die, coming at Audra's back with two short swords. Incredibly quick. She whirled the blades in a disorienting flash. From the corner of her eye, Audra could see a second woman aiming a crossbow. *Distraction.*

Audra stepped toward the first woman, drawing the aim of the other closer to her mate. Then, she circled out. Slowly. She waited until she saw the trigger-finger of the other tense, starting to pull, fire. She took a sliding step in her circle, forcing the other woman to turn into the bolt. It caught her in the back of the head. Her blades fell. Her eyes shut. Her legs gave out. After all the clatter, Audra snapped a knife at the archer. It buried itself in the woman's chest.

The last two were men. Older. Sagely waiting to see how the others fared. When their fellows were downed, they hemmed her in front and back. This would not be so easy. Knives would never work on men who'd been at killing a good while.

To her right, on the table, the freshly bottled wine sat, impertinent. While the two men watched, she grasped several bottles from the table and smashed them on the ground in front of her. The ground there was now slippery and sharp. The man in front of her would need to take some care. It would give her a half-moment's time with each of them. More than enough.

"Clever," said the one in front of her. He then began to dance through the glass as nimbly as a surefoot—a cutter class known for negotiating rooftops and ledges.

Audra didn't have time to vacillate. She turned and charged the man coming at her from behind. He smiled, revealing several browning teeth. He pulled a pair of hand axes from his belt. Not good cutter weapons, which made her think he was challenging himself. She respected that.

He set his feet, put one ax up in a defensive posture, and cocked his other arm to strike. He shook his head, as if acknowledging her mettle. A stride from him, she faked a knife strike at his defensive arm, making him think she meant to go hand-to-hand. Then, using her momentum, she dropped, slid, bringing her knives up into him. Not to his manhood. Such was a simple woman's attempt to declare her superiority, or anger. No, Audra took him in the two arteries that passed down the legs. They'd bleed fast. He wouldn't suffer overmuch. She afforded him that mercy for showing her a measure of respect.

Then something struck her in the back. A wine bottle. *Apropos*, she thought.

She whirled in time to see the last cutter throw another bottle, taking her in the chest. The bottle splintered and broke, splashing wine all over her and knocking the wind from her lungs. This was the crew chief, no doubt.

He stepped to the warehouse floor and drew three long needles from his belt. These he shot with an interesting finger motion, sending them deep into Audra's shoulder, cheek, and stomach. They weren't killing blows. And he'd not have descended to poison in combat. That was for theatrics, really. Not a test of face-to-face skill. These were nuisances. These showed he could hurt her in multiple ways.

"You're doing quite well," Jenn called from the far wall. She didn't sound concerned, or overly interested.

"She'll keep hiring out your death," the man said.

"So, I should give in?" Audra smiled.

"Hells, no," said the man. "I just want you to understand that killing me isn't a win. And, for my part, killing you isn't a brag. I hate to see skill wasted."

Audra nodded to that. She didn't give another moment's thought, rearing with both hand-knives. One she threw at the man's boot, the other at his chest. Smart as he was, he eluded the fatal blow with a twist, taking the other full in the top of the foot.

He'd now be a half-beat slower than her. She could see in his eyes he knew it. Audra drew her sword. She struck. He parried. She struck. He countered. She struck. He struck back.

They danced for several minutes. Evenly matched. She looked for an advantage.

Behind him, maybe ten strides back, an unbroken bottle of wine lay on the floor. She began to press, forcing him to give ground. She took a few nicks from his blade, but nothing she couldn't sew up later. She never let her eyes drift to the bottle, but kept it in her peripheral view.

And she guided him. She'd need him to take a full step back in order not to simply shuffle it out of the way. She waited, watching his feet from the edge of her vision. Then she jumped at him, slashing hard. He stepped back with his right foot, his heel coming down on the bottle. He slipped and fell back, catching himself. But before he could recover, her sword was in his chest.

Blood immediately flowed from his mouth. He looked up at her, respect in his eyes.

"A damn bottle of wine," he said, and eased himself down.

Audra let him die with her sword still inside him. No painful removal. No further blows.

When he'd been still a good ten seconds, Jenn came up beside her. "Well, that didn't go the way I'd hoped."

ON THEIR LAST NIGHT IN THE VINEYARD, THEIR LAST night of the wine-making season, they sat on a fieldstone terrace beneath a lattice overgrown with ivy, taking a fine meal with a few dozen other visitors. It was the final leg of the journey, where they'd drink wine drawn by the same process they'd shared over the past week. They'd talk of what they'd learned. Use metaphors. Share regret at having to leave, but eagerness to relate what they'd learned from the wine-making process.

Audra sat with Jenn, who'd yesterday tried to have her killed.

"They teach you wine making as a Dannire?" her employer asked. It felt like an examination.

"Actually, I don't drink wine," Audra revealed.

They both laughed at that.

"Am I going to get a glass lined with poison?" Jenn asked. "Or maybe tainted duckling?"

Audra knew they weren't real questions. After all the years she'd spent as the second counselor's assistant—and now that Jenn knew Audra's unique skills—the woman would have realized Audra could have killed her at any time. Perhaps she wasn't sure if Audra's Dannire days were in the past. Whatever the truth, she was fishing. A bit clumsily for her, but then she'd probably never been quite as close to killing as she had in the last few hours. Ordering death on a piece of paper is an entirely different matter from watching it take place. Or doing it yourself.

"I think the meal is going to be quite tasty," Audra replied cryptically. She wasn't above a bit of fun at the counselor's expense.

"How does it go in the storybooks?" Jenn asked. "The master of the house has someone taste her food to ensure it's safe?"

"Now that you mention it, I *am* rather hungry," said Audra with a gambler's absence of certainty in both her tone and expression—more ambiguity to unsettle the woman.

Jenn sat back, collecting her wits. "I wish I'd known years ago how subtly deceptive you could be," she said. "I could have put those talents to work. Or do you only take commissions from the Reconciliationists?"

"Dannire mostly work for themselves." She sipped from a glass of wine. "But it's true enough that on principle we share more with them than any others."

"You're talking about values. Morality," Jenn said with sharp condescension.

Audra gave her employer a careful stare before replying simply, "Decency."

"I'm indecent, you're saying." Jenn quaffed her glass of red.

"You're ambitious," Audra clarified.

"Which you find indecent," Jenn replied. She'd fallen into the role of counselor, examining with indelicate precision.

And that worked fine for Audra, giving her the perfect opportunity to relate an important visit. She took a slow pull from her wine, dragging out time. Arguers hate opponents who don't succumb to their cadence of back-and-forth verbal barbs. There's a rhythm to debate and justice. Audra kept her own clock about it. A long one. Patient.

But she eventually placed her glass back on the table, and drew a deep breath. "One more story."

I SAT IN THE SHADOWS OF THE FIRST COUNSEL'S bedroom, where he and a lower court judicature counselor rolled and rutted in the bed like sweating pigs.

This was part of it. Being present to gather information. Wherever and whenever that may be. Tonight, it was while two people consummated a mutually beneficial arrangement. I didn't have any particular aversion to watching two people have sex. I wasn't a prude. And to be honest, it has its appeal—watching, I mean. As much, anyway, as I could see through the heavy shadows.

Eventually, the rolling and rutting ceased. There were heavy gasps and quiet sighs and the ceasing of bedsheet rustle.

Through the dark, the First Counsel spoke with a hint of regret. "Improvement, to be sure. But not enough to warrant a promotion into the higher courts. Thank you, Angela. We'll try it again another time."

The woman—an eighth year defender of the strong law in the most strenuous lower court—aspired to defend law in her country's high court, where the First Counsel presided. She'd learned that ability wouldn't be enough. She'd have to do some bedwork. *Aggressive* bedwork, as it turned out.

The woman slipped into a robe and exited the room as discreetly as she could. The protuberant First Counsel—Wilem was his name—sat up on the edge of the bed, cutting a vague silhouette in the darkness.

"Not to your satisfaction. Again," I said, quietly interrupting the mellow after-sex mood.

Wilem didn't startle, but turned his head in my direction. "I don't cave to extortion. And a simple shout will bring eight city guards. You should leave while you still can."

"Two on the roof," I said. "Another in the room to the north, and another in the room to the south—each side of this cozy philanderer's nest."

He shifted to face me, squinting through the dim light.

"One in the room below," I continued. "One in the room above. One at the stair. The last in the lobby. You protect your infidelity quite thoroughly."

"A clever extortionist," Wilem said with a laugh of genuine delight. "What will it be? Money? Pardon for a family member?"

"You're not quite understanding the nature of my visit." I stood, taking a step into the weak fall of moonlight from the nearest window.

He looked me up and down, his appraising eye following the lines of my body—easy to assess in the tight-fitting pliable cloth I wore by trade. A lecherous smile tugged at his lips. "Do tell."

Only a man of law is so self-assured that he assumes an intruding woman would rather have his cock than anything else he possesses. Even his life.

I crossed the room and sat beside him on the edge of the bed, like a pal might. In the moonlight, his puckered bulging flesh looked like that of a dead bloated fish. He made no effort to cover his shriveled member.

"The woman," I said, speaking as though it were perfectly normal for me to sit next to strange naked men, "she's a colleague. You lie about promoting her to get her to give up her box to you. Why does she believe you?"

I knew the answer. But as usual, I liked to lead them down a path. Helped them realize their culpability in the inevitable.

"Oh, that's easy," Wilem answered with a warm chuckle. "I advance one or two from time to time. Capable law counselors, mind you, but truly *professional* in bed."

"And these few serve as examples of the possibility," I clarified for him.

"Exactly." He patted my knee rather softly with his meaty hand.

"And along the way, you steer them toward your most recent obsession." I'd witnessed enough of his rendezvous to have seen more than one inclination. "Of late, you tend to like it…rough."

The smile came more in his eyes, glinting in the moonlight, than his lips. Desperate need. Reckless. "Nothing is indecent between two people who consent to giving each other a bit of pleasure."

"And this one—" I nodded toward the door where Angela had just departed, "—she gave you those?" I pointed to a pair of bites on his neck.

He raised a hand and rubbed the marks, which had broken the skin. "Some women do struggle with control. But then, I'm hardly innocent of that myself." His hand crept up my thigh.

I put a hand over his to stop the advance. "And the claw marks on your back?"

"Oh, you saw that did you?" He laughed again. "I'll confess. I enjoy that quite a lot."

"No," I said, answering his casual question. "I didn't see it."

His expression turned puzzled. "Then—"

"She did that for me," I said smiling.

The look on his face became a twisted snarl of desire. He thought he was hearing some strange fantasy. And the oddity of it excited him. But there was more to it to than that. And it had been on Angela's fingernails.

"Yes, let me ask you, did you happen to notice Angela's hands tonight?"

"Red nails," he answered immediately. "Very provocative. I made her use them—"

"And later, she raked your back with them," I cut in, ready to get to my purpose.

His eyes glazed. His manhood began to thicken. He was reliving the moment. Probably taking the fantasy further in his mind. "Oh, yes," he said with a flutter in his voice.

"Broke the skin, those nails." I examined my own fingernails as a visual counterpoint—mine were kept trim for a different kind of night work.

Wilem's eyes focused now. "I'm sure they did. A little anyway." He glanced at my knives, and again at my tightly wrapped body. I knew he was seeing the utility of my dress now, and not the body beneath.

"You're a cutter. A dimwit knife-and-alley gal." He shook his head the way one does to clear it when six whiskeys deep. "And you've not plunged your knife into me…because Angela delivered your poison for you."

"That's quite good," I told him. "What else?"

Fury began to burn in his eyes, keeping the drug in his system at bay. For now. "Angela would never do this willingly. Oh, she hates me. But she also still believes in the strong law. She'd never break it for personal gain."

"Right again."

He was now fully aroused. Anger did that to some men, but I knew this wasn't anger.

"There'd be some risk to *her*," Wilem added. "She could get whatever you put on her nails into her own blood." He shook his head again, like a dog shaking water from its mangy fur. "You think this is all rather poetic, don't you? Delivering your poison by means of my personal appetites."

"I don't find it *un*-poetic," I answered.

"Unimaginative," he added, slurring now. "It smacks of the spurned lover. Like a wagging finger. Must make you feel… Wait—" he blurted, his eyes lighting with hope. "There's always an antidote. Yes. You're here with your casual way to ask a price. Tell me. What will it take? Hurry!"

"But it's not the poetry of the delivery that I'm particularly fond of…" I paused, making him wait. "It's the substance itself that I find…appropriate."

"Certainly doesn't feel…bad," Wilem offered. The sweat now running down his cheeks and neck might have been part panic. But there was more to it than that.

"There's a seed that grows in the hill climbs of Daria," I explained. "Comes from a ground plant known as Cypress Stiltoe. It can be brewed with alcohol to produce an aphrodisiac that helps young courtesans get through those first nights with demanding kings and queens."

Wilem began to tremble. His skin rose with chill bumps. His arousal now looked painful.

"Sounds lovely," he remarked, his words slurring badly now. He licked his lips a bit slower than a woman likes to see a man do.

I eased him back onto the bed. "Through successive distillations, a large pot of the aphrodisiac can be condensed to a few drops. A few drops may be stirred into the paint a woman uses for her nails."

"Sounds lovely."

"The condensation makes the aphrodisiac potent to the point of death." I patted his slowly rising chest.

Caught in the rapture rushing through his veins, Wilem hadn't made the connection until I gave it to him. The sobering fact dimmed his rush a bit. "Death! This feels nothing like that. This feels…nice."

"You've felt death before, then?" I quipped, knowing he was all but unaware of me now. "I'm not sure it's really a poison," I remarked, affecting the air of a sophist. "I mean, can one really die of too much sex? Seems incredible, don't you think?"

"What's happening to me?" he asked with the voice of an addict—enraptured, already anticipating the next time.

I loved this part. "The body has normal functions to govern how *excited* it allows itself to become. Some of this is in your mind." I laughed. "A good deal of it is in your heart."

"Heart?" he slurred.

"Not the metaphoric heart," I said. "The blood-pumping kind. You see, my dear First Counsel, your stimulation is galloping away from you just now. It's broken down every barrier you thought you might still have for personal gratification. And your heart is accelerating to keep pace. At some point, it will be unable to keep up. It will tire. Catastrophically tire."

The First Counsel began to thrash atop his bedsheets now. He looked a bit like a beached carp.

I took my leave. No one questioned another woman making her way from his bedroom.

"YOU KILLED THE FIRST COUNSEL?" JENN ASKED, incredulous but also glaring hard at Audra.

"Just before our wine trip." Audra sat back. All the careful preparation. The hours. Months. Years. To bring it to this moment, taken in the sanctimonious garden of the upper-crust, merchants and lawmakers come to play at civility.

"Dead gods," Jenn whispered.

"Indeed," Audra sympathized with thin regard. "How's it go again? When a member of the High Court dies, the appointment is passed first to a member of his family, if anyone in the family is *lettered*, trained in the strong law."

Jenn looked across at her, her stunned look stiffening with violent intent. "You would already know his wife is lettered."

Audra gave a satisfied smile. "Just as I know that you rose to your seat as Second Counsel in the High Court of Judicature by *satisfying* Wilem, and that his wife knows it, too."

For maybe the first time since Audra had known her, Jenn was speechless.

Audra nodded at the obvious conclusion. "She's removed you from your appointment. You're now just another lettered woman needing a client."

"So, I'm the end of your story, then?" Jenn leaned back, gathering herself, forcing calm. "I'll make my way back."

Audra reclined, too. She waited a good long moment before finishing it all. "When I defended the pedophile at the public court, you'll remember I did so in disguise."

Jenn eyed her closely.

"I was disguised as you, my dear former counselor." Audra gave it a moment to sink in. "Public opinion of you, while not something you would know or care about—since you spend all your time in the rarified air of the high courts—well, let's just say the people hold you in rather low regard."

"That so?" Jenn said with more smugness than Audra had thought she'd have left.

"That's so," she affirmed. "I wouldn't give a thin plug for you in the streets after dark. Defending a child-rapist and killing that child have ruined any reputation you thought you had. Or ever could have. And the story of it has made its way into every city across the Eastlands."

Jenn was seething. "You whore. You said the child was sick anyways."

"She was." Audra shot her a look of easy contempt. "Would have died soon, to be sure. I saved her some pain."

"Well then—"

"But all that the people know is you're a heartless bitch." Audra didn't deliver this news with any vindictiveness, but as a piece of information like any other. *Evenness to bring one low*, the Dannire saying went.

And as far as the young girl, Sarah, she'd known what her death would also bring. This moment. And it had given her some purpose, and courage. Audra was sure of that.

Jenn raised her chin, her assured smile returning. "Cunning. But reputation is the lesser part of authority. Especially where the courts are concerned." She leaned forward so that Audra might not miss what she said, or how she said it—condescension and victory bright in her expression. "I will buy my way back to a seat at court. Might find a cutter like you to help make that path an easy one, too. Maybe start with you."

This threat always came. As predictable as sunrise. It disappointed Audra, particularly coming from Jenn, who usually found such creative solutions to her problems.

"You're welcome to try," Audra said, "but you may need to find someone to back your play. You see, the ministry banker I told you about? Her name was Jan. Your personal banker."

Jenn began to shake her head in denial. "I was told she'd traveled to Nallan on bank matters. What did you do?"

"All your accounts have been liquidated," said Audra, dealing this piece of the kill. "All the foreign accounts you've seized. All your government kickbacks and grafts. The percentages you collect from those you've granted legal favors. And the businesses you own, besides. All of it. Gone. Redistributed to counselors who defend those who cannot pay for service. And to orphanages. And to porridge lines. I had Jan see to this before she tasted the metal's edge. And it was all carried out the day we set out for this winery."

Jenn's brow furrowed deeply. She clenched her teeth. Her chest heaved with the force of her angry breathing. "I will kill you myself."

Another empty threat. And predictable. Disappointing. After all her might and time in the high court, Jenn was the same as all the rest—those Audra visited, anyway. She thought more of herself than was healthy. The problem of arrogance is that it makes you believe you condescend from a higher, better place than those you belittle and treat poorly. Truth was, arrogant folk stand the same height as the all the others. Bleed the same. And they tend to feel pain more intensely, because it's always a surprise to them.

Like the surprise that began to dawn in Jenn's face when Audra said, "And the young girl, from the Society of Ruin? The little leader…her name wasn't Ann. It was Cate."

Jenn's mouth fell slightly agape. "The one you set all her friends against…"

Audra let the realization set in, then confirmed it. "Your daughter. A lot like you she was. Crafty. Mean-spirited. And it got away from her much younger than it did from you."

"Lies!" Jenn slammed a fist down on the table. "I would have known of this Society of Ruin. It's all lies. She was a good girl." The words sounded like a defense and eulogy all in one.

"No, Jenn, she wasn't. She was good at keeping secrets. And she was good at destroying lives. Not in the same way as you. But often with the same lasting result." Audra paused, making sure Jenn was hearing her behind her distant stare. "Several took their own lives once their reputations were shattered. That's the legacy of your little girl."

Jenn looked up, a broken expression in her face. A hint of genuine contrition, maybe. "She could have changed."

"You loved her," Audra observed, leading Jenn the final mile. "The way you love your son. And husband."

New dread bloomed in Jenn's face. "Dead gods, not them, too."

Audra nodded toward Bur and Kaleb, who'd approached from behind her, and came to stand near the table. But not too near.

Jenn was visibly relieved, and held out her arms for Kaleb to run into.

Bur gave Audra a concerned look, searching for confidence to do a hard thing. She showed him a simple smile. He'd make the right woman a good husband some day.

"We're leaving, Jenn," he announced. He did it with a quiet tone, trying not to draw too much attention.

"Speak up," Jenn chastened, wagging her arms a bit to encourage Kaleb to come.

Bur let go his son's hand, and the boy stayed put. "We're leaving," Kaleb repeated.

"Nonsense," Jenn said without real conviction. She turned to Audra. "What is this?"

"A man isn't there to be trodden on, even if you have the means and will to do so." Audra spoke in a soothing tone, so as not to frighten the boy. "And sometimes all it takes is a reminder that he is better than his worst moment. Though you would have him live forever in its failure. To maintain control."

"So you plotted with my husband to take my child from me?" Jenn's eyes carried a threat.

Audra readied to answer, but Bur held a hand up toward her. She happily yielded to him. "No plot, Jenn," he said. "If you need a reason, it's because I won't let Kaleb turn out like Ann. And he would. If I do nothing, he would. Because he'd see you, everyday, doing it to others. I can't let that happen. I won't."

"You can go," Jenn snapped. "My son is staying here."

"No," Audra interjected, "he's not."

There'd be no argument on this. Audra triggered a boot-knife and kicked into the meat of Jenn's outer thigh.

The second counsel gritted her teeth, but didn't cry out.

"Your next choice will leave a lasting impression on your son." Audra twisted the knife inside Jenn's flesh. "Think about how you want him to remember you."

Jenn glared true hatred at Audra. But in the time it took to turn toward her son, her face changed. Softened. Bur patted Kaleb's back, and the boy ran into his mother's arms. There are times you see the face of regret and loss. Usually it's over the barrow of someone gone to their earth too soon. Audra saw it more often than that.

And saw it again now.

"Da says we have to leave." Kaleb sniffled against Jenn's breast. The words were hard to understand. The feeling wasn't.

Jenn didn't find anything to say for a long moment, then she whispered, "I'm sorry, Kaleb."

The boy pulled back. "Do we have to go?"

Perhaps the hardest thing a parent does is give the answer they know is right when their heart would have it another way. "Yes, sweet boy, you do."

He grabbed her close again. "Fix it, ma."

She wrapped him up, breathing in the scent of him. "I love you. All my silent gods, I love you. Don't ever forget that. No matter what you hear. Don't ever forget."

"I won't," he promised.

She hesitated to let him go, but released him at last. The boy returned to his father. Jenn looked up at Bur. There was regret in her eyes toward him too. But the damage was a long one. And not something to forgive in a parting moment. Then he did something Audra had rarely seen. He gave Jenn a smile. A small one. And there *was* a measure of forgiveness in it. Maybe some weariness, too.

She nodded, seeming to accept the small grace of it.

Then he took his son by the hand, and they departed down a row of empty grape vines.

Dinner conversation rolled back in. But Jenn and Audra held a long silence at their table. The wine—a featured centerpiece to their days here in the vineyard—now stood impertinent on the linens between them. All its considerations—latitude, altitude, soil, fertilizer, irrigation, harvest time, yeast—all of it so thoughtfully chosen to produce this vintage. So like the many things Jenn had controlled to create the life she'd known. And none of it meant a good gods damn to her now. That was the look in her face. That was the feeling that encircled them.

Audra had taken everything. But taking family cut deepest. It made the grief complete.

"This is the Dannire way then, isn't it?" Jenn said. It wasn't really a question.

"Not always." Audra pulled the knife from Jenn's leg—the woman didn't even wince. "But usually."

Jenn looked at her through vacant eyes. "So what now? Take me back to my rooms? Cut my throat?"

Audra considered a hundred replies, and used none of them.

Jenn nodded to some internal thought. "My last hell, you're all I've got left." Her laugh came weak and empty.

The feeling circled back in. That absence. It was failure and anger and sorrow and aloneness. It was empty husks when autumn harvest was gone and stalks stand dry against the coming of winter.

Jenn's gaze sank to the dirt below them. "I'd prefer if you killed me." Her tone had a plea deep down inside it.

Audra took up her glass. "Let's have another glass of wine."

THE CARATHAYAN

R. SCOTT BAKKER

– Second Apocalypse –

USTER SCRAUL DRUMMED HIS FINGERS UNDER HIS nose the way he always did when events took perplexing turns. They smelled coppery…sticky. And this was not a good sign *anywhere*, least of all *here*, a timber hostel abandoned for the winter, marooned way out where the forest *crawls*. The structure was windowless, but raised crudely enough to be threaded by lines of outside light. The flame in the great fieldstone hearth in the common-room had finally taken, so they were warm at least—those still alive that is.

The little Master was dead, his little left hand amputated and his little skull transformed into a grisly little flower pot. The Lady had slumped unconscious after he had gagged her, praise Seju. But her husband, the rotund Angle-Lord of Bayal continued his vicious assault, weeping at Uster's feet, pawing at his knees, blubbering like a leper at temple. Uster kicked the caste-noble, not savagely, but the way a hard yet decent man might kick an annoying dog. Perhaps this was what unlatched the outrage.

"*Madman!*" the breasted Lord bellowed to the rafters. "I curse th—!"

Words, Uster had learned, were easier to spear than fish in icy water. He lurched forward in his bobbing way, raised a boot to kick the jerking caste-noble clear his sword…

He scratched his head, attempting to recollect how his blade had found its way into Lord Bayal's stomach. Nothing came to him, so he shrugged, reckoning it meant more heat for the rest of them.

The Lady Bayal pulled herself from her slump and resumed screaming as best as she could manage with her little boy's severed hand jammed into her mouth. Uster graced her with a rare smile that became a frown when she shrank at his approach. He reached out and tugged the little left hand from her mouth.

"My sister Yild," he mumbled, persevering despite her rudeness, "says to tend honest effort like a *garden*."

The Lady Bayal gagged for breath, for sanity, then resumed her screeching.

Uster beamed his appreciation, not so much celebrating her racket as his own spirit of generosity. Nodding, he turned and strode across the vacant common room. Uster never walked, you see. He *strode*, taking vast stomping steps, as though the ground drummed a special song just for him, a boom that only his ear could detect. He was tall, yet narrow shouldered, large of foot, face, and hand. He should have been rangy, the grizzled product of a gangly youth, some Galeoth yeoman's son, perhaps, shy for involuntary looming, stooped for low ceilings, humble for being so slight-shouldered. He should have occasioned hilarity. But when he strode, or when he peered, or when he talked, a shadow fell across all hearts present, for he betrayed a peculiarity of manner that blotted the holy borne between life and death, good and evil.

As Yild liked to tell him after this or that accident, "Uster, you are aimed all wrong."

He swallowed the length of the hostel's common-room with seven great steps, cracked wide the oaken door, lowered his face against showering winter light. It was the solstice, no less, and the days were short to begin with in Galeoth: the sun was already shimmering across the snowy back of the land.

"Safe now!" he boomed in a crooning holler. Then he clomped back to regard the Lady Bayal. Subdued by this unexpected turn of events, she now stared at the open door with a look every bit as hopeful as it was terrified.

A shadow darkened the sunset glare behind him, one smaller, more slender. The Lady Bayal expelled an audible gasp.

"Sorry about your little brother," Uster called out over his shoulder. The door clapped shut, a sound like kindling rattling across the floor. "Like a vicious little monkey, he was. Course, killing him got your mom squawking like a goose and I was... I don't know... nervous, I guess, *jumpy* so—I mean, it was in my hand already!—so I just shoved it—your brother's hand, which was in *my* hand—into *her* mouth... Then your father...he comes roaring out the back door, there, and he...got killed...somehow. *After* I shoved your brother's hand into her mouth, his...mother's mouth...that is... *Before* I took it out, there, just a moment ago... It's over there, now."

The slow clump of clapped boots resolved into a tall, raven-haired adolescent, girt in ermine-trimmed, Oswentan winter-fines the same as everyone except Uster.

"I'm explaining it wrong..." he mumbled.

The girl looked to him in horror. The now roaring hearth-fire laid bare her and her mother's impeccable beauty, and Uster found himself cowed, as he so often was, by the evidence of breeding. The House of Samp had enjoyed their fair share of unlikely prosperity, given that Bayal was little more than an impoverished frontier march. No House so far from the capital could boast such blood—nor such returns from such savage lands.

"But, you see, the thing to *understand*, Mirrim, is that's the way these things quite often go..." As his sister Yild would say, people were always following the wrong nose, thinking they're aimed this way, when they're running that. "That's why people like me charge more for these jobs, because, you know, of all the people like them they end up kil—"

"Shut up, Uster," the girl said, her voice as glassy as her gaze. She turned to peer at the quivering, buxom heap that was her mother. "My brother *was* a little turd. And my craven father soiled his breaches before he died, I'm sure. Smell's li—"

"That sometimes happens," Uster interjected.

Mirrim cast a glare over her shoulder. "Why must you expla—?"

"My sister Yild says that I can only understand things by *saying* them, that I'm not really explaining anything to anyone bu—"

"Time to *shut up*, now, Uster... My Mom and me..." She paused, turned to the Lady Bayal with a slack grin that shouted malevolence and a love of sport. "We have a few matters to discuss..."

The Lady Bayal had watched their exchange with lunatic fascination, her lips trembling about a sob, a snarl, a grin. Uster, who was mystified by expressions most of the time, found her difficult, even painful, to look at. Faces, he had long ago decided, were far and away the most obscene things. Wrinkled. Gnarled with knobs of flesh. Flabby about wet orifices. Pimpled with kinked hair.

"I-I very much liked your husband, Lady," he hooted down at his feet. "I knew him for only fifteen and a half days, yet he became as a *father* to me…"

Even though this was entirely true, its significance was diminished, somewhat, by the fact that Uster felt that way about almost *all* older men in his company—as if they were his fathers. He had no less than 477 fathers by this point in his life.

He was collecting them.

The Lady Bayal blinked. "But you just *murdered him*, murdered his-his…" She had to pause, look out on an angle to life to find her way back to the matter at hand. "*Son.*"

"No. That was an *accident*, Lady. I had nothing to do wi—"

"I just *watched* you murder my husband and my-my—!" Her face crumbled into anguished creases. "His son."

"Noooo. Murder? Nooooooo. My body, Lady, it does whatever the bodies about it *tell it to do*. Your husband and your son are only dead, I assure you, because *they made it so*."

Both Mirrim and the Lady Bayal squinted at him.

"Uster," the girl said, "*you* murdered them. Let's not count straws of ha—"

"Noooo. It onl—"

"You *murdered* them!" Mirrim screeched. "*You did it*! Sweet Seju, will you just *shut up*!"

Uster Scraul's face froze in comic indecision about an unspoken retort.

"I *would* tell you he's a madman," the Lady Bayal said, turning to regard her daughter, "that you are doomed to kill yourself using the likes of him…"

"*There* she is…" Mirrim said, resuming her dark scrutiny.

"But then we're *doomed* anyways."

"*There's* the hard, heartless woman I know. My Mummy."

The Lady Bayal laughed. "I'm the wife of a soft-hearted Angle-Lord! What else could I be? I've speared *Sranc* in my very nursery, child. And what have you done, aside from seducing this ungainly wr—"

"That was not her fault!" Uster cried. "Her body was simply doing what my body wa—"

"Shut up!" Mirrim cried. "Aaaaah! I will rip off my ears if you do not shut up!"

"But I like your ears!"

Mirrim searched the rafters. "Then! Shut! Up!"

Just then, the fire coughed like an old man buried under powder. A coal bounced smoking across the greased floors.

"Yes…" the Lady Bayal said, regarding Uster narrowly. "He likes your ears…"

"Uster and I are in *love*, Mother."

"My bosom heaves for you…as does my stomach."

Mirrim chortled in disgust. "Yes! *There she is*! The woman who told his daughter's father that it was for the best because… What was it you said Mo—"

"I said you were becoming *tiresome*!"

"Ah ye—!"

"I said what I needed to say to be able *to see this through*!"

Real regret had bubbled up about these words, the bovine dismay of a mother aghast at what she had done, incredulous… This shocked her daughter enough to winch uncertain fingers to rigid lips, and throw questioning eyes toward Uster Scraul.

"THE ODD HEAR NO LAMENT," THE *CHRONICLE OF THE Tusk* warns. "They frolic where the righteous weep."

Uster Scraul was Odd.

He knew this not because he could *feel* it (he felt as normal as normal can be), but because he had been told as much by countless people. "Odd! Odd! Odd!" the other boys would cry after Temple. "Odd in the 'ead'! Odd in the rod!" He had thought it a game, at first, one celebrating his gifts. He had nodded in confirmation, giggling for all the divine attention. They were *laughing*—he could tell by the sounds they made, how their cheeks tried to touch their ears—and he loved nothing so much as making people *happy*, (because that, as his sisters always told him, was his *special gift*, the ability to bring joy to others).

The game only turned sour when they began throwing rocks at him. Not that he minded, it was just that he could throw so much *harder* than they could, and more accurately too. At first, he had thought the fathers had simply joined in the fun, what with so many mouths pinned to so many ears. And the blood! And then his sisters had to go burn the whole town to the ground… Ugly stuff, that…but, kind of beautiful too, the way they all danced shining out across the snow.

"Uster," Yild said, "we had hoped to send ye to some Heaven, but it looks like you're built for Hell…just like the rest of us."

To which he hooted, "It wasn't me!"

"WARE HIM," THE LADY BAYAL SAID TO HER DAUGHTER. "Death falls from him like potatoes from a skirt."

The tracery of pale lines had vanished from between the timbers of the hostel. Either the fire had brightened, or the sky beyond the walls had grown dark.

"You don't know Uster the way I do."

Her mother chortled. The violence of her communications had loosed hair after hair from her felt habit, so that a blond nimbus encircled her face and jowls, alternately deranged and angelic, depending on the firelight.

"I know you think him simple…" the Lady sneered. "Simple and *ferocious*. I understand that feeling—I think all women do. The fierceness of a man, the violence—these are things that should warn us away, and yet we're drawn to them like moths to candle-flame. We think we can seize such men, tame them, especially when they're simple, make a harness of their desires, *aim* their danger as proof against a dangerous world, not realizing that they are *lodestones* for strife and discord, that the hand quick to beat the stranger is also the hand quick to beat the child, take the lover, choke the wife!"

"Such fine sentiments," Mirrim said, her gaze cold, "for a woman who endlessly savaged her husband for being weak…"

The Lady Bayal smirked. "Avoiding the dangerous, my dear, does not mean loving the tender."

Mirrim shook her head in wonder and pity. "Such an *empty* life you've lived."

"*Because I dwell in emptiness!*" her mother roared. "Pompous, entitled brat! What do you know of my world? I'm a child of the capital, sent *here* the very year she dripped, to while away her days being pumped by a wheezing old brute! I should be gossiping on the Floating Court, making eyes and passing droll on the Ay-Dinai! But there I was, larded with an heir to the House of Samp—*you*, Mirrim!—thinking, maybe, maybe I could squeeze some joy out of such a bitter fate! Only to be told that child *did not belong to me*! That I had no—"

"You had a choice! Mortgage the Estate! Pay for a Schoolman to come and *protect me*!"

"Child… *There is no protecting* you. You think me cruel—*me*!—the one who has loved you, cherished you! knowing this day must come!"

"Then why have me at all?"

"I didn't want to!" the Lady Bayal cried on panic's edge. "I did not want to, but then you came, and you were so…so beautiful, so *perfect*, and what was I to do? Drown you? Brain you with a stone? Or let you live and love the span allotted?"

"I don't believe you!"

"And even if I had possessed the will, none would have allowed it! Why do you think they always adored you, the menials, always hovered like protective hens? This whole country *knows what you are*! This whole country understands what your death *means*, Mirrim. They know which way the trencher tips! For them, your blood is harvest, heavy purses, children rollicking safe in the meadows."

"Liar!"

"Then kill me and be done with it! The sun is setting! The *Carathayan knows* by now! She's likely racing here even as I speak!"

Mirrim turned to Uster apprehensively. "What do you think?"

"She looks a lot like you…save the hair and fat."

"No… What do you think about *the Carathayan*? She obviously *believes* it."

"I think so too."

The girl fairly stamped for exasperation. "So should we…you know…*flee* or something?"

Uster shrugged. "It's just starting to get warm."

The Lady Bayal began laughing in her delightful, savage way. "Your idiot is wiser than you know, dear. There's no *fleeing* the Carathayan. She will take you because you've *always* belonged to her. Why do you think your hair is *black*? Her finger was there the very moment you were born!"

"Shut up! Shut up!"

"*She's your mother now!*" The Lady shivered for the sincerity of her mad cackle. Her bosom sloshed like beer in a barrel. "I'm nothing but a common thief—as are you, Uster Scraul! None of us shall live to see morning!"

"But it is *warm*, though," Uster meekly offered.

Mirrim mimed the act of strangling herself.

CHILDREN LAUGHED WHEN HE RAN, IT WAS TRUE, BUT no one else. Dogs slunk away, never barked. Nothing wild would come near him, in fact. Warring for the Aspect-Emperor across the Secharib cane fields, he once found himself face-to-face with an elephant cobra possessing a hood the size of a Tydonni shield. The whole company had watched him *stare the thing down*, not so much with fury as with vacant *curiosity*. 'Ermû'kipillal,' they began calling him, the Iron Mongoose. The rumour spread so wide that the Lord Palatine of Eshganax summoned him to dine at his palace the following week—exactly as Uster's sister (the Other one, not Yild) had prophesied the previous winter.

Uster did not like rehearsing the details of what followed. All he would tell those who dared ask about the rumours was that he had loved the Palatine dearly, as a son might love a father, and that this had made his other son jealous.

THE LADY BAYAL LAUGHED IN THE FEY MANNER OF matrons who pretend to be pestered into sharing what their heart has been shouting all along.

"Your grandmother, of course, was kind enough to explain it to me, you see, the way it works in the gloomy wilds of Bayal. She told how she had been snatched from Oswenta the same as me, and how she, like every other wife of Samp, had given birth to a girl and then, seven years later, to a boy—the first to be fed to the forest on the first day of her fifteenth year, so the second might grow old and rich and fat!

"I remember I laughed when she said it—I thought she was mad, you see, but she was my new mother, so I thought it better to pretend she was joking… She flew into a rage, of course, screaming about her first born daughter, *her* Mirrim. 'You must hate them!' she raged. 'Hate your daughters! Or be lost, doomed to hear them crying out on the wind… '*Mummy-mummy! I'm cold! Please, mummy…*'"

The Lady Bayal hung breathless upon the memory. Mirrim looked upward, as if balancing eyes like overfull bowls.

"I asked your father about it," the Lady continued. "I can still remember how I shook, *bodily*, like a sack of piglets! listening to him *confirm* everything his wretched mother had said. The *Carathayan*, he called it, a demon from some faraway desert waste, come here to bless and to hate!"

"Yes, Mother, I *know*," Mirrim said, pupils beneath fluttering lids.

"And then you know that we are *doomed*!"

There had been real terror in her screech, that gurgle that speaks of bodily panic. The ensuing silence fell upon them as a muzzle.

"Well…" Uster ventured. The hearth popped and crackled. "You *two*, maybe…"

Mother and daughter stared dumbfounded.

"Unless the Carathayan is a Bashrag," the mercenary said on an inexplicable lurch. Mother and daughter exchanged a glance.

"You know," Uster continued, "those big, misbegotten brutes, soulless, with hands flapping from hands, little eyes gazing out from their cheeks?"

Mirrim slapped her forehead with both palms simultaneously. "Uster? A *Bashrag*? Really?"

"Because that's the only thing that can kill me. I gotta watch out for them…"

"And ho—?"

"Bashrags. I got to avoid them as best I can."

Mirrim closed her eyes in prayer. "And how do you know that, Uster?"

The scales of his hauberk rattled for his shrug. "My sister says..."

"Yild?"

Uster scowled at the stupidity of her mistake. "No... How could you even think that?"

"How about," Mirrim replied, "because *I don't even know your lunatic sisters?*" Scarce a fortnight had passed and yet her exasperation had the overtaxed twang of one who could pretend no longer. Uster was forever mistaking the boundaries of things, assuming that everything obvious to him had to be equally obvious to the entire Race of Men. "What *is* the name of your other sister anyway?"

The mercenary swung on a stoop, acting as if amused at a silly question. "Oh, no-no-no-no," he laughed, his eyes rounded more in fear than hilarity. "We-we don't...ah...do that."

"What? Call her by name?"

"Ha-ha-ha..." Uster said, shuffling in anxious imitation of dancing in laughter, or something of the sort.

Lady Bayal had been peering at the blood-soaked thug the entire time, leaning with what seemed ever more avid attention. "My husband hir—?"

Wood cracked like gravel. The front door did not so much explode open as *yield* before some brisk entrance—only one *lacking a traveller*. Uster, Mirrim, and the Lady whirled to the vacant threshold, peered more at than into the blackness blotting the once shining outdoors.

"Behold!" Lady Bayal cried, finding confirmation in her own demise. "The Carathayan *has come!*"

"If we're *lucky*," Uster muttered.

Terrified as she was, Mirrim spared her protector a witless glance. "We should have fled!" she cried under her breath.

"You two, maybe," Uster rasped.

Both women spared him a witless glance this time.

"Unless, a *Bashrag* comes through that door."

The hearth burned behind them, the heavier hardwood logs now crumbled into glowing heaps, so that the whole pulsed between glow and shining flame. Its light dimmed the further it reached across the common room, until it merely limned the joints between shadow and absolute black about the door.

"That," Uster observed, "would be scary."

Cold winter air rushed across their booted feet, bearing with it the scent of frozen evergreen.

Something boiled in the blackness.

Not one of them possessed the words to describe what entered that portal and approached them—if it could be said that *anything* 'entered' let alone 'approached,' for all three could feel the presence hanging about their neck, *inhaling heat*, watching as they did, watching *its own approach*, first a wraith walking there, then a wraith walking here, countless horrid glimpses advancing on all angles simultaneously, a thousand spectres, all closing upon themselves, at once singular and divided.

Lady Bayal began screaming.

Tut-tut…reality groaned. **No noise**…

The buxom caste-noble bit back her terror as best she could, choked her curdling scream into a pathetic keen.

The oath has been broken…

Mirrim fled to Uster, embraced him about the waist, only to find herself unceremoniously dumped on the floor below the great hearth.

Now the wheel must be reset.

The voice sucked all breath from them. The hostel's great timbers shuddered and creaked, the sound of deep joints pestled. A girl Mirrim's age did not so much appear as shimmer like a reflection upon tar, a point where the eyes refused to fasten, no more than three paces from any of them.

Uster turned to the Lady Bayal, scowling, baffled. "Is *this* the Carathayan?"

The woman glared at him from the corner of her eyes—the way a horse in a burning barn might. "You're mad! Can't you see *we're dead?*"

Uster shook his head, dismayed by her coarse manner. He turned to the small maelstrom of glimpses boiling in ink and cold between them.

"Are you the one they call the Carathayan?"

That names, a dozen cadaverous lips replied, **only my *terror*.**

"Yes!" Uster cried, nodding amiably. "Your *true* name is *Cacollub…*"

Not one of them possessed the words to describe what ensued.

"USTER… YOU DO REMEMBER THE SPIDERS?"

His nostrils flared. "Yes-yes. But not as *me*. As someone *else*."

"Well, you used to be fascinated by spiders, drawn to them like a robin to meadows. *See how he aims*, our Sister would say, and I would turn, look, and there you would be, skinny as a rag-daughter, bent over some spider."

It tickled his bones, hearing Yild laugh. Plucked his marrow.

"The most common ones you killed outright, and others you drafted into your mad little boy games, and some of them, the rare ones, you *befriended*, Uster, or at least attended with a reverence far, far too grave for a boy your age. Then there was this *one*, a sinister bluedevil—as shiny as an opal, I swear!—that had taken up in the witch-orchids on the back gantry. That had been nothing short a love affair, that one! And then do you remember what happened?"

"Yes. But not as me."

"So it wasn't *you* who came bounding into the manse weeping?"

My, how his neck was itchy! "No. I'm pretty sure I've *never* wept, Yild."

"You have wept. Do you remember why?"

"The wasp?"

"Yes! A blackjacket had come and paralyzed your beloved bluedevil, carried it away for her baby worms. And do you remember what it was our dread sister said?"

His bottom lip bulged. "Wasps don't weep for spiders."

"And *who* was it she said that to?"

"Me."

"Yes! And all this time you were fascinated by spiders *because…*"

His brows knitted into a scowl.

"Because I eat them."

A FLESH AND BLOOD GIRL STOOD SHIVERING BEFORE them clothed in nothing but forest filth, convulsions tearing down each incredulous glimpse. A sound like a cat coughing escaped her, but somehow they all knew it was a shriek, one too great for such a slender throat.

Mirrim drew her Seleukaran rapier, leapt forward and skewered the wretched girl mid-furball. She yanked the blade clear the girl's folding collapse, ran her through again as she flopped across the corduroy floor.

"Noo!" Uster cried out, wagging two giant palms as if waving down an approaching horse team.

"What just happened there?" Mirrim gasped.

"You murdered that girl!"

"*Seju and Angeshrael!*" Mirrim cursed in disbelief. "What happened with *you*, you idiot? How is it you can just speak its name and turn it into something so easy to kill? *How did you know the Carathayan's name?*"

Uster squinted at the raven-haired beauty, shook his head in amazement. "So you didn't know?"

"His sisters," the Lady Bayal said, approaching her daughter from behind. "Your *sisters* sent you, didn't they, Uster?"

A single stride took the gaunt mercenary to the dead girl. He dropped to one knee, grunting the Galeoth equivalent of, "Yawp."

"Sisters?" Mirrim cried, tearing her shoulders from her mother's clasp.

"Leave it be, darling," the Lady said, her eyes imploring Uster as he laboured to decapitate the girl. "So does this mean the curse is…is *broken*… That Mirrim and I are *saved*?"

The mercenary stood, slinging the girl's head over his shoulder by the hair. The grisly trophy slapped on his back sideways, regarded mother and daughter with an eerie, almost philosophical detachment before he turned.

"Are we?" Lady Bayal pressed. "Are we *saved*?"

Uster paused for a moment, his bottom lip furrowed. "No…" he finally said. "If I were God I would have damned you a long tim—"

"Sweet Seju, Uster!" Mirrim cried. "*Is the Carathayan dead?*"

Nodding, the awkward giant held the severed head out by the hair, let it swing about like a carpenter's string circling plumb. "You have to *live* with this, Mirrim. Do yo—?"

"Uster, I will tear your *eyes* out I swe—!"

"But I like them even more than your ears!"

All three souls stood staring one to another, the girl's severed head swelling, draining blood like melted butter. The fire fairly whooshed behind them, pulsing with blessed heat.

Mirrim's eyes bulged for the grisly madness of the head, then managed to focus on the mercenary. "Are we…*safe*…safe from the curse?"

Uster Scraul shrugged. "*You?* Sure."

"B-but n-n-n-not *me?*" the Lady Bayal cried, backing away, starting at the bump of a table corner, fairly undone for this one last dignity.

Uster deposited the severed head into a sack he had pulled from the back of his war-girdle. He looked like something truly savage then, cruelly armoured, spattered in gore, lacquered in boiling firelight, a soul too elemental to leave its vessel uncracked.

"Nope."

"Sweet Seju, *why?*"

"No one ever tells me anything," he groused, taking a great stomping step toward her.

At long last, Mirrim began screaming.

Evil is a Matter of Perspective got you aching for more grimdark epicness? Get your fill with

Never miss an issue, subscribe today!
www.grimdarkmagazine.com

www.ingramcontent.com/pod-product-compliance
Lightning Source LLC
Chambersburg PA
CBHW020514110726

47899CB00004B/1109